'Ismaïl destroys the concep[t]
saga" by feeding it through th[e]
shredder. Funny, tender,
Ruby

'A book of big, heady ideas . . . captured in intense,
minute, unflinching detail. Ismaïl is very strong on the
interior desolation of immigrants . . . showing a collapsed
family unit that doesn't know it's collapsed'
Guardian

'A satire of capitalism, a parable of money, a saga of
"statelessness" and diaspora, and a most heartfelt chronicle
of fractured families. Delicious, harrowing, gutting, hilarious
and deeply necessary, *Hyper* is a masterpiece'
Porochista Khakpour

'*Hyper* weaves parallel worlds into a broken tapestry of
finance, familial disruption and the remnants of
internationalist aspirations. Flash crashes briefly illuminate
desperate journeys over borders, Dubai malls and the US
armoured vehicles of Baghdad. It is not only the best but also
the most contemporary novel I've read for a long time'
Hito Steyerl

'A fascinating, thrilling novel'
Samira Ahmed, BBC Radio 4 *Front Row*

'Both a rich novel of ideas and a moving family saga . . .
Hyper is notable for the fully rounded characters it brings to
life . . . Agri Ismaïl is a master of dramatic tension, too'
Times Literary Supplement

AGRI ISMAÏL

Agri Ismaïl is a Kurdish author based in Sweden. His work has appeared in *The White Review*, *Guernica*, *3:AM Magazine* and *Asymptote*. *Hyper* is his first novel: it won the Catapult Prize (2025) and was nominated for the August Prize (2025) and the Borås Tidning Prize for Debut Novel (2024).

AGRI ISMAÏL

Hyper

VINTAGE

13 5 7 9 10 8 6 4 2

Vintage is part of the Penguin Random House group of companies

Vintage, Penguin Random House UK, One Embassy Gardens,
8 Viaduct Gardens, London SW11 7BW

penguin.co.uk/vintage
global.penguinrandomhouse.com

First published in Vintage in 2025
First published in hardback by Chatto & Windus in 2024

Printed and bound in Great Britain by Clays Ltd, Elcograf S.p.A.

The authorised representative in the EEA is Penguin Random House Ireland,
Morrison Chambers, 32 Nassau Street, Dublin D02 YH68

A CIP catalogue record for this book is available from the British Library

ISBN 9781529931945

Penguin Random House is committed to a sustainable future
for our business, our readers and our planet. This book is made
from Forest Stewardship Council® certified paper.

To Amanda

When Anacharsis was asked what the Greeks used money for,
he replied: ' for reckoning'.

(Athenaeus)

Deposit (1978)

A SALESMAN'S HAND STRETCHED OUT towards the prospective buyer, cupped into a universal signifier. His fingers flexed slightly towards the palm, in case Rafiq Hardi Kermanj, the potential future owner of the AM/FM radio on display, had trouble understanding: money was to be exchanged.

Rafiq suspected that the anxiety suffusing the market had made any pickpockets unlikely to be scoping out potential shoppers. Still, he gave a quick glance around him before he pulled out his money from the inner pocket of his blazer. In his hand, it felt as though the stack he'd slid into his blazer that morning had somehow become smaller.

As Rafiq Hardi Kermanj's life in exile had begun, so had the gradual transformation of his belongings from material objects – houses, furniture, cars – into immaterial wealth: dinars, dollars, toman. By the time he, his wife Xezal and his children illegally crossed the Iran–Iraq border at night, just about everything that they had once possessed had been replaced by a stack of crumpled bills, folded and taped to Xezal's chest under the pouch that contained the items of jewellery that she had refused to part with. Gradually, as a new life was purchased for them in Tehran, the bills disappeared, in ever smaller increments. The first, largest stack had been given in Iraqi dinars to the smuggler who took them from the outskirts of their native city of Slemani across the mountains into the Kermanshah region where a car was waiting to drive them into Tehran. The second consisted of US dollars that had served as a deposit on a furnished two-bedroom house in the Doulat neighbourhood. Then there had been a car to buy, bribes to pay, a school uniform and supplies to purchase as Mohammed, the oldest child, began his education. The bills that he used to purchase the wood-panelled AM/FM radio in the Grand Bazaar were the last of that original stack.

Rafiq, having come to terms with the fact that he needed to recon-sider his relationship with money, bartered with the salesman for longer than was his custom. Two bills returned into Rafiq's hand upon his pointing out that the wood panelling on the side of the radio was scratched and that the knob felt rather flimsy. Neither assurance of German manufacture nor of superior sound quality suf-ficed to get the bills back into the salesman's palm. It wasn't until a hidden compartment in the radio's back, perfect for stowing contra-band, was demonstrated and explained with a conspiratorial whisper that Rafiq relented.

'Something is happening, my friend,' the salesman said, gesturing to the shop in front of them, its graffitied metal door still rolled down. 'You will need a good hiding place.'

Rafiq handed over the bills and was left with nothing. New money would now have to be made.

The deal done, the money exchanged, the salesman began rapidly wrapping a rope around the radio for Rafiq to be able to carry it to his car. While the man performed his well-drilled ribbon dance, Rafiq lit a cigarette and looked out over the people milling around, buying soaps and sponges, sweets and spices, carrying their purchases in identical flimsy black plastic bags, bathed in the multicolour glow of the light coming through the bazaar's stained-glass windows. Though Rafiq knew the shopkeepers in the bazaar were prone to exaggeration and fearmongering – for years they had claimed that the Shah's desired technocracy would mean the end of traditional trade – he did sense that the people around him seemed particularly anxious that day.

In fact, the entire city of Tehran was in thrall to the notion that something was on the verge of happening, a rumour that had begun spreading earlier that day when several stalls at the bazaar were boarded up. A closed stall was always cause for suspicion: the owner's entire family history would be reviewed in order to ascertain whether or not they could know something that most others wouldn't. The youngest chewing-gum seller would adopt the conspiratorial tones of a seasoned Kremlinologist, seeing signs and premonitions in every event. The market was where you could sense a coming crisis before it even happened, where news was amplified, distorted and downright invented well before it ever made it into a newspaper. And so, when it was deduced that the four boarded-up stalls belonged to the same family, and that this family had an in-law who was a member of the Imperial Army, agitated rumours quickly began spreading across the city.

There had been a period of relative calm in Tehran, Rafiq felt, and so it was perhaps time for an attempted coup, for a demonstration, for a new crippling edict. It had been over a decade since Ruhollah Musavi Khomeini had objected to the new modernised dress that the Shah had ordered, an order that had led soldiers to stand outside bathing houses tearing off women's headscarves, but the protests had lasted only a few days, after which Khomeini had been imprisoned then exiled, relegated to sending cryptic apocalyptic missives from a distance as though he were the returning Twelfth Imam himself. The Iranian Youth Movement in Europe were still chanting May '68 slogans ten years on, but they were based in London and Paris and might as well have been on the moon for all the influence they had over Iranian society.

The fact remained, however: there were four closed stalls.

The shopkeeper announced that the radio was ready and Rafiq flicked his half-smoked cigarette towards the open sewer that ran through the bazaar corridor, jettisoning tiny explosions of ash as the bright orange of its tip followed its ballistic trajectory. Rafiq thanked the shopkeeper and hurried out of the bazaar's maze-like structure to find his car.

While Rafiq was spending the remainder of the money he had been able to bring with him to Iran, his wife Xezal was leafing through dated magazines on her second-hand couch, the previous owner's cigarette burns covered by a green fabric of hers that was now in turn covered in the plethora of stains children produce. She didn't need to know the language to understand what the glossy photos of singers like Googoosh or Mahasti draped in jewels were intended to convey, daydreaming about times when she herself would not have looked out of place in these pages.

At the time the radio was purchased, in 1978, little separated Rafiq and his family from the rest of Tehran's many Kurdish Marxist refugees, who enjoyed the freedom of being allowed to criticise the Iraqi government, as long as they avoided including in their criticism any mention of the Shah. Only ten years prior, however, before the 1968 coup that had brought the Baathists back into power, they had been one of the most influential Kurdish families in the whole of Iraq. In the years following the coup Rafiq threw away (Xezal's words) a lucrative career in medicine to be able to participate in that most honourable of endeavours (Rafiq's words): leading the Communist Party across the contentious political minefield that was the issue of Kurdish independence. To Xezal's grand and vocal consternation, the only discernible accomplishment of the political party he founded was that all the drivers and servants were gradually given notice until it was deemed that the Baghdad house was too big for Rafiq and Xezal to manage on their own, which precipitated a move to a much smaller house in Slemani.

Xezal had long grown accustomed to her position in society and enjoyed the way her neighbours would ooh and aah over a new garment her dressmaker had sewn, a new bracelet that the goldsmith had made especially for her. Her silks were uniformly from the great French houses (though these were a few seasons old by the time they settled in Slemani), and her perfume – an extravagant blend of ylang-ylang, rose and jasmine – was purchased from Harrods in London and flown in first semi-annually, then annually, then not at all.

After they moved back from Baghdad, she found herself no longer spending nights at dinners aside brilliant men and their dazzling wives, but bringing bowls filled with pistachios to her husband, who would be sitting on the floor in a circle with a handful of moustachioed men, smoking cigarettes, drinking counterfeit whisky, and discussing the various exploits of Lenin and Marx. At night, at least one of the children would wake up from the sound of a drunk man reading aloud from Marx's *Capital* as though it were juvenile love poetry, and if Xezal were to voice a complaint Rafiq would just smile, his eyes trembling with liquor, and tell her that it was important for the children to hear this too. So Xezal would bring either of her toddlers, the youngest having yet to speak her first word, to sit late into the night listening to Rafiq and his friends recite the effect of circulation time on the magnitude of capital advanced.

One day, to Xezal, completely without warning, her husband announced that he was rejecting his birth name, tied as it was to the Islamic conquering and subjugation of the Kurdish people, and that he was changing it from Mohammed to Rafiq (meaning *comrade*), a name that better suited his newfound beliefs. Xezal knew then that this was not just some brief folly of his that she was to indulge as a loving and supporting wife. Nonetheless, she remained committed to the man who had shown her, a mere girl with neither wealth nor family name to speak of, the world and everything in it. And she did remain immensely proud of him when she saw how much the people of Slemani respected the work that he was doing. There wasn't a house that wouldn't be honoured to welcome them for dinner, and the pamphlets that Rafiq would print and distribute illegally became much sought-after totems of a revolution to come. So when she returned from the bazaar one day and found a printing press in what was little Mohammed's room, she accepted it, just as she accepted Rafiq's bizarre insistence on naming the third child Laika after that Soviet dog who was sent to space. Xezal, who had been raised from an early age to aspire to be a good wife, accepted all of this. She knew that her husband was a brilliant man, and that brilliant men were known to do stupid things.

It wasn't until four months into their exile in Iran that she found that she did, in fact, have a limit. As she put the children in the back seat of their Paykan, she heard her husband – fighting the ignition of the car to get it to start, as he did every morning – casually mention that Xezal might have to sell some of her remaining jewellery. Rafiq Hardi Kermanj, the man who had once showered her with gifts so lavish that she was the envy of Baghdad's entire Mansour district, now had the audacity to tell her to pawn it off. She shut the door to the back seat, went around the car to get in the passenger seat and steeled herself for the part that she realised she now would have to play. Any good wife knows that sometimes their husband needs to be guided back in line, so she ran through her options: a migraine that would render her bedridden for days, a cascade of tears, a barrage of threats. As the car's engine finally sputtered into a purr and her safety belt clicked into place, she drew a deep breath. Guilt. Guilt would do.

'Rafiq. Our homes have been taken away, all of our belongings you have sold, you take the food from our mouths, from the children's mouths, to give to the *people*. And this we do not complain about, this we have accepted. But what have they ever done for us, the people? You tell me that, Rafiq. No, really: tell me. This ring,' Xezal pointed her middle finger in his direction, 'this ring was given to me by Faisal himself. You want me to sell a king's ring to feed our children, I will do it, I will do it right this minute.' She put the thumb and index of her other hand around the band, as if to demonstrate her willingness to rid herself of the ring. 'But you don't want to do that. You want me to sell my only remaining belongings so that you can print more pamphlets. It's not enough that these damned machines take up half our house, stain our hands and clothes with their ink, now they need to be fed our possessions? Mohammed Hardi Kermanj, by God, this I simply will not do.'

The pouch that she had strapped to her chest as they crossed the border did indeed contain one ring given to her by Faisal II during the years of respite when Kurds and Arabs ever so briefly found an uneasy, fragile peace. The other bracelets, rings and necklaces, however, were often of far more humble origin, yet in future iterations of this quarrel – and there would be many in the years to come – it would be this one ring that she used as the core of her argumentation, as though suggesting to sell the flimsiest gold bangle found at a disreputable souq was tantamount to selling off Iraq's crown jewels.

Rafiq, incensed by his wife's use of his rejected name, swerved to the kerb and pulled the handbrake to a chorus of honking cars.

'These jewels of yours, Xezal, they're mere baubles, it pains my heart to see you so easily duped by shiny commodities.' He used a more heightened register of Kurdish as he spoke to her, not so subtly indicating that whatever Xezal enjoyed pretending to be, she was still the plain-spoken peasant girl who had been lucky enough to marry him. 'These items, they have no use-value to us. Capital that is not being used is dead capital. You hear this, children? Repeat after me:

capital that is not being used is dead capital. Only exchange provides commodities with utility. We will not be hoarders of commodities, Xezal, I will not allow it. As Marx said: "Value does not have its description branded on its forehead, rather it transforms every product of labour into a social hieroglyph." Your jewellery is the fruit of the labour of men slaving away in mines all over the world, the fruit which we have decided to accord an arbitrary value to. So: let us use the value! Let us use the gains against capitalism, against the feudal Arabists and western imperialists of this region who are striving every day to dispossess your children of their freedom.'

(Rafiq was not above invoking the plight of his children for the sake of winning an argument either.)

Now, as she went through the beats of this argument in her mind, riling herself up at her husband's words once more, Xezal noticed Mohammed was standing next to her.

'Story time?' he asked, reminding her of their daily ritual. She banished her husband from her mind, slapped her magazine shut, and called the other children to join her.

She could no longer remember if it had originally been her idea or her children's, but for the past few months she had found herself gathering them around her like dolls at playtime in order to imagine their glorious destinies. It was a way to pass the time, a way to make sense of the lives they found themselves living, to connect the strands of the chaotic events that had brought them there, and weave those strands into a cohesive narrative of their lives.

'You, Hama,' she said, licking her thumb, rubbing some imaginary dirt off Mohammed's cheek, 'you will be a famous, successful doctor, like your father was. Maybe you will be a beauty specialist and work with all of the world's celebrities. I can tell by your hands, my dear, you have such good hands. You will go to the best universities and do so well; you will come first in the whole country. Maybe you will discover the cure to some disease . . . or a new medicine. You will have a beautiful, glamorous wife . . . but don't you go forgetting your old mother then! No, you'll be a good son, I know you will. I will intervene on behalf of our family to talk to the girl's parents – your father will be useless at that, let me tell you. Yes, I'll

9

see to it so that even if we don't have two fils to rub together, they will know that our family's name echoes through the annals of Kurdish history.'

She then turned to Siver, who sat anxiously waiting her turn.

'Siver, you will marry a rich, handsome man. Someone who is good to you, the kind of man who showers you with gifts. And you will love him and provide him with great joy. You're going to be so, so beautiful, covered in jewels.'

Every so often the call to prayer would be heard from the nearby mosque. A loud, distorted wail that had initially led the children – who had not heard these sounds in their old neighbourhood in Slemani – scurrying under the kitchen table believing it was a siren announcing an upcoming airstrike. The sound would always momentarily stop Xezal from conjuring the fate of her children, her lips moving as she retraced the future she had described before the interruption.

'Ah yes, jewels! And your children – you will have two children, a boy and a girl – will be beautiful, just like you, my dear.' She smiled, patting her daughter on the head.

The only one she worried about, though she would never say this aloud, was Laika, little Laika with his ridiculous name insisted upon by his father, with his inability to string together the most meagre syllables hinting at 'mother' or 'father', even though he was almost three years old. Of course – for her own sake as much as for the child – she would concoct a glorious destiny for him as well, even though she felt he would be the most difficult to mould into happiness, to steer onto a productive path. Her efforts, however, would ultimately bring her joy, she knew, assisting him in his struggles, helping him navigate the path to a successful marriage.

Oh yes, her three children would be successful, and happy, and they would make their parents proud.

Soon, the demonstrations did indeed start, amplified echoes of the recent protests in Qom and Tabriz, which led Rafiq to pace the living room and proclaim ecstatically that this was it, this was the end of the Shah, that imperialist puppet of the West. The students were in the street, they were demanding their rights, a just socialist society; this would be the first communist enclave in the Middle East, freedom would spread, ring across the continent, remove the shackles of a people oppressed for far too long. 'Come, bring that book,' Rafiq said to Mohammed, who diligently carried a heavy tome from his father's stacked shelves. 'Children, this, this contains all of human history, here, in these pages. Today, these empty pages at the back are being filled. Remember today, children: a new chapter begins.'

Later, when their house went up in flames and they had to leave their second country in a decade before being granted asylum in Europe, they had to leave most of the books, which burned with the house. In the truck that took them across the border, Rafiq asked his children if they'd brought the concise encyclopaedia, then berated them for choosing to bring their toys and stuffed animals instead. 'All of human history,' he muttered as he counted the cash that his family was now left with. 'All of human history.' Until he died, poor and forgotten in a London suburb, he would keep referring to this one book. Even as they had to sell King Faisal II's ring to pay the rent, as the children grew up traumatised and apprehensive, all that Rafiq ever would admit to regretting was having left the encyclopaedia behind.

But all of that was yet to come. When the protests began in 1978, he still had the book in his hands and looked at its final pages with a fervour that the children would never forget. 'A whole new chapter,' he said to himself, then, noticing his audience: 'Can you hear that?' he said to his three children sitting on the floor observing him the way they would a monkey at a zoo. 'That is the sound of freedom marching this way. Listen!'

The children tried to hear the sound of freedom, but all they could hear was the corner grocer yelling out the low, low price of cantaloupes.

ONE

Testament (2010–2

THE DARK BLUE PASSPORT with its golden eagle and its Koranic calligraphy on the cover opened to show the laminated photograph of a child awkwardly distorted, looking more computer-generated than human.

Baghdad photographers, keen to show off their image-editing skills, would Photoshop the pictures of anyone who asked for a passport photo: blemishes and birthmarks would be erased, cheeks reddened, eyes enlarged. A passport photograph looked less like the person it was meant to help identify and more like the photographer's ideal version of said person. In the case of Siver Hama Hardi's daughter Zara, this ideal seemed to be a slightly effeminate potato.

The immigration officer at Dubai International Airport squinted, trying to match the smooth artifice of the photograph with the flesh before him. Iraqi passports had yet to incorporate any advanced biometrics, and so, without any fingerprints, facial-recognition systems or iris scans digitised and embedded in the passport cover, he only had the photograph to go on. A photograph that had authority over the body: only the body could be deemed to be incorrect, never the photo.

'Lift.'

Siver, lost in thought, didn't understand what was being asked of her.

'The girl, lift, I need to see.'

'Oh.'

She picked her daughter up, a sharp pain running through her right bicep as it supported the child's weight.

'Zara, honey, look at the nice man,' Siver said, trying to shake the girl out of whatever funk of slumber or shyness had befallen her.

'I'm sleepy!'

15

'Honey, if you can just be awake for a little while longer, I promise I'll buy you something, OK?'

The child obeyed.

After a slight head-tilt and a glance back down at the laminated potato, the immigration officer finally seemed satisfied. He closed the child's blue passport and opened Siver's red one, both colours muted on the gleaming laminate counter.

'Take off your sunglasses.'

She did as she was told, removing the oversized glasses she had kept on for the duration of her flight. He looked at the passport photo, taken nine years ago, when Siver was barely twenty-eight, then up at her, then back at the photo. Yes. She had gotten old.

'Siver?'

'That's me.'

'How long you stay in Dubai?'

'Oh, a month. We're on holiday,' she lied.

The immigration officer, dressed in an immaculate white thawb, leafed through the passport, visibly bored, and yet he kept flipping the pages back and forth, to find either a blank page or an incriminating stamp. He looked at Siver once more, scanning her face, her body.

Siver's designer jacket – a present, but one she had chosen for herself – was beaded in Romania after the shell had been sewn up in Bhutan, the fashion house whose name was on the jacket's tag taking advantage of the changing regime to set up factories in a country where cheap labour was suddenly both plentiful and legal. The finishing touches to the jacket were added in a traditional atelier in the Yvelines outside of Paris, where the leather piping to the sleeves and collar were applied and the buttons were fastened. This could, of course, have been done in Romania as well, the skills requiring no real expertise, but having it done in the Yvelines allowed the fashion house to put the coveted 'Made in France' label on the garment. The jacket looked expensive. It was made to look expensive.

'Why she not have same passport as you?'

Siver started to explain, her husband was Iraqi and—

'You must learn Arabic.'

Siver pursed her lips as the man stamped their passports.

'Go,' the passport controller said, waving them away.

On the flight from Baghdad to Dubai, she had spent most of the journey re-enacting the day when Karim told her that he intended to marry a second wife. She was surprised at how moments seemed preserved in an almost hyperreal state, while other moments were blank, as though the events of that day were comprised of short scenes. She remembered the light just as it entered through the kitchen windows – the dull, heavy light of late spring – illuminating in its path swirls of dust, dancing in the air, cutting across the kitchen until it sharpened into a corner where Siver had noted, not for the first time, a procession of ants, hugging close to the wall of her Baghdad home, its paint cracked with heat and humidity. She remembered thinking she should do something about the ant problem. Then nothing, nothing until Karim was home from work and dinner was already on the table. She remembered the shirt he was wearing, a light blue poplin plastered to his belly, his upper back, his arms, spots that seemed translucent from sweat. She remembered the moment he asked her what she thought of him getting a second wife, how he was scrolling through his phone when he said it, either because he couldn't look her in the eyes or because it was to him such an uncontroversial question that he may just as well read the news while asking it.

She remembered laughing, thinking that he was joking, and then, as he looked up, realising that he wasn't. 'Nothing will change between us, habibti,' he told her, getting up from his seat to kiss her forehead. 'I just think that it would be good to have someone else, yahni, to help out with the house? What do you think?'

Siver blinked. 'You're describing the need for a maid. We already have one of those.'

Karim, whose eyes had been soft and loving the way they always were when he asked for something, stiffened, his eyes now flat and impenetrable. 'No, I mean a wife. It is very normal, you know.'

She did not know.

She did not remember the rest of what the smashed plates testified must have been a memorable argument. She remembered no violent gestures, though bruises on both of their bodies attested to that effect, and she did not remember her daughter crying as they argued. She could only see herself in the bathroom, already in her nightgown, rubbing anti-ageing cream on her cheeks with ferocity, as though she were applying warpaint. 'You're being so unreasonable,' she remembered him saying from the bedroom as he got into bed.

She did not remember sleeping next to him.

She did not recall whether she actually entertained the notion of sharing her husband with another woman, but her leaving was not immediate. She would find herself mulling over the memory of when her mother had, a decade or so ago, told her that Rafiq had been unfaithful. 'Many, many times. It brings me shame to say this. Even when we went to Paris, remember when he went out all night? Someone had left him a phone number. I did not say anything, of course.' Then, after a beat, 'I stayed for you, you know.' At the time, the revelation had only made her irritated: her mother blaming her own cowardice on her children while sullying the memory of their trip to Paris, the one birthday present she cherished. But then, once Siver was faced with a similar dilemma herself, she wavered as well. Men were men, after all. She should not be so naive as to expect anything from them.

She did get a passport issued for her daughter and put her affairs in order so that she could keep her options open. But she did not leave, not at first.

But then. She went to his office one day to drop off a tablet he had left at home which contained a presentation that he needed, and saw the woman he had in mind. The moment she was pointed out to Siver by a conspiratorial employee, she knew this was not something that she was willing to accept.

She was a child; what could she be, eighteen, nineteen? Definitely younger than Siver was when she had met Karim. 'She has nobody,' Karim told her that night or whatever night Siver brought the subject up. He was trying to appeal to her sense of empathy by telling her that the girl had recently lost her father. 'Her brothers were all martyred by Saddam. She has nobody.' 'Oh, I see, so you want to fuck her for her own good, is that it?' Her use of profanity incensed Karim, who, she knew, found such language unbecoming. 'I cannot talk to you when you're like this.'

She remembered the moment she looked at her husband and saw a stranger. Though she imagined that the end of her eight-year marriage would feel more substantial, it only took a moment for a man she had loved deeply ever since they met at university to turn into someone who had the same traits as someone she used to know. She remembered flipping open her wallet and counting the hundred-dollar bills inside, checking various bank accounts, making sure she had enough. She remembered packing her bags, packing her daughter's bag, him shouting, 'If you leave, I will not be supporting you, you know that?' as she tried to fit a life into suitcases.

She did not remember leaving.

———

The moment she wheeled her wobbly luggage cart out of the perfectly air-conditioned terminal to where the taxis had been waiting for hours, Siver was overcome by the city's extreme humidity. She could almost feel her pores opening, sweat being conjured all over her body, sleeper agents called to task.

'How was your experience at Dubai International Airport today?'

Before she could join the taxi queue, she needed to answer a robot's customer-service request. The robot, fixed cartoon smile on its face, airport logo on its forehead, encouraged her to press a screen on its belly where four figures were illustrated, faces that went from red and irate to green and beaming with joy. It wasn't clear whether it was a functioning robot or just a humanoid iPad holder. Siver pressed the greenest of figures.

'Ma'am, ma'am, please this way,' a uniformed man said as soon as her interaction with the robot had been completed, one of a dozen human beings performing the job of a single sign. He motioned with a wave of his arm for her and Zara to approach the row of parked Lady Taxis.

Siver couldn't remember seeing these the last time she had been to Dubai: garish pink minivans with female drivers dressed up in polyester uniforms that resembled off-brand Aladdin outfits. It was a nice addition, she thought, not having to be creeped out by a male driver the moment you land. Once, before Zara was born, a cab driver had berated her for not wearing a veil. Another time a driver had leered at her through the rear-view mirror so long he was seconds away from crashing into another car. Karim wanted to report this last driver, but Siver made him promise not to. 'He'll be deported immediately. You really want an entire family's suffering weighing on your soul?'

'When did you become a Buddhist?' Karim said, putting down his phone.

Having greeted the budget Disney princess in the driver's seat, Siver fiddled with Zara's seatbelt as a man put their luggage in the trunk. 'Where to, ma'am?' the female driver said, with a surprisingly spot-on British accent.

'The One & Only, please.'

'Which one?'

'The One & Only hotel?'

'Yes, ma'am; there's two One & Only hotels. One on the Palm, one on the Marina.'

Flustered, Siver got her phone out and went looking through her emails.

'I'm sure I have the hotel confirmation here somewhere . . .' A Lady Taxi behind them started honking. 'I'm sorry, I didn't know there were two.'

'No problem, ma'am. Take your time,' the driver said, glancing anxiously in the rear-view mirror.

There. Finally. 'The Marina. Royal Mirage.'

'OK, ma'am.'

They left the airport complex behind, got on the city's main high-way which stretched out in an almost chronological line from the old heart of the city where the airport lay. Buildings became ever more ambitious, their architectonic features morphing into the future. It was soothing, this feeling of leaving the past behind.

Entire clusters of towers rose far into the black of night, towers that had not been there on her last visit, between swirling roads and glitzy malls that had sprung from the desert. When she had first seen the city she was shocked at how such decadence and modernity could exist there, surrounded by countries that were in the throes of a brutal medieval LARP. 'How is this place not bombed to pieces?' she'd asked Karim, marvelling at the prostitutes in designer wear with their Cartier shopping bags. 'Money needs sanctuary,' Karim had shrugged. 'It's why Switzerland was spared. Money needs cities where it can be safe. And this is one of the safest cities of all.'

'Where are you travelling from?' the taxi driver asked, her cheap turban bobbing with the movement of the car.

'Iraq,' Siver said. This would have to do. She did not owe the driver her entire life story.

'Ah, inta t'kallam arabi?' the driver asked her, in the broken Arabic of someone who had learned the language from studying the Koran. Where could she be from? Pakistan? Siver said yes, yes she did, but neglected to ask a follow-up question, hopefully indicating that she was not in a talking mood. Zara, as was her wont, had fallen asleep the moment that she got into the car. Siver should really have brought a child seat, she realised. A six-year-old should still be in a child safety seat, she was pretty sure. Suddenly, and not for the first time that day, she was overwhelmed by the feeling of being a terrible mother.

'And your husband, he lives here?' the driver continued as they sped through the buildings that were erected in the late 90s, all blue anti-reflective windows and crude Lego-looking shapes, to the future, to the future.

No, no her husband was not here.

'He is, yes,' she said, looking out the window.

They met in Advanced Ethnographic Study class, in her second year at SOAS, though later he would admit to her that he had attempted to speak to her several times, but not dared to do so. 'You had a look that said "don't talk to me",' he laughed. 'Wollah, you terrified me, Siver.'

The once wealthy Rafiq Hardi Kermanj was by now poor, and only a combination of loans and grants permitted Siver to pay the yearly tuition fee, but Xezal had never allowed them to *look* poor, insisting throughout their childhood that they wear the best clothes that they could afford. 'Your father doesn't understand these things,' she would whisper to her children, telling them not to mention how much their Global Hypercolor T-shirts, OshKosh B'gosh jeans and Nike Airs actually cost, 'but as long as I'm alive, you will have only the prettiest clothes.'

Though she referred to 'pretty' clothes of 'good quality', she mainly bought the children whatever was in fashion at the time, having a keen understanding of how fashion situated a child in a particular social context. Xezal knew, of course, that the United Colors of Benetton sweatshirt that Mohammed wanted was of no better quality, really, than one she could get for a fraction of the price at Hennes & Mauritz, but she was aware of what such a sweatshirt meant: a message she was adamant her three children would in fact convey.

So when Siver sat in that fateful Advanced Ethnographic Study class, she had tied around her neck a Fendi scarf that Xezal claimed to have found at a jumble sale (Siver knew better than to enquire further). Karim, in his crisp shirt and pleated khakis, leaned across toward Siver, smelling like every boy did at the time, doused as he was in Francis Kurkdjian's omnipresent blend of bergamot, cinnamon and cloying artificial vanilla. She had noticed him in lectures, with his scruffy hair and neat beard, the way that his limbs, always tanned from the sun that imprinted itself on rich people, draped over armrests, the backs of chairs. Even when she did not know his name, she saw a man who seemed perfectly at ease in his own body, and for this Siver both resented him and desired him. 'Nice scarf,' he said, giving her a wink, like a character in a TV show. He had little dimples high up on his cheekbones, little quotation marks that appeared whenever he was being kind or sarcastic. Siver didn't know if anyone had ever winked at her before. She'd been leered at, hollered at, felt up and harassed. But winked at?

After she finished sixth form, she spent the next few years working the odd menial job, which allowed her parents to pay their bills on time, until her father sat her down and told her to apply to universities, that her life was too precious to be wasted away slaving for capital.

So when she started her BA in Politics and International Relations, she was already a few years older than her classmates, viewed with suspicion by the freshly turned eighteen dressed in an assortment of post-grunge outfits and Spice Girls-derived crop-tops. She didn't look young enough, she felt, for the boys in her class to show any interest in her and she wasn't emotionally mature enough, in her view, for the older boys to be into her. And, mostly, this suited her just fine. Boys were trouble, boys got you into trouble.

After the lecture she saw Karim awkwardly lingering outside the classroom, pretending to look for something in his bag. 'Hey!' he shouted out as she passed him. 'Want to get a coffee?'

She was about to say no. She always said no, it was more reflex than anything at this point. And yet when she opened her mouth she found it forming the word yes instead.

'Where are you from?' he asked as they walked out towards the unoccupied storefronts around the Brunswick Centre, a question that annoyed her when other people asked it, since it put her in a position where she had to justify her heritage, while jumping into a fifteen-minute soliloquy about the 1923 Treaty of Lausanne and the consequences of the First World War on the Middle East. She stole glances at his bare arms, arms covered in peach fuzz, the gentle ripple of his muscles. She wanted to reply 'Sutton', the way that her friends were able to, but when she limited her answer to the name of an impoverished London suburb, she would get a cocked eyebrow and a 'No, but, like, *really*.' She did not like the question, and yet, coming from this boy, she did not feel insulted. So she said 'Iraq', though she would usually have said 'Kurdistan'. A betrayal, one of endless betrayals, to be loved, to be worthy of love.

'Wollah? So am I!' he said as he squeezed her hand, sending an electric charge through her, and he smiled that awkward, wonky smile that broke her heart just a little. Damnit.

The Lady Taxi drove up to the hotel's massive domed entrance, a train of golden camels towering above them, the intricate statues lit up from below making them look like malefic phantoms.

'I don't like them,' Zara said as the taxi parked in front of the entrance.

'They're just statues, monkey,' Siver said, rummaging in her purse until she found her wallet.

A man appeared to whisk the suitcases out of the cab and into the hotel while Siver handed the Lady Driver some of the local currency she had from her previous trip. 'Keep the change,' Siver said, knowing that she couldn't be handing out money like that in the future.

As another man guided them into the hotel, they walked past a guest shouting at the staff, his voice vibrating with anger, rising with each sentence. Before the automated glass doors shut behind Siver, she'd understood that he was demanding his car be parked in front of the hotel, while the disconcerted staff kept apologising and referring him to valet parking. There was a Rolls-Royce, a Maybach and an Aston Martin already parked outside the hotel almost as advertisement, the owners' wealth reflecting on the hotel's exclusivity. The complaining man stood next to his Maserati, realising his status wasn't what he thought it was, and offsetting his humiliation on those around him.

'I'm so sorry about that, ma'am,' the man escorting her through the dazzling entrance said, the spectacle ruining the hotel's well-drilled introductory routine.

'Welcome back to the One & Only,' a woman said, taking over from the man, a tray of champagne flutes filled with orange juice perfectly balanced on one hand. How this woman knew that Siver was a returning guest, she had no idea. 'Would you care for a non-alcoholic beverage while you check in?'

'Zara honey, do you want a drink?'

The woman crouched so that Zara could get a glass, gingerly balancing it between the child's small hands, as Siver approached the check-in counter with her membership card in hand. She prayed Karim had accrued enough points over the years for a week's stay, that she would be allowed some breathing space as she attempted to cobble together a new life.

'You have points for six nights,' the unreasonably chipper man at the desk informed her. 'Should I put your final night on your credit card?'

She should have changed her reservation, told him that she didn't need the last night. Surely this man who barely earned enough to survive would understand her predicament. And yet she found herself fishing out her Trade Bank of Iraq credit card, heard the faint slap of its plastic against the hotel's marble counter. The man behind the desk gave her a smile as the card was swiped, and handed her two key cards in return.

'My colleague will escort you to your room; we trust you'll have a pleasant stay with us at the One & Only.'

Once she had received her suitcases and been shown the room's various features and amenities, she undressed Zara and tucked her into the king-size bed. It didn't take long for a light snore to emerge from under the duvet and Siver could proceed to count the money that she had, the stack of crisp hundred-dollar bills she had accumulated during her years with Karim. She'd counted the bills so many times, and the result never changed. Five thousand, three hundred dollars. That was it; that was all the money she had.

She locked the money in the safe, grabbed her handbag and went down to get a drink.

Of the hotel's fourteen bars, the Lobby Lounge was her nearest option. A Disneyfied ode to colonialism, the decor consisted of skulls, pelts and feathers belonging to animals that had never lived in this desert. A menu appeared on her table before she'd even taken off her jacket.

Glancing over the drink list, her heart sank. Was this the price of cocktails in these hotels? Ever since she'd walked into her first five-star lobby, holding Karim's hand and marvelling at the way he did not seem uncomfortable in these spaces, she had never needed to think about money. Suddenly, she regretted coming to this hotel. Even with the free nights, the meals alone could end up costing her more than a modest two-star hotel, but she wanted Zara to feel like this was all a nice holiday, the kind of holiday Daddy used to take them on, where they stayed only at the best hotels, ate at the best restaurants. Siver wanted to ease Zara into their new life gradually. Though, she realised, there had to be a way to do this without staying at a place that sold a Sazerac Ellipse for over a thousand dollars. She ordered a glass of house white.

When the wine arrived, the glass was already filled for her, requiring no pretence that the cheapest item on the menu needed to be tasted beforehand. She sipped the wine that had been chilled to such an extent it was no longer possible to tell if it was any good, and began browsing through a magazine she'd taken from the plane. She glanced at an article about a famous author's writing shed. The author had the shed made as his house was filled with five children, a dog and a spouse who was also a writer, and thus the author found the home 'a very busy place, far too busy to write in'.

The article did not specify what the wife, the family's other work-at-home writer, could do to escape this very busy place, this place far too busy to write in.

He added her on AOL Instant Messenger the same evening they first had coffee, and the sight of his screen name in her contact list made her feel something close to terror.

She tried to bat away the feeling the way one does with an irritating gnat. She focused on her coursework, tried (and failed) to get through her second-hand copy of *The God of Small Things*. She masturbated in the shower, anxious that the time she took in the bathroom would lead to her mother's stern reminders that they were not made of money, that she couldn't waste hot water like that. She took long walks, asking everyone in the flat whether they needed anything from the shops, letting the breeze rush over her arms, feeling almost like a touch. She read fucking poetry.

And still, every night, after everyone else had gone to bed, she found herself sitting in the living-room corner where the computer was located, before Laika commandeered it and relocated it to his room, waiting until 1 a.m., 2 a.m., 3 a.m., waiting for the creaking-door sound that would announce his presence online. And then, once he actually did come online, she would simply stare at his screen name, willing karkrash99 to make a move. And then, after a minute, ten minutes, the sound of a door slamming shut, his blue screen name turning red. She would play little games, convincing herself that if he came online at exactly 01:11, that meant they were meant to be. If he was online for an even amount of numbers, that meant she should forget him and move on with her life.

As she waited each night for Karim to appear, she spent her time in various Yahoo! chatrooms, calling herself James, pestering those with female-sounding monikers with *A/S/L* until someone was game to talk to her, someone female who – Siver often imagined – was in fact male. She would quickly veer the conversation into sexual territory, and, if the other party was receptive, begin describing what he (she) would do to her (him). She would glance over her shoulder repeatedly as she wrote, even though she knew from a lifetime of experience the sounds that preceded either of her parents coming out of their room: her father's phlegmy coughs, the slaps of plastic as her mother put on her slippers. Often, she wanted to touch herself right there, in the living room. Sometimes she did.

One night, as karkrash99 logged on, she noticed that he had an away message: *please could you stop the noise I'm trying to get some rest.* When he logged off, again without saying anything (why had he even added her on AIM if he wasn't intending on writing to her?), she spent another hour online thinking of an away message of her own. In the end, she went with a Fiona Apple lyric: *you can't illuminate what time has anchored down.*

The next time she saw him online, he'd changed his away message to: *and we don't need them to cast the fate we have.* This was not a lyric she recognised, so she searched for it on HotBot and, as she scanned down the lyrics online she felt a chill run through her: *I don't want to hurt you / no reason have I but fear / and I ain't guilty of the crimes you accuse me of / but I'm guilty of fear / I'm sorry to remind you / you but I'm scared of what we're creating. / This life ain't fair.*

She read the lyrics again, and again, as if there was something that she'd missed the first time around. Did he mean for her to do this? To look up these lyrics? Were they aimed at her? She changed her away message to *the world is a vampire* and disconnected the modem, reconnected the cable to her father's fax machine that would sputter out dispatches from another world in squiggles she had once been able to read but now only served to remind her of a childhood she'd rather just forget.

Then, the next time she came online,
karkrash99: Hi ☺

But why Dubai? Why that wretched place? . . . I understand, but once you've renewed the girl's British passport, you can go anywhere, can't you? I will never understand you, my daughter. Why not just come home to Slemani? Come and take care of your mother, leave that desert to the Arabs, may it make them happy.

The day after their arrival in Dubai she arranged to meet with an estate agent she had found online – a pushy, leggy woman who was gruff to Siver but always trilled whenever she answered the phone – who showed them four apartments in quick succession, the recent Dubai World crash having resulted in a multitude of vacant properties.

One was located in the Marina, a lavish space that was way above what Siver had indicated she would be able to afford.

'It has a walk-in closet. I'm not going to need a walk-in closet.'

'That's the maid's room,' the estate agent said slowly, as though she was trying to explain inflation to a cat. 'The walk-in closet is by the master bedroom.' Siver peeked into the windowless room she had mistaken for a closet and shrugged. 'I'm not going to need a maid's room either.'

Another was located on the thirty-eighth floor in a tower that had only one elevator. It took them almost fifteen minutes before they could fit in the elevator, constantly hurrying up and down the tower. A third was furnished with a circular waterbed, and a disco ball in the living room. 'The previous tenant was a banker,' the estate agent said, as if that explained the decor. The fourth one they viewed, a large two-bedroom apartment in a dusty, desert-defying development called Discovery Gardens, was cheap enough for Siver to afford, approximately 9,000 dollars for the year, 750 dollars a month. 'I'm sure the owner can leave the furniture here if you want it. The previous tenant left rather quickly.'

Zara was pulling at Siver's dress, she was hot and she was bored and could they go back to the hotel?

Siver signed the lease that same day.

Karim would ask if she wanted to go for coffee, and then just sit there, quietly, reading some shitty tabloid filled with half-naked women while she stared at him. At the way the muscles in his jaw tensed when he saw something he didn't like, the way he licked his thumb before turning the page. Every so often, he would look up from the paper and ask her a question, as though something he'd read had just made him think of it, like what do you think of Tony Blair, or who was your character on Mario Kart. Other times he'd launch into impromptu analyses of various Disney movies, about how the servants in *Beauty and the Beast* did not deserve the fate that befell them by the sorceress, who condemned them to a life of servitude when they were already oppressed, or how the upcoming *Mulan* was created by Disney to atone for *Kundun*, the Scorsese movie about the Dalai Lama that led to China boycotting all Disney films. 'Henry Kissinger was sent on an, um, diplomatic mission. It was to find out what the Chinese wanted to let Disney movies be shown again,' he said, looking into her eyes as though he were relaying state secrets.

Siver would just stare at him, wanting to scream. What was his deal? If he desired her, why wasn't he making a move? What was the point of all this fucking coffee and these stupid Disney movies? She'd leave the café each time bewildered, frustrated, angry with herself. She would promise herself that the next time he asked to have a coffee after a lecture, she'd tell him in no uncertain terms to go fuck himself.

But then, when he'd ask, she'd say yes, time and time again.

———

Online searches would often result in a big blue exclamation mark and a message indicating the site was blocked, containing 'content that is prohibited under the "Internet Access Management Regulatory Policy" of the Telecommunications Regulatory Authority of the United Arab Emirates'.

Though it was never entirely clear what specifically was being objected to on the sites Siver tried to access during her job search, she had a hunch. Job forums were rife, after all, with the sort of reports of employee abuse that the United Arab Emirates were keen to eradicate from its history. This was not to limit liability or minimise the risk for litigation: the law did not acknowledge the possibility of abuse. When the UAE labour ministry replied to a critical report by Human Rights Watch on the state of labourers in 2005, they maintained that immigration laws did not apply to the UAE, as labourers were merely to be seen as temporary employees, not immigrants. Even applying for residency required providing a permanent address abroad, hundreds of thousands of workers pretending that their home was not their home, that they in fact resided with a mother, a brother. You were only ever an employee at Dubai Inc.

No, the censorship was due to something else, something more elusive. No criticism would be found in Dubai's museums, television channels or bookstores either, in the same way that there weren't any references on the Hugo Boss website to the fashion brand's founder having designed the SS uniforms and used forced labour to make his clothes. A brand ultimately tailors its history in order to correspond to an image. What would become Dubai's history, then, was nothing more than PR puffery, a glorious tale of visionary leaders.

Siver needed to accomplish a similar trick with her CV. She needed to sell herself, construct a successful history through sheer willpower. She needed to make her years spent as a daughter and then as a wife sound less like a life and more like a career, to shape the fits and starts of her education and the random assortment of jobs taken for the sake of money as a coherent narrative, an understandable series of events that presented her, Siver, as someone who should be employed.

She got her first job at eighteen, selling ice cream in Purley, quickly learning to put the flavours nobody wanted (liquorice, vanilla, peach) furthest away from her so that men and boys wouldn't leer at her bending over to scoop their flavours. She then briefly worked as a cashier but was fired for showing up late one too many times. Her third job was working at the KFC in Sutton, all oil and fat and grease, forever making her gag at certain smells. Then she had a job folding clothes and selling clothes, followed by university where she met Karim and, when they moved to Iraq, a job at his construction company in Baghdad, her university degree's main purpose having been to make her a more valuable wife, and then she got pregnant and when she suggested going back to work he told her it would be unseemly. 'It's not proper to make my wife work and have strangers take care of my child; what would people say?'

How could any of that be turned into the shimmering corporate lingo that suffused every text in Dubai? The hotel they'd stayed at invited her to 'indulge in abundant space, luxurious rooms and suites, nine inspiring restaurants, and dramatic, Arabesque architecture', the mall she went to for the free Wi-Fi was a space where 'shopping, dining and entertainment come together with history, culture and the story of a remarkable adventure'. What was luxurious about her? What remarkable adventures could she promise an employer?

They went to see *Titanic* together. She wasn't too keen as she had heard the movie was three hours long and that sort of time would need to be explained to Xezal. Besides, what was there to see? It was a boat, it sank, the end. He insisted on buying her ticket, which she objected to but was shamefully happy for in the end. All those cappuccinos were starting to add up.

They sat in the dark room, curiously alone even though the movie was rumoured to become the highest-grossing movie of all time any day now, awaiting ads and trailers, moving about in semi-comfortable chairs in order to find an ideal position.

'Can I ask you an indiscreet question?' she heard him ask, and although her eyes were on the blank cinema screen, she felt his look upon her.

'Sure,' she replied, although she wasn't really sure. She felt like the sky was about to fall, and not talking about it might prevent it all from happening, at least for the time being.

'Are you in love with anyone?' he asked, a slight tremor in his voice.

She shook her head and whispered

'No,'

so faintly she wasn't sure he had heard her. She wanted to say yes. She had told herself 'yes' for quite some time now. But 'no' was the answer she gave.

She'd recently read the poems in Edna St Vincent Millay's *Collected Sonnets*, a book she'd bought at WHSmith as part of a *buy 2 get 3* deal on paperbacks, a book she hated herself for buying as Xezal was no fool. She would know what it meant to be reading poetry; after all, she too had been in love once. Three verses from the seventh sonnet stood out to Siver, as though they had been written especially for her: 'A silly, dazzled thing deprived of sight / From having looked too long upon the sun. / Then is my daily life a narrow room'.

Had the words been embroidered on a pillow, she would have cringed at the sentiment, yet while poring through the poems for some way to put her feelings into words, she had found a neon clarity to those verses, and knew that if she didn't surrender to whatever was going on inside of her, she would return to the narrow life she had been living before she met him.

Karim, who had stayed silent after her rather wistful 'no', found the courage to press on. 'Have you ever been . . . ?' he began, but then trailers appeared on the screen, not minding the fact that they were interrupting something, and she sat silently by him for over three hours, never once losing herself in the movie long enough to not be acutely aware of how close his arm was to hers, how little it would take for them to touch.

Once outside, as the chilly London air enveloped them, he began complaining that Leonardo DiCaprio clearly could have fit on that door, that the whole thing was just a manipulative tear-jerking exercise.

'It's all so stupid, like he had to die for us to feel something, like . . . Siver? What's wrong?' he said as he noticed her crying.

She slashed away an errant tear with the side of her hand and narrowed her eyes at him out of spite. She turned to leave, then turned back, pushing him against a poster of *Spice World*, and kissed him, grabbing his hair hard, hard in her fist.

———

The skyscrapers lining the path between the Mall of the Emirates and Dubai Mall were a mix of the iconic and the cheap: for every sleek Burj Al Arab that was rumoured to not recoup its construction costs for a hundred years, there was a gaudy green-and-gold monstrosity like the slapdash Al Attar. For every architectural feat, like the majestic Atlantis atop the artificial Palm Islands, there was a childish novelty like the dolphin-shaped DAMAC towers. For every Four Seasons Hotel there was a Two Seasons Hotel.

As the silvery middle finger to the West that was the Burj Khalifa appeared on the horizon, the taxi driver turned down the volume of the Koranic recital he had been listening to, and said – quietly, as though someone might listen in on their conversation – that the building contained a secret extension that could be deployed in case a taller tower was ever built. 'This way, it will always be the world's tallest building.' He glanced into the rear-view mirror, hoping to catch the eyes of the mother and daughter in his back seat.

Zara's eyes widened at the marvel of this purported technology, while Siver politely nodded, doubting the veracity of what she was being told. She had grown accustomed to these embellishments being relayed to her in the back of every cab. 'The young Emiratis, they go to the moon to drink and party,' more than one driver had told Siver, which seemed a particularly outrageous anecdote until she realised that there was an artificial archipelago named The Universe, which was meant to be shaped like the Solar System until the money ran out, and that the 'moon' was a crescent-shaped island which people apparently sailed out to at night to have illicit get-togethers.

Having penned a corporate profile and passed it off as history, the rulers of Dubai had inadvertently led to the emergence of a vibrant oral history. Knowing that documentation of events could lead to deportation or prison, truths were instead whispered conspiratorially, without ever being recorded. Stories of events that would never make it into the press, of high-profile decadence, dust-ups at gay bars or demonstrations quashed by police, were endlessly transmitted by the transient inhabitants of Dubai.

Earlier that day, she had attempted to open a bank account at the Emirates NBD branch in Mall of the Emirates, but when she finally got to see an Account Manager, she was told that without an Emirates ID there was nothing that could be done. 'Maybe try the HSBC in Dubai Mall; they have a special expat policy,' the Account Manager said as Siver left with Zara in tow. And so, another cab to another mall. But whatever policy the Emirates NBD Account Manager had been thinking of was not one that anyone at HSBC had heard of.

'Maybe we have this policy, ma'am, but I cannot see anything about it in our system.'

In her third taxi of the day, going back home, the driver told the story of a worker who, being denied his annual leave, went to the 148th floor of the Burj Khalifa to commit suicide. Nowhere could she find confirmation that this had happened, though that did not make it any less true.

She got her first mobile phone a month or so after they'd gone to see *Titanic*. A Nokia 6110 in a shimmering purple, which cost £80 with a two-year contract. Mohammed and Laika both had phones before she did, so she didn't think her parents would be suspicious regarding her need for one. Xezal was even pleased, to Siver's surprise. 'I get so worried when you're in London, Sisi my soul. Now I can call you at any time.' Siver saved Karim's number under the name Sepideh, a university friend she had often spoken of at home. Karim would text her a 'hello', then, if Siver answered, would not respond for several minutes, sometimes hours. Siver began to ignore his messages for as long as possible, forcing herself not to leap over as soon as she saw the screen light up, forcing herself to not read what he had to say for as long as she could withstand it. Texting with Karim made her feel anxious, and giddy, and confused, and horny. Withholding instant gratification from herself felt like taking a shot of whisky and feeling the alcohol course through her veins.

I miss talking 2 u he would write, and she would stare at the message, wondering when they'd ever talked.

Every time Zara missed her father, a hundred dollars would have to disappear from the stack. Trying to take Zara's mind off the fact that her parents were now separated, Siver would take the girl out for a movie, for a milkshake, for something, anything, that could be purchased and temporarily fill the emptiness.

So when Zara asked if they would see Karim for Eid, Siver booked tickets to At the Top, the observation deck at the Burj Khalifa. Another hundred dollars. Siver's stack had within a few weeks dwindled to just under $3,000. Some of the money had been spent on necessities: sheets and towels, cups and cutlery. Most of it had been spent on indulgences.

The line to the elevator that would take them to the 124th floor slithered like the queue to a popular ride at an amusement park. Glass panels bearing photographs of the building's architects and developers were set opposite inspirational quotes and trivia regarding Burj Khalifa's architectonic wonders. Zara was impressed by Burj Khalifa being the world's most photographed building while Siver was amused by the fact that construction had been supervised off-site at something called the Work-Action-Resolution room, stylised everywhere as the WAR Room.

At the top, a group of tourists were huddled in a crescent, their backs turned away from the observation deck's floor-to-ceiling windows. They were observing, Siver saw as she got closer, a gold-coloured ATM selling gold bars at whatever the price of gold was at any given moment. 'Can we get some?' Zara wondered, and Siver tried to avoid a potential tantrum by saying they would have to wait their turn, hoping she could somehow make Zara forget about the ATM by showing her the clusters of towers they could look down upon, the cars speeding below like frenzied ants.

A tourist was indeed interacting with the machine, his finger above the digital purchase button as the price of gold fluctuated, which allowed Siver to successfully coax Zara over to one of the many binoculars instead. 'Look how high up we are, monkey!'

Zara dutifully stepped on the platform by the high-tech binoculars and stretched upwards on her tiptoes to reach the device.

'I can't see anything! It's all empty!'

Siver looked through the binoculars and saw that it was set to show the city not as it appeared on the other end of its lenses, but as it was in 1975. What the binoculars showed was Dubai as it once was, beginning to shed its old identity as a small port city, a less-than-reputable trading post for merchants from Iran and India. When new government policies and years of drought had led the Bedouins to abandon their nomadic traditions, when their myths and poems ceased to be recited over the fires, when their laws, derived from Koranic suras, began to fade from the tongues of the tribal elders. All that the binoculars showed were wide swathes of desert, the odd road slashing through the sand, a skeletal structure or two, daring to exist.

'You're right. Everything is empty.'

As they went to take the elevator back down to earth, Siver noticed the tourist was still standing in front of the ATM, his finger still primed to buy at the perfect moment.

Why won't you let me visit you? I want to make sure you and my only grand-child are safe. I don't understand, I went to see Hama in London, he sticks me in a hotel, it was like a coffin, and I never see his home. No space, no space. It's like you children purposely live in small rooms so you have an excuse not to see me. And now you live in a country that is younger than your own mother. How can you tolerate a place with no history? It wasn't until petrochemicals bled over the sand that anyone even knew that place existed. I remember it hap-pening. This was during my lifetime. They may pretend to be a city of the world, oh with all their tall buildings, but I remember.

Eventually she told her parents about Karim. It was a Sunday after-noon, Rafiq at the dining table reading *Asharq Al-Awsat* while drinking tea, Xezal on the couch watching MED TV as the cassette player in their bedroom played worn-out tapes of old Kurdish love songs, the shrieking trumpet sound of the zorna drowning out lyrics about a sixteen-year-old's pomegranate breasts. Siver had been fret-ting over this conversation all weekend but had made a vow to herself that she wouldn't go back to university on Monday morning without having told them. Mohammed was out doing God knows what, Laika was in his room playing video games, and her parents looked bored. There wasn't going to be a better time.

'Daya. Baba.'

Her parents looked away from their media sources, towards her.

'There's someone I like.'

Her parents looked at each other with terror, Xezal literally gasp-ing, always more adept at performing life than actually living. After a moment of confusion, where her parents looked uncertain as to what they should do, Xezal went to sit by Rafiq, and he put his hand on hers. This was the worst thing Siver could ever tell them, and they would face this disaster together.

36

It was Xezal who spoke first.

'You will not be one of these whores who gets into bed with these British men. They're not like us, Siver, they do not respect women.'

'Mum, he's not British. He's from Iraq, like us.'

Xezal beamed, baring the gold fillings of her teeth, but Rafiq squeezed her hand, shook his head.

'Is he Kurdish?' he asked quietly, not looking at her.

Siver looked out of the window, at the tree where years ago a cat had got stuck for days and her parents were too afraid of the UK authorities to call someone. A neighbour was blasting that song where two women both claimed that the boy was theirs. In the background the Kurdish singer lamented the young woman not giving him her flower.

'No,' Siver said.

'Arab?'

'Yes.'

Rafiq said nothing more, simply took up his newspaper again.

'After all they did to us, the Arabs, you go and *marry* one?' Xezal said, raising her voice as though Siver were all the way across the street rather than in front of her.

'I didn't say anything about marriage.'

'*Ahstakhfirullah*, I will not allow my daughter to be a whore!'

Siver clenched her teeth, didn't want to say something she would come to regret. Xezal began to cry; Rafiq folded his newspaper neatly and went to his room to read. For the next two weeks he only emerged to eat his one daily meal, in silence. Afterwards he came into the living room and told Siver, without looking at her, that if she wanted to see this Arab, she was free to do so, but he would never give his blessing.

Still, what could they do? In the end she did marry Karim and all that remained of the struggle to get there were faded scars of the things her mother had said to her.

She had high hopes for her first job interview. It was at an upscale hotel adjacent to the Dubai Mall, with reasonable working hours and a salary that was advertised on the website. Her interview was at nine in the morning and she guessed that she would be the first person they saw for the position, so she needed to make sure that they remembered her at the end of the day. To that effect, she wore a long-sleeved cotton blouse with a floral broderie anglaise and a skirt in silk muslin paired with heeled almond-toed sandals in walnut, prepared to impress the hotel's HR department with her old wardrobe.

In order to save money, however, Siver elected to take the Metro instead of a taxi. This was a mistake.

Dubai had complied with the western narrative of a new city emerging out of nothing, a true neoliberal dream without any cultural baggage for investors to have to take into consideration, a city of transience. And so the names of the metro stations in Dubai would change every few years, as different companies bought the rights to specific stops. It was the ultimate statement of the capitalist city in eternal flux that today's First Gulf Bank station could become tomorrow's Equiti station. Siver could not work out where she was, as the corporate stations bore no relation to actual locations, but she thought at least that she knew where to go: surely the Dubai Mall stop would let her get to the Dubai Mall.

But although the Metro was being heavily advertised as the world's longest driverless metro, it achieved this feat by going in a straight line. Its stations were, then, plopped around Sheikh Zayed Road with little to no proximity to the places it was meant to take a person to. As Siver exited the air-conditioned glass orb, with an hour until her interview, she saw the mall far in the distance, across a tract of desert sand.

She asked the security guard stationed how she was to get there, to which he just laughed. 'The shuttle buses start at nine. But you can walk, madam, no?'

After a fruitless, desperate search for a taxi that could take her to the mall, she began walking, dragging her feet through the sand. Even though it was early morning, the sun was already weighing down on the back of her neck, a drop of sweat slaloming down her spine. The mall appeared mirage-like, right there in front of her but somehow impossible to reach.

By the time she reached the mall, twenty minutes later, she couldn't find her way up the ramp where the taxis dropped off visitors and so entered the mall through the lower floor, joining a throng of Filipino women who made their way through the corridors, getting some final conversations in before they began their silent servitude as shopkeepers, manicurists, waitresses. Those already in uniform had not only their employer's name printed or embroidered on their backs but also their own names pinned to their chest. Ruby, Girly, Cherrylove. A row of labourers were standing alongside the building's wall, backs as close to the wall as they could to remain in the shade without burning themselves on the hot concrete behind them, with the unfortunate effect of looking like the world's longest police line-up. The labourers, aliens in this glitzy commercial space never intended for them, a space that they themselves had built, didn't have their names on their uniforms, only that of the company hiring them. As Siver walked past them and into the miraculously cool air-conditioned mall, she felt several of the men leering at her, making her suddenly very aware of her bare arms and legs, of the blouse's neckline and how she looked to the world. Even men who had no power whatsoever still had the power to make her feel like meat to be devoured, discarded. If she were to complain to a supervisor, the worst offenders would certainly be beaten or deported, which seemed like an incredible overreaction to some ogling. And yet it wasn't nothing either: once she'd found her way to the hotel, she could not shake the feeling of discomfort, a stain that would not rub off.

Her state of mind, it turned out, could not have mattered less. The walk from the metro station had led her heels to be caked in dust, the heat and humidity had made her make-up transform her face into a grotesque death mask of liquid foundation. Her intricate blouse now looked baggy and misshapen, sweat patches forming on her chest, across her entire back. The moment the woman from HR looked at her in the lobby, looked at what had become of the designer wear she had hoped would impart a sense of wealth and professionalism, Siver knew she would not get the job.

She had seventeen days left before her visa expired.

Before Siver's parents accepted that she was serious about Karim, they orchestrated a set of proposals from young Kurdish men who admired Rafiq and wanted to marry into a family that had once had

39

renown and wealth. 'Just to let you see what your options are,' Xezal told her, as Siver groaned and rolled her eyes.

Two men proposed to her. The first was a young man whom she had never previously met but who seemed to know all about her. His proposal was traditional, with the young man's father accompanying him and telling Xezal and Rafiq that they had 'a flower in their garden that they wanted'. The suitor's tucked-in shirt, a size too big, ballooned at his waist. His moustache was neat, his hair cropped in the latest fashion, his perfume reaching the other side of the table. He spoke abstractly of love and duty, using words that nobody, including himself Siver suspected, actually understood. He made eye contact with each person in order: father, mother, her. Father, mother, her. He spoke of his law practice and of his uncle who had once been a minister in the Kurdistan Regional Government. When asked, that evening, what she thought of the young man, Siver found no more diplomatic way to tell her parents than the truth, which was that he repulsed her. Her father was able to save everyone's face by letting the young man know the following day that she was still in school and that until she graduated from university, there'd be no talk of marriage. That night, Siver apologised to her father, who kissed her goodnight. 'You will never have to marry a man that you don't like.'

The second man was older, had already been married once, but his business (selling split air-conditioning units) was booming and he wanted a new bride. He had a thick, bushy moustache and the eyes of a child. He wore traditional Kurdish clothing, but even so, Siver could tell that he was much larger than she was. He never spoke to Siver, instead talking only to her father and glancing approvingly at her every now and again. She said no. Her father repeated the decision to let her graduate before any talk of marriage and kissed his daughter goodnight. She woke up, however, to her parents arguing. 'Your daughter thinks too highly of herself! What, she will be an old maid?' she heard her father say in the voice he acquired after two or three glasses of whisky. 'You want your daughter to marry that old lecher? You want her to be an old man's second wife?' 'Well, what about that first boy? There was nothing wrong with him! I think she's forgetting her age. She's lucky that she has this many proposals.' 'There is always the Arab, Rafiq.'

There was always the Arab.

The Manpower offices in Dubai were in one of the city's older buildings, built in the early oos, and the two men who were assigned by the firm to find Siver a job met with her at the coffee shop in the lobby. Siddartha, the older of the two, had a south-London accent, and wore a garish purple shirt and a woven pink tie. Gil, the younger man, wore a crisp white shirt with an open English spread collar and spoke with an unplaceable European accent. They both wore black brogues, polished to a sheen. They both spoke as though they were in charge of the whole emirate.

'What can we get you?' Siddartha said, removing a Mont Blanc pen from a Mont Blanc pen case that was in a Mont Blanc messenger bag.

'A tea is fine, thanks.'

'Gil, go get Shiver here a cuppa. Cheers.'

Siddartha looked at her minimalist CV, turned it over for effect, as though looking for something that he obviously knew would not be there.

'So when did you arrive in Dubai?'

'A few weeks ago.'

'Oh, right. Right. You're brand new. Good.'

Gil returned with Siver's tea, having got her a black tea, not asking her preference. He reached into his bag and brought out another printout of Siver's CV, glancing over it.

'So, I'll be honest with you. Your experience in Iraq won't be of much use here. And that's all you have, along with some retail experience in the UK.'

'What you *do* have,' Gil – clearly the good cop – said after Siddartha's put-down, 'is a British passport, and good language skills. So that's not nothing. Especially in Dubai.'

'Do you have any intentions of having another child?'

'It says here that you are single. Employers could see this as a red flag, that as soon as you find a boyfriend, you'll leave the company.'

'And you're not young any more, you're what? Almost forty?'

'No, you're not young any more.'

Siver drank her tea, even though it was still too hot. This attempt at hiring a recruitment agency had been her last hope. The two men said they would try to find something, perhaps secretarial, perhaps within retail. 'We can't promise anything,' said one of the men she would owe half her first salary to and clicked his pen, indicating that this meeting was now over. 'But it was nice to meet you, Shiver.'

The feeling of futility that this meeting engendered in her lasted longer than the burned roof of her mouth.

She never took his name. It was not customary for Kurdish women to take the names of their husbands and she felt, on some level, that her marriage to Karim had inflicted enough pain on her parents. She could at the very least keep the name she was born with.

Once, during a parent–teacher conference, her biology teacher, Mrs Baker, had asked Rafiq and Xezal why Siver did not have the same name as them. 'There's three of you, and you all have different last names. I must say I was a bit, well, suspicious at first.'

Rafiq, overdressed in his finest suit and tie to impress upon Siver's teachers that he was an educated man, launched into a tirade about Kurdish nomenclature in his broken English.

'We have our name, then name of our father and then name of our grandfather. My name is Hama, it is like Mohammed, and my father Hardi, and my father's father Kermanj.'

Mrs Baker looked as though Rafiq was talking to her in another language altogether.

'So, same: Siver has her name, Siver, yes? Then my name Hama, then my father's name Hardi. We see history in names, not like here.'

'Oh.' Mrs Baker shot a confused look down at her sheet of paper. 'I thought your name is Rafiq.'

'Yes, yes, Rafiq. I change it.'

'This is all quite confusing, I must say. You have very funny names,' Mrs Baker said, an awkward smile to indicate she was sorry to have ever asked the question.

'To us, Baker is a funny name. Mrs Teacher is better name for you,'

Rafiq said with a grin as Siver, sitting between her parents, wished she could melt through the floor.

With time, she grew to appreciate the stratigraphy of Kurdish names, the way that you could tell someone's relative age by seeing where the schism between traditional Muslim names and the Kurdish names occurred. It was a century of apostasy and Leninism and nationalism all writ out in one's three names.

And yet, when Zara was born, she didn't even think to insist any of her names be given to her. Just like that, her history ended.

The English department store owned by a Bermuda-registered, Hong Kong-based conglomerate was the first shop you'd encounter upon entering the mall, premium real estate at a premium price.

Siver had received an email from the Manpower agency earlier that day, instructing her to go to an interview for a Senior Salesclerk position. She had worn a professional, minimalist suit by a Japanese designer she had once purchased for a funeral, from a few seasons ago, and coupled that with an expensive necklace made of black pearls and metal logos.

At the entrance a barrage of smiles, of expensive foundations and lipsticks stretching over perfumes to spritz. 'This is Joy, want to try?'

'Who buys scents on a whim?' Xezal had said to her once, at the Allders in Croydon, before the developer Minerva PLC put Allders into administration. Siver had picked up a matte-black Calvin Klein bottle that she had seen Kate Moss advertise on TV and Xezal was not impressed. 'A lady is loyal to her scent, does not flit willy-nilly like some commoner unsure of her identity.'

Siver asked a bored woman behind the Make Up Forever counter for Jeff, the man who the email said had called for the interview. The woman shrugged. She didn't know a Jeff. But did Siver want to try the new Ultra HD Stick Foundation?

She walked past the rows of sunglasses (all manufactured by the Italian firm Luxottica Group, all with different logos on their temples, all with a 1000 per cent mark-up), and went up the escalator to the women's department where skimpy child-sized garments hung sparsely on chrome racks. She asked two more people for the elusive

Jeff, and eventually she was led to a door hidden while in plain view, down a corridor where limbs and torsos of naked mannequins lay beside racks of clothes still wrapped in the manufacturer's plastic. A crime scene: all plastic sheets and body parts.

In a small, cramped office packed with cardboard boxes from which garments were jutting out like the entrails of dead animals, Jeff emerged from behind an old computer. Siver introduced herself, arm stretched out, and Jeff either had forgotten or pretended to forget he was supposed to meet with her at all.

'Well, I guess you're here now so . . . have a seat.'

He looked at her as though she were a snake charmer and he the cobra, swaying his head, eyes at breast level. 'Tell me: why should I hire you?'

Siver rattled off a few platitudes about her work ethic, about her extensive experience in the retail market, her knowledge of brands.

'Where do you see yourself in five years?'

A terrible question, one of the worst parts of the job interview ritual. She knew the answer should be something that simultaneously showed that she was a loyal employee, but with ambition, but not with too much ambition, yet when he asked, she tried to imagine her future and saw nothing. It was as though Karim had erased whatever future she had imagined for herself, forcibly removing anything that she could cling to as certain, worth gambling on. She was left with a blank canvas, improvising. Five years from now? She didn't know where she saw herself at the end of the week.

Siver, why don't you call your brother, be a good influence, tell Hama that he should find a good girl, remember that the time has changed in London, he's now four hours ahead of you, I guess Emiratis don't know how to change their clocks, they have to be so special. Call him now, he's still up, tell him he's not a child any more, he needs to think about getting married, I keep telling him that Kak Goran's daughter has just got her master's in engineering, mashallah, she's a good girl from a good family, she's very handsome -- you remember Kak Goran's daughter Chra? You two were friends, remember, you used to play with those Barbie? But of course he doesn't listen to his mother, none of you do, with Hama it's just work work work, money money money.

When the UK started the National Lottery in 1994, Siver and her brothers would put down a pound each at the beginning of the week and spend the days until Saturday dreaming of what they would do if they won. These daydreams would make each week surmountable, and though the televised draw would ultimately lead to disappointment, a new dream could commence the very next day.

'I'd get a McLaren F1, in blue, first thing I do, I'd just drive up and down Harrods all day so all of London can have a look at me,' Mohammed said during one of their many joint sessions where they spent their imaginary winnings. Every other week, he dreamed of a different car, but the gist was the same.

'I'd buy the parents a house, three flats, one for each of us, and I'd never work a day in my life,' Siver said, looking at the row of numbers she played every week, believing that the probability of her eventually winning was higher that way.

'As opposed to all the hard work you've done so far, you mean?' Mohammed chuckled.

'Fuck you, Mo; you're not getting a flat from me.'

'A house would be nice,' Laika said. He picked out a different set of numbers each week, thinking that perhaps some form of otherworldly inspiration would give him the correct numbers. 'Just to have a place that was ours, you know? Other than that, I honestly don't know. I just don't want Mum and Dad to worry.'

At first, the weekly lottery tickets were purchased in secret, to avoid Rafiq launching into a rant about how lotteries were nothing but taxation of the working classes, a government-sanctioned notion that money would solve all one's problems. After a while, however, he began giving Siver a one-pound coin every Monday, alongside a series of numbers inspired by historical events (18, the year of Marx's birth; 46, the year of the Republic of Mahabad; 51, the year the Kurdish linguist Bedirxan died, and so on), always in silence, as though he were committing a sinful act. As though dreaming was not something he should do.

With nine days left on her visa she got an interview in a designer store on the first floor of the Mall of the Emirates.

Siver had selected various items from said brand to wear for her interview and to her astonishment, the manager, a French woman by the name of Isabelle, who'd had impeccable work done to her face and was thus of indeterminate age, immediately began speaking to her as though she already had the job.

'Nothing against the others,' she said so that the young woman dusting off the glass case where the small leather goods were kept could hear, 'but they have as much knowledge of the history of our brand as they do of nuclear fission. You know, we are not for the teenagers who come in here with Daddy's credit card, we are for the madame who has her own money.'

Siver nodded, as this was what was expected of her.

'I think it is only admirable that a woman with actual, you know, style, represents our brand to the customers. I think you will work here very well, Silver.'

And that was it.

They shook hands, Isabelle promising to send across the necessary paperwork to her email later that day, and Siver walked the long path from the mall to the metro station in tears, as though months of stress had just been released, emotions pinballing through her. She didn't know why she couldn't just be happy that she'd managed to do it, finally, to get a decently paying job. Maybe it was because after all that, she was just given it, she couldn't even feel like she'd done anything special to get this job, that she'd accomplished it. It was just a fluke.

Still, by the time she got home she had put a smile on her face, dancing with Zara in their new apartment, promising she would buy her that doll she so wanted. 'We're going to be OK, monkey, I promise,' she told her daughter, who looked confused, and a bit scared, as if not being OK was never something she had actually considered.

———

Ever since her father had died six months ago, she spent most of her time at Karim's place, dreading having to return home, seeing her mother's judgemental frown. Xezal never said it outright, of course, she never said that news of Siver's engagement with an Arab man was what had led to Rafiq's heart attack, but Siver still felt it hanging in the air, she felt it in her mother's gestures, the way she would barely look up when she barked at her to do the dishes, to make an appointment for her at the GP.

'She's just lonely,' Karim told her as she began complaining again about Xezal. 'She's lost the love of her life,' he said, rubbing Siver's knuckles.

Siver cackled. 'Love? Don't be ridiculous, Karim. There was no love there.'

'Still. You should be there for your mother.'

'If you want me out of here, just say so.'

'That's not what I meant,' Karim said, his voice dropping.

'She's got Laika living with her. Mohammed is there at the weekends. I don't know why I'm always the one who has to take care of her.'

'You're her only daughter, Siver. You know this.'

'I don't want to talk about this,' she said, reaching for the remote control.

She turned on the TV just as the second plane flew into the South Tower.

———

When Siver went to a car rental franchise intending to rent something reasonable to be able to get to work and to drive Zara to school once she started in the autumn, the employee told her of the car park near the airport where all manner of cars were left to die. 'Ma'am, if you go to our airport branch, they for sure will give you a good deal.'

On her cab ride over to the airport, she noticed construction had been halted on all the massive architectonic vanity projects across the city. The World, an artificial archipelago formed to resemble a Mercator projection of the world that had been intended for development, was left to sink back into the sea. She'd read that the owner of the 'Ireland' island had committed suicide, and the owner of the 'Lebanon' island opened a bar, ferrying customers over to serve them watered-down cocktails as the world sank around him.

Construction had also stopped on the Falconcity of Wonders, a massive real-estate project that would have included to-scale copies of the Eiffel Tower, the Great Pyramid of Giza, the Taj Mahal, the Leaning Tower of Pisa and the Great Wall of China. Shame, that. She had been looking forward to taking Zara there.

The notoriously bad traffic down Sheikh Zayed Road had improved considerably, the taxi getting her to the airport in a previously unthinkable half-hour, but it was hard not to notice the skeletal structures that cluttered the skyline, undead reminders of a future that was, temporarily at least, put on hold. The financial crisis had, finally, reached Dubai.

The manager at the airport branch of the rental firm took her down to the rows of dusty vehicles that the rental company had bought at a recent auction, the windscreens all carrying instructions to WASH ME and juvenile scribbles of I WISH MY WIFE WAS THIS DIRTY. There were impractical sports cars, swirls of lightweight carbon fibre impossible to conceive outside of a computer, giant SUVs with tinted windows, expensive German sedans. The remnants of wealth that had now evaporated. 'Pick what you want. I give you a good price.'

She picked an SUV, something that might keep them safe from the speeding cars and the many accidents that she saw every day on the road.

'Very good choice,' the manager said, barely looking at the car she'd pointed out.

He called two young men, dressed in faded blue overalls, to clean the car, wipe off months of sand, as he took Siver out of the oppressive humidity back into his office to sign the lease agreement.

As she drove away, she sped far beyond the speed limit, slid down all the windows and imagined what it would feel like to drive into a wall.

Karim received the call from his mother one Sunday afternoon while he and Siver were eating at the Tate Modern. They had been in the middle of a conversation debating whether the fact that proper nouns were written in parentheses in Arabic meant that Middle Easterners were less individualistic, when the phone rang. Siver picked at her Thai salad, looking over the Thames and the wobbly bridge that linked Southwark to the City of London as Karim's voice trilled with the frenzied staccato rhythm of warring violins. It was a tone she had not previously heard him speak in.

'That was my mother,' he said once he'd hung up the phone. 'My father collapsed in his office yesterday.'

'Oh no. Is he OK?'

'I don't know . . . Siver, maybe I have to go to Baghdad.'

'When?'

'I don't know. My mother wants me to run the company, so that my father can rest.'

Karim had been sent to London to attend boarding school at Westminster eight years ago, his father believing it important that his son get his education in London. The family owned an apartment in Marylebone that they had purchased in the 80s, not knowing whether it would be safe to stay in Iraq in the future, and so once Karim got his A levels, he moved right into the family apartment that had been vacant for over a decade, save the odd summer holiday spent therein. When his parents began enquiring when he intended to come back to Baghdad, Karim stopped frequenting Mayfair nightclubs and applied for university, hoping to draw out the time he had at his disposal in London.

But now, on the seventh floor of the Tate Modern, he was considering returning. 'It won't be right away; of course we will get married first, and besides, I might not be so long, I can just go, a few months, come back. You don't have to come, habibti. Baghdad is no place for you.'

They ate the rest of their meal in silence, a solemn audience to the clattering orchestra of plates and cutlery around them.

Work was easy, what was hard was to appear at all times like you enjoyed the work. Siver's colleagues, after interactions with particularly awful customers, would often sneak into the back of the shop to have a quick scream. But the work itself was easy.

It was immediately clear to Siver what her role was: to comfort expats, to soothe them with her British accent and her western references, to not make them believe for a single moment that they were somewhere they did not belong. In this way, Dubai was much like a generic airport, engineered to make the surroundings feel familiar, effortlessly herding people through its geography. The mall was the ultimate generic construct with its identical and instantly recognisable luxury brands that stretched out over a space that was designed to be easily navigated and understood: the same fast-food chains, the same signs and structure typologies, all in order to instil a sense of calm in its visitors, the feeling that this was just like home, only better. What chatty customers would often describe to her as the best thing about Dubai was the access to the best parts of home without having to deal with the least pleasant parts.

The main import to the Gulf from the West was not western culture, but rather western brands. NYU and the Sorbonne, the Louvre and the Guggenheim were no longer site-specific institutions but global brands that could be purchased. Despite Dubai's showy newness, what the city ultimately peddled was nostalgia. And it was Siver's role to cater to that nostalgia. The British still had an empire, the French still were at the centre of the world, the Americans still came from the Best Country on Earth.

It was all an illusion, but an illusion Siver had a knack of maintaining.

When she eventually joined Karim in Iraq, Siver landed at BIAP, Baghdad International Airport, the very day they were removing the letters from the side of the building that spelled out Saddam Hussein International Airport. It had been renamed by Coalition Forces months ago, but the former sign had remained. As her plane taxied, she saw three men atop an orange platform, one scraping off the oversized letters making up the name of their former dictator, the other two simply witnessing. Once removed, the space beneath the metal letters remained the original green that the building had been painted decades ago and so still showed Saddam Hussein International Airport and would for months, a slowly fading spectre of a previous identity.

It was her first time in the city since she was a baby. Though both she and Mohammed had been born in Baghdad, she had not been back since her parents left for Slemani when she was still a toddler.

She remembered nothing of the place, Mohammed telling her before the move that he seemed to recall it being nice, but of course he didn't remember much of anything himself, aside from the fact that there was good ice cream.

She had found life in London unbearable without Karim. Initially she enjoyed her free time, having his apartment to herself, going to galleries and movies on her own. Her friends from uni made an effort to see her for dinner, but gradually they got swallowed up in work. Mohammed did enjoy the odd drink with her, but he was travelling to Africa every other week buying air from villagers or whatever it was he was doing. Seeing Laika meant seeing Xezal and she was still not on the best terms with her mother after she refused even to show up for her wedding. She looked at the photos Karim would email her from his life in Baghdad first with some bemusement, then, as time went by, with something resembling longing. And, yes, she missed the sex.

It didn't help that she no longer felt at home in London, a city that was doing everything to push her away. In the streets people were protesting a war in a country that they had never been to, had no knowledge of, seeming to indicate that they would prefer her people get slaughtered by Saddam Hussein's regime for all eternity, as long as they didn't have to think about it. She was tired of going to job interviews and being told she was overqualified, while never being able to land an interview for a job she was actually qualified for. She was tired of being told that she had such a good British accent. She was tired.

So she called him. Said she would try it out. She'd move to Baghdad.

Xezal barely spoke to her in the run-up to the move. When Siver and Karim had got married at the Sutton Register Office, after it turned out the Suleymaniye Mosque on Kingsland Road had a month-long waiting list and Karim needed to return to Baghdad to care for his ailing father, Xezal had told Laika that she had a headache. She said this when he asked if she was ready, that they were meant to be there in less than half an hour. A headache, Siver scoffed when Laika told her what had happened at the register office – a beautiful house just a few minutes from where they lived in their cramped flat. 'That's all we ever are to her, headaches,' she said as Laika tried to console her.

It wasn't until the minicab came to pick Siver up for her flight to Baghdad that Xezal confronted her, deeming this a good time to tell her daughter not to leave. 'I don't understand why he can't just live here. What, he doesn't have enough money, this man of yours?'

'Now you tell me this? When the car is already here?'

'We left that wretched place for a reason, Sisi. And now you're going back?'

'You always said how much you loved it there,' Laika said, looking up from his book.

Xezal took Siver in her arms.

'My heart is worried about you,' she said, crying now. She always knew how to turn on the waterworks.

As Siver got in the cab she saw her mother waving from the street. She was still waving as Siver turned around one last time before the car turned a corner and her mother and the building she'd grown up in were gone.

———

BIAP's interior, designed and built by the French firm Spie Batignolles in 1979, looked dated even for the late 70s: drooping stalactites inspired by Islamic architecture and painted a wretched green. As the only people who could fly through the airport at this time needed documentation that the vast majority of Iraqis lacked, there was the need for not only a VIP room but a VVIP room. A small duty-free shop sold perfumes and not much else (a Shiite cleric had recently objected to the sale of alcohol) and a café with Pepsi-branded refrigerators showed a Spanish football match.

Siver collected her bag and got into the shuttle that would take her to the concourse where Karim would be waiting, as visitors were not allowed past the many security checkpoints where dogs sniffed luggage and travellers had to show documents to American soldiers pointing rifles at them. She squeezed in among the other passengers for the duration of the ride to the outdoor car park where scores of waiting family members stood. She saw Karim and his mother as soon as she got off, both visibly uncomfortable in the scorching heat, a film of sweat covering the small, pudgy mother's face, patches under Karim's pits. The mother took Siver's face in her hands, kissed her hard, spoke words in Arabic that Siver did not understand. She put something in Siver's hand, a gold ring, and Siver felt relaxed for the first time at the prospect of having another mother in her life. This one seemed more eager to please than her own.

'It's dusty here,' Siver said, squeezing Karim's clammy, comfortably big hand, looking out of the window at the cement maze constructed by the Americans, fencing in the city of Baghdad amidst modular blast walls that with time would morph and twist at will, creating new neighbourhoods, new geographies.

'It's the war,' Karim said, leaning in to whisper in her ear, his breath warm on her nape. Siver initially thought this was a metaphor, but it was indeed the war that created Baghdad's many sandstorms: the marching troops and the vehicles roaming around the desert had created a climate where sand swirled ever stronger.

At the home, *her* home, he showed her the lavish entrance, the many bedrooms, the fully equipped kitchen, then pointed out a crack in the wall he saw her notice. 'It's the humidity that does that to the paint. It's nothing to worry about; we'll just paint over it.'

This was not a metaphor either.

———

She had been working at the mall for a few weeks when posters appeared all over the city announcing the upcoming Dubai Shopping Festival. An ad for Damac Properties advertised a free Lamborghini Aventador Roadster for anyone who bought property in their exclusive Damac Maison. The world's largest shopping cart was installed in the atrium of the Mall of the Emirates, prompting a ribbon-cutting ceremony, local journalists and gawking tourists holding their phones up to the giant steel object as though they were shielding their eyes from a new sun. Isabelle sent an email to the staff informing them of the store's opening hours during the festival.

'Wait, we're expected to be here for twelve hours?' Siver interrupted her colleague over lunch as she scanned the email on her phone. She already felt a weight in the pit of her stomach for letting

Zara run feral in the Discovery Garden complex while she was at work during the day. Now she was supposed to leave Zara from nine in the morning to nine in the evening?

The colleague that she interrupted, Linela, was in the process of telling her about a failed modelling career. She was from Bosnia-Herzegovina and had been on several top-brand runways, but encountered consistent visa issues ('I have the same last name as a famous terrorist. So.'), which made American casting directors less inclined to include her in the New York Fashion Week runways, for which her body type was more suited. She stabbed a piece of lettuce with a blunt food-court fork and shrugged. 'Ah yes, I hear the Saudis have paid for the malls to be open later this year, so they can shop at night when there are no westerners. It is what it is. Maybe you can find a babysitter? It's only a week. Anyway, so . . .'

By the age of twenty-four Linela had realised that she would never have the kind of modelling career that she aspired to, and so initially moved to Moscow to 'find a partner'. She enrolled in what was colloquially called the Gold Digger Academy and paid a thousand dollars a week to learn how to find a man (module 1), get a man (module 2) and keep a man (module 3). She quickly found herself a boyfriend, an oil trader and small-time gangster who set her up in a two-room mistress apartment, sent a Maybach to pick her up for their dates and showered her with expensive trinkets, but just as quickly grew anxious in Moscow, she said, mouth full of mâche, as her boyfriend had installed security cameras to ensure she didn't bring other men to the apartment and increasingly spent their dates ogling the gaggle of eighteen-year-olds who were lying in wait for him the moment he was done with Linela. She was too old for the mistress game, she said, shrugging. That's a teenager's game, getting in and accumulating enough money to be able to modestly retire by twenty-five, twenty-six at most. So she flew to Dubai, signed up for an Arabic course, got a job at the store, and spent her evenings going to networking events and cooking classes.

Siver was only half-listening at this point, thinking of how little money she had left, her first salary that she wouldn't receive for another two weeks, the fear of trusting a stranger with her child.

'You have to get to a point where you stop worrying all the time,' Linela said matter-of-factly, to sum up her life's ambition.

Everything in the Baghdad house had to go. Karim was a doting husband, but he did not have taste. Siver leafed through Turkish and Italian catalogues selecting new couches, new beds, new everything. 'This looks like it was decorated by Saddam Hussein on an LSD-trip,' she said by way of explanation and Karim did not object. His mother would agree with her, telling Karim to listen to his wife (or so Karim told Siver). In the end it was his mother who suggested a solution: the family owned another house that needed renovation, a house that was going to be rented out to the Korean government for them to use as their embassy, and so the furniture Karim had chosen himself was sent there, to make room for Siver's selections, which were trucked to Baghdad in the following months. The only thing she kept, aside from the televisions and kitchen appliances, was a painting Karim had purchased in a souq. It wasn't anything special, your run-of-the-mill oil painting of a cottage in a field, but Siver found it appealing for some reason, some memory sparked by the cottage. It couldn't have been their house in Slemani, there were no photographs of it, and she could not remember living there. It was kitsch, of course, but still she felt there was beauty being conjured in the idyllic scenery.

It was hard to remember that she had once been happy. Though she had a hard time learning Arabic (her private tutor much more interested in practising his rusty English than forcing her to learn grammar), Karim did his best to get her acclimatised to the city, introducing her to family members and friends, getting his mother and cousin to take her to get manicures and haircuts at the best Lebanese salons in the city, and they had a cleaner, and a chef, and errand boys who did her shopping for her. 'You just relax,' he told her when she wondered what she was supposed to do.

After a few months, he took her to his place of employment and put her in charge of liaising with all the firm's western clients. Karim's family had started the construction business in the 60s and had known how to stay on the right side of Saddam's regime, so there was substantial wealth. Karim's father, a frail, cancer-ridden man whom Siver barely saw, had handed the daily operations over to Karim, who saw the new Iraq as a place where one could finally do business with international firms. He met with representatives for hotel chains who saw Baghdad, Karbala and Basra as future business hubs and would hire Karim to build their four- and five-star hotels for them. Siver, whose Arabic was improving but not quickly enough for her to do more than talk to her staff about the most mundane things, handled communications with the various company representatives, sending out documents to be legally translated, and spent her days answering emails, assuring nervous Europeans and Americans that the place they were bombing had a future. There was money to be made here.

'Use your sexy English,' Karim told Siver, her London accent putting the company representatives at ease. 'They hear my accent and they don't trust me. They hear you and can see you as one of their own,' he said matter-of-factly. Although she had never had a savings account, and though she had never been able to buy any of the things that Karim now regularly provided her with, her tongue was more a marker of wealth than Karim's broken English ever could be. 'But I'm nobody,' Siver once told Karim in the car from work when he told her she should chair the next meeting with the people from Kempinski Hotels. 'Never say that,' Karim said, taking his hand from the gearstick and placing it on her thigh.

She knew she had been happy then, she knew it had been true, but she did not remember the feeling at all. She recalled this time the same way she thought of that painting she had found beautiful once, but which now left her cold, unable to see whatever it was that had evoked such marvel in the first place. It was just stuff, all of it.

With her new life in Baghdad came new social obligations. Every other night, Karim would drive her past the many armed checkpoints to the home of a friend or a relative, where other friends and relatives were gathered. The living rooms were all virtually identical: large spaces with baroque, uncomfortable chairs lined up against the walls. The men would sit closest to the host, loudly debating politics, while their wives would whisper gossip to one another further down the rows. These were people who had been well-off during Saddam, who were still well-off under the Americans, who would be well-off regardless of what happened next. Most of them had swapped their expensive SUVs for more modest vehicles, fearing being kidnapped for money as many of Baghdad's wealthy residents were, but their newfound humility was only for show. When safely at home, servants would bring a multitude of bottles of alcohol, all counterfeit, and place them on a centre table alongside plates of nuts and various mezze. The contents of the bottles – always blended whisky, always labelled Chivas Regal, Royal Salute, Blue Label – was identical, distilled as they had been on ships moored alongside the Aegean Sea, but there was great pride in presenting the most exclusive bottle to one's guests. Whenever Siver was surrounded with Karim's family members, she was allowed to drink, but as soon as there was someone outside the family in attendance she was forced to sit with cans of Pepsi or Mirinda, trying to understand what they were talking about in Arabic, snapping up names like *Bush* and *Saddam* and inferring the rest. She tried to memorise the names of the wives, want- ing to fit in, but could never keep up as the men kept taking second and third wives. Every so often, one of Karim's relatives would realise that she did not understand what was being said, and would give her a pained smile and offer some food. The women would compliment her clothes, show off their latest designer handbags for her approval. To them, oddly, she was not a Kurd, someone they'd barely deign to speak to let alone look to for fashion advice, but a Londoner.

Whenever Karim spoke he would launch into one of his tirades which she would recognise even if she did not understand the language he spoke them in. Often, he'd launch into an attack on Roman numerals. He saw this as snobby European imperialism at its worst, insisting on these inel- egant numbers above the far more versatile and useful Arabic numerals. Before Arabic numerals reached the West, a European scholar would still be using an abacus, like a child, he would growl, swivelling his tumbler of whisky clouded with fingerprints. Back at their house, while Siver craved some calm, trying to replace the foreign words and sounds swirl- ing in her head with silence, Karim would return to this topic, talking well past the point of being interesting. 'Do you think it's a coincidence that western universities insist on using Roman numerals, still to this day, to let us know at what point in the Middle Ages when we were developing algebra and geometry and trigonometry, they put three stones on top of each other and called it a university? They want to rub our noses in it, as if history is theirs and we are just ahistorical sand people.'

And so, Siver had to admit, when she saw that the Dubai school she decided to enrol Zara in proudly claimed to have been 'Est. 2007', she was disappointed. He would have been happy with her choice. She did not want him to be happy.

Coeus International School, Est. 2007, had a logo inspired by medieval heraldry and followed the British curriculum, while offering its students myriad after-school activities such as skiing (at the Mall of the Emirates), horseback riding (at the Ibn Battuta Shooting Range) and diving (at Dubai Mall). It lay in the relatively underdeveloped Jumeirah Village Triangle area, a beacon of primary education surrounded by desert.

The tuition fee for a six-year-old who would be finger-painting most of the time was 20,000 USD per academic year, a sum that Siver did not have at her disposal and (she eventually concluded) she would have to ask Karim for. She could take the high road when it came to her own finances, she would refuse to take a single penny from him until the day she died, but she would not subject her daughter to any disadvantage due to her own sodding pride. This was her philandering husband's responsibility. Just because Karim had decided he wanted to sleep with teenagers, he could not shirk his duties towards his own child. The cheque having to be with the school in five days, she did not have the luxury of delaying the matter. She considered, briefly, having Zara call up her father and ask for the money but she could not bear to do that to the child. This was her responsibility, her email to write.

Subject: Zara school

Message: Your daughter needs money for her schooling – this is the school: coeusinternationaleducation.com. I would appreciate 20,000 dollars asap to pay for the tuition.

Siver

She looked at the message, appreciating its directness, but still annoyed at her own tone. 'I would appreciate'? No, 'she needs'. That was better. She needs 20,000 dollars asap.

She removed her name from the bottom of the message.

Before she had time to obsess further about the email's contents, she hit send, immediately beginning the process of obsessing over his reply. She imagined him sitting at one of his relatives' gaudy houses around Harthiya, drunk on whisky as he received the message, interrupting one of his soliloquies as his teenage wife sat at the end of the room, partaking in the latest gossip with ease. Siver stared at her laptop, aimlessly browsing news articles she could not focus on, until her email client pinged and a new message from Karim appeared.

Re: Zara school

I will give you the address to a hawala to pick up the money tomorrow. Bring ID.
It's good to hear from you.

Karim

Siver did not know what she was expecting from him, but it certainly wasn't the email she was staring at. She had steeled herself for a long, protracted argument about his responsibilities and his need to be there for his daughter. Now he'd robbed her even of that argument. And what was with his send-off? 'It's good to hear from you'? A declaration of victory from his part; she'd blinked, she'd reached out to him, he'd won. Son of a bitch.

Perhaps he hadn't even given this any thought, maybe he just replied in the car, while waiting at a red light. Maybe he ended all his emails with 'it's good to hear from you'.

She scrolled through her mailbox, reading email after email from him, sending links, reminders, short missives of iloveyou, from before he had gone and eradicated her life, her very identity.

It was dark by the time Zara came up to her, saying that she was hungry. Siver called for a pizza and continued reading until the delivery man arrived.

————

Whenever she called her family from Baghdad, regardless of her mood, she felt that it was her duty to act as an ambassador of Karim's, of her life in Iraq. Mohammed would boast about the many deals he had lined up, as if Siver wasn't aware of his financial situation, and Siver would talk about how successful Karim's firm was. Laika would talk about how much he liked Berlin, how you could feel the emptiness left by the wall, a scar through the city, and Siver would describe Baghdad's sunsets, the fiery orange sun hanging low over the horizon, bigger than she'd ever seen it.

Her mother had moved back to Slemani, and whenever Siver would fly over with Zara to visit her for the weekend, she found herself saying how much more beautiful Baghdad was, how much history there was there. She heard how obnoxious she was being, how little of what she said was intended as honest communication. She had turned into a PR representative for her own life choices.

'You've forgotten where you come from,' Xezal would reply with disgust, as her maid – who Siver later learned was a relative of theirs – brought them tiny cups of coffee. It was a curious accusation, Siver always felt. After all, she could not forget what she had never known.

When Karim sent the funds for Zara's school he resorted to a hawala in Dubai's gold souq. Iraq's banking system was still in its infancy, and a telegraphic transfer could take weeks as the Iraqi bureaucracy coupled with international due diligence held the money up at every step of the way. Which left hawalas, a system for financial transactions across the Arab world and Asia that had existed since the eighth century, where one agent would receive the money and inform a broker somewhere else in the world that the money had been received. The second broker released the money in exchange for an ID or a password.

Once Siver got the address from Karim she took a taxi, as there was nowhere to park a car near the souq, and wandered amidst the hundreds of stalls selling identical gold bracelets for the better part of an hour before she saw a handwritten cardboard sign in the window of one of the stores indicating that this was indeed Mohammed Ahmad General Trading, the location that Karim had told her to seek out.

Sitting behind the glass display case, in which diamonds and emeralds glittered under spotlights, was a short, bearded chipmunk of a man, wearing a stretched-out T-shirt picturing a cartoon skunk uttering a vaguely sexual invite. Siver showed the man Karim's email, handed him her passport, which he proceeded to photocopy. He opened a safe and put two stacks of bills in a money-counting machine.

'Twenty thousand,' he said, making her sign a document that the money was well received.

She fumbled with the stacks, forcing them into her handbag, briefly wondering how it was possible that those nimble briefcases in the movies could contain tens of millions of dollars. Clutching the bag to her chest, she walked the streets of Deira trying to find a taxi to take her to the nearest mall so that she could deposit the funds into her account. She was suspicious of every person that she saw, fretting that she would get robbed, and it wasn't until her money disappeared into an ATM and a receipt indicated to her that the money was now truly hers that she could relax.

Small things she remembered, long after:

Karim watching a movie featuring a pneumatic blonde, legs that made up 70 per cent of her body, hair expensive and flowy, walking down a set of stairs wearing a dress that was poured rather than sewn. Him telling her, 'You would look good in something like that.'

Siver crying watching the news, seeing an earthquake in Iran that had devastated an entire village, Karim coming up to her concerned, his arm around her. 'Did you know anyone from there?' he asked, to which Siver shook her head. 'It's just so sad!' Karim's arm receding, him suddenly annoyed. 'Siver, you can't scare me like that, I thought something had *happened*.'

Karim telling her she should not wear red. 'It's not, yahni, *appropriate*, for a woman your age, habibti.'

Siver announcing she was pregnant and Karim falling to his knees, kissing her belly, praising God.

Karim whispering that night in bed, as he was caressing her head gently as though she were suddenly breakable, or more breakable than before, 'Do you think it's a boy?'

Karim's face during orgasm, how he temporarily became a demon, how the way his face contorted terrified her, how she had to turn off the lights before sex.

Siver forgetting the pin code to her online banking and Karim sighing. 'Why are you so useless?'

Siver asking him what he wanted for dinner, met with the same look every time, face scrunched. 'Anything is fine.' 'So chicken?' 'I'm tired of chicken.' 'OK, a lamb stew then?' 'Siver, I can't make every single decision in this household. Pick something.'

(This was their dance, they knew the steps well. Sometimes she would joke that she had two children. It wasn't really a joke, rather a cliché: a truth so dull it wasn't even worth mentioning. Sometimes she would ask him things not because she was wondering what the answer was, but because she wanted a fight, and wanted him to be his unreasonable self so she had a reason to scream at him.)

————

As a reward for working longer hours during the Shopping Festival, Isabelle gave the staff free tickets to Ski Dubai. Siver did not ski: at university those who skied would often profess to long for their family's chalets in Gstaad or Val-d'Isère and, invariably, once they got to fulfil their annual dream, would come back to lectures with a broken arm or leg. And then, the following year, they would sigh wistfully once again at how fortunate they were to be able to break a limb in the Alps. It was one of those rich-people things that Siver would never fully comprehend, natural selection for the wealthy. Still, the indoor ski resort at the mall also had a small park where children could interact with penguins, so on her day off, she took Zara there.

She was told that the free tickets were only valid for a meet-and-greet with three penguins; if she wanted to pay more, however, they could meet up to twelve penguins at a time.

'Three is more than enough, thank you.'

What surprised her was the extent to which the penguins shat, a constant stream of excrement following the birds as they waddled around Zara. Siver had difficulty framing a photograph so that the shit wouldn't be visible, wondered if she could crop the photo later or edit it somehow. After forty minutes of Zara excitedly hugging the three penguins in the river of shit, someone appeared whose job it was to clean up the excrement, to make the snow park ready for the next visitors.

After their visit, Siver would receive a weekly update email about the penguin that Zara had claimed to be her favourite, McFatty. Every week a new picture and a short paragraph of what McFatty had been up to. There was never any shit visible in any of the photos that the team at Ski Dubai sent her.

———

When her father died and she travelled back to Slemani for his burial, along with Mohammed, Laika and her mother, a man introduced himself to them at the border as their uncle Ali. Ali had made all the funeral arrangements, attending to them with the seriousness of someone who has something to prove. He insisted on driving them back to his house in a new but dusty Land Cruiser and had set up bedrooms for them all to sleep in. For the week that they were there, Ali would be generous to the point of obnoxiousness, consistently making sure the feasts that his poor wife would slave over were to their liking, asking them if they needed new clothes, if they needed to use his satellite phone to call the UK.

The day before they were meant to go back, he came to the room where the siblings had gathered, three envelopes in hand. Inside each was a thousand dollars, in crisp banknotes. Mohammed, having undertaken some sort of traditional elder-brother role during this whole trip, refused the money, saying that they couldn't possibly accept it, but Ali insisted, making them promise not to say anything to their mother.

'I could never be there for you kids; my brother's life made it unsafe for him here and our family was robbed of the chance to grow up together. I remember you, Mohammed, from when you were a little boy, as stubborn then as you are now, but I only saw Siver once and Laika, I only ever saw you in the photographs your father sent home. Let me do this for you, please. Things are going to be hard for you without a father. Let me do my part. I know your father would have done the same for my children should I have passed.'

They took the money. On the plane back to London Siver asked her mother what Ali did for a living.

'Oh, who knows? Something with cars; he just likes to show everyone that he's the one who is affluent now, little show-off that he is. If it wasn't for your father he would be a starveling, you know that, don't you?'

Once the cheque to the Coeus International School had cleared, Siver received a phone call. The woman on the phone, with an impeccable British accent, introduced herself as Jamila, and said that it would be hard for Zara to be interviewed before Thursday, but that the following week was more open.

'An interview?' Siver asked. 'She's six.'

'We interview all of our prospective students. It's an integral part of the Coeus education, to ensure that we have the best and the brightest amongst us, we want to ensure that every student reaches the standards required by the school.'

'But again . . . she's six. You want her to count to ten? What kind of interview are we talking about here?'

'We just want to ascertain Zara's suitability. Like I said, we attract the best and the brightest.'

'I mean, she's going to be able to talk in complete sentences . . .'

A forced laugh from the other end of the phone. Jamila's voice was now strained, impatient.

'Mrs Hardi, please. We have a team of highly qualified educators. They are more than able to ask the pertinent questions to see whether your daughter is a good fit for our school. Now, how does Sunday at eleven sound?'

The following Sunday Siver dressed Zara in one of her nicer dresses and drove out to the school. The interview took the better part of an hour, with a young British woman who had the title Lead Educator asking Zara what she wanted to do when she grew up (Zara's answer was policeman; Siver couldn't tell whether this was a good or bad answer) and if she liked school (Zara's answer: I don't know, I haven't been). The hour over, Zara fidgeting in her seat, the Lead Educator stood up and told them that she would get back to them.

That night Zara was desolate. *Ummi, what if they don't like me?* Siver consoled her, saying that they would have to be idiots to not see what a fantastic and wonderful little girl Zara was. Once Zara had fallen asleep, Siver locked herself in the bathroom and cried until the bathroom's motion detector no longer detected any motion, turning off the lights.

———

Whenever she reacted to an outrageous news article about the Middle East, a woman being stoned for having been raped in Saudi Arabia, say, or a draft law that would let Iraqi men marry six-year-old girls, Karim sprang to the defence of the countries she spoke ill of. The British put us in this mess. Yahni, we didn't even have tribes here in Iraq any more until the British recreated them to divide and conquer us the same as they did with the Indians. They get to play morally superior, when this entire mess is their fault. Siver thought that after a hundred years of independence, maybe Iraq was freed from its colonial shackles just enough so that they would know that marrying six-year-olds is a pretty disgusting thing to want to do. Karim sighed, an exaggerated sigh to indicate how unreasonable she was being. 'The West, with its so-called feminism, do you know what happened when women started working? Suddenly it was impossible to live on one salary. Before, one person could feed a whole family; now both need to work to survive, and need to outsource everything – food, child-care, elderly care – all in the name of equality. It's a con; the whole thing is a con. At least here in the Middle East we have not fallen for it. Read Marx, you'll see, purchase-power was lowered when women entered the workforce. The whole thing set the family unit back.'

'What is it with men and bloody Marx?'

'Besides, marriage has always been about property. Never about sex, or love. In France you could marry dead people. If your husband died in the war while you were engaged, you could still legally wed him, because the contract between families was what was important. The rest did not matter.'

'You're speaking as though I've insulted your family. I'm talking about these idiots.'

'But they are my people, Siver. That's what you're not understanding. They *are* my family.'

At the mall, people came and went in waves. Labourers came first, left last. Siver rarely saw them, their spaces separate, starkly utilitarian, not meant for lingering. The cleaners and service workers were next, arriving in buses that quickly dropped them off at the lower parking, its 7,000 spaces still empty of cars.

Then came Siver and those of her ilk. Many changed from the sportswear they had been wearing into brand-mandated attire in the restrooms, capitalism having been exported to a place where the heat ought to have prohibited suits and long skirts and crisp white shirts and ties and yet that is what everyone wore because that was the professional uniform. So everyone sweated and flopped and melted due to their ridiculous insistence on wearing clothing devised by people who could never have conceived of such heat or humidity, let alone lived in it.

Tourists were the first of the consumers to come, looking with awe at the stained-glass roof modelled after that of Paris's Galeries Lafayette, giggling at the children's stores that carried Dior, Gucci, Lanvin. They would rarely buy anything, content with observing the sheer tonnage of entertainment available to them, taking pictures outside of designer stores, their fingers raised in a victorious V, as though the store's brand-value would rub off on them merely by being in the same photograph. Often too nervous to ask how much something cost, since prices at Siver's place of employment were never marked on any of the items for sale but instead required a conversation with a salesclerk like herself, they would instead marvel at how beautiful various items were before scurrying out of the shops, ashamed to ever meet Siver's eye.

The odd group of pupils would be next, on one of the many school tours that took them around the malls. Though Mall of the Emirates was less popular than Ibn Battuta Mall – a mall divided into sections named after the various places the Moroccan traveller had been to, thus allowing for a history lesson amid the Costa Coffees and fourteen-screen cinemas – there were still three or four classes that came every day, bored children being told of the mall's many records and achievements, pestering their teachers for a Krispy Kreme donut or a cup of frozen yoghurt.

The unemployed Emiratis were next, and this was when sales would occur. The employees at Siver's store were instructed to disregard the HQ employee handbook which suggested clients who seemed uninterested in purchasing items be ignored to focus instead on HVTs. This was deemed to be a successful policy in Europe, where people's net worth was perhaps easier to ascertain, but not in Dubai, where the unfathomably wealthy could walk in wearing ill-fitting T-shirts and flip-flops and buy half the store. So, they would put on their brightest smiles, their dimmest voices, and assist everyone with their various queries, hoping that the shoppers would walk out of the store with a $10,000 handbag or two.

After the Emiratis came the expat housewives, between a session of the latest exercise fad and picking up children at school, looking uniformly great in their high-end athletic wear, buying a new top or accessory to wear to the next Friday brunch, the weekly chance to demonstrate before their peers how well they had it.

As the women left, the expat businessmen came, in-between work and home, hurriedly buying a toy for a child's birthday they had forgotten to delegate to a PA, a bracelet for a wife who had been feeling neglected, lingerie for a mistress who had yet to be fucked.

Then came the teenagers with their skateboards and spiky hair, milling around the mall, going to the cinema, having elaborate milkshakes before taking a taxi back home as though this space were a cosplay of 50s America on steroids, which of course it was.

Then it was time for her to pack up and leave, locking the scarves away, putting the writing instruments and watches back in the safe, changing out of her suit back into whatever she had worn in the morning.

On her way to the car park, Siver would always walk past the many banks on the mall's lower level, where South-Asian men and women were standing in long lines, waiting for a teller number given to them by a woman whose job was to make as many of the people there do their business online instead. As most of the people were sending money back to their families, they had no use for the internet, cash-transfers being the only way the money made its way home.

Siver would get into her car and drive off, towards the school where Zara would be waiting for her in the after-class room, often the last child there, playing with a ragged doll or bouncing a ball against the wall by herself. Soon she'd be able to afford a nanny, Siver promised herself as she drove out, the mall receding in the rear-view mirror.

The mall was never closed, not really. On weekdays, stores stopped letting customers in at 10 p.m., at which point employees spent half an hour or so performing whatever necessary and brand-imposed end-of-day rituals had been decided upon. The French multinational hypermarket closed at midnight, as did the cinema and the indoor entertainment venue Magic Planet. Once the mall was emptied of clerks and consumers, the food court workers jettisoned the fat and the trash, and buses arrived with cleaners to clean the mall from the day's human residue. They would work for hours, scrubbing the mall's 2,400,000 square feet until the events of the day had been removed. Then the doors would slide open, the mall's other employees flowing back in to open their stores and stalls, for the whole thing to be repeated again and again and again.

During their first few years in the UK, Xezal barely spoke. The kids would come home, dismal grades in hand, complaining about the difficulties they faced in a school system where they could barely speak the language, and Xezal would just sigh and go into the kitchen to rinse some rice for dinner while their father fiddled with the radio, focused on events that took place on a different continent altogether. They would later joke that Xezal's constant barrage of complaints was due to so much having been bottled up during her silent years, a dam eventually bursting and wave upon wave of bile washing over those around her. There was nothing that didn't annoy her: the loose-clad British women on the BBC, the veiled women

68

on Al Jazeera, the condescension of their British neighbours, the stupidity of visiting Kurds. Whenever Siver would call Xezal from Baghdad, to assure her she was settling in just fine, it was as if Xezal had prepared a whole new list of topics to be aggrieved about. On this day, Xezal was incensed at the Abu Ghraib scandal. In the run-up to the war in Iraq, she had found herself watching more and more English news, but found the time spent on the prisoner abuse scandal an insult.

'It shakes my heart, all this,' Xezal said, and Siver assumed she meant the photographs of naked men in a pyramid.

'Me too, isn't it awful?' Siver said, leafing through a magazine. This call was a ritual that consisted entirely of spending a few minutes exchanging polite trivialities. Her mother's insistence to talk about the news wasn't ideal, Siver knew, as she never could find the right words to agree with her mother, the conversation invariably ending in an argument. A conversation with her was a permanent study in the defusing of bombs, of steering the conversation out of hostile territory.

'No, not the photos. Although that's bad. What really extracts my soul is that after all these years, that prison will be known not for what happened to us there, but what happened to them.'

'Yeah, but it's disgusting what they're doing to them, the Americans. Just because we had it rough there doesn't mean these people deserve to be mocked and tortured.'

'You call that torture? Pah! Acrobatics! We got raped by broken bottles. We had children who were forced to watch and clap when their parents were eaten by wild dogs. Abu Ghraib was a name to strike fear in the hearts of the Kurdish people, and now it's been taken over by this shit-eating? Nobody cared for us one dust, not one dust.'

Siver waited for Xezal's dramatic monologue to come to an end, there was no point trying to get a word in when she was like this. 'But that wasn't these people,' she said, once her mother was finished. 'And even if it was, they still don't deserve this. Nobody does. It's not fair.'

'Nothing is fair, Sisi. You'd do well to remember that. Nothing is ever fair.'

Siver said nothing more. She knew Xezal had been unfairly miscast as a housewife her whole life, forever struggling to be believable in the role. All casting is a lie: Travolta as a teenager, Astaire as a minstrel version of Bill Robinson, Siver as a loving daughter. Some lies are just easier to swallow than others.

'OK, well I have to go, Mum . . .' Siver said, indicating that this particular scene was about to end.

When she told Karim about her conversation – another ritual, the post-brawl analysis – he bitched about Xezal and Siver let him.

Siver? Siver? The line is bad. The Emiratis can't afford phones? Hai. I saw Haji Bawar's daughter today, she looked so beautiful, you know she's remarried? A lovely man, oh, I haven't met him myself but they say he's delightful. Why don't you come back here, Sisi dearest, we can find you a nice Kurdish man, why are you forcing yourself to stay in that desert full of Arabs and whores? That's the problem with you: always preferring the Arabs to your own people. Why don't you think about your daughter growing up like a nomad with no country to call home?

Sometimes, if Linela wasn't working, the men would try to flirt with Siver, while browsing expensive gifts clearly intended for other women. It always struck her that the only way men in Dubai knew to flirt was to launch, unprompted and uninvited, into what they did for a living, their inner eHarmony indistinguishable from their LinkedIn.

There was the man who sourced the aquatic creatures for the underwater restaurant Al Mahara, who promised to take her to dinner there. 'I'll show you my favourite oceanic manta ray,' he said with a wink that made Siver wonder if she'd missed an innuendo. There was the man who bought three handbags for over $25,000, who said he did legal work for the Louvre in Abu Dhabi and that he would let her touch the 'Ain Ghazal statues. There was the young man who fondled several scarves without buying anything who claimed he had received a grant to build robot pets. The sheikhs intended to make Dubai the happiest city on earth in time for Dubai Expo 2020, and the man had, he claimed, sold them on the idea of robot pets as a way to maximise happiness. 'Think about it: a dog you never have to walk? It's perfect.'

He showed her photos of his various prototypes: a cat, a dog, a rabbit and, for the discerning customer, a Bengal tiger. He then handed her his phone and told her to put her number in. 'If you want to have a good time.' Then there was the guy who imported restaurant concepts and who claimed he could get a table at Hakkasan, Zuma or Nobu any time he wanted, and the westernised Emirati in Lanvin sneakers who was tasked to suss out which camels in the annual camel beauty pageant had cosmetic surgery. 'Botox injections to inflate the camel's lips are easy to spot, but it's much harder to know if there is silicone in the hump, that requires real talent.'

The strangest of these wannabe Lotharios was the impossibly tanned Italian man who, every week, would buy the brand's silk twill headband for 350 dollars and instructed the staff to embroider a name on it for an additional 200 dollars. Every week it was a different name, Siver alone had sold him headbands embroidered with Eliza, Rebecca and Laurene. The staff would gossip, wondering if he had dozens of daughters, or if he gave an infantilising headband to every woman he dated, or if they were kept in a perverse trophy case, until Isabelle told them to stop their gossiping. The man spent thousands of dollars in their store every month, and should be treated with respect. He often invited the staff to parties on his yacht, handing out his business cards with his mobile number already scribbled on the back, and so eventually it came to be Siver's turn to be invited. His job, it turned out, was to import sand from Australia for Dubai's most exclusive beaches. Dubai's own desert sand was not comparable, he said, with the featherlike white sand from Whitehaven Beach. 'If you go to the Burj Al Arab, you will want a better experience than anyone else around you. We provide that.'

Mostly, however, the men would keep to themselves, taking photos of the items their partners had instructed them to get, before they called and confirmed size, colour, model.

'If I get this wrong my wife will kill me,' they would say, smiling, and Siver would smile back.

None of the women ever came in saying that their husband would kill them. Maybe because that wouldn't be funny.

While flicking through the hundreds of satellite TV channels at their disposal, they landed on the 1991 movie *Not Without My Daughter*, with Sally Field. Siver had never seen it, but remembered her parents being aghast that the Kurds in the movie who helped Sally Field escape Iran through the Kurdish mountains did not speak Kurdish. 'They couldn't find five Kurds in all of America?' her father sighed, and launched into a rant about the horrors of imperialism.

'Yahni . . . this fucking movie,' Karim said as Sally Field conspired with an Iranian friend in the kitchen. It was the first time Siver had heard Karim use the word 'fucking', so she shifted on the sofa, her eyes wide.

'I take it you don't like it?'

'Oof, no, it's really a terrible, terrible film.'

'I thought you hated Iran.'

'It's not that. Every white girl I dated, every single one, had mothers who had been traumatised by this stupid film, who would stare at me from across the room as though I was about to force their daughters to wear a hijab and move into a cave with me. This movie has done more damage to interracial dating than any piece of Bush propaganda.'

'Well, if you hadn't had such a horrible time dating white girls, maybe we wouldn't have ended up together. So we have *Not Without My Daughter* to thank for that.'

He hugged her close, kissed her head.

'I guess you're right,' he said, changing the channel.

When Siver saw a paperback copy of Betty Mahmoody's memoir at a Dubai bookstore years later, she smiled. He'd been right to fear the movie. His wife would eventually leave him, and take their daughter away, after all.

———

Within six months of arriving in Dubai, Linela found herself a sheikh, appointing a law firm to oversee the prenuptial agreement before she'd even chosen a wedding planner. *You're admirable and strong. Best of luck,* Siver wrote in the goodbye card that the employees signed upon her departure. She realised, on her way home, that the message seemed cold, but she did not mean it that way. She genuinely admired Linela, a mere girl who knew how to play the game better than Siver ever would.

Her replacement was Tanya. Half-French, half-Lebanese, with the blessings of youth and beauty that meant that she could arrive at the store with her hair in a tangle, having applied only the most rudimentary mascara and lip gloss and yet she was the only thing that husbands would look at while their wives were selecting handbags. Siver tried to keep up with the intricacies of Tanya's love life but realised that every other week the boy she was having troubles with was a different one, and gave up trying to follow this particular soap opera.

On Tanya's first day, while Siver was showing her how to fold a scarf – a scarf that cost USD24 to produce and retailed at USD699 – to the exact specifications that the brand required, Tanya interrupted her monologue about why she was where she was, why she did what she did.

'Was he not a good man?' Tanya asked, perhaps as nothing more than a way to indicate that she was still listening, still part of the conversation.

For days Siver thought about this question.

Siver could never find out how badly Karim's father was doing, everyone from Karim himself to the doctors and nurses at the hospital kept repeating that *inshallah* there was nothing wrong with him, that he was getting better when she could tell there was no improvement at all. The man had cancer and inshallah wasn't going to cure cancer. Yet, gradually, she learned to ignore what her eyes were telling her, and began trusting what she was being told. Though communication with Karim's parents was minimal, they both had such affection towards her – always sending over gifts with their driver, always giving her wet, sloppy kisses when they saw her – that she grew to love them in return. If they complained about her to Karim, they were kind enough to do so behind her back, and Karim smart enough to not share this with her. Even though her own parents had been *there* her whole childhood, they always felt far away, concerned with things that had nothing to do with their children, who were treated at best as an afterthought, and more often than not as an inconvenience. So when Karim's father finally died, and Karim's mother passed away as well, quite unexpectedly, only a few months later, Siver took it hard. She felt that the stability she had so long craved had been snatched away from her by a vengeful god and she rapidly flitted between the stages of grief, pinballing between anger, depression and acceptance in any given moment. Xezal and Mohammed texted her, telling her to give Karim their condolences, which riled her even more. Nobody was offering *her* any goddamn condolences. While Karim was dealing with his parents' passing with the stoicism that was required of a male child, her grief was seen as a necessary performance rather than something authentic.

The men held their wake at a nearby mosque, Karim standing in line at the entrance, greeting people as they came and went. His job, along with his other male relatives, was to stand still and solemn. For hours he would have to stand, staring out in empty space, his feet and legs dull with pain, showing the people of Baghdad that what is worthy of love must be endured. He later told her that his uncle had hired a photographer to go up and down the aisles of the mosque taking pictures of those who showed up, for the family to pore over later to check who had attended the wake and how long they had stayed for. Siver massaged Karim's feet as he came home from the mosque, as he told her how disconcerting it was to stay standing throughout the wake in front of all the mourners, as though he had an audience.

'I had to keep as still as possible, determined not to dishonour the memory of the deceased by fidgeting or yawning. It's exhausting, wollah.'

Siver did not burden Karim by telling him of the women's wake, held at an aunt's house, where Siver was relegated to bringing trays of tea and water for the mourners while they performed their grotesque masquerades of emotion. Siver had never seen so much wailing, so many women hitting themselves, trying to one-up each other by showing how much they were suffering. More than once, Siver noticed women blithely chatting away in the back before they remembered what they were supposed to be doing and resumed tearing at their own hair. Karim's family had even hired professional wailers to give the proceedings a suitable volume of grief.

Once the wakes were over and they returned to their now emptied lives, Siver found herself in tears one day as she noticed a pair of plastic slippers Karim's mother had brought for her, telling her that the floors were cold and she would get pneumonia walking around barefoot.

Karim put his arms around her.

'Why are you crying? It's not like she was your mother.'

The massive curvature of the single glass panel that stretched around the entire store, specially constructed for the designer brand by the architecture firm Foster + Partners, had a slight distorting effect that made the people inside look taller, skinnier, not entirely unlike mannequins. You grew aware of the distortion when confronted with the disappointed looks of men who had walked into the store expecting one type of woman and being faced with another. The employees were always observed, always scrutinised by the gaze wielded by passers-by. Even when the store was completely empty of customers, Siver needed to keep up the performance. She wondered if this was like being in a reality show, like that British one where they remained for a year on an island after the show had been cancelled, with the cameras still rolling but with nobody watching on the other end.

Karim's plan was always for her to give birth somewhere else. Amman maybe, Istanbul. 'London, if that's what you prefer.' Plans were made for Amman, as flights there flew regularly, and their hospitals were known to be the best in the region. Then Jordan decided to stop issuing visas to Iraqis at the border and required a visa to be applied for in advance. Karim, who only had an Iraqi passport, went back and forth to the highly militarised embassy area over the course of several weeks until, finally, he received his visa. By that time, however, Siver was too pregnant to fly. They discussed driving across the border, but they were both afraid of Al-Qaeda and Shiite militias and wanted, if at all possible, to avoid being kidnapped and appearing on Al Jazeera wearing orange jumpsuits with a machete to their necks. 'Orange

75

isn't my colour, Karim,' Siver quipped, and suggested just staying in Baghdad. After all, successful childbirths took place outside of internationally renowned hospitals all the time.

But then Siver's contractions suddenly became unbearably strong after 5 p.m. and they had to break the city curfew to make their way to a Baghdad hospital. He called his aunt, told her that they had to leave, to not worry.

'It would be ironic if we got shot by some Amriki on our way to give birth,' Karim said, hunched forward towards the steering wheel, speeding through Highway 8. Siver was about to point out that she didn't think that would constitute irony, but a contraction shut her up. 'Everything is going to be fine, habibti, I promise,' he said, eyes peeled wide for trigger-happy security contractors.

Xezal had always told her that you forgot the pain of childbirth the moment it was over, but Siver remembered the agony of it all, the hours of her screaming and the doctors scrambling only to tell her that they were out of epidural anaesthesia. How she was told that the laughing gas was efficient pain relief but all it did was give her a headache. Karim, bless him, stayed in the room even when the doctor said that it was not necessary. 'This isn't Europe, we can handle everything on our own, go have a coffee,' the doctor said, tilting her head under Siver's gown. 'I'm fine here,' Karim said, squeezing Siver's hand while pretending not to notice a nurse rolling her eyes.

Once Zara was born, after a long, brutal delivery that lasted almost fifty hours and required eight stitches, Siver didn't feel any of the things that she knew she *should* be feeling: all that talk of nothing ever comparing to the joy of seeing your child, the sheer life-changing force of holding your baby, none of that. She saw before her a red, angry, wrinkly little alien that looked so unlike either Siver or Karim that she thought, for a moment, to ask whether the nurses hadn't mixed the baby up with another. It felt less like becoming a mother and more like a stranger handing you an infant and telling you that you now had to take care of it. That much-vaunted new-born smell everyone kept talking about? Sour milk. She was more impressed with the sight of her placenta, which glistened like marble from an alien planet, than the weird stop-motion creature they put on her chest. Skin to skin after birth releases a wave of oxytocin, the books had told her, yet she felt nothing at all.

But then she saw Karim crying, the first time she ever saw him cry, and his tears awakened something in her. If he could show love, then surely she could too.

Take a few deep breaths, in through the nose, out through the mouth.

Siver fiddled with the flimsy headphones that came with her phone, trying to get them to fit in her ears as snugly as possible. She switched on airplane mode whenever she used her meditation app, so as to not have her intended relaxation be disrupted by a barrage of promotional text messages. This was session four of the 'Stress' bundle, though she had been trying to get through said bundle for over a month now. She'd receive notifications from the app, instructing her to 'Remember to Relax!'

And with the next outbreath, you can close your eyes, and begin breathing as you normally do.

It had been seven months since she had left Baghdad. Zara was happy at her school – having found a friend – and Siver was having an easier time making ends meet. Everything was, finally, improving, and yet she couldn't shake the persistent feeling of panic whenever she received an email, or a call, or a text message. She felt that everything she had could vanish in an instant, that they would be out on the street, unable to fend for themselves.

Scan through your body, from head to toe, just checking in, seeing where there is tension. Don't focus on the pain. Simply notice it and move on.

Was this anxiety temporary? She didn't think so. Dubai, after all, was a transient city. This was not somewhere you were encouraged to stay. If you were let go from a job, you had thirty days to find a new one or you had to leave the country. Landlords could raise rent as they pleased, even though the authorities had tried to stop them from doing so too egregiously, and the ever-persistent rumour of the UAE introducing VAT, making her purchases untenable, loomed in her mind. Compared to the lack of workers' rights in Dubai, a supposedly cut-throat city like London seemed almost quaint with its acceptance of rudimentary human rights, its insistence on perpetuating vague notions of freedom and liberty. To be in Dubai was, the city almost aggressively reminded you, a pit stop, a temporary measure. But what came next? What was she going to do once this was over?

And now just let go of any focus, let your mind wander freely.

She found herself wondering what it meant when Dubai was described as an 'artificial' city. After all, every city since the dawn of time had been a human construct, and yet the same term was not used in reference to Jericho, Babylon or Rome. Perhaps what it meant was that this particular city – with its futurism derived from the automobile-centric utopias of 1950s America, its giant glass cacti emerging from the sand, hubristic indoor ski slopes and all-you-can-hug penguins – should not exist *here*, in the middle of the desert. It was incongruous, and as such it appeared unreal.

But maybe there was something else to it as well. Something to do with the fact that you no longer needed to travel to Paris for a favourite hot chocolate or macaroons now that you could simply get them at the Dubai Mall's Angelina and Ladurée. The Ladurée store had created a little patio outside it with grass and Parisian bistro tables, creating the illusion of being outside, even though you were still inside a mall. In creating hyper-specific, exact replicas of the world that surrounded it, perhaps what made Dubai seem particularly artificial was the uncanny valley. Ultimately, Dubai inspired the same eerie sentiment as a forged painting: it may look identical to the real thing but just by knowing it was fake meant that one would always keep looking just that little bit closer, hoping to catch the tiny detail that gave away the game.

And now, when you're ready, you can just open your eyes in your own time.

As she switched her phone off airplane mode, she received a notification. From Karim. *I love you.*

She stared at the message for a long time, trying to use the techniques her meditation app had taught her to figure out what she was feeling. She could never name her emotions, she only saw colours. The colour now: black. She deleted the message, so as to never have to look at it again, and tossed the phone at the wall.

The joke was that whatever movie Mohammed, Laika and Siver watched, it would turn into hardcore pornography the moment their father walked into the living room. They could be watching all three hours of *Titanic*, Mohammed quipped, and their dad would invariably walk in during the one minute where Kate Winslet's tits were out.

On this day, rare because Mohammed and Siver were both home the entire weekend, they decided to watch the classic comedy *Airplane!*, only to find, as always, that their father walked in during a moment when two naked women were on screen. Mohammed quickly changed the channel, hoping their father hadn't seen anything, and rolled his eyes at the other two. 'What are the chances?' Siver sighed, always feeling like their father catching *her* watching nudity was especially shameful. The boys, they were supposed to do it in secret, but for her it was wrong, perverse somehow.

That day, thankfully, Rafiq was too preoccupied to notice the bouncing breasts on the television. 'Has anyone seen my cigarettes? I had a packet, it was right here.' The children all shook their heads, each thinking one of the others had stolen it. 'Can one of you go and get me a packet?' he said, giving up on his search. Mohammed looked over at Siver, mouthed for her to go. It was always her.

'I'll go, Baba,' she said, getting up to put on her shoes and jacket.

'Come, let me give you some money,' Rafiq said, looking in his pockets for a few pound coins.

'It's fine, I have money.'

'Nonsense, here,' Rafiq counted the coins in his hand and gave them to Siver, who knew better than to insist.

'I'll come with you,' Laika said, to the surprise of the others. Laika rarely left the apartment, and never volunteered to run these errands. Siver, trying to act as though this was normal, shrugged and told him to hurry up.

The air had the electricity of a coming snowfall, too clear for November, betraying its intentions. Siver, who had expected a much warmer day from looking out the window, immediately dashed back into the building to get a scarf and gloves. 'You sure you're not going to be cold?' she said to Laika, who shook his head.

'This is fine, I like it.'

Laika had grown into a gawky, wiry kid, ill at ease in his body, his limbs jerky, as though he had no control over them at all. He was preternaturally shy, unwilling to complete his schooling and without any aspirations to go to any university whatsoever. To make money, he built websites for people, people he would never have to see or interact with. They were all worried about him, about what would become of him, but every member of his family had their own worries that superseded whatever was going on with him. He seemed happy at least, in his room with his computer.

'OK, I'm ready, let's go,' Siver said, a woolly hat and a pair of mitts in hand. 'I couldn't find a scarf, but whatever.'

They walked the road to Sutton High Street in silence, as though they were two strangers who just happened to be walking beside one another.

'Is everything OK with you?' Laika finally asked.

'What do you mean?'

'I just. I don't know, I noticed you were more anxious lately, checking your phone more often, like you're waiting for something bad to happen.'

Siver smiled. 'It's nothing bad. Honest.' Then, for the first time, she told him the truth. 'I've met someone. A boy.'

Laika nodded, as though he had received the solution to a riddle that made sense but maybe didn't satisfy him entirely. 'Good. You deserve it.'

'I haven't told Mum and Dad yet, so . . .'

'Obviously. Omertà rules.'

They went into the corner shop and bought two packets of cigarettes, one to give to their father right away, one to replace the one that had been stolen before, to be casually dropped behind a couch or a table to be serendipitously found a day or so later.

'Want anything else?' Siver asked her brother, before handing the cashier her debit card.

'You know, if you ever need to talk about this. I know I'm not the ideal person for one-on-one conversations but. If you need it.'

Siver smiled. 'Yeah, no offence, but I don't see us braiding each other's hair and talking about boys all night.'

On the way back she wondered why she hadn't just thanked him, why she had to make a joke about it. She wanted to apologise for the quip but instead found herself talking about something else altogether.

———

There was, at the back of the shop, a small room where the staff would show their wealthiest clients their most exclusive wares, handbags made of crocodiles and pythons and sharks, with diamond appliqués and white gold clasps. This room was decorated with only the finest furniture: the table on which the bags were revealed had been designed by a famous Dutch autodidact and cost more than Siver's annual salary. The couch, a tangle of midnight-blue velvet ropes, was intended to allow for all sorts of seated positions, but intimidated most to the extent that they would keep standing.

While the customers waited for the near-mythical handbags to be brought out, they were offered a non-alcoholic beverage of their choice, and encouraged to leaf through one of the magazines the store subscribed to. There was one fashion magazine (French *Vogue*), one lifestyle magazine (*Tatler*) and one travel magazine that catered to owners of private planes (*Elite Traveller*). To Siver's knowledge, no customer ever touched the magazines, but they were useful for when the staff took a break.

It being Dubai, any nudity in the magazines would be censored, but each of Dubai's censors clearly had differing opinions as to what constituted immoral imagery. Sometimes the low neckline of a *Vogue* model would be left visible, other times a completely abstract painting would be blacked out, the censor seeing something in the artwork that he did not deem acceptable. Siver would pore over the models dismembered by censorship, their striking alien faces no longer connected to their long, Photoshopped limbs, the black boxes drawing her attention to what some man somewhere had found sexy. It was often possible to forget that you lived in a religious theocracy. It was the little things, like the hand-drawn streaks of magic marker running through every single magazine in the country, that brought you back to reality.

———

At one point, when they all still lived in London, Mohammed started dating a dancer by the name of Tatiana. Karim suggested that they all go out for dinner, the four of them, and Mohammed somehow said yes to this, choosing La Petite Maison on Brook's Mews, which he was happy to let Karim pay for. Throughout the entire dinner, Tatiana looked bored, staring out onto the street behind Siver and Karim, barely deigning to answer the questions asked of her, seemingly content that Mohammed act as her spokesperson as she unenthusiastically picked at some burrata with her fork.

'What do you see in her?' Siver later asked her brother, when they were alone and she'd had half a bottle of cheap wine.

'What do you mean?'

'I mean just that. I can see that she's hot, obviously, but what do you like about her? Don't you find her, I don't know, somewhat bland?'

Mohammed, drinker of the other half of the bottle of wine, recoiled from her as though Siver had just vomited all over his couch, his eyes narrowing in disgust.

'We like the same things! She likes movies, I like movies. She likes food, I like food.'

Siver cackled then, a laugh that seemed much crueller than she had intended.

'You're describing every human being on planet earth there, Mo.'

'Well go on, tell me what you see in Karim other than a big fat wallet, then, missy.'

'At least we have conversations.'

'Aren't you describing every human being on the planet?'

'Clearly not Tatiana,' Siver said, dragging out the name syllable by syllable to make it sound haughty and ridiculous.

'Fuck you, it was your man who insisted we go on that stupid dinner, I would have been more than happy to stay at home and watch a movie.'

'Ah yes, I forgot, those esoteric movie-things that you and the love of your life have in common.'

'Not everyone you date has to be the love of your life, Siver.'

'I just don't know why you'd bother if it isn't.'

Mohammed shrugged then, and made an exaggerated motion of the wrist so as to indicate that it was getting late, that Siver should be on her way home. Usually when they wound up at his place late at night, he offered for her to sleep on his couch, but it seemed her criticisms of the movie- and food-loving Tatiana had put an end to that tradition.

She walked up to King's Cross station, debating whether to take a taxi to Karim's or the night bus to Victoria where she could catch a train home. Usually she'd be loath to make the trek all the way to Sutton, sneaking into the flat like a child, but Mohammed's counter-question, about what Siver saw in Karim, was lingering. She could rabble up a list of clichés as to why she was initially attracted to him: his good looks, his odd sense of humour, his way of focusing his attention on her as though she were the only person in the world. But now, now that she was engaged to him, what was it that she saw in him?

Realising her initial question to Mohammed had been unfair, she texted him an apology.

No worries sis, we had a lot to drink, no need to apologise.

She chose the night bus.

Next to the store where Siver worked was a watchmaker, a Swiss brand that advertised its products by showing fathers and sons sailing, playing golf. The watch was a tradition, to be given from one generation to the next.

The Spanish man who worked there, mostly on his own, sat most days behind a desk, waiting for customers that might enter his store once a week, if that. Every so often he would stand outside the store, doing ridiculous little squats after hours spent immobile. Siver began saying hello to him whenever she walked past him and then, one day, he asked her out.

Siver flushed, feeling like a warm liquid had just spilled inside her. He looked confident, the Spanish man, as though nothing she could say would make him feel one way or the other, a mischievous tug of his lip as he said, 'I'm a pretty good date, if I do say so myself.'

Siver smiled. 'I'm sorry, I can't. I have a daughter, and . . .' The Spanish man nodded, not letting it show whether this information made him consider her differently in any way.

'OK, but if you change your mind, I'm next door.'

Isabelle, who had witnessed the conversation, confronted Siver as soon as she walked back into the store. 'Are you crazy? You deserve a night out! Look at him, he's gorgeous!' She kissed her fingers like a TV chef.

'I have Zara. You know this. I don't have time to date.'

'I'll watch her for you! It's one night, it's not like you're eloping with him!'

That night she masturbated, thinking of the Spanish man while squeezing a nipple hard, the man becoming Karim, becoming Karim's new wife, becoming Kate Moss in the 90s, becoming Noah Mills in an Armani ad, becoming himself again. She hoped Zara was asleep, she hoped she was not being too loud.

I was just so worried about you, my heart was with you, I'm always so worried, how could that son of a dog do this to you? You are more beautiful than any of those Baghdad women. I know what they're like, I lived there, I know them. I won't give you a headache, telling you about my woes, but you should call more often, I never hear from you, you really should make more of an effort to reach out to your old mother, you know.

As a precautionary measure, Siver had entered recurring reminders on her phone to call her mother every four days. Some days she would not feel like having her mother judge her for ten minutes and so she'd leave the call for the following day, but that would be stretching it. If she waited a whole week, Xezal would call to berate her. Once, Siver had foolishly asked her mother when the last time was that either of her sons called. *Oh my darling boys, they're so busy.* It was always Siver who would be the Bad Daughter, even though she was the one who made a point of visiting her mother, of calling her, of making sure she wired some money to her every month.

She could see her now, berating the maid she kept in her employ in a deranged love–hate relationship for some inconsequential inaction, combing her hennaed hair while she swore at politicians on the news. Siver understood that her mother had a need to vent, but she resented that she was the only outlet for said venting. 'I'll send you some money this Friday,' Siver had interrupted her mother last time they spoke, so as to underline that she was doing all that she could for the woman. *Oh, don't worry about that, my lovely son has sent me so much this month.* Who, Mohammed? Had he found a new job? *No, my darling Laika.* Siver scoffed, sure that this was one of her mother's mind-games. If even the perpetually broke Laika could send her money, then Siver doing so wasn't a very big deal at all.

She envied the times before all these apps made it possible to speak for free for hours on end. It used to be too expensive to say more than hello, I love you, goodbye. Now her phone was crammed with green, blue and purple icons all making it possible to say whatever you wanted, for as long as you wanted. It was a terrible thing, technology.

One low-risk, high-reward method of keeping in touch with her mother was of course to just send a photo of Zara, a particularly cute one could mitigate not calling for several days. Most days Xezal would merely wish to be sacrificed for her granddaughter's smile, post a jpg of a nazar to ward off the evil eye, and that would be that. Some days, however, Xezal had comments on the photos. *Why is she angry what's wrong?* and Siver had to explain that no, that was her being happy. *Who is that man?* she would ask about a worker in the background of a photo, as though Siver knew the name of every single construction worker in Dubai. *Why are there holes in her trousers do you need money I can send you money* when Zara was wearing distressed jeans. And eventually, the photos would lead to a request to talk soon, so as much as Siver tried to pimp out her daughter in exchange for silence, a conversation was ultimately inevitable.

It always took her several minutes to muster up the courage to press call on the app, and, once over, the calls would put her in a foul mood for hours, if not days. She found herself instantly reverting to her teen self, all spite and rancour. And, in the end, the suspicion that her mother was right. She was a bad daughter.

The food court at the mall contained everything from the traditional fast-food chains to a café that served shots of 92 per cent Valrhona chocolate mixed with 24 carat gold and a restaurant that shaved black or white truffles over every single dish.

Lunch was taken in twos while the rest manned the store. Often Siver would be paired off with Tanya who'd insist they eat after everyone else at the store. 'It's nicer this way, not having to rush back, worrying about the others waiting for us, hungry,' Tanya said one day as she went in line for a salad bar at the mall's food court. Siver was really in the mood for something more substantial but she already felt like enough of a monster in front of Tanya without eating gross fried things in front of her. She got a Caesar salad, dressing on the side.

Something bad had happened to Tanya in the spring, it was unclear to Siver what exactly, but she once heard Isabelle mutter that she only had herself to blame. Siver tried to grow closer to her, suddenly feeling a kinship with this woman whom she had believed to be an alien from the planet Youth only a few weeks ago, but her advances were rejected by Tanya, who did not need pity performed by a single mother. Their relationship was simple: they had lunch, Siver looked at Tanya with awe and Tanya expanded on her life.

They each got a plastic puck that would vibrate when their meal was ready, and Siver took the opportunity to find the nearest toilet.

Before heading back out she applied a new coat of lipstick, flashing her teeth in the mirror to check for errant lipstick stains, and sure enough found some bright red on her front tooth. Before she wiped it off with her finger she realised how she looked: fangs bared, blood on her mouth.

Back at the food court, Tanya spoke effusively of the numbing quality of the city, like an anaesthetic. She hated having to travel home and deal with her father's dementia, her mother's bad hip. 'It hurts too much to look at them and know there is nothing that I can do.' Her eyes welled up just by discussing it, then her Ruby Woo-accented smile flashed. 'It's easier here.'

They left their trays when they went back to the store, knowing one of the mall's many cleaners would whisk it away in no time at all.

———

In all of her years in Baghdad, Siver could count on one hand the number of times Xezal took the forty-five-minute flight to visit her. Xezal wouldn't even entertain the idea until Zara was born. Upon her first arrival, she insisted all of the baby's features were in fact her family's features, that she was a carbon copy of Siver as a child. There were enough photographs to prove otherwise, but they all sat politely around Xezal as she concocted a reality suitable to her. She would give these barbed comments, about how the house was beautiful but too big. 'Nobody needs a house this size. But I guess you like this.' But even as she would walk through the house dragging her finger across surfaces to check for dust, and complain about her morning eggs ('Our Kurdish eggs are so much more flavourful. These Iraqi eggs taste like plastic.'), Siver was still glad to have her mother there somehow, seeing her hold Zara as though it was the most natural thing in the world to hold an infant that could not even keep its own head up, the way she would gently press down on the baby's third eye and immediately make her stop crying as though it were witchcraft. For the first time, her mother's presence calmed her.

When it was time for Xezal to leave, Siver actually tried to make her extend her trip. 'What will I do here?' Xezal had asked, packing her suitcase slowly, as if her fabrics could break.

'I don't know, help your daughter, maybe?'

'You have help here. You have more help than I ever had. You don't need me.'

'Well, I don't need you, fine, but maybe I want you to be here? It's not as if you do anything in Kurdistan, just sitting alone in that house.'

'You should know I'm plenty busy.'

Whatever entente they'd had during the stay was deteriorating into the eternal cold war between them, Xezal made that perfectly clear. Subsequent visits were polite, distant affairs during which Siver counted the days before her mother left. So in the aftermath of Karim's desire to have sex with teenagers, Siver did not feel that she could call upon her mother. She knew what her mother thought; she didn't need to hear it. Mohammed would probably only care insomuch as he would feel obliged to help her out, and Laika, while supportive, had so little life experience that he would just tell her he was sorry, as if he had been the one who had blown up her entire life. She had had friends once, but after years in Baghdad her only friends were his friends, his family. She realised, suddenly, that she was completely alone in the world.

She contemplated reconnecting with some of her old university friends through Facebook, asking about their life, gradually becoming close to them again, to eventually after some time (one week? two?) be able to confide in them. But even that felt wrong, manipulative. Also, she didn't want to seem like a failure. She was well aware of what everyone thought of her moving to Baghdad of all places, to a city where she didn't speak the language, that was being bombed to pieces; she knew how it looked, her marrying this very wealthy man. It served her right, everyone would say. What did she think was going to happen?

It was perhaps naive of her, but she had believed him when he said that he loved her. She believed him when he said he wanted to live the rest of his life with her. And now here she stood, in the kitchen of her Baghdad home, while he was in the living room watching the news, unable to go to bed because she didn't want to walk past him to get to the bedroom.

Her phone vibrated, and an old photograph of Mohammed appeared. Just seeing his face made her well up.

'Hello?'

The sandstorms that week had disrupted the mobile phone network and she couldn't hear anything that he was saying, he was speaking quickly, as though something had happened. Her heart sank. He needed help with something, probably.

'I can't hear you, do you need help?'

The line went dead. Siver stared at the phone for a minute, unsure as to whether she should try to call him back. She was too emotionally exhausted to take care of her brother's problems, whatever they were. In the living room, Karim had turned down the volume on the television, trying to hear what was happening in the kitchen.

The phone vibrated briefly in her hand again. A text message.

Just wanted to tell you I closed this really huge deal, I had nobody to share it with and I just thought to tell you. I miss you. Hope you and L'arome are fine. Give my love to the little one x

Then a second text: *I mean Karma obviously.*

Then a third: *KARIM! I HOPE KARIM IS FINE! FFS DUCKING AUTOCORRECT!*

She smiled at that, and sent him a reply, telling him that she was happy for him, that Karim said he always knew he'd be successful. A lie, of course: Karim thought Mohammed was a wheeler-dealer who was more likely to end up in jail than he ever was making serious money.

She then started typing another message.

Listen. Things aren't great here. K wants another wife, which . . . yeah. And I honestly don't know what to do. He's serious about it, and if I leave him which I am thinking of doing I don't know . . . where the fuck do I even go? What do I do? Honestly, this is a shitshow Mo, a total fucking shitshow. ps obv don't tell mum she'd flip

Siver stopped typing and looked at her message. No, no, Mohammed was having a good night, why should she ruin it for him? She deleted the message and sent *Rly proud of you xx* instead, putting away her phone and walking to bed, pretending not to notice her husband.

The store's one especially exclusive handbag sold only to customers in the small VIP room was made entirely by hand in France, and had, in every other country in the world, a year-long waiting list. Now that most luxury items were no longer made-to-measure, the same airport stores selling the same 'exclusive' scarves and handbags, brands needed to do more to create the illusion of scarcity. If one in four Japanese women owned a genuine Louis Vuitton handbag, for instance, how exclusive could those bags really be? Most brands opted to highlight the newly released and therefore elusive in order to grant the bags, and by extension the brand, a sheen of exclusivity: the 'it' bag was a concept born from this desire to create an object that was a 'must have'. The bags needed to be easily identifiable, well-marketed and given to the celebrity du jour to wear to as many events as possible. Fendi's 1997 Baguette and Chloé's 2002 Paddington were some of the first to succeed at attaining this status, Fendi using the popularity of *Sex and the City* to cement itself, Chloé aligning itself with the actress and model Sienna Miller to boost their bag's popularity. The many presentations Siver and her co-workers were made to sit through outside of office hours explained time and time again how the concept of the 'it' bag had died a quick death with the financial crisis, as their frivolous nature seemed indicative of the spending habits that had led the world to the brink of the abyss. Instead, customers had reverted to the bags that they had grown up coveting, the status symbols such as Chanel's 2.55 or the Louis Vuitton 'Speedy'.

Sales of the especially exclusive handbag at Siver's store also skyrocketed, to the point where there was briefly actual scarcity, not just a brand-imposed one. Once production was ramped up and Isabelle had correctly identified the manner in which the notion of exclusivity could be maintained in a country where consumers were not inclined to wait for much of anything, the Mall of the Emirates store had set up a special room filled with these handbags that customers who wanted to purchase one (or more) could be brought to. The sales per unit area of the Mall of the Emirates store rose considerably after Paris agreed to Isabelle's proposal, and it was deemed that her suggestion had been so revolutionary, so in tune with changing values in up-and-coming markets, that she ought to be promoted. One day, after the store had closed, Isabelle therefore asked the employees who were working that shift to stay a few minutes: she had an announcement to make. She was going back to Paris, she said, and was going to join the executive team as Senior Vice President of Retail. They were sending in a new store manager from Paris in the next two weeks, but she had given firm instructions that her procedures be kept as they were.

For Isabelle's leaving party, she snuck in a bottle of champagne, which the staff proceeded to drink in secret in the room with the especially exclusive handbags. They had all pitched in to buy a ceramic bracelet that they had noticed Isabelle looking at more than once. The staff hugged her, some cried, and she promised them that she would keep in touch.

Outside, the cleaners milled about, waiting for whatever it was that was going on in the store to end, so that they could do their job.

By the end of her first year in Baghdad, when Siver felt that she had finally settled in her new life, the statue had long been toppled, and the Iraqis' initial song and dance greeting the Americans had faded from the collective memory. Bremer, the American in charge, had fired 100,000 Iraqi soldiers on a whim, thereby giving Al-Qaeda and all their offshoots 100,000 new armed and trained recruits, and Blackwater USA had begun shooting up civilians in the middle of a crowded street for no earthly reason at all.

The early days of US soldiers being able to wander safely around Baghdad to buy fake watches or take a joyride in a looted car were by this time demonstrably over.

During her time at Karim's construction firm, the driver who would take her and her husband to the office and back had an almost supernatural knack for finding the best route. Every morning, certain roads were closed off due to visiting dignitaries, various VIPs, suspected IEDs, aftermaths of terrorist attacks, or entirely redrawn due to the modular security walls being persistently shifted to contain new groups of people, new neighbourhoods. And every morning Faizal, the driver, would know exactly how to navigate this ever-changing landscape, avoiding the over-militarised security firms, avoiding the militias keen to kidnap anyone worth a ransom.

She heard traces of the violence, of course. The echoes of explosions near and far quickly became routine, but through luck or Faizal's efforts, she was spared the sight of much of the destruction, barring the odd smoking shack which had once been a restaurant known for its arak.

At first, friends back in London emailed her after every news report of a bombing in Baghdad, her mailbox a long list of *are you OK* subject-matters, but as time went on they emailed less and less until they finally stopped reaching out to her at all. Siver's initial consolations to them seemed witty to her, but probably glib to them: *Don't worry, if I die you'd hear about it. Suddenly in the eyes of Her Majesty's Government I would, finally, be deemed British. It would be on the front page of every newspaper, the news of a dead Briton haha.*

Siver was rarely afraid of the sound of bombs going off, even the time when the neighbouring house, where Saddam Hussein's judge's brother lived, was bombed and her entire house shook, she simply did a quick check to verify that nothing had fallen over or broken in the tremors and went back to bed.

You got used to it. The bombs were useful in their own perverse way as she never needed to set an alarm: *something* would explode before 9 a.m. on any given day, ensuring that you were well awake in time for work.

Then one day, Faizal was driving her on her own to the office as Karim had had an early-morning meeting. As the large, unwieldy SUV weaved through the dull, dusty streets of the Qadisiya district, she saw a man bleeding on the ground, the blood soaking his clothes visible even behind the blue tint of the window. The man kept shouting for help, in Arabic, over and over, his cries so loud they pierced through the bulletproof glass of their car.

'Faizal, stop, we have to do something!'

The driver shook his head, kept driving.

Siver's initial polite requests grew in intensity until they were commands, upon which Faizal turned around and, like a parent having to control an unruly child, told her to be very quiet.

Later, at the office, Karim told her that this was a preferred method for certain terrorist cells to maximise the damage of their attacks: shoot someone in the belly, put explosives on and around the body and wait for onlookers to gather and try to help before you call a mobile phone that acts as a detonator.

And still, even as she heard the man's cries for weeks when she lay in bed trying to sleep, still she told Xezal that everything was fine. Still she replied to her friends' emails with bad jokes.

The only time the city went silent was during the 2006 World Cup, when suicide bombers kept themselves alive during football matches. It seemed to Siver that to bring peace to Iraq, all you had to do was ensure that there was football on at all times.

Even a Saudi cleric's well-publicised fatwa against the sport did not make the jihadists change their minds. The fatwa, which was printed in many of the newspapers that wound up on Siver's kitchen table, claimed, according to Karim, that one should 'play in regular clothes or your pyjamas or something like that, but not shorts and numbered T-shirts because they are not Muslim clothing' and 'Do not follow the heretics, the Jews, the Christians & especially evil America regarding number of players. Do not play with 11 people.' Even so, the World Cup remained a brief but near-total respite from bombs and explosions. Once Italy won the final, normal order was restored. The terrorist factions of Baghdad resumed bombing the city to pieces, thinking that they were somehow responding to the Evil West's mischaracterisations of them.

The instant Siver slammed the brake pedal, in order not to collide with the SUV that had performed an illegal U-turn in front of her, she knew her car would not be able to screech to a halt in time. Her car's metal bloomed as it folded into itself, like a sheet of paper being crumpled, as the radio's weather forecast continued to extol the sunny weekend ahead. Everything felt as though it was happening in slow-motion, the actual moment of impact, the smell of rubber erupting from under her, the half-eaten protein bar that slid from the dashboard onto her lap, its aluminium wrapper sparkling in the daylight, until the airbags activated with a force that brought Siver back into the moment. Her only thought, once she could yet again formulate thoughts: *Thank God Zara is not in the car.*

A young man stepped out of the car in front of her, shook his head while assessing the damage. His dress indicated that he was an Emirati, a slight wobble made her believe the crash had left him in a daze. Siver started to panic: everyone knew that if you got into an accident with a local, the accident was deemed to be your fault. He produced a Vertu phone while Siver flapped her way out of the vehicle, pushing aside the airbag. He was calling the police. Siver should call Zara's school, let them know she was going to be late to pick her up. Only the sight of a group of workers on the side of the highway waiting for the transport back to their camp calmed her nerves. They had seen everything. She had witnesses.

'Are you OK?' he asked her once he'd hung up. His eyes made Siver realise that he wasn't in a state of shock: he was drunk.

'I'm fine.' Siver wondered what it would take for her to one day assert that she was not fine. What was her threshold?

'Uff . . . This had to happen today. I still haven't gotten my licence back. Ya Allah.' He shrugged, and went back to sit in his car, blasting a song by Nancy Ajram.

The police arrived shortly thereafter, and her initial suspicion turned out to have been correct: in spite of the fact that he was visibly drunk and could not produce a driver's licence, the young man was given a handshake and told he could drive off. Siver was told to follow the policemen to the station, was told that the accident was deemed her fault, that they would need to send the report to her insurance company.

'Ask them! Ask them what happened!' Siver said, careful to not raise her voice, to not get herself entangled in a worse situation than the one she was already in.'

'Ask who?' one of the policemen said, genuinely curious, as though Siver had invoked a tree as her witness. She realised that the workers were not a Greek chorus, even though they saw everything, knew everything. They were deemed part of the landscape, expected to remain forever silent.

———

'What are your parents like?'

Siver and Karim were on their second date, having gone to a British-owned Asian fast-food chain after seeing a movie about a mailman who traded Shakespeare plays for food, and she was starting to feel like she needed to ask him the important things, to know whether or not this, whatever this was, was something worth fighting for. She knew his thoughts on virtually every Disney movie ever made, but she knew very little else. If his father was a fundamentalist cleric or had been involved in the ethnic cleansing of Kurdish people, needless to say she would have to break it off before she got in too deep.

Part of her was hoping that he would tell her something that she could not live with. That would be easier than having to go through with this relationship that, she knew, her parents would be less than happy with.

Karim put down his chopsticks and wiped the corner of his mouth with a black paper napkin. 'My parents?'

'Yeah, I mean, I realised I know nothing about them, about you,' Siver said, hoping her tone indicated that this was no big deal, just the type of conversation people had, regular people with no emotional baggage, people who didn't have to take into consideration the entirety of the Kurdish independence movement when selecting a mate.

'Oh, they're lovely, if a bit neurotic. Yahni, my parents are the kind of people who go abroad not for holidays, relaxation or amusement but to see doctors – "This year we're going to Thailand, they have a great specialist for brain tumours" – and if you want to be cynical you could call them hypochondriacs or say that they are somehow faking it or playing up their very real diseases for attention but it's very true nonetheless that everyone tends to notice the perverse glee with which they speak of their trips to the doctors. Anyway, inshallah they will always be healthy.' He made a motion to knock on the table but, realising it was not made of wood, gave his head two short knocks with his knuckle instead.

Siver smiled. This was not what she was expecting.

'It's like they can't just come and visit me, they have to book an appointment at a Harley Street clinic and use that as the excuse for their trip. Because otherwise they think people would see them as frivolous. My father started his construction company in the late 60s, and wollah I don't think he has ever taken a trip that wasn't pretending to be because of work or health. It's just how he is.'

'And your mother? How did they meet?'

'Oh. They're cousins, arranged marriage. My father was told to pick one of three sisters, and he picked my mother. So if I seem a bit weird to you, it's because I'm an inbred!' Karim laughed at his own joke.

'I don't know if you know of this tradition, but on your wedding night in Iraq in more traditional families, the man sometimes kills a kitten.'

'A . . . kitten?'

'Wollah, it's what they do. It's . . . it's weird. Basically it's to demonstrate the husband's role, they go to the bedroom at night, and the husband presents the wife with a kitten, and he is to say something like, "If you're a good wife, then I will be good to you, like so . . ." and then you pet the kitten. Then you go on, "But if you're a *bad* wife . . ." and you're meant to break the cat's neck or slit its throat, I don't know honestly how you're meant to kill it. But you do. And then you make the wife clean it up.'

'Jesus.'

'Yeah . . . so my father was told by his relatives that he had to do this, and he refused. He asked them how could he be in a happy relationship with someone if that was the first thing that he did. And the family, even my mother's own father, made fun of him saying that yahni he was going to let her run all over him if he didn't set clear boundaries and show who was boss. But he never did. And mashallah they have been happy, for a long time now.'

When she got home, she asked her mother if she had ever heard such a thing as men killing cats on their wedding day. Xezal was surprised, wondered where Siver had heard such a thing.

'Oh, it's just something my friend Sepideh mentioned.'

'We used to hear this, but honestly I think it is a myth. I don't think that men actually do this. Your father certainly never did.'

That night Siver kept dreaming of murdered cats, of her picking up a kitten to stroke only to find when the animal was in her hands that it was a lifeless fluffy mess, with nothing left any more but blood and fur.

Her car was totalled. Except, of course, it wasn't her car. She had leased it. The company that owned the car and the insurance company were engaged in a month-long battle that, until it was resolved, meant that Siver did not have a vehicle at her disposal, even though she still had to pay the monthly leasing fee. This, on top of the now daily taxi fares she was paying since there was no public transport that went anywhere near Zara's school, meant that she was yet again on the precipice of poverty, yet again fully aware of exactly how much money was in her bank account at any given time. And then there were Zara's incessant demands, the never-ending requests for new toys. She'd complained about not having this stupid toy hamster for weeks and finally Siver had relented: 55 dirhams less in her account; 876 dirhams left until the next salary.

'Ummi! I didn't want Pipsqueak! All the kids at school already have Pipsqueak! I wanted Num Nums!'

'Baby, I couldn't find it. This was the only ZhuZhu Pet they had in the store.'

'I *hate* you!'

In barely a year, Zara had transformed from a shy, introspective girl to, Siver had to be honest here, a right little shit. Every other day she would come home from school with a request for new toys or insipid accessories that she 'needed' because all the other kids had them and she would die if she didn't have one too.

A few weeks ago, Zara had been invited to a classmate's seventh birthday party, and the kid's parents had rented out an entire park in the five-star Jumeirah Beach Hotel, with a clown, a three-layer cake and even a sleeveless shirt-wearing DJ. Siver, unaware of what birthday parties in Dubai were like, had bought a children's book about an elephant in love, and saw the mound of presents other parents had brought, immediately realising that Zara's social life would suffer due to the gift that Siver had chosen. 'How could you be so *stupid* to get Vanessa a *book*?' Zara cried in the taxi on the way home and then pestered her mother for a birthday party of a similar scale. Siver had expected this sort of behaviour once Zara turned thirteen or so, not while she was still barely able to dress herself.

Every week there was something new, the school calling to propose another ludicrously expensive outing to the mall that she had to pay for; every week Siver had to sit her daughter down and explain the harsh economic realities that precluded the purchase of that new thing; every week Zara would find a new way to make Siver feel small. *Daddy has money, why don't we ask him?*

So when Siver received a call from the school the day after the failed ZhuZhu Pet purchase while she was at work, she let it go to voicemail, thinking it would be another mind-bogglingly expensive excursion that Zara would pester her about. It wasn't until her lunch break that she listened to the message.

'Mrs Hardi, this is the nurse at Coeus International. Unfortunately, Zara had an accident in the playground today and broke her arm. She's been taken to the American Hospital with one of our staff. You can reach her on zero five five thirty-two, forty-four seven.'

Siver felt as though the entire mall had just gone dark; she wanted to replay the message, as a soft buzz in her ear had stopped her from being able to focus, but instead of replaying the message by pressing two, she deleted it by pressing one. She looked around, people with shopping bags, laughing, as though she were outside of time entirely. And here she was, having for four hours ignored a message from her daughter's school that her daughter had broken her arm. Siver left her half-eaten lunch on the table and rushed through the food court, up the escalator and back into the store to tell her co-workers that there was an emergency and that she had to go. She took a cab to the American Hospital and once she got there she was faced with cold hospital light and myriad signs to various departments. Where would she be? Osteopathy? Emergency? Paediatric Ward? She asked a bored woman at a desk by the entrance, who told her to check with the Emergency Room. Siver rushed through the mint-green maze, following directions, until two doors opened automatically and she found herself under a sign that said EMERGENCY. The man at the desk confirmed that Zara was indeed there, in room 204. He was typing something into a computer, and didn't look at Siver directly; when he turned and saw whatever it was that Siver's face exuded, he became instantly more considerate, told her that Zara was fine, the doctor had seen her, and if she would only fill out this form, she could go see her daughter.

Siver struggled to focus on the form, its rectangles blurring together, but filled it out to the best of her ability.

'Perfect, thank you. Can I have your insurance details as well, please?'

Siver rummaged around in her handbag to find the insurance card that she had been given by her employer.

The man squinted at the insurance card as if he were a bouncer trying to determine whether to let her in. 'I'm sorry, ma'am, but your insurance is not valid at this hospital.'

Siver blinked.

'What?'

'You should have taken her to another hospital, ma'am, because you are not covered here.'

'But I didn't bring her here, her school did. Listen, can we talk about this later? Can I just see my daughter?'

The man handed Siver her insurance card and strained to be pleasant. 'Please, one of our nurses will take you to her.'

A nurse appeared and instructed her to wash her hands with an antibacterial solution. 'We have to be very diligent,' the nurse said, before she led Siver down a corridor where broken men and women sat, awaiting help.

And there, in a light-blue room with one of the school administrators, was Zara, sitting on the hospital bed, her arm already in a cast.

Siver immediately started weeping. She had been such a terrible, neglectful mother.

'I'm fine, Ummi, it doesn't hurt any more.'

After Rafiq died, Xezal spent months admonishing Siver and Laika for touching anything that belonged to him; they couldn't even throw out the yoghurt in the fridge, or change the channel on the television, without her screaming at them. Then, one day, she handed them some garbage bags, and told them to get rid of all the stuff.

'Mum, are you sure?'

'I'm not going to live here for ever. The little time left I don't want to be reminded of him every minute of every day.'

It amazed Siver how quickly their lives could be packed up. Siver and Laika rushing around with bin bags, Mohammed arriving from work to give them orders like a self-appointed supervisor. Surfaces scrubbed with diluted Dettol, faded Spider-Man stickers peeled off bedroom doors, and hundreds if not thousands of documents discarded.

The pamphlets went first, those little screeds he had spent so much time and effort on for so many years. Then the bundles of newspapers and magazines Rafiq had kept, encircling any article that mentioned the Kurds. Then the postcards showing the victims of the Halabja bombings, their images now faded. 'God, I used to hate these pictures,' Siver said as she tossed a handful in a bin bag.

Once they thought they were done, and the outlines of an apartment without Rafiq had begun to emerge, Xezal told them there was still much to do.

'You need to get rid of his clothes, too, and the rug, and that table, and that god-awful radio. What am I going to do with a radio?'

'Mum, where are we going to eat? We need a table.'

'We can get another table. One that your father wasn't sitting at before he left us.'

After deliberating with Laika, Siver called for a four-yard skip to be delivered later that day. 'It might be a mistake, but it's her mistake to make,' Laika told her. If she wanted the memory of their father purged from the flat, who were they to tell her no? In time her grief would in all likelihood find a way to coexist with her love, becoming inseparable from one another, but for now they obeyed her grief, and when the skip arrived they proceeded to toss a life's worth of belongings into it.

Each bin bag filled with Rafiq's tattered clothes, each piece of furniture that she could no longer live with, Xezal would lay her hand on before her children took it out of the apartment and down the stairs, as if she was saying goodbye. 'This is the last of it,' Laika said, struggling to find a good grip on the radio that had followed them since Tehran, the only item Xezal did not seem to want to touch before it was disposed of.

Having carried the radio successfully down the stairs, Laika misjudged a step just outside of their building, tripping just as he approached the skip. The wooden radio cracked open, letting its shell and innards spill over the pavement.

'Careful!'

'Bit late for that,' Laika sighed, crouching to pick up the pieces.

'Careful you don't hurt yourself on the splinters. Do you want me to get gloves?'

'Siver. Look at all this.'

Siver walked over, saw the documents sticking out from the broken radio. 'What is all this?' There were maps of Paris, several photographs of the same bespectacled man, a timetable scribbled in Rafiq's handwriting.

'Who is that?' Siver said, pointing at the man in the photos as she tried to find some recognisable traits in the man's beady eyes behind oversized tinted glasses, in the speckles of white across his neat moustache.

Xezal shouted at them from the window, telling them to hurry up. Siver suspected that her children lingering around the detritus of Xezal's former life made her briefly doubt her decision.

'We found these things inside the radio!' Siver shouted, holding up the maps. 'Do you want to have a look at them?'

'I want nothing to do with that disgusting radio! Throw it away!'

Laika pocketed one of the photographs before tossing the rest into the skip. 'We should find out who it is, right?'

'Just don't let Mum see you with it.'

When they went back upstairs, Siver noticed that what was once a home had become property once again.

Jerome Lang was introduced to Siver and the other staff members by Isabelle on her last day of work. A young, brash-looking man with a well-groomed stubble, dressed in an impeccable tan leather jacket and carefully distressed jeans, he spoke with a heavy French accent and stared intensely at whomever he was talking to.

He had been brought in from Paris, promoted from being second-in-command at the Rue du Faubourg Saint-Honoré store, and explained at once that he would not, as Isabelle had, be spending much time in the store itself, but rather be working from the brand's offices at the Dubai International Financial Centre. Isabelle's role had been to successfully launch the brand in Dubai, and now that everything was set up, Jerome would be coming by once a week only to make sure that things were in order.

'He's handsome, no?' Tanya said to Siver, ogling their new boss from afar.

'Sure, if that's your type,' Siver said.

'Oh chérie, that's everyone's type.'

In the weeks following his appointment, Jerome would come by the store every Thursday and hold one-on-one meetings with the staff in the back room. Tanya claimed that her meeting with the new boss consisted merely of him flirting with her for twenty minutes. When it was Siver's turn to talk about her future, she found him standing behind the monstrous table. He gestured for her to sit on the cluster of velvet ropes.

'This is the thing, Siver: I know how Isabelle liked you. She put in a note for me to say you were one of her favourites, so, I know. But we want to make the shopping experience more attractive to younger people, you know?'

Siver, struggling to find a position on the couch that did not make her feel like a trapped animal, stopped fidgeting. In her hand she held a folder containing a series of printouts that outlined her accomplishments.

'And so I have decided to hire some younger women, who can be, uh, inspirational to the customers, yes?'

'Wait. Am I being fired?'

'Non, it is nothing like that, not at all. We are simply restructuring this boutique. Which . . . does sadly mean we will have to let you go. It is best for you as well, no? I hear you have been leaving work to take care of family; maybe a full-time job is not what you are supposed to be doing? Now you can take care of your children.'

Siver opened her cardboard folder, looked at the numbers she had been so proud of, sales effected, customer satisfaction, upsales. She had thought it mattered, that Jerome would care about her quarterly results. She closed her folder and struggled to get up from the couch, one final humiliation.

'We are just, ah, moving in – how you say it? – a different direction,' was the last thing he said before she left the store with its bags and ties and scarves behind.

———

Karim was at the pub, having already had three pints by the time Siver arrived. The South Western trains had been cancelled due to swans on the tracks, and she'd had to take a bus to Purley and then wait half an hour for a train to London Bridge.

'I wish you lived closer to me,' Karim said, hugging her tight, his eyes wobbly with booze.

'Yeah well, not all of us have apartments in Marylebone,' Siver said, taking off layer after layer of clothes, subtly checking that she didn't smell, and proceeding to wipe her face with a tissue before getting a cider at the bar.

'You could live with me, you know?' Karim said, once she had returned, to which Siver cackled.

'Yeah, like my parents would allow that. Don't be ridiculous, Karim.'

'They would if we were married.'

'Well, you'd have to propose first.'

'So: will you marry me?'

'Stop it. You're drunk.'

'Habibti, you are the most amazing person I have ever met. I want to spend the rest of my life with you.'

Siver put down her drink, realising that Karim – perhaps – wasn't joking.

'What are you saying?'

'I'm saying will you marry me?'

Her first instinct was to ask for some time to consider this. After all, her parents weren't exactly pleased about the whole her and Karim thing to begin with, and was he the one? Was it not reckless to marry the first man who showed any interest in you? Surely she should wait, think about it, find out if this was something that she actually wanted. She thought all this, and yet

'Yes.'

———

'Do you need anything, baby?' Siver asked as she put the finishing touches on a drawing of a sun with a smiley face on Zara's cast. 'Are you hungry? I can make you a snack.'

She kissed Zara's forehead and went to the living room. She needed to make a decision. Her car was gone. Zara's hospital fees came to over $6,000. And now she was unemployed. Meanwhile, it was time to renew her lease, and her landlord had raised the annual rent by 5 per cent. It was time to pay for Zara's school again. Her visa would expire in three weeks. It was time to redo everything Siver had done a year ago, the job search, the scrounging and begging for money from her husband, looking for a new apartment. It was like starting from scratch.

She was tired.

She scrolled down her list of contacts until she reached Karim. He could still help; she should be smart about this. He'd sent her a text saying that he loved her; if she could just swallow what little remained of her pride, he could make all of this go away.

In a moment of weakness, she had almost told Xezal everything. 'I can hear something is wrong in your voice,' she'd said and a year's worth of frustrations and humiliations almost welled out of Siver. But what could a poor old woman in Kurdistan do for her? It's not as though she had money to spare.

A text message, from the Undercover Happiness Police. *Are you happy? Reply YES or NO to 2664.*

As part of Dubai's priority to be listed amongst the world's happiest cities, the Undercover Happiness Police had been formed to ensure everyone was as happy as they could be. If you were seen doing something good, holding the door open for the person behind you, say, or letting someone go ahead of you in a queue, you could be pulled over by the Happiness Patrol, who would give you a Happiness Voucher to spend at your mall of choice. This one-word survey was another in a long line of methods devised to promote happiness. If you answered no, someone at work had told her, a police officer would call you up and ask you why you weren't happy.

Siver did not answer the message.

She couldn't have a future in Dubai, it was impossible. Nor could she go back to London and force Zara to live in squalor, sharing an apartment with roommates as though Siver were a teenager. Zara needed stability. They both needed stability.

Siver clicked on the contacts tab of her phone, scrolled down. Karim. Scrolled down two more names. Mum. Karim, Mum, Karim, Mum.

The dim roar of Sheikh Zayed Road could be heard, the thousands of cars driving to and fro. Outside, the faint red and white lights from Dubai's skyscrapers flickered. The lights were scattered across the sky so that planes could distinguish buildings when flying in at night, but the effect for those on the ground was a persistent flickering of red and white, making Dubai glitter.

That night an extravagant display of fireworks splashed over the skies in honour of the Dubai Shopping Festival, which would begin the next day. She didn't remember seeing any fireworks last year, and wondered if this was a new addition to Dubai's major holiday. She walked into the bedroom, its walls reflecting the explosions of colour taking place outside.

'Zara honey, do you want to come look at the fireworks? They're really pretty.'

'But I'm tiiiiired,' Zara moaned, pulling the duvet over her head with her one mobile arm.

Siver didn't insist, even though she knew this would probably be the last chance Zara got to see Dubai like this.

'OK, monkey, just sleep.'

Back in the living room, Siver picked up her phone, about to call her husband, when her phone rang, an American number. She looked at the unknown number as the phone twitched in her palm, as though it were one of those Magic Eye 3D optical illusions, and the caller's identity would become clear if only she looked at the number long enough. She answered.

'Hello?'

'Sisi? It's me, Laika.'

INTERLUDE I
Worth (1984)

Rafiq Hardi Kermanj looked up at the rearing horse towering above him, the armoured knight about to strike down a broadsword. He had to kneel under the horse to see the plaque on the museum floor. 'Armour for man and horse, c. 1480.' An old man wearing a security uniform sat in the corner, surrounded by rusty swords and lances.

'Excuse me? Where restaurant?'

The man looked up at Rafiq's scrawny frame, confused for a moment as though he could not remember how he had come to be sitting there, on that chair, before the clouds over his eyes parted and he pointed Rafiq in the right direction.

'Right through there.'

It always made Rafiq sad to see the aged and trod-upon in uniforms; how the need for a salary, the need to survive in the world, allowed those in power to pit the proletariat against itself. The history of all hitherto existing society may have been the history of class struggles, but Rafiq did not recognise the world any more, now that the struggles had been whittled down to fit into each and every heart, burdens to be carried alone. A Mars a day helps you work, rest and play. Not solidarity with your community, not the struggle for a more just society but the fetishism of a piece of chocolate or a carbonated beverage to be purchased. The possibility of consumption provided the only remaining arena where a person could reasonably dream. This was the era of a cowboy president in Washington, and a crippled geriatric in Moscow struggling to even walk up the stairs to Lenin's mausoleum. All the hopes of the twentieth century had amounted to nothing more than this. If revolutions were the locomotives of history, it had been a long wait at the station.

Rafiq made his way through a corridor with dozens of portraits in gilded imposing frames. The gold-painted moulded plaster on the gold-painted wood indicated by its ornate nature that the history contained within was an illustrious one, a history of aristocracy and empire. Men and women but mostly men, all made to look wealthy and important, some with their belongings prominently placed beside them, some in pelts and minks, all painted unto the world. Rafiq did not know what any of these people were famous for, but he was sure it had at least a little to do with the subjugation and exploitation of others. There were no portraits of the workers who had built this museum, who had built the world.

At the end of the corridor, just as the security man had said, a courtyard appeared, as though he had walked through a magic portal to a garden somewhere other than this drab, grey city. Covered by a vast pyramid skylight, an assortment of small trees jutted out of terracotta pots, their leaves casting a playful flicker of shadows as the sun glimpsed between the clouds overhead.

Abdulrahman and Lawko were already there, waving him over. It was Abdulrahman's idea to meet at this restaurant nested inside a museum, itself nested in Manchester Square, an idyllic pocket in the very centre of London. The sort of enclave capital required for itself.

'Stop gawking, Kak Rafiq, you're acting like you've never been here before.'

'But it's true, I haven't.'

'Yes, but the people around us shouldn't know that. Also, you could not wear something nice? You look like a pauper; this is not a bus station.'

Rafiq looked down on his crumpled shirt, his lint-speckled corduroys. He knew what black calf Oxfords like the ones Abdulrahman was wearing were likely to cost, he had owned a similar pair himself back in Baghdad, tanned single-leather sole, subtle punching details on the toecap. He remembered that he wore shoes like that on the day at the tea house when he convinced two comrades the time had come to start a Communist Party in Iraq, to turn their backs on their bourgeois aspirations, back when he still harboured a dream that the world could be changed. He looked down at the cracked fake leather of his boat shoes. He almost trotted out a well-worn phrase about the subjective theory of value, the totemic nature of clothes as status symbols, but sat down quietly instead. This was not a time to argue with his co-conspirators.

A waitress provided Rafiq with a stiff piece of cardboard on which the day's menu was printed, her bosom appearing white, proud, jutting from a crisp shirt and a tight waistcoat. Her face had the innocence Rafiq had only seen in westerners, not even Kurdish children could carry such a face, eyes like those of a cartoon character, a mouth ever so slightly agape at all times, in eternal anticipation of something wondrous. We mistook it for beauty, this proof of an unburdened life.

Ten pounds for some tea and sandwiches?

Perhaps sensing that Rafiq was bristling at the prices, Abdulrahman casually mentioned that this was on him, to which both Rafiq and Lawko objected loudly, somewhat scaring the waitress in the process.

As soon as the waitress had left the menu of teas listed like the spoils of their conquered lands – Assam, Darjeeling, Huoshan Huangya – Rafiq unfolded a sheet of paper from his pocket.

'I have the timetable.'

'You don't need to whisper, it's suspicious behaviour. Do you see anyone here who looks like they understand Kurdish?'

It was true; none of the well-heeled old couples and brightly dressed young women surrounding them looked like they were from the Middle East. It was the reason they had chosen this place, after all, to be able to discuss the matter at hand in peace, away from their wives and other Kurds. They needed somewhere they could discuss the plan that had come together months earlier when Abdulrahman had come to visit Rafiq. He had brought gold-wrapped chocolates to impress Xezal, and matter-of-factly enquired whether Rafiq had any money to invest in his flailing kebab shop on Edgware Road. Rafiq, always too proud to state outright that he had no money, would often hand out whatever cash he had, but the amount Abdulrahman owed to his bank was of such a magnitude that Rafiq couldn't even pretend to entertain it. When he turned him down, Abdulrahman flashed a quick smile, as if to indicate that this was no worry at all. He pivoted immediately into the second reason he was visiting, by showing off a counterfeit fifty-pound note, stating that he was more than willing to sell these at half price. 'See if you can find any flaw in it,' he'd said to Rafiq and Xezal, who pretended they knew what a fifty-pound note was supposed to look like. The idea intrigued him, but Xezal made it very clear they weren't interested. After all, if the notes were as good as he claimed, why couldn't he pay off his debt to the bank with them?

To save face, Rafiq had launched into a tirade about Tariq Aziz's state visit announced in the day's paper, of Mitterrand being a filthy hypocrite, that while his wife was supporting the Kurds, the old lecher was inviting the foreign minister of a fascist regime to come look at weapons and nuclear power plants. 'He cannot say he doesn't know what the Baathists will do with this technology. What, he does not speak to his wife? Tariq Aziz will walk the red carpet, he will be given the full diplomatic treatment in Paris like he's some dignitary and not an animal.'

'Someone should kill that son of a dog in Paris,' Abdulrahman said, finding, as he was uttering those words, that he meant them. Just by stating it out loud, the two men saw a potential for the words to become reality. And so began their tentative plan to assassinate Iraq's foreign minister.

'Have you decided what you'll be having?'

Abdulrahman shot a peeved look at the waitress, who had re-emerged, and ordered three Earl Greys to be rid of her.

It had first been a joke, or rather an intellectual exercise. *If* they were to do it, how would they go about it? What would they need? How would they avoid getting caught? The more they discussed it over the following weeks, the more seriously they began taking the idea. For Abdulrahman it was a way to reclaim some lost pride: he had been one of the first Kurds in London to open his own business, and was used to being called upon for help. As soon as his money ran out, he felt invisible among his Kurdish friends, like there was nothing to him other than his wealth. He knew people were laughing at him behind his back for selling forged bills, even as they would happily buy the banknotes off him. He was becoming a joke, and they were laughing extra hard because he had once had all they wanted. He had not been active in the struggle back home, forced to provide for his family by smuggling electronics between Iraq and Iran before he fled to the UK in his late teens, and could not compete with the tales of war everyone around him brandished like medals of honour. This, this would be a way to assert himself. He may be a failed businessman, reduced to selling counterfeit bills to make ends meet, he may not have fought in the mountains for Kurdish independence, but he could drive a stake through the heart of Saddam Hussein's regime.

For Rafiq, he admitted one night to himself as he was running through the possibilities in his head, the appeal lay mostly in being able to say that his life had not been in vain. The Kurdish independence movement had run out of steam, its leaders all exiled or holed up in the mountains, and what remained of his former party was Marxist–Leninist only on paper. Of the three founders, he was the only one still alive, and his role had been mostly forgotten, his work had been lost in flames, his essays and political pamphlets unable to reach anyone back home any more. Instead of storming army barracks and shouting down a fascist gendarmerie, here he was, merely surviving on the teat of the imperialist power that had caused this century-long subjugation of the Kurds in the first place. Standing in line to collect welfare from Her Majesty to be able to provide a measly meal for his children, it was degrading; his entire existence had become devoid of dignity. At least by killing a core member of that fascist regime, his name would be etched into history. So when the question was raised, after weeks of skirting the obvious, Rafiq said that he would be the one to pull the trigger. If they were caught, or killed, Rafiq wanted his name to be the one associated with the man's death. Abdulrahman's best kebab-maker Lawko was brought in to drive the getaway vehicle, Abdulrahman himself was to be the lookout, and the plan was set in motion.

When they met for tea at the museum, the state visit was two weeks away.

'Here, the official timetable of the visit,' Rafiq flattened out the piece of paper on the table. He had reached out to some former revolutionaries who had fled to Paris and now earned a living doing caricatures of tourists at Montmartre. How they'd managed to get the schedule, Rafiq did not know, but it wasn't until he got it that it was decided, truly decided, that the plan would go ahead. They had already found out that Aziz would be staying at the Hôtel de Crillon, and imagined that catching him entering the hotel after his last event of the day would be the best way to get him. They all had different flights into Paris, different excuses for being there. Abdulrahman would meet with the owner of a shawarma restaurant in Belleville, claiming that he was looking to make his London shop a franchise. Lawko would visit a friend from Slemani who was enrolled at the University of Nanterre studying engineering, and Rafiq was treating his family to a trip to Paris, claiming he wanted to celebrate Siver's birthday. They each had a wad of Abdulrahman's fake bills to pay for flights and hotels, while Lawko was given an extra thousand pounds to buy a gun from a dealer that a member of the PKK had recommended to them. The car of a recently deceased Kurd had been purchased. Everything was set.

'So he will be visiting the Élysée Palace at seventeen hundred hours to discuss military aid to Iraq.'

'Those whores don't seem to need military aid when they fire rockets on Kurdish civilians.' Since Abdulrahman had no real experience with Baathists, had never fought them in battle, he felt he needed to assert his loathing of them to Rafiq at every opportunity. It was endearing, but also tiresome.

'Then there is a dinner with the minister of foreign affairs at this restaurant, Jamin, near the Eiffel Tower, at seven. Let's say the meal lasts two hours. Then he will return to the hotel. That will be our moment, as he returns from the meetings. Kak Abdulrahman, you will be positioned outside the restaurant and call us when they leave; we will somehow have to give each other the numbers of whatever phone booths we will be close to. At that moment I will go into the hotel and wait at the bar near the lobby, and Kak Lawko will be parked somewhere nearby so that if I manage to escape, we can get out of there.'

Abdulrahman and Lawko nodded. The way Rafiq described it, killing a high-ranking member of the Iraqi government was easy, as though anyone who wanted it enough could do it.

'We have to memorise this timetable, we cannot be seen with it at the airport,' Abdulrahman said, tapping the sheet of paper with his finger.

'I have a good hiding spot,' Rafiq said, thinking of the radio at home with its hidden compartment where Abdulrahman's forged bills were already stashed.

'Good. Try to get hold of some pictures of him. Look at the photos whenever you can. Make sure you'd recognise his face as though it were that of your own parent. They use body-doubles, these sons of whores, make sure it's really him.'

'So we are doing this? We are really doing this?' Lawko asked, his first contribution to the day's meeting.

The waitress returned, and put on a smile as she brought them towers of tiny sandwiches which hovered in the air for a moment while Rafiq scrambled to put the documents back into his pocket.

Marx wrote that 'a house may be large or small; as long as the neighbouring houses are likewise small, it satisfies all social requirement for a residence. But let there arise next to the little house a palace, and the little house shrinks to a hut.' Rafiq was reminded of this when he saw the disappointment on his children's faces – the hotel he had selected would probably have made them all perfectly happy, since it was the first hotel they had ever stayed in, but they had gone down the wrong street at the roundabout by Franklin D. Roosevelt and so before they saw their perfectly serviceable three-star hotel, they passed the luxurious Plaza Athénée, where royalty stayed, where Jackie Kennedy and Mata Hari had roamed the halls. Suddenly the cramped lobby and dirty rugs of their hotel became a hut, and the children needed a moment to muster up enthusiasm again.

Upon check-in, as their passports were being carbon-copied for the hotel's files, Rafiq was informed that someone had left a number for him at the lobby. This would be the number of the payphone Abdulrahman was using, from where he could observe the entrance of the restaurant.

As the concierge slipped him the phone number on a sheet of hotel stationery, he noticed Xezal giving him a look. She knew he was up to something, she knew a trip to Paris was an outrageous birthday present for an eleven-year-old. Of course she did. That woman was always too nosy for her own good, but he could not tell her what was about to happen. He did not want to implicate her, and he did not want her to stop him. Soon none of it would matter anyway. She could have her suspicions.

After they made their way through the hotel's corridors and into the room where they would stay for two nights, Rafiq checked the time. He had just over six hours to kill before he was supposed to meet Lawko at the Concorde by the Luxor Obelisk that the Egyptians had given the French in exchange for a broken clock.

'Come on, children, hurry. Wash your faces and get ready, we have a lot to see.'

Walking the wide boulevards, he began explaining the history of the Paris commune, the barricades that were erected, the devastation wrought on working-class families by Haussmann's destruction of Paris to create these impressive streets, impossible to barricade, impossible for ever more to hinder the French army's oppression of its own people. He had wanted to take them down to the Bastille, to tell them about the real revolution that nobody ever spoke of in the West: the Haitian slave revolt of 1791, how once the French had their revolution they decided that the others did not deserve any of their own, how they had brutally cracked down on Algeria's attempts at freedom, but he noticed his children yawning, Xezal sneaking peeks into designer stores. None of them were interested in history; they kept wanting ice cream and pancakes and to drink Coca-Colas at cafés. Everything he had taught them, all the stories he had told them about the plight of the common man, and here they were, distracted by commodities like puppies glimpsing treats. He almost got angry with them but swallowed his irritation; this could, after all, be the last day he spent with them. So, he turned towards the Trocadero instead, to have them look at the Eiffel Tower, that vulgar monument to nothing. What was it Barthes had said about it? That the structure was unique only because it had no use. Now, of course, it had a restaurant for over-eager tourists to dine in, but originally it didn't. The Eiffel Tower, which had come to represent Paris more than any other symbol, honoured nothing but itself.

The children, however, loved it, pestered him to buy cheap (yet expensive) Eiffel Tower keyrings and T-shirts from the Moroccan street vendors who kept a constant eye out for police as they tried to hawk their souvenirs. An odd word, that: souvenir, as though memory could be embodied in an object that way, an object that could be purchased for others, transferring the memory of a trip the recipient had not even been on.

'Rafiq, tell me. What's wrong?'

He turned to his wife, who unlike everyone else at the base of the tower was not looking up at the four giant beams conjoining together far up in the sky. She was looking at him.

'What makes you think something is wrong?'

'You seem distant. As though you never came here with us. Is it money? I know this trip must be expensive.'

He gave Xezal a pained grin. 'Everything is fine, my love. I promise.'

———

At exactly two minutes past seven, Rafiq emerged from the Art Nouveau vines of the Concorde metro station. The children were chatting away in their double bed, hypnotised by the baubles they had bought during the day, and he had told Xezal he was taking a walk, that he would be back late, and to her benefit, she knew better than to ask anything further. He tried to not look too conspicuous as he scanned the crowd for Lawko, whom he eventually saw pacing anxiously around the Obelisk. There was something about his agitated movements, his arms flapping at his sides like an agitated penguin, that made Rafiq feel like something had gone terribly wrong.

Rafiq felt adrenalin coalesce into metal in his mouth as he waited for the traffic light to turn green. Lawko had not seen him yet, he was walking back and forth as though looking for a lost object. The green stick figure allowing him to cross the street appeared, along with the percussive ratatat tone that reminded him of a distant machine gun. He noted two police officers standing by the corner and was mindful not to attract their attention by running across to Lawko. Whatever had happened, he would find out on the other end of the zebra crossing. He tried to imagine what had caused Lawko to look so out of sorts: the visit had been cancelled, or the schedule was incorrect, or they had skipped the restaurant and gone straight back to the hotel.

There, finally Lawko saw him.

'I couldn't get the gun!' he hissed the moment Rafiq reached him.

'What do you mean? Didn't you find the guy?'

'He didn't take pounds!'

Before Rafiq could say anything, a family of tourists held a camera out towards him, made a hand-gesture to indicate they wanted him to take a photograph. Centring the family in the viewfinder, in spite of everything that was happening, Rafiq thought for an instant that he should have brought his family here, with the sun setting dramatically behind the Obelisk, the arcs of water from the nearby fountain shimmering in the background. He waited for the camera's light to flash green and pressed down on the shutter-release. The father of the family gave him a thumbs-up of gratitude as Rafiq returned his camera. Once they had stepped away, he grabbed Lawko's arm hard, digging his nails through the sleeve of his jacket.

'What do you *mean*? Of course he didn't! You were meant to exchange the bills!'

'Well, I *tried*, once he said he needed francs, but at the bank they knew they were fake! They tried to confiscate the bills, they were going to call the police but I ran away!'

Rafiq massaged his temples as he tried to come to terms with Lawko's stupidity. For weeks he had been painstakingly exchanging the bills in small increments, going to Marks & Spencer, the Thomas Cook travel agent, any place that wasn't going to look at the bills too closely. And this dimwit had walked straight into a bank with thousands of forged pounds. On the day it was all meant to happen.

'You should have told us. We could have come to a deal with the guy. But now? Now it's too late for anything!'

'I didn't know how to reach you, I swear. Anyway, I got this.' Lawko shoved a plastic bag into Rafiq's jacket pocket.

'What in the name of God is that, Lawko?'

'A knife. I managed to get a knife.'

'And what am I meant to do with a knife? Give the man a shave?'

'It's all I could do!'

Rafiq, aware of the tourists around them, of the police standing across the street, knew he couldn't raise his voice, couldn't call too much attention to himself. He tried to compose himself, breathed in deep, and hissed through clenched teeth, 'Did you get the car?'

'Well. No. At that point . . . no.'

Another breath.

'I swear, Kurds like you are the reason that we don't have a country. Just go. No, no really go. Just leave before you somehow put even more shit into this than you already have.'

He stood for a moment watching Lawko scurry away, his dumb childlike body waddling towards the metro, and wondered what he should do. This couldn't be the end of it, it couldn't. He could not go back to his life, to that cramped apartment where the hot water was never enough for everyone's shower, his own family looking at him with disdain, his neighbours who treated him as though he had a mental deficiency just because he was not fluent in their language, the bureaucrats at the Home Office and the Department of Health and Social Security who considered him a pest, an insect to be waved away. Every day invaded by thoughts of money, money for rent, for groceries, for bus fare. His mind had once felt vast, a space where the entire world could fit, where he could converse with the world's foremost thinkers. Now it had narrowed into a constant worry about making it to the end of the month. There was nothing, nothing in his life that he still looked forward to, nothing he hoped for, nothing he felt able to strive towards.

He checked the time on the massive clock across the street. It was half past seven. He tightened his grip around the plastic bag in his pocket. To hell with it, he was going to go through with this.

Tears of rage and ineptitude were gathering in his eyes as he left the Hôtel de Crillon just after midnight, the impossibly tall valet wishing him a *bonne nuit*. A joke, everything had been some terrible cosmic joke.

Oh, Aziz had dined at the restaurant. Abdulrahman called the payphone on the rue de Rivoli to let Rafiq know that the convoy had departed just after 9 p.m., and Rafiq made his way to the hotel to wait for him at the bar. It shouldn't have taken longer than thirty minutes to get there, even with traffic, and yet Rafiq had sat there for hours, his heart beating so hard he felt like he was on the verge of vomiting any time someone walked through the corridor. But no delegation, no Tariq Aziz. He had ordered a glass of Chivas Regal with ice, not wanting to arouse suspicion sitting there on his own, and he believed the whisky would give him some courage, help calm his nerves. But as he had sat there for an hour, and then another hour, watching the blissfully ignorant parade through with their shopping bags, one whisky had become two, then three. By the time two Arab men in suits came to have a drink, Rafiq was already drunk, so drunk that it took him the better part of another hour to realise that these men were Tariq Aziz's bodyguards, that he'd arrived long ago and been taken into the hotel through a back entrance while Rafiq had been sitting there, sweaty palm wrapped around the knife in his pocket. All this time, Tariq Aziz was in his room, wearing his hotel bathrobe, ordering room service. The whole plan had been an embarrassing fiasco.

He began his walk back to the hotel where Xezal would be waiting up for him, would be reading his face to know how she should feel about his late return. How should she feel? She had married an imbecile, a useless cretin whose only joy in life in these past three years had been to concoct this hare-brained scheme with two morons. All those years going door to door with his pamphlets, convincing the Kurdish people to join his cause, to come together and with one voice demand a more just society, pry self-determination from the fists of their oppressors, had led to this abject failure. Crossing the street, a car honked at him. After a few seconds, Rafiq gave it the finger and shouted a fuck you into the night. He could not remember ever giving anyone the finger before, it seemed such a vulgar, western act, but here he was, saying fuck you to a vehicle that had already driven past. Had he really thought he could accomplish this? What, because he had so many life accomplishments to his name? The main effect of the many demonstrations he had convinced his comrades to participate in was that Iraqi soldiers began shooting ever more indiscriminately into the crowds; all his words did was encourage his neighbours to march to their deaths. Once, in London, he had organised a demonstration to denounce Iraq's genocidal Anfal campaigns and managed to gather so many protestors in front of the Iraqi embassy that buses and cars had to be rerouted. Everyone swore at them for the inconvenience, all *bloody* this, *fucking* that. The police hauled him into one of their vans, charged him with a breach of the peace. This was his greatest political success: disrupting some traffic. He tossed the knife in a bin, gave the metal can a kick for good measure. All of this, for nothing. All those years of struggle for the Kurdish people, and yet they were still being massacred, while he was holed up in Britain, eating pan-fried fish fingers because chicken was too expensive to have on a regular basis. He really believed his life would amount to something glorious, which he only now, waddling through the streets of Paris, realised was the source of his downfall. All that talk about community, about working together for the rise of the proletariat, all of it was nonsense: it was about him, his own self-esteem, wanting to secure *his* place in the world. He truly was the worst kind of hypocrite.

He made his way past the concierge at the front desk of his hotel, up the creaking stairs that led to the second floor and down the corridor with its sickly yellow lighting. He found himself praying for the first time in decades that his family would be sound asleep, that they wouldn't bear witness to this humiliation. But of course they were all still up, the children huddled around the television watching something with teddy bears fighting robots in a forest, giggling at the French dubbing. Xezal in her nightgown, leafing through a fashion magazine she'd bought earlier that day.

'Did you have a good time?' Xezal asked him as he stepped through the door, broken and drunk. He gave a quick nod, because what could he possibly say? That his entire life had been a failure? That this night destroyed any remaining hope he had of ever doing anything that mattered?

He took a deep breath, hoped his family wouldn't notice a quiver in his voice.

'So, children, what should we do tomorrow?'

TWO

Account (2009)

LOMBARD STREET WAS AN UNASSUMING STRETCH with a long history: paved in the first century, it had been one of the main roads used by the Romans through the city of Londinium, named after the goldsmiths from Lombardy who set up shop in later centuries. It was here, in Lloyd's Coffee House, that the global insurance market emerged in the eighteenth century, a fact commemorated by a small blue plaque by the entrance to a Sainsbury's Local supermarket. For centuries, the buildings had identifying signs of various animals, of the kind that gave the bank Barclays its avian logo and most pubs their names, to help the largely illiterate populace of London find their way, but of the hundreds of signs that once littered the street, their sole remainder was the golden grasshopper hanging above 68 Lombard Street. An exact replica of the grasshopper first erected in 1563, when Thomas Gresham set up London's first bank there – a bank that had stood for over 400 years until Margaret Thatcher's Big Bang of 1986 changed the financial world for good, relegating Lombard Street from being the most important banking location in the world to simply being another banking location.

The Big Bang – a name insisted upon by the press – was the popular term for the deregulation of the London stock market, a Thatcherite project to claw London's financial dominance back from the post-war usurper that was New York. Overnight, traders and stockbrokers were effectively replaced with screens and algorithms, rendering the London Stock Exchange on Old Broad Street obsolete, its trading floor an unsightly reminder of a time when humans had to do work that required perfection, before the realisation that we were nothing more than the bottleneck of the entire financial system. The new, post-Big Bang world order needed to be reflected in the city's buildings and bridges and so a confused mongrel breed of classicism and brutalism was erected, a virtually office-free space for worship at the altar of the terminal. The building was located next to St Paul's Cathedral, a statement of intent, the old gods in the shadow of the new. Deep in the London Stock Exchange's bowels a server room was built, housing computers belonging to the world's biggest trading firms, the room lit only by the flicker of white and blue LEDs and the odd throb of red. It was a cosmological re-enactment.

It wasn't long before banks and trading houses all across the City of London packed up and moved as close to the London Stock Exchange as their balance sheets would allow, freeing up valuable property in what had hitherto been the beating heart of capital. Rental prices in the City morphed rapidly, the market adjusting to this new reality. When the mid-market trading firm Hilliard Drake Capital PLC began conducting preliminary research on whether to upgrade the firm's office space, then, they found that they could rent four of the ten floors that were available at 68 Lombard Street, recently acquired by the workspace provider Regus, for the money they had intended for half the office space. The rental contract was signed, a press release drafted and issued, and the employees informed.

The markets interpreted the move as a bullish sign of confidence on behalf of a London firm with modest market cap, leading to record share prices for Hilliard Drake Capital PLC and significant end-of-year bonuses to the firm's managers. When the profits of the next two quarters did not correlate with the market's aforementioned optimism, Hilliard Drake's parent company as well as the board of directors felt it necessary to assuage worried investors by voting out the CEO who had presided over the firm's growth, Lloyd W. George, and appointing in his stead the well-respected Charles Allencourt, who had served as the chief executive officer for the London subsidiary ever since.

It was the time between the completion of 30 St Mary Axe (*aka* the Gherkin *aka* the Spirit of London *aka* the Butt Plug *fka* the Swiss Re Building) and the construction of the Shard (no known aliases), when people lived in fear of the double dip and were not yet above all things austere. Towers had fallen, tubes had been bombed. The notion of leaving the European Union with its faceless bureaucrats in order to regain control of the country had yet to be voiced into necessity. The price of Crude Oil, Dated Brent was 45.02 USD per barrel. The Bank of England had reduced the base rate of interest to a then historic low of 1 per cent. People tried to understand what had just happened to their lives, online clips of economists explaining the subprime mortgage crisis with the aid of cartoons and simplistic metaphors were eclipsed in popularity only by the viral music video to Rick Astley's 1987 hit 'Never Gonna Give You Up'. People still called what was taking place 'the Credit Crunch'. The narrative was still being formed. It was not yet their own fault, as it was soon to be.

There was, still, money to be made.

Mostly, this money was made by cutting costs: at Hilliard Drake a 'restructuring' had been implemented, which meant a wave of redundancies and the termination of the firm's lease on two floors at 68 Lombard Street, which injected much-needed cashflow into the London subsidiary's quarterly results. And that led to this here, now, with a courier walking into the building with the golden grasshopper sign, his bicycle folded and carried in one hand, an envelope for M. M. Hardi in the other.

II

MOHAMMED HAMA HARDI DIDN'T KNOW when it had happened, but at some point, the villains in movies stopped being Soviets and, instead, started to look like him. Being saddled with the name Mohammed was, then, not the best leg-up his parents could have given him to succeed in the cut-throat world of corporate finance and so he chose M. M. Hardi as his name on Hilliard Drake's business cards. Though his friends had called him Mo since his early teens, he preferred the Flemingesque initial M and tried – largely in vain – to be referred to as such.

As the courier approached the reception with a plastic envelope in hand, M was running late for work. He had, upon the customary third snooze, remembered that he hadn't picked up his shirts the day before, and so rushed to Lamb's Conduit Street in his sweatpants, only to find that the dry-cleaner didn't open until ten. A frantic scramble through the basket of already worn shirts ensued, a sniff of the armpits, an inspection of collars and cuffs for remnants of Londonian grime. Fishing out the least offensive shirt, he instead took a scalding-hot shower, the crumpled shirt hanging off the shower curtain rod in the hope that the steam would make the shirt, and by extension him, appear somewhat presentable. A quick scrape of a disposable razor over his cheeks, a slap of cologne, a swirl of silk around his fingers to tie a half-Windsor knot, and he was ready to go.

Outside his building, he checked the Transport for London app to determine the quickest route to work. Northern Line: Reduced Service; Central Line: Part Closure. He gambled on the Central Line and turned from the cul-de-sac where he lived on to Gray's Inn Road, that long and intestinal grey stretch near King's Cross, its heroin and prostitutes recently replaced by a treadmill of young men in ill-fitting suits, well-dressed women in trainers, kitten-heels in hand, cat-called by the boys in front of the corner shop who, on account of being poor and brown, were not boys at all, but rather *youth*. Smile, luv, gap-toothed men in yellow vests shouted out. Smile. M swerved down the street to Chancery Lane station, slaloming between people, making sure to not step in the puddle of vomit in front of the strip club, a remnant of a seedy past that would soon be eradicated completely. All around, billboards encouraging people to find out why millions of people across Britain saved with NatWest, claiming that more people chose to save tax-free with Halifax than anyone else, while BP offered assurances that there was energy security in energy diversity. The averted glances of people devising real-time stratagems to avoid the men and women in green raincoats emblazoned with the logos of well-regarded charities. Do you have a moment for the children of the world? Do you?

M disappeared down the gape of Chancery Lane, his phone informing him that he was already eight minutes late for work. By the time he emerged from the byzantine tangle of corridors at Bank, it was 09:22.

Hilliard Drake weren't stricter about punctuality than any other workplace in London, but M was not oblivious to the fact that there were those who did not feel that he deserved his place there, that he was a token hire taking the position of someone else, someone more fitting.

Certainly, his path to the position of Executive Manager of Corporate Finance was unconventional, in comparison to the other two executive managers on his floor. He was neither of the Eton- and Harrow-educated MBA-wielding ilk, combining ambition with an interest in the weekly *Financial Times* supplement 'How to Spend It', like Daniel Chamberlain, nor the working-class trader extraordinaire who had worked his way up from cold-calling pensioners and who spoke often and effusively of the School of Hard Knocks, like John Morris. M did not fit any of the available corporate finance narratives; he had been lucky to make it as far as he had, and he knew it.

Not that anyone in his family ever acknowledged this. To them, the very fact that he was working with *money* (Xezal would barely deign to speak the word) was a betrayal of everything the family had once stood for. 'Prostitutes deal with money,' Xezal would say. *Having* money, according to his mother, indicated good standing, but actually *earning* it was a tawdry act that one should never draw attention to. 'Remember, you wanted to be a doctor, whatever happened to becoming a doctor?'

What happened: after the revolution in Iran had gained the epithet *Islamic*, Rafiq Hardi Kermanj reached out to his network of Marxist dissidents and through them struck a deal with a smuggler who got the family out of Tehran and back into Iraq, where Rafiq's contacts at the British embassy – from an era when the United Kingdom ever so briefly considered supporting Kurdish statehood – got them on a cargo plane to London.

The night they left Iran was one of burned-down houses, of talking their way out of death at checkpoints, and whatever happened to his mother that was never spoken of in spite of it rendering her virtually mute for a year, but M couldn't remember much of it, and it only informed his notion of who he was in the way that, say, the Blitz did for someone born in the UK. What M did remember was that he had a blue bunny, and blue bunny was left behind, and the loss of this raggedy stuffed toy with a dangling eye and frayed arm was something that he still sometimes thought of.

When they arrived in the UK, Rafiq reached out to the few Kurds he knew who had made it to that green and pleasant land for whatever reason and through whatever miracle (usually assisting the British against the Ottomans in the Great War) and eventually found a small flat in the outskirts of Surrey, south of London, from where the Struggle could continue. Since M's grades had been lost in the fire, they were unable to prove to the Home Office that he had been attending school in Iran for three years already. This, coupled with the fact that he could only read in Arabic script, led to him having to start in Year One, sitting with five-year-olds when he was almost nine. And so began the process of trying and failing to fit in.

At school he was called a Paki and was assumed by just about every teacher to be lazy and/or stupid due to the fact that he was so much older than everyone else. After his A levels he wound up at Croydon College, which was free and close enough that he could still live at home. There were arguments over money, over food and lack thereof. Xezal cried a lot. Rafiq, unable to find any work in this new country, became quiet, spending time reading and rereading the few books in Kurdish and Arabic that he had been able to bring with him and writing a memoir that he never finished. The radio he had insisted they bring with them to the UK was displayed prominently in the living room of their flat, put upon a small table as a relic or prized statue, its power cord slithering across the living-room floor, causing every member of the family to trip over it on a regular basis. Every night alien squeals and sharp laser sounds would emerge amid the static as Rafiq would try to find a faint broadcast providing news from home. He would squint every time he heard something that could be a human voice, as though attempting to see faraway stars through a cloudy sky, and on the few nights that a broadcast was found it always sounded as distant as their home country now felt. He would infer the news from chopped-up syllables, trying to convince Xezal and himself that the revolution would come, any day now, while the kids were left to fend for themselves, the odd plate of reheated leftovers ready for them when they got home from school.

One day, without informing Xezal, Rafiq took M with him on the bus to Croydon and bought a computer. M remembered the box the machine came in, a futuristic purple swirl and the words Pentium II printed across the black background. Xezal, knowing what this meant with regard to the food situation, spoke neither to Rafiq nor to M for several weeks, instead instructing the other two children to carry passive-aggressive missives across enemy lines. But Xezal stopped being angry eventually and they still had the computer. It's easier to receive forgiveness than permission, Rafiq said to his son as he clicked through the languages on the Encarta encyclopaedia, delighted to find Kurdish in there. He played the set phrases so often that the children went around mimicking the computer's recorded voice for years. A few months later, Rafiq came home with a little grey box that they connected the phone wire into. M's first search on AltaVista, one day when he was left alone with the computer, was 'samantha fox naked'.

The first time he got drunk (on shots of tequila with his mates

Rakesh and Pradeep) he vomited all over his Next shirt and thought, the following day, that he had a hangover. Decades later when experiencing crippling paranoia and unable to get out of bed to open the door for the pizza delivery man, this would bring him some amusement.

The first girl he loved (the active choice of defining a feeling as love was, he thought, what made it love) moved back to Bangladesh with her parents after nine months. They kept in touch by fax for a while but the letters grew less frequent and then one day stopped entirely. He kept those letters for years and when he finally moved out of his parents' flat found that the fax papers had faded, impossible to read, impossible now to remember what he ever saw in her that made him think that the madness inside him was love.

The family rarely went to central London, instead referring to where they lived as London, the high streets of Croydon and Sutton being the extent of what they saw. One day, at the Sutton train station, M saw a man shouting into his phone. M had heard people shout before, at home he heard it on a near-daily basis, but this man (dressed in a suit, wearing shoes that glistened) did not do it out of anger or powerlessness but rather from a sense of confidence. The world would bend to what he wanted it to bend into.

A guidance counsellor, a person with an antiquated sense of the job market and naive understanding of the world, told M that his grades weren't going to get him into many fields, but he could always become a trader. Your brashness could well be appreciated there, she said, stifling a yawn before she saw the next student.

His parents weren't happy that he wanted to go into finance, deeming dealing with money beneath them. There were a few arguments but by this time both of his parents had fought too much and too long. They gave up quickly.

He graduated. Barely. His father and Laika did not come to the graduation but Xezal and Siver did and he remembered how out of place they looked, Xezal dressed in what remained of her old clothes, her jewellery shining conspicuously, Siver's body forced into a dress she hated. There are no smiles on the one photograph they have of that day, but there is a photograph.

He got an internship at Credit Suisse but had to quit after a week because it was an unpaid internship and it cost him £16.80 to buy the travel card to get into the City every day.

Then he found a job in sales and then he lost a job in sales.

A year later he managed to bullshit his way into a junior analyst position at Hilliard Drake. The joy of finding stable employment made him forget that he earned less than others at the same firm with the same title, made him forget that his job consisted of making money for other people, made him grateful that they gave him the honour of making them money.

After his probationary period ended, he finally moved out from the family flat, prompting, he believed, the rapid deterioration and demise of his father. His mother eventually decided to move back to Slemani, the 2003 Iraq war making it possible for her to return to the home she'd left behind thirty years ago. Siver had married a wealthy Arab and moved to Baghdad. Laika did whatever Laika did, moving first to Berlin for two years, then to Paris, then to New York. The flat they had lived in was a rental and the landlord complained about the state it was in and refused to pay back the deposit. His father didn't have a will and had £12.31 in his current account and £0.83 in his savings account at the time of his death. The furniture, along with all of Rafiq's pamphlets, were thrown into a skip.

M began going to the gym and hated everyone there who looked glistening and sexy and perfect as they worked out while he sweated and essentially looked like he'd been violated, devoured then regurgitated by a washing machine. He would stare at his increasing bulk with pride in the mirror each night, his body a sculpture of his own making.

He got a handheld computer which replaced his old phone (a tiny thing he had mainly played Snake on) and this became the single object he looked at the most in any given day.

He moved every six months for two years, trying first to find acceptably hygienic roommates and, when this proved too difficult, a place he could afford to live on his own. Then he got a raise and a promotion and he found an apartment just off Gray's Inn Road where he would live for six years. The building had once belonged to one family but now was divided into twelve illogical apartments to fit as many rent-paying humans as regulation allowed. On the right side of the elevator lived Beryl Rathbourne, oldest resident, former Olympic ice-skater and now a nobody. Above her lived three art students from the nearby Slade School of Fine Art, who were sharing a one-bedroom apartment before being forever priced out of Zone 1. Two of them would spend their lives bobbing above the poverty line, hustling their way from one bill to the next until old age made them bitter and full of the singular regret of having followed one's dream to find it did not actually exist. The third one would make it, where to make it meant being well respected and coveted by famous galleries and curators, while of course still barely bobbing above the poverty line. And next to them lived M, in a rundown one-bedroom apartment, with mould stains on the ceiling and carpet on the bathroom walls which he rented for £1,890 per month. This was, as was true of the living arrangements of most Londoners, a temporary arrangement.

'M. M. Hardi? I have this for him,' the courier said in the lobby at 68 Lombard Street, presenting an envelope to the receptionist, who glanced up from a copy of the *Financial Times* scattered with ominous headlines disclosing the aftershocks of the financial crisis: the claim that inflation was looming on America's horizon, that Chrysler had filed for bankruptcy, that AIG had paid out 200 million dollars of its government bailout money to give bonuses to its financial services team.

M, just about to swipe his access card when he heard his name, turned back towards the courier.

'Oh, that's me, I can take that.'

The courier eyed the man, built as though he would be good in a fight, hair colour and skin tone hinting at a Middle Eastern heritage. Didn't look like a Hardy. Out of place in a building like this, navy suit and tan flap-over briefcase notwithstanding.

'Can we see some ID, mate?'

The courier saw the man claiming to be Hardi roll his eyes as he handed over a passport.

'Says here your name is Mohammed.'

M gritted his teeth and presented a business card instead.

'Whatever,' the courier said, handing over the envelope.

In the elevator, M clicked through the messages and emails he had received while on the underground, deleted all the spam, flagged an email that was to be replied to. A message from his sister. *Mum wants to know that you have her arrival time. She's looking forward to seeing her FAVOURITE CHILD*, to which he was about to reply that he'd seen her flight details so often that they were practically etched on his retinae, but he found himself focusing instead on Siver's quip about him being the favourite child. She was always saying that, and yet when it came down to it, whose birthday was it that had led to the family's one and only holiday abroad? Who was it who had been helped and encouraged to go to a prestigious university? It sure as shit wasn't M. Irritated, he pocketed his phone and checked his shirt, fiddling with his wrinkled collar as though he could make the fabric conform to his will, before he gave up and straightened his tie instead – knowing that Charles Allencourt cared excessively about the ties his male employees wore: the suitability or lack thereof of various tie-knots, the number of folds in the silk, and the fashion houses that had put their labels on the back.

Allencourt was known for rash, impulsive gestures, the kind of extravagant acts of profanity and violence that invariably led to hagiographic profiles in the trade papers as well as the odd lawsuit by those who were clearly not suited for this industry. One of the hobbies for which he was known (which, in fairness, had only happened twice but it was in the best interest of the Hilliard Drake shareholders that it be believed this was a regular occurrence) was to walk around the office with a comically large pair of scissors and flip the ties of his male employees. If the label on the tie was not one of two designer brands (one French, founded in 1837, the other Italian, founded in 1910) he would simply cut the tie in half and instruct the employee that another mistake like that would lead to immediate dismissal.

Still, for all of Allencourt's faults, he was eccentric and successful enough to sidestep company policies as and when he pleased, and had personally intervened when HR hadn't deemed M's credentials to be 'of the calibre that Hilliard Drake applicants aspire to', by claiming that he, Allencourt, saw a drive in M's eyes and that he should therefore be given a chance. 'Besides, the man's CV is written in Gotham. Never dismiss a man who takes his fonts seriously.' M was thus given a chance at Hilliard Drake, based on something in his eyes and a font he had chosen at random. As anxious as he was to prove that he deserved his place in the ecosystem of Hilliard Drake Capital PLC, he also knew that Allencourt himself had given him a chance when nobody else would hire him. As long as he remained in his boss's good graces he would be fine.

And with that thought he got out of the elevator and passed through the glass doors to the Hilliard Drake offices where Charles Allencourt was currently suffering a massive ST-segment elevation myocardial infarction.

III

IN A FEW HOURS HEADLINES WOULD APPEAR, informing the world that Charles Allencourt was dead, aged sixty-two. Journalists in what remained of the UK's newsrooms would scramble together a few details about the CEO of the financial advisory firm Hilliard Drake Capital PLC having had a heart attack, lying dead in his office for over an hour before anyone called an ambulance, cobbling together the semblance of a narrative for the editors to approve as the articles went live on hundreds of news sites, an important enough event to warrant prominent placement above the scroll, not important enough to warrant push notifications to people's phones. The specialist papers, the *Financial Times* and the *Wall Street Journal* chief among them, would use Allencourt's name, while others would refer to him as 'City banker' in their headlines. By the time the physical papers arrived, the next morning, the news story would have been pushed aside to make room for new developments in the world economy, the death of Charles Allencourt already a historical footnote.

Paramedics, when they finally arrived, reported that they may well have been able to save his life had the staff not waited almost ninety minutes to call an ambulance. The reason the Hilliard Drake employees neglected to act was that Allencourt had retired to his office and instructed anyone within ear's reach to not disturb him, under any circumstances. This was usually the only way that Allencourt could ensure fifteen or so uninterrupted minutes, during which he could attempt to break his high score on Minesweeper, and so he would sit at his desk (his office phone off its cradle in an effort to fool the receptionist into thinking he was on a call) clicking through squares, avoiding digital landmines. He would then go back out to the office landscape, indicating by his presence that he was yet again available to be pestered about minutiae by his incompetent staff. On the day that he died, however, his finger slipped, exploding a mine that made him lose the game, upon which he suffered a heart attack.

Many did in fact hear the sound of him crashing to the floor, dragging with him his laptop and a pen-filled coffee cup, and though several of the firm's employees exchanged concerned looks, Charlie, the firm's receptionist, who had been at the London branch ever since she got her A levels, hurried to position herself between the rest of the staff and the door to Allencourt's office, a French-manicured finger to her lips. In a hissed whisper, Charlie reminded everyone of the time that Richard Pryce had heard Allencourt scream (due to his failing to beat the aforementioned Minesweeper high score) and knocked on his door to make sure that he was OK. Pryce no longer worked at Hilliard Drake. So the staff returned to their desks, concerned that they had not heard any sound from Allencourt's office since the crash but too scared to actually check on him. Charlie briefly considered sending him a quick text but, afraid for her job, convinced herself that the man was fine, and focused on the spreadsheet that was open on her company-issued laptop.

M walked through the corridor where Hilliard Drake's employees stood muted, anxiously milling about, gradually realising something was amiss. 'What's happening?' M asked Naveen Agarwal, the specialist in financial modelling on his team, as he logged into his computer, aware that even though his co-workers were too busy to notice his tardiness, the company's productivity-monitoring software would know all too well he had arrived late.

'We heard a sound from Allencourt's office, and now everyone is scared to check on him.'

'Some of us have better things to do, frankly,' said Jane Tilly, M's due diligence officer, as she furiously typed something on her computer.

Aside from being the sort of man whose employees were scared to check whether he was still alive and whose family had the net worth of a small country, Allencourt was also known for Punctuated Equilibrium, his pioneering company structure, which had led to a bestselling book of the same name published as though Allencourt himself had written it and implemented throughout the corporate group. A bastardisation of a term in evolutionary biology (chosen by Allencourt not because of the term's aptitude, but because it sounded both disruptive and authoritative), it consisted of dividing a company's salesforce up into groups of three or four and making them compete with one another. When a company's competition is another company, the life-or-death nature of business becomes an abstraction, Allencourt's ghostwriter wrote, and it is easy to forget that business consists of vanquishing other people and gaining control of their assets. The junior analysts, the accountants, the HR department and the in-house lawyers were to be kept in the middle of the office layout, available to all, whereas the Corporate Finance teams would operate individually, consisting only of the few individuals needed to close a deal. When M got his raise and became an Executive Manager of Corporate Finance, he was given the chance to form his own team. He fought for Naveen, having seen the magic the man could work with a spreadsheet, but did not get his first two choices for due diligence officer, as they both held out for a more experienced group leader. Jane, at the firm for three years already without a promotion, was assigned to M, who was initially concerned that an attractive woman would be distracting to prospective clients (and to him and Naveen).

'You know, this is how Stalin died. All alone in his office with his staff too scared to check on him,' M said over the clacking of Jane's keyboard.

'If you're so concerned, why don't you check in on him?'

'Well no, I'm not an idiot.'

It wasn't until Charlie in reception slipped Hilliard Drake's unpaid intern £20 from the petty cash that the door to Allencourt's office was finally opened. After this, it took the ambulance twenty-one minutes to arrive and although the staff were understandably distraught at the death of their CEO, they also knew that the productivity-monitoring software installed on their terminals would indicate that they were not working during this time. As nobody at Hilliard Drake had died during office hours before, it was unclear what proper etiquette was. Charlie let a few tears fall, but upon looking around and noticing nobody was paying attention to her, she got back to work.

There would be some criticism in the following weeks of how the Hilliard Drake employees handled the immediate aftermath of their CEO's death – a typically maudlin *Guardian* think piece asked 'Employees at Hilliard Drake Capital kept working as their CEO lay dead. Does the City lack heart?' – but ultimately not assisting those in danger was not a criminal act and the whole thing was forgotten as soon as the next financial scandal hit (which was the revelation that the Houston-based Finvexia Financial Services was operating a multi-billion-dollar Ponzi scheme, which led to hundreds of suddenly destitute clients and a swift rebranding on the part of the company).

No sooner had the paramedics left and the news of Allencourt's death spread out of the confines of the Hilliard Drake offices than the board of directors, in order to quell the nerves of shareholders and attempt to put a positive spin on the day's events, swiftly sent out a press release to Reuters and AP, ccing all@hilliard-drake.co.uk, wherein they offered condolences for the loss of the 'visionary' and 'beloved' Allencourt, before noting that the company COO, Nathalie Hardy, would take over as interim CEO, with a permanent replacement being chosen at the next board meeting.

Only minutes after the email arrived, Daniel P. Chamberlain, Executive Manager, commandeered the boardroom with his team – a boardroom one usually needed to reserve through Charlie – and began projecting a series of spreadsheets. M saw through the boardroom partition that Chamberlain was comparing the projects that they currently had under mandate. Cheeky fucker. It was not news to anyone that Chamberlain was ruthlessly ambitious; he'd been gunning for CFO of the British operation since the day he arrived at Hilliard Drake. M *was* surprised, however, at just how brazen he was being, calling attention to himself as though he were making a declaration: he intended to submit his successful closings, and ingratiate himself with his good friend and Chairman of the Board Lord Harbinger so as to make himself a viable candidate to the board of directors.

For someone like Chamberlain, the death of Allencourt presented an opportunity, one to be grasped, swiftly and efficiently. Chamberlain had, on paper, the same Executive Manager title as M, but they were different in every way that mattered: he dressed in bespoke suits that cost more than M's monthly salary (indicating as it did that since Chamberlain did not need money, due to the fact that he came from money, he was thus more deserving of money), and had the demeanour of someone who had never doubted, not for one moment, that he was owed and would receive everything that he could ever desire. More than once, in an emulation of Allencourt's behaviour towards his subordinates (though in Chamberlain's case more cruel than eccentric), he had reduced co-workers to tears, often by mocking what they wore. A junior analyst, fresh out of business school, had never returned after the humiliation of being caught out on laundry day wearing socks with a 90s cartoon character on them.

Chamberlain's play was shameless, and unlikely to succeed, but even M recognised that he had a shot: the options available to the board at this juncture were to appoint a person who was already well regarded by the market as a CEO, or to promote from within. Seeing as the firm's next quarterly board meeting was in a month and the board would at that point have to reassure the market that the London subsidiary remained in capable hands, the board's ability to lure a big-name CEO on such short notice would be limited at the best of times, let alone during a period when the market was in the throes of a 1930s-style meltdown. Nobody with a reputation to maintain would be likely to leave an existing position when it would be all but impossible to generate profits for the shareholders. Whoever got this job would be in the position for one quarter, two tops, until the board voted them out. That made promoting from within a viable option. And though in-house promotions to the CEO position came almost exclusively from operations, Hilliard Drake's COO was a woman, which would give off a vibe of fresh optimism and a contemporary outlook in a bull market, but in times of crisis a struggling firm did not have the luxury to be promoting equality at the cost of maximising revenues. This was therefore not an option to be entertained, as the email made clear by assuring investors that her interim status as acting CEO would merely last until the next regular board meeting. As for the Hilliard Drake CFO, he had been poached by rival firm Spearmint Capital a few months ago and had yet to be replaced.

So even though the board would never appoint an Executive Manager under anything resembling usual circumstances, this confluence of various factors meant that, as unlikely as it seemed, someone like Chamberlain had, perhaps, a shot at this undesirable job and could then for ever more be in the running for CEO positions merely on account of having been one once, albeit unsuccessfully so.

For M, the death of Allencourt did not present an opportunity so much as a challenge. He knew that with his background, redundancy was a more likely consequence than promotion. It was, after all, Allencourt himself who had vouched for M when nobody else cared to. The dawning realisation that he could soon be back on the job market made him feel queasy. It suddenly became very important that he close a project before the next board meeting in order to cement his status as one of the value-adding employees at Hilliard Drake.

M opened his folder, which contained the projects that he was currently working on. Not one of them was developed enough that he could reasonably close by the time the board was meant to meet. The Iranian shipping deal was on hold due to sanctions, the Lebanese bank merger was mired in a byzantine bureaucratic approval process, and the dogshit-cleaning app seeking financing was, frankly, just a ridiculously dumb proposition.

M glanced at the couriered document on his desk. He ripped the yellow plastic pouch open and saw therein a countersigned copy of a mandate document, quickly scanning the document to ascertain which project this was.

'Naveen, we got exclusivity on the Islamic Credit Card deal for three months. Can you provide me with a revised estimate of revenue?'

'The Islamic Credit Card?' Naveen asked, his voice ever so slightly inflected with a sense of weariness but too polite to come out and say what he actually meant, namely that the project had never made much financial sense, before he nodded himself into action and proceeded to tinker with his spreadsheets, sufficiently advanced to a layman to be indistinguishable from magic. The Islamic Credit Card project was not one that M had chosen himself, but rather one that had been assigned to him. The reasoning behind this was evident to everyone at Hilliard Drake even though it had never been stated out loud. It was the same reason that M was assigned the Four Seasons Mecca Hotel Project (did not close, due to the fact that the Saudi government decided to give the plot of land that lay atop what was once the second oldest mosque in existence to Kempinski rather than the Four Seasons), the Halal Meat Project (did not close due to the fact that the company founder was currently doing four years in prison for securities fraud) and the Emirates Renovation Project (did close, but came with so much equity that it would have been a fireable offence to fail to structure the project successfully). These were the kind of projects that were deemed to be M's expertise. Chamberlain, of course, was deemed to be an expert in projects like the Barclays Bike deal (closed), the EAT restructuring (closed) and the DF&H merger (closed). These were things that he – Eton, King's College Cambridge, internship at Bain Capital – was thought to excel at.

The Islamic Credit Card was not a great project, by any metric. It was hard to gauge revenue, it was difficult to determine whether or not the damn thing even worked, but they had hit a moment in the global economy when, ever so briefly, Islamic Financing was thought to be perhaps the great saviour, structured to appear as though it did not rely on usury or interest, and after the *Financial Times* ran a well-received article claiming that the Islamic Finance industry had emerged from the global credit crisis relatively unscathed, the general idea in the City was that this newfangled concept (which had existed for 1,600 years or so) may just be the Next Big Thing. It was the rare moment when the notion of an Islamic credit card could possibly seem like a sound investment.

A text message, again from his sister. *? Did you get my message? Mum is driving me crazy wanting to know if you have her flight details. Why she can't just call you herself I don't know x.*

Now was not the time, Siver. Christ.

M picked up his phone and flipped through a series of business cards that he had collected at the PepsiCo-sponsored Islamic Finance conference two weeks ago at the Grosvenor. The third card he picked out to call, belonging to someone at Deutsche Bank about whom M had unhelpfully scribbled 'loose handshake, nondescript face', led to a fairly positive result. The man on the other end of the line, Benjamin Freeman, Vice President, Project Finance, Asset Finance & Leasing, Corporate & Investment Banking, had read the same article in the *Financial Times* and knew that Deutsche Bank, having made billions upon billions of dollars on the subprime mortgage crisis in the United States, was looking to invest in new markets. 'This Islamic card could well be it, well be it.'

'I'm very glad to hear that,' M said, looking over his partition to see Chamberlain wildly gesticulating in his performance as successful financier over in the boardroom. If Deutsche Bank actually moved on this, or at the very least came in as the main lender in a consortium, then that would be a huge get for M. He could well survive the oncoming shakeup. Game on, fuckers. 'So, when do you think we could schedule a meeting? Maybe a quick dinner?'

IV

A GREEN RECTANGLE APPEARED, glimmering under the chandelier of a fashionable London restaurant.

'So this is it. This is what it looks like. As you can see, we wanted it to be stylish, to give owners a sense of exclusivity, think Palladium or Centurion. And the investment needed to make the soft rollout is minimal. It really is, Benjamin, like printing money. If you have someone willing to do the hard groundwork.'

M mimicked rolling up his sleeves to demonstrate 'hard work', which gave him an excuse to reveal the clasp of the rose-gold watch on his left wrist, in order to show this man from Deutsche Bank that he was not some rube trying to con him, but someone to be trusted.

'Gentlemen,' the waiter now, timing his precise positioning of the plate in front of M to be simultaneous with his colleague, who did the same for the Vice President, Project Finance, Asset Finance & Leasing, Corporate & Investment Banking, 'this is your first course. For you, sir,' here he gestured to M's plate of tiny jewels, 'a seared duck foie gras, with a purée of Jerusalem artichoke and hazelnuts topped with 24 carat gold leaf. And here,' the waiter swivelled over to the Vice President and the cubist assortment on his plate, 'we have the seared tuna belly, straight from Japan, flew in this morning, that Chef has prepared with an assortment of caramelised fruit, matsutake mushrooms, Densuke watermelon emulsion and a drizzle of 150-year-old vinaigrette. Bon appétit.'

'You know how they make that, right?' the Vice President said, suddenly looking straight at M, a wenge-wood chopstick that had been provided for this course pointing vaguely at M and the plate in front of him. 'They force-feed the thing, it's brutal.'

M, surprised at this sudden burst of sentiment, wanted to point out that a tortured duck or two paled in comparison to the havoc wrought by flying in fresh ingredients from Tokyo but instead just laughed – 'Ah, those bloody French, eh?' – and proceeded to ruin his plating by digging into the circle of liver with his fork. He needed Deutsche Bank's money and didn't have the luxury of having morals the way the Vice President did.

'But let me tell you a bit about myself. You know, I joined Hilliard Drake five years ago, and I didn't need to. I didn't need to work, Benjamin, for me this is a lifestyle business.'

A waiter, not the same one as earlier but then again maybe it was, appeared out of nowhere to pour more wine into both glasses and then vanished.

'Our offices are on Lombard Street – you should come visit someday, we should do lunch – and I hired a team of young, hungry people, the best. Just the best people. And we have a motto, that we will only take on projects that we truly believe in, and this, this is—'

The Vice President's phone that had, like M's, rested by the bread knife throughout the meal as though it were part of the cutlery, now woke to life, twitching on the tablecloth like a wounded insect, its silence conspicuously loud.

'I'm sorry. I have to take that,' Benjamin said and reached over to the phone. 'Freeman. Yes. Yes, I understand. We were going to leverage their jet, though, remember that.'

Their plates were whisked away, someone brought a silver utensil designed to swipe breadcrumbs off a tablecloth and rendered it pristine again. The wine glasses were filled anew.

'Well, no, the project as such doesn't exist yet, but I think. Yes. What time is it now in New York? What about Singapore? Well, let's set up a confcall in, say, two hours? Yes. We can do that, yes. I just, Bill, I just don't want the value here to evaporate. You know as well as I do, the due diligence on this is done, but who knows where the market will be in six months, right? So.'

M stared at this man whose attention was the difference between him bringing in hundreds of thousands of pounds to his firm and bringing in no pounds. The Vice President was young, too young to be doing his job; but then again, who knew what his job was? His business card read like the menu of an Asian restaurant in a small town, providing everything and nothing. Everyone was a Vice President of something these days. Benjamin Freeman's voice hadn't yet managed to be scrubbed of a Mancunian youth and his suit was cheap, ill-fitting, but his shirt was expensive, and his cufflinks branded. M didn't mind having to go through a Cerberus or two to get to the guys with the authority to sign a cheque, he told himself. He could wine and dine dozens of these little twerps if that's what he had to do.

Deeming it rude to look at his own phone, M first feigned interest in the water menu left standing on their table, consisting of thirty pages of flowery descriptions of mineral waters from every corner of the world, from Arctic fjord water flown in from Norway to the carbonated oasis water from a Saudi desert, but M quickly grew bored of this and instead looked around the restaurant. This had been, only a few months ago, one of the most difficult restaurants in London to get a table at. You would call at 09:00 on the dot, exactly one month before your desired reservation date, and if by some stroke of luck you were fortunate enough that a snooty person deigned to answer, you were either told that sorry, the day is fully booked – you can try again tomorrow, even though it was only 09:02 and they couldn't possibly have taken thirty reservations already – or that yes there was one table, by the kitchen, at 21:45, would that do? We can only hold the table for two hours, they would always say, a newfangled haute cuisine concept where the entire meal is planned and packaged so it lasts exactly 115 minutes, thus maximising the number of tables turned per night, optimising revenue. M had been to this restaurant before in order to impress clients, something it never failed to do as it had been the town residence of the Prince Regent between 1785 and 1824, and preserved to give diners a sense of regalia as they sat at tables engraved with the names of the historic people who had eaten there before (that night, M and the Vice President sat at the Winston Churchill table, which was to the right of the T. S. Eliot table and to the left of the Wayne Rooney table). One archaic touch that M bristled at was that the menus for guests came without prices, making it harder for the people M was inviting to know how much he was paying for them, but since the extravagant prices of the restaurant were well known, the lack of concrete evidence perhaps wasn't needed. On previous visits he had been surrounded by City boys drinking bottles of champagne so large that their nomenclature needed to consist of obscure biblical figures, whereas now, while governments were throwing money at financial institutions and weekly magazines ran headlines claiming that we were all socialists, you could call the restaurant a day before and they would be pleased, *delighted*, to have you. Any particular time that you would prefer? The only other diners there that evening were three young people decked out in designer wear who ate in complete silence and took photos of every single dish with their phones and an older man with a conspicuously younger date, who had either an incredibly expensive designer handbag or the knockoff of said handbag on a little stool next to her chair.

'I'm so sorry, I'm going to have to leave soon,' Benjamin Freeman said, putting the phone back down, its screen upwards this time. No sooner had he done this than the main courses appeared, precariously stacked food in the midst of giant circular plates. Again, these were put in front of the both of them simultaneously, before the waiter delivered the artist statement.

'And here we have for you, sir,' the waiter's hand angled slightly towards M, 'the squab, from Anjou in France, Chef recommends to nibble on those bones with your hands, and with this, poached pear served with a blood orange sauce and a heart of artichoke deconstructed baozi.'

'And here,' a nod in the Vice President's direction, 'the Kobe beef, marbled grade nine. Our beef is from a particular farm just outside Kobe in Japan where the farmer, a former alto at the Tokyo Opera City, every evening sings the cows the aria from Gluck's famed *Orphée et Eurydice*. The steak is on a bed of caramelised grass from Kobe and a black truffle smashed potato on the side. Enjoy.'

'So, in a sentence,' said the Vice President, impaling a pink slice of beef with his fork, 'why should we invest in an . . . Islamic credit card?'

M, struggling to dismember the pigeon, gave up and took a gulp of his wine instead.

'Think of it this way, Benjamin: the Islamic finance sector was the only one that came out unscathed from the events of last year. The only one. And we've done the research – I can show this to you all later, we have a fairly comprehensive investment memorandum prepared that your numbers people can peruse at their convenience – it shows there is enormous appetite for something like this not only in the Middle East but also in Europe. It is ideal for a Muslim family: it donates the 2.5 per cent of Zakat automatically with each purchase – Zakat, as I'm sure you know, is the charity that every Muslim must give – and we can then synergise with various charities so that we can create value together. But also, the card ensures that you can only buy halal products. And that, Benjamin, is really our killer feature.'

The waiter filled up their wine glasses again, letting the final drops drip into the Vice President's glass. 'I'm so sorry, gentlemen, would you care for another bottle?' the waiter said, suddenly heartbroken.

'Sure, what do you think Benjamin?'

'Actually, if you don't mind . . . I need to be fresh for a conference call in just over an hour.'

'No worries, Benjamin, of course. That'll be all, thank you.'

The waiter slinked away, the empty bottle clutched to his chest as though it were a wounded bird.

'Here. Hold it, that's the card. Feels good, right? So, if you are out buying an item and you have picked up groceries with, say, gelatine in them, then what will happen is your card will be declined. Or, say, you are out and you succumb to the temptation of ordering a beer. Well, you can't. It's a card that ensures that the Muslim man stays true to his faith. And Muslim women, they can be given one of these by their husband, and they have their freedom, their financial freedom, yes? All while the husband, of course, gets text messages informing him not only of his wife's purchases, but also of her whereabouts. It really is an all-in-one solution, one that has already been developed, the product is finished. It works. Now all we need is roll-out capital.'

Benjamin Freeman looked at the green metal card in his hands. 'This is very interesting.'

'I knew you would feel that way, Benjamin.'

'I'm going to bring this up with our Islamic Finance team, see if we can't set up a meet.'

'I appreciate that, Benjamin.'

'Gentlemen, would either of you care for some dessert?' Two leather-bound menus were presented to the diners, with three suggestions written on white background in a sans-serif font so small M had to squint.

'I'll have the chocolate cake. And a double espresso.'

'The reimagined chocolate fondant, excellent choice.'

'The tart for me, please. And an Earl Grey.'

'The mille-feuille. Perfect.'

'I'm really glad to hear you are interested in the project. This is something that I think can be good for both sides. I think this could be incredibly lucrative, and there is no reason, if we make this work, we can't just wet our beaks a little, right? I am sure that Deutsche Bank can liaise with the big Saudi and Emirati banks, there is no reason this can't be rolled out as an option to the wealthier Muslim nations.'

Their desserts arrived, this time sans exposition, remarkably soon. M saw the small pile made of gelatinous geometrical shapes in front of him and raised his hand to summon one of the waiters. 'Sorry. I ordered the chocolate cake.'

'This is the chocolate fondant, sir, Chef has reimagined it.'

'Oh. Right.'

They ate their desserts in silence, slurped down their beverages.

'I'm not going to keep you, I know you have to leave. I do appreciate you taking the time, I do. Let's catch up soon, yes? Garçon!' M's hand shot up, his credit card between his fingers in an approximation of the National Lottery logo, 'This obviously isn't the Islamic Credit Card, haha, not with what we've had to drink tonight!'

V

POLICE IN RIOT GEAR ARE PREPARING for clashes with anti-capitalist activists in London's West End. They're demonstrating at the Bank of England today ahead of this week's G20 summit in London. Staff at some of the world's largest banks, hedge funds and private equity firms have told employees to take precautions and to 'dress down', while banks have boarded up their windows in preparation. Authorities claim // *Shares of UK bank HSBC briefly surged 2.4 per cent in morning trading today with market watchers blaming a trading error for the move. At approxima* // the master suite takes up at least a third of the apartment. At fifteen times the size of the average house in the UK, who says size doesn't matter? It is an apartment with a stunning view, for the lucky few for whom money is no object. What is the cos★

M turned off the TV, put the empty bowl in the sink and got ready for work. The news of the G20 demonstrations had put him in a foul mood, and he took off his white shirt, remembering what the news anchor had said about dressing down, which correlated with the contents of an email that had been sent from hr@hilliard-drake.co.uk to all@hilliard-drake.co.uk the previous day. A bunch of scroungers, the lot of them. M picked out a flamboyant lavender shirt, fiddled with his finest cufflinks and instead of his regular Thursday suit, which he had purchased straight out of university, he put on the one bespoke three-piece he had had made with the bonus from 2006 from the same tailor that Chamberlain used (the last consistent bonus the employees at Hilliard Drake would be receiving). He wrapped the tie, a thick cyan silk, around his hand, pulling and tugging until it had become a full Windsor knot, not something he usually favoured (the symmetry of the knot had been frowned upon by Allencourt) but somehow entirely suitable for the day's events.

The screen of his phone lit up, the first few lines of an email legible.

Dear Customer,

We've decided to take our customer service to a whole new level of accessibility

He swiped away the notification, stacked atop notifications of missed calls from his mother. She kept insisting she bring him something from Slemani, soap or nuts or honey, as though these were rare Kurdish treasures and not something he could just pick up at any Tesco. He had told her a hundred times he did not need anything, and still she kept calling. 'You have to let me know soon, I'm coming in less than two weeks,' she would badger, pretending she'd scour the bazaar for him when in reality she'd just send her maid.

He'd call her back later.

He ran a pair of stockings he once paid an escort extra to leave behind across his tan brogues, her thinking that it was part of one of the many kinks that she was paid to indulge, when in fact nylon stockings were a great way to get a quick shine on your shoes without having to spend all that time getting the glaçage right by polishing.

Before he left, he glanced at his weather application (no umbrella needed today) and the London Underground application (Central Line: Good Service; Northern Line: Severe Delays) in order to decide the best way to go to the office before he put his phone to sleep, slipped it into his pocket.

Walking from his apartment to Chancery Lane station brought out a particular anxiety where M was aware that he was too often unaware, resorting to the bubble of his phone with its maps and eternal endless entertainment and the world's entire music collection that he carried in his pocket. But if he were to try to *be* aware, to see his surroundings, he would be confronted with a horde of people who wanted things from him. People giving out pamphlets, asking for money, wanting to shanghai him into their charities. Young women in T-shirts that said 'Free Hugs'. On every street was an insidious scheme constructed to root out and take advantage of your humanity, ploys to get your attention long enough to sell whatever it was they were selling.

The music M had been listening to, a piece of corporate pop that was on a weekly playlist constructed for him by an algorithm, faded out and a happy voice informed him that for just £9.99 he could play any song, anywhere, with no audio ads and no commitment. He then listened to the overexcited voices of radio ads for a minute before the music that just about made his journey to work bearable began anew. A handwritten sign outside a run-down corner shop read 6-PCK STELLA £5.99. The following month the shop would be gone, and M would try, every time that he passed it, to remember what had once been in that space.

The girl who approached him that morning looked dishevelled. Not homeless-dishevelled but been-out-drinking-dishevelled. Just need enough for the bus. My friends they're waiting, and I was supposed to call them, and my phone is dead and and and. How odd that the word we use when our phones run out of battery is 'dying'. He looked at her. Pretty. This made him more likely to give her the money. He hated himself for it, he recognised it, but he couldn't stop it. The same way that he was more likely to give money to someone who wasn't actually in dire need of it. A true homeless person he would have been able to pass without thinking twice about, but this middle-class-looking girl, this girl he felt inclined to help. He gave her a five-pound note, more than she asked for, not an insubstantial amount. She was surprised, he could see that, but she managed a thank-you and was on her way. For a moment he felt good about himself, but found as the escalator took him down into the underground that he felt bitter about the encounter. Plot holes began to niggle him as though a movie he had just enjoyed had turned out to make no sense: a literal esprit d'escalier. Why didn't she ask to make a phone call to her friends rather than ask for money? Surely she could find a way to log into her social network of choice and get help. How could she know that her friends were waiting for her?

Why did he feel so uncomfortable at the idea that he had just been scammed?

He had to wait for two tubes before one emerged that he could squeeze himself into, immediately feeling a trickle of sweat run down his back, a dampness under his arms.

Just as they left Chancery Lane, he heard someone deep into the carriage exclaim that someone had fainted. M sighed. There wasn't a week where someone didn't faint or, worse, jump in front of a train. Both events caused delays, but the fainting would last ten minutes, just until the paramedics arrived and someone could drag the body out onto the platform. Suicides, however, took for ever, with the entire underground network ground to a halt. As the train arrived at the next station there were a few minutes of shuffling, of having to take the woman out of the train, of relaying information over crackling walkie-talkies. Many were tutting to themselves and one another, complaining that they were now going to be late for work. *Every day*, someone muttered loud enough for M to hear. *Every bloody day*. Others brought out their phones in the vain hope that they would be able to text their superiors, to inform them of their now inevitable delay, only to pocket their devices once they'd ascertained that today, like always, there was No Signal. Two men behind M were claiming that there were more rats in London than people. M wanted to verify this fact once he was above ground, but when he left the underground and had access to the internet again, he had already forgotten it.

The conductor apologised a few times for any delay or inconvenience and assured the cramped passengers that they would be along as soon as he received the go-ahead. Some passengers decided that they could walk to their destination and exited. Eventually the eternally calm voice announced *this is St Paul's* and that they were on a Central Line train, followed by the sharp whistle preceding the closing doors, the sonic upward loop as the carriage gained speed, culminating in a monotonous low rumble and then the squeal of the brakes as they arrived at Bank.

Once he reached the escalator that took him up, M's phone whirred in his pocket. Two missed calls. Six new emails. Breaking: *AIG shares plummet*. Message: *Pick up your phone Mo, I've been—* Notification: *Extra Security at G20 Summit*. He braced himself for the walk between the station and the office.

He understood it, of course. The discontent that spurred protests like the one taking place today. Everyone felt that something was wrong, and they wanted to blame systems and invisible forces. M had grown up with that sort of thinking and knew the appeal of it. His father was told, upon reaching the UK, that neither the medical degree that he had earned in Baghdad nor his many years of experience were of any use to the United Kingdom and that he would have to go back to university and get his degree all over again if he wanted to work as a doctor. Rather than try to find a way to do just that, Rafiq had given up, lived off welfare for the rest of his life while complaining about colonialist powers and the ravages of Empire. Just because things did not go his way, everything was the system's fault. M had vowed not to fall into that complacent trap, of blaming his fate on everything but himself. He had earned his job at Hilliard Drake, and he was going to do his utmost to keep it. So the teenagers and deluded hippies could chant all they wanted for their daydream utopia. M was going to work harder than anyone at his office until he got what he deserved, the rest of the world be damned.

Out on the street, the pandemonium he was expecting was nowhere to be seen. Where were the malcontents with nothing better to do, no job to go to? Those who chose to live their one life complaining about everything: the anarchists, the environmentalists, the communists, the anti-globalisation people, the conspiracy theorists (the ones who thought that Bush, who couldn't even swallow a pretzel, could orchestrate a terrorist attack to take down the Twin Towers, blame it on some cave dwellers and Nobody Would Find Out), the hippies with their hemp trousers, the disaffected, the angry and the massively misinformed, where were they? M glanced at his watch; it was 09:04. He should have known better than to think that they would be able to get out of bed early. Revolution? Yes, sure, but only if we get to nap until noon in our parents' spare room first. He smiled at his own wit and greeted a few of the policemen who had begun prepping the area, all anachronistic bell-end hats and yellow vests.

'Move along, please,' one of the policemen sneered, waving him away as though he were an unpleasant smell. Somehow, he didn't seem to understand that M was on their side.

M was reminded of the hundreds of demonstrations his father had dragged him and his siblings to, how the police had stared them down, daring them to throw something at whatever embassy they stood in front of. Once, Rafiq was even arrested, M saw him in the distance being beaten up and put inside a police van, as Xezal rushed the children away, making up some lie about Rafiq having run into a friend he hadn't seen in a while. Maybe the police could still sense it, that once they had been on opposite sides.

The receptionist at 68 Lombard Street was a sullen girl, neither attractive nor friendly. It always angered M to walk past her, all these pretty unemployed girls in the City who would ritually murder family members for a job, and it was this moody cow who sat there, doing fuck-all and getting paid.

It was an employers' market: Naveen on his team was an over-educated Indian doing most of M's work, often working until the last train back to wherever he lived, for just under the national average. Jane was a graduate from LSE and did the due diligence for less money than if she were to work at a shop. The trick, the trick to keep them at Hilliard Drake rather than at menial jobs that would pay them more for fewer hours, was the promise of a future. M would drop tantalising hints of upcoming bonuses, of raises that he would have his team parse. They were fiercely loyal, the two of them, and wanted nothing more than one of the many projects that M was mandated to secure financing for to actually happen, for Hilliard Drake to receive the 8 per cent success fee.

'Good morning,' Charlie intoned as she put down the breakfast bagel she was eating. M didn't have the heart to tell her that she wasn't earning enough to spend five quid on a bagel every day.

'Good morning,' M echoed, going to his partition. No sooner had he sat down than Naveen emerged.

'Mo?' M waved him over and Naveen sauntered towards M's desk, a stack of documents in his arms.

'Wasn't there supposed to be a demonstration today?' M asked.

'Oh?'

'It's all over the news, Naveen.'

'I follow the market. Nothing has happened yet. Anyway, here is some financial modelling I did on the Islamic Credit Card project. It's looking good.'

'Yeah? Let me see that.'

The charts and graphs, several coloured pages of them, meant very little to M. But it could be money. It could be real money.

'Mo?'

'Yes. Sorry. What were you saying?'

'That the IRR is the only thing that I worry about even slightly in the best-case scenario model. But if you look here at the—'

'That's fine, we'll just be presenting the investors with the best-case scenario. They have their own team, if they want to run the numbers on this they can, but why should we downplay our own product? Right?'

'Right.' Naveen nodded, having long since lost the will to disagree.

M began scrolling through his emails. *Re: Deutsche Bank Web Inquiry Mum's flight plan (I'm sorry I know you already have this) Last Week For Discounts KYC Questions* delete delete delete delete.

Outside he heard a ruckus forming. He stood up and saw protesters fighting against police, a wave pushing forward and then being drawn back. M had to squint to see the slogans that were written on the banners. One mentioned the war in Iraq. Another had a dubious statistic regarding oil spills. A third said No Borders No Banks.

'Guys, come see this!' he called out as the police began kettling in protestors in small batches, rendering violence inevitable. Later that day, a man would be found beaten to death, and it would make the news for almost an entire day. A few of the Hilliard Drake employees came over, looking over the ledge.

'Can you believe this?' M said, wondering how he'd get to the Pret a Manger across the street now that the entire road was blocked off. 'Did anyone bring lunch?'

Chamberlain, of course, had brought a sandwich. 'I can give you a bite if you want,' he said, nudging M with his elbow while looking down the ledge at the protesters.

Recently Chamberlain had announced that the project that would be most worthwhile to focus on was the expansion of the Brands Hatch social club, a project that wealthy private investors would be more than inclined to partake in as it granted them free and perpetual membership to the club which otherwise would require an arcane and frankly unintelligible process. The projected earnings weren't great, but still there was an estimated IRR of 7 per cent and it was deemed to be a quick close. They already had an assortment of earls and marquises who had shown a willingness to invest in the project. 'Until this is closed, no meals outside the office for me, matey. I bring my sandwiches and will sit at my desk until this baby is done.'

'Anyway, you look well rested,' Chamberlain said to M as he looked away from the fighting masses. The latest craze at Hilliard Drake was sleep deprivation as an indicator of work ethic. Eric Pontén, a Swedish corporate financier down on the second floor, had started the fad by purchasing a device that measured his sleep and proudly showed his co-workers his average sleep time of four hours twenty-one minutes.

'The thing is, old chap,' Chamberlain had once said to M as he was showing off his slightly more expensive sleep-tracking device than the one Pontén had demonstrated, 'that where we're at now, sleep is the final frontier really. Everyone is working every day, reachable by email at all times. What separates the successful from the less successful is the hours we gain by not sleeping as much. Do you think it's a coincidence that the greatest prime minister that this country has ever had only slept four hours a night? Time for human rest and regeneration is now simply too expensive to be structurally possible within contemporary capitalism. Sleep is the only remaining barrier, the only enduring "natural condition" that capitalism cannot eliminate entirely. But if we try, matey, if we try, we have a leg-up on all these other suckers.' This was before Allencourt died, when Chamberlain would regularly ask M to have a pint with him after work, where they would both present their projected future selves to each other, both trying to find out if there was any way the other person could be used to their advantage. Now that M was struggling to remain at the firm while Chamberlain was gunning for CEO (not that either of these two goals had ever been verbalised), there were no pints to be had.

M didn't sleep much himself, not necessarily due to any formalised notions of wanting to somehow hack capitalism (as Pontén had once described it) but rather because the anxiety of missing an important message, of not hearing a call that would change his life, would keep him up for hours every night. He would regularly check his phone in bed, the bright cold light of his device shocking his body into a state of alertness. Nothing. Then he would check Yahoo! Finance, his Facebook, properties on Sotheby's filtered by most expensive, at which point he checked his email again and so it went for hours and hours until his sunrise-emulating alarm clock showed that it was well past two in the morning and he would then not be able to sleep because he kept thinking of how he had to be up in less than five hours.

'Everyone,' Daniel Chamberlain said to the pen, turning away from the window, 'just so you know, I'm going to be needing the boardroom at four today, the investors for the social club project are coming by.' This, of course, was a statement of intent, delivered so that everyone could hear his progress. All he had to do to book the boardroom was to inform Charlie, who would put it into the system. The fucker already had investors coming into the office, M thought, returning to his computer, refreshing his mailbox.

'Naveen, can you include the latest numbers on the card project in a new draft of the investment memorandum?' M said, louder than was absolutely necessary. 'I want to send this across to Deutsche Bank before close of business.'

A shoe hit M's window, startling him.

'How on earth can you throw something that high?' M asked nobody in particular.

'Hmm?' Jane said, reading the *Financial Times*.

'A shoe just hit my window!'

'I'm sure Naveen can calculate the probability of that happening,' Jane said, stifling a yawn.

The shoe ineffectually flopped away from the reinforced double-glazed window and landed on the windowsill, where it would remain for weeks until the cleaners came and removed this last vestige of the demonstration.

It was a nice shoe, too, M thought. One of those trendy trainers that cost more than Goodyear-welted shoes even though they were made in Bangladesh by some seven-year-old. Outrageous profit margins on those things.

A crash was heard outside, followed by sirens. M checked the BBC website to see if anything had happened.

'Should we go before the investors come?' Naveen asked, referring to a Punctuated Equilibrium-inspired Hilliard Drake tradition to leave the office if another team was making enough progress to be seeing investors.

'I don't know; I'd like to stick it to them but it's mayhem outside. What are we going to do, join the protests?'

'What do we want? Dan with egg on his face. When do we want it? Now,' Jane whispered in a monotone.

When the investors came through late in the afternoon, frazzled from having to witness the aftermath of the demonstration, Chamberlain gave his best smile, shook hands intently and guided the doddering old men who oozed centuries' worth of accumulated wealth into the boardroom, whereupon he barked to the intern to bring them all coffee and sparkling water. The Indian numbers guy on his team – M forgot what his name was – proceeded to project the calculations pertaining to the expansion project and Chamberlain spoke with authority about how this was a no-brainer, how the relics of an empire that once was would be fortunate to have the opportunity to invest in such a prestigious project. He was good at this, making people feel grateful to hand over their money. It was a skill M had never developed: he always felt faintly like a criminal whenever the dotted line was signed, and he believed the investors could sense this, that a man who wasn't quite British even though he spoke with a manufactured accent indistinguishable from Chamberlain's had just fleeced them of their money.

From the boardroom there was loud, purposeful laughter. Chamberlain had said something that the investors agreed with. M's last email was from Pizza Hut, asking him how his meal had been and did he have time for a five-minute survey.

Ping. New email.

It was Naveen, sending him the new investment memorandum.

M gave a thumbs-up in his direction, not sure if Naveen could see him over the partition, and proceeded to write Benjamin an email.

Subject: Islamic Credit Card

Dear Benjamin,

It was a pleasure to see you the other day. As discussed, here is the investment memorandum for the Islamic Credit Card project for you to peruse at your convenience.

Please do not hesitate to contact me if you need any furter information at this stage.

Sincerely yours,

M. M. Hardi

He left in the typo, believing it showed an email written in haste, in-between several other very important emails that M was typing. *Swoosh*. M began killing time by reading the online edition of the *Financial Times*, which Hilliard Drake had a corporate subscription to and which was one of the rare websites that did not trigger the firm's productivity-monitoring software after four minutes, resulting in an automated email to HR at the end of the day that included the employee's surfing history that day. Something happening in Ghana. The world's most expensive apartments were up for sale in Hyde Park One. A column about the need to reassess the UK property market. Three articles with the word 'recession' in the headline.

Chamberlain's meeting had ended and he began walking the three men to the door, all thumps on backs and handshakes. We'll keep in touch, he said to one. Great to finally put a face to the name, to another. Lovely to see you again, to a third. He then went back into the boardroom, where the staff began unplugging laptops and collecting the investment memorandums that had been glanced at and left behind. Chamberlain gave his team awkward fist bumps and Good Work Mateys and Let's Get Back to It.

As the stacks of investment memorandums were being shredded another email arrived in M's inbox.

M, having no one to give fist bumps to in his vicinity, smiled. Outside, the sound of sirens abated, the complicated slogans to overthrow
the financial system long since faded.

When M left work that day Lombard Street was clear of any
remains of the protest. As he walked towards the underground station, he was surprised to note that from just looking around, it was as
though nothing had happened at all.

His phone began chirping in his pocket. His mother. He uttered a
deep sigh and answered the call.

VI

Ever since they got settled in the UK, Xezal had claimed she wanted to return home. 'Home' being Kurdistan, even though M remembered how she would complain about the lack of reliable electricity, the terrible roads, the inability to get anything from anywhere. 'This,' she'd say, sipping on her PG Tips in Slemani, 'is made all around here, all the countries close to us, and we struggle to import it back to us from the British. What's left for us here is the garbage tea that nobody else wants.' And yet, no sooner had she settled in a country where PG Tips were plentiful, than she began expressing a desire to go home. 'We're barely wanted guests here, in every corner of this city we must always act like we are in someone else's home, never relax, never break anything, and always be grateful for the hospitality of our hosts.'

And so, once the Iraq war made a return possible, Xezal packed two suitcases and moved back to Slemani, claiming that she missed her sister, that she felt tired pretending to belong elsewhere.

All of which was fine, except the minute she arrived she started complaining about the lack of electricity, about how lonely she was, how she missed her children, and in two weeks she was visiting London to stay with M. She'd sent her flight details at least a dozen times, still terrified of travelling even though she'd had a British passport for years and was no longer harassed at borders, and M noted that she only ever sent her departure flight. He had no idea how long she was planning to stay with him. 'Just ask her,' Siver had sighed, exasperated, when he asked her for the third time if she knew how long she'd be in London.

'Yes, absolutely, she will totally not read that as a sign that I want her gone as quickly as possible.'

'You *do* want her gone as quickly as possible, though.'

Though that had been somewhat too harsh an assessment, he did find himself gnashing his teeth as the purpose of his mother's phone call became clear.

'Mum, I already told you, you don't need to confirm your flight, you have a ticket, that ticket is the confirmation.'

'Your father and I once were denied boarding in Batman because we had not confirmed our ticket.'

'Well, what can I tell you, that's not how things work any . . . Wait, you said Batman denied your boarding?'

'Yes, the airport in Batman.'

'You're telling me there's a city called Batman. With an airport.'

'You really should know your own home better. It's a very important Kurdish city.'

'And it's called Batman?'

'Can you call the airline and make sure I am confirmed?' said his mother, suddenly irritated.

'I'll do it when I get home, I'm on my way back from work.'

'Why what time is it there?'

'Seven thirty.'

'They make you work like a dog, they don't appreciate you my son. If you were here everyone would know who you are and treat you with respect.'

'OK, I gotta go, Mum.'

'I don't even know what it is you do for a living.'

He'd told her many, many times what was written on his business card, namely that he was Executive Manager of Corporate Finance, but he had to say this in English as he didn't know any of those words in Kurdish. He had half a mind to tell her that his job consisted of writing emails. He received and sent emails. In a day he would receive anything up to a hundred emails; most of these weren't directly aimed at him but were simply nuggets of information that he needed to be aware of, his ID buried deep in the nest of carbon-copied recipients; others were emails that other people didn't want to have to deal with, a fwd message preceded with the mere acronym FYI, a way to say that he was lower than the sender on the food chain so it came upon him to deal with it. Other times he would receive emails directly aimed at him, emails he would have to reply to, so he would have to go online and find out what it was that he was supposed to know about before he composed a vague and tentative reply, praying, as he clicked send, that he wouldn't be thought of as a complete idiot.

He knew that in the twenty minutes it would take him to get home he would receive eight to ten new emails that he would scan quickly in the elevator, flagging those he would have to reply to. The worst was in the mornings, though: no sooner had he switched off his daily alarm than he would see the twenty to twenty-five emails that had arrived during the night from America and then later from East Asia. He would already be behind on his day's work, and he hadn't even got out of bed yet. If he were honest about what he did, then, he would say he read and wrote emails. He suspected that this was what most office workers in the UK were doing for a living.

'I help companies make money, I have told you.'

'They seem to have no problems making money on their own, these companies.'

As M took the stairs down to the underground, he glimpsed the headline on a discarded *Metro*: 'Financial crisis will add £1.5 trillion to national debt'.

'They have some problems in that area right now, Mum. Listen, I'm getting on the train, so the call might cut off.'

'Don't forget to call the airline!'

'Bye, Mum.'

VII

THE AUTOMATED EMAIL THAT reached the mailboxes of every Hilliard Drake employee at exactly 09:00 on the last Thursday of every month contained a list of the employees' names and a star rating next to them, consisting of the weighted average of each employee as voted on by their co-workers.

The implementation of this system, coinciding with the publication of Allencourt's follow-up to *Punctuated Equilibrium* called *Let the MVP Eat Cake*, served to decide who was the employee of the month, the MVP in sanctioned Hilliard Drake nomenclature. It was a privilege that came with a cash bonus and a lunch out at any restaurant of the MVP's choosing, and allowed for infighting not among groups as the Punctuated Equilibrium system was designed to encourage, but on an individual level. However, when Hilliard Drake had their surge in share price and subsequent expansion in 2007, the monthly MVP lunch was capped at a certain amount, as management deemed that there were suddenly too many employees to treat to expensive Mayfair lunches. Later, when the company implemented a wave of redundancies, the monthly lunch was scrapped altogether, seen as a frivolous expenditure that did nothing for the company's productivity and value-adding. The weighted-average star system, however, remained as the last vestige of the previous system, it being deemed that IT had spent too much time and effort on it to delete the system completely.

So what was once a source of joy, announcing as the email did that they might be going to a Michelin-starred restaurant, was now a source of anxiety as each employee would obsess over the meaning of the stars. M had just received 3.5 stars and, not knowing how each individual person had voted, it was impossible to know whether the weighted average was brought down by one or two petty co-workers who had given him one star or if indeed every employee saw him as decidedly mediocre. He spent the rest of the morning obsessing over his score.

The fruit basket from BasketHead Fruit & Veg arrived between 10:30 and 11:45 on weekdays. BasketHead was the fourth company in seven months that Hilliard Drake had signed with to get fruit delivered to the office, there always being a new start-up with more competitive prices to switch to once the trial period of a company had expired. The bananas disappeared immediately, being the most coveted fruit, followed by the apples and the pears, if there were any. Left at the bottom of the basket until they were eventually thrown out were the kiwis, requiring as they did a knife and/or spoon to be able to eat, which made it hard to do in meetings where no knives or spoons were provided. M once suggested to Naveen that they start a business that only did banana baskets, as that seemed to be the only thing people actually wanted, to which Naveen asked if he should run the numbers on such a project.

A joke, Naveen, that was a joke.

As it was never certain that the person who first reached the fruit basket on one day would reach it first the next, several bananas were taken by those who had the opportunity, stashing said bananas in drawers (where they often rotted eventually), eating them on other days or using them to barter with when someone had to make a phone call that they did not want to make. M once got into an argument with Chamberlain over his repeated pilfering of the bananas, which he laughed off with an 'it's first come first served, here don't get upset, take a banana. No go on, have one, I know you like them.' Which had the effect of making M feel small and petty and that he was overreacting to the whole banana situation. Charlie had sent out a multitude of emails reminding Hilliard Drake employees that they should only take one banana per person, and management briefly increased their order to two baskets each day but that only resulted in more rotting kiwis and so after a two-week trial period everyone was back to fighting over the bananas.

It was deemed important, for some reason that was never made clear, that the least time possible be spent having lunch. They all had forty-five minutes, contractually, but nobody spent more than twelve to fifteen minutes getting their sandwich and eating their sandwich before they logged back into their systems. Whenever someone took too many half-hour lunches, an automated email would inform them that their total hours logged in that week had dropped below the company average.

Similarly, when it was time to leave it was only Charlie who picked up her purse and uttered a quick 'take care' at five. The others would sit as long as they possibly could, wearing each other out, an endurance piece in honour of company ethics. The times M had managed to be the last person to leave it was well after 10 p.m. It was an arduous task but it needed to be done, especially when the company was reviewing its employees.

Every Thursday, someone would try to corral the others into a post-work drinking session at the Counting House during their happy hour, and just about every Thursday such attempts would end in humiliating failure for the person proposing said drinking session as nobody wanted to go unless upper management was going, which virtually never happened on account of prior commitments.

Every Friday, a 'have a nice weekend', was trilled as the employees exited through the glass door, a vain hope considering most of them would end up spending their Saturdays at the Hilliard Drake offices.

And so the week would end and begin anew.

VIII

IF M HAD AN IMPORTANT MEETING – and today's meeting with Deutsche Bank certainly qualified as such – he would arrange for the bodies to be assembled. Since the culture at Hilliard Drake encouraged each corporate finance team to be in direct competition with the others, it was not in everyone's immediate interest that meetings at the office go well. Both Chamberlain and John Morris on his floor had a tendency to take their teams and one or two stragglers out for a coffee or lunch at whatever time M would have booked the conference room and so, to present to investors the appearance of a well-oiled machine, some bodies were needed. Said bodies consisted of a handful of good-looking out-of-work men and women in their twenties who would dress up in their nicest suits and stand around the Hilliard Drake offices looking busy for £20 each and a lunch at YO! Sushi. Often they were models or wannabe actors, but sometimes they would have some form of legal or financial education, which meant that M could get actual work out of them. Usually, M liked to be part of the audition process as Naveen was often a tad too generous on what constituted 'good-looking', but he had been too busy preparing for the Deutsche Bank meeting to have time to leer at twenty-year-olds.

The parade of hot young people arrived at the office at 08:30 and were instructed to sit at the desktops, transcribing articles from the *FT*. Once an article was finished, they were to print it out and pass it to someone else, who would write it anew and so on and so forth until the meeting was adjourned.

The tray of pastries was placed on the table in the boardroom, glistening glutinous pastries originating in France and Denmark and now made all over the world in bakeries with French- and Danish-sounding names, next to tiny bottles of sparkling water from a Swiss lake bottled and flown over to London. The pens and legal pads put in front of each chair had the Hilliard Drake logo on, both manufactured in China.

The representatives from Deutsche Bank were punctual, two men (James Erdinger, Director of Finance and Risk Management, and Paul Grayson, Associate Director and Equity Researcher) and a woman (Pauline Mann, Executive Director Corporate Finance), all dressed in modest grey suits, presenting their business cards as they shook M's hand. M gestured for them to sit, and they exchanged cards with Naveen and Jane. M tried to take them in. In spite of their impressive titles, they all seemed too young to be able to say yes to anything but perhaps they were senior enough to be able to say no.

M arranged the cards on the table in front of him in the order in which the people from Deutsche Bank sat so as to know who was who. This was one of the methods he used to make sure that every potential investor felt like they were somehow special to M aside from the fact that they had money. A trick that Jane had taught him was to have a notebook in which to write down what he was wearing whenever he met someone so that when he had a second meeting he would not by mistake wear the same suit and tie. M had looked at Jane's vast spreadsheet in which she also included what she wore and cooked when she had friends over so as to not repeat meals and outfits and even a section where she wrote down what jokes or anecdotes she had told during meetings or social gatherings. 'The worst thing in the world is to become one of those people who tell the same story over and over again and everyone around you has to smile politely and pretend like they haven't heard you say this a million times already,' she had said as M and Naveen attempted to mock her spreadsheet once.

'So. Welcome, thank you very much for making the time to come and see us. We are all very excited about the prospect of working together on this card and hope that you will be as excited as us. We will show you the presentation that we have prepared shortly, but let me just begin by giving you some background. As I'm sure you all know, the world of Islamic Financing was the only part of the financial system left intact after the events of last year, and more and more financial institutions are looking at Islamic Financing as a potential windfall. Of course, Islamic Financing traditionally prohibits the sort of profit motif we are contemplating, but the products offered by Islamic banks go around the prohibitions of usury by imposing a fixed fee, which is halal, rather than charging interest. This is really a giant emerging financial market, the high net-worth individuals in the Gulf are looking for ways to use their money and this card can be an important step in that direction.'

M looked at each of the people from Deutsche Bank as he spoke, not allowing them to look away, to grow bored. The small red light on Paul Grayson, Associate Director and Equity Researcher's phone blinked several times, indicating that something was happening that its owner needed to tend to, making Paul glance uncomfortably at his screen, trying to both be politely attentive and read the notification.

As for James Erdinger, he was constantly leering at Jane Tilly. Though Jane had not been M's first choice as due diligence officer, it was undeniably positive that there was at least one white person on his team. That she was a woman was a slight inconvenience, as James Erdinger's lack of concentration proved, but she was a consummate pro, pretending at all times that she was being listened to and not just looked at.

M asked Naveen to present the numbers, and the shuffle as Naveen connected his laptop to the projector snapped the two men from Deutsche Bank back into focus. For some reason the projector refused to recognise Naveen's computer and someone from IT was called to resolve the issue.

'These machines, they never do what you want them to,' M said, extending a smile to the bankers. Discussing people's relationship to technology had in recent years begun to usurp small talk pertaining to weather, and M had found there was nothing safer to discuss during awkward lulls in the conversation than the latest hassles with phones, computers or websites.

Someone from the second floor came up, dressed in the informal uniform of IT people all over the world. Naveen briefly explained the problem ('it doesn't work') and the IT guy hunched over the laptop.

Naveen had a lasting and often nightmare-inducing fear of connecting his laptop to the projector, fearing that somehow rather than the graphs from his Excel sheet appearing, a hardcore pornography clip would pop up, exaggerated orgasmic moans pouring through the boardroom's surround-sound speakers, or that while googling a fact during a presentation, he would type in the letter p and Google's autocomplete function would fill in, say, pornhub.com. He never kept any video files on this, his work computer, and whenever he surfed porn he made sure to put his browser in Explorer's InPrivate Browsing mode, but he still feared he could have missed something in a post-masturbatory haze and that his surfing habits would be revealed to all of his peers.

Once the IT person had demonstrated the magical keystroke to make the computer show up on the projector – a keystroke that everybody in the room would proceed to forget in under a minute – Naveen tentatively clicked his way through the worst-case economic model, praying under his breath that nothing would appear that would make the others ridicule him.

'So you see, gentlemen, there really is enough return on investment even under the worst-case scenario that Naveen has modelled; this card is as close as we are going to get to a sure deal in today's climate. The synergy that it offers with other parties is frankly limitless; if we are able to sign up various well-known counterparts that we can send the two and a half per cent Zakat to, it will create value for everyone involved and, let us be honest here, it will look very good to provide a financial service that ties so directly to our various CSR departments.'

Pauline Mann, Executive Director Corporate Finance (had M addressed them all as gentlemen just now, dammit, he had, hadn't he?), was jotting down every number that Naveen was bringing up on the monitor. Was this a good thing?

'We can of course send you these spreadsheets later, right, Naveen? Benjamin sent me the countersigned non-disclosure agreement, so we can send these to you right away.'

'That's right,' Naveen agreed, jotting this down in the notebook next to his laptop. 'We will be sure to add this as an action item.'

At this Pauline looked up from her notepad, smiled and nodded at Naveen and returned to transcribing the numbers on the screen.

Jane then presented the risks inherent in this project, a presentation that was not unlike answering the question about one's worst personality trait at a job interview: the goal was not so much to present actual risks that would make potential investors nervous but to show that they were realists who had done the necessary due diligence and who were able to turn each of these risks into an opportunity. So there was no mention of the card's owner's somewhat sketchy past but instead she focused on how the card's parent company had so many other successful projects that were ongoing that they might not have the manpower to work on this project as much they needed to, but of course they had received assurances from the board that they were open to hiring more people, something that would not be a problem considering the profits that they had just declared in their latest annual audited accounts.

'We know that there is an inherent issue with trusting new financial mechanisms, and a risk that we will face is how to persuade Muslims to put down their Visas and Mastercards and to instead use this product. That's why the backing of an important bank such as Deutsche Bank, with its stellar reputation in the Arab world, is important, as it will instil that trust and also, we have some ideas on how to convince Muslims that the cards they are currently using are — what's the word there, M? Haram? Haram, right, so not in accordance with their beliefs. We have some well-regarded religious figures on board who are more than willing to denounce credit cards as an evil invention of the West at odds with the core tenets of Islam and to present this card as a wholesome solution.'

The three bankers nodded at Jane, then turned towards one another and nodded among themselves.

M provided the closer, a brief summary of what they had discussed, and asked whether anyone had any questions, to which James asked a question that Naveen had already addressed twice, but which M was more than happy to repeat the answer to. Pauline told Naveen that she might have some questions about the numbers but that she would send those across to him later by email. 'I'll revert back to you later today,' she said, still jotting away on her pad. M could see at the bottom of her sheet beneath the series of numbers she had diligently written down, she had also drawn little skulls and crossbones and lightning bolts. It reminded him of a child's drawing, something he himself used to draw, and seeing that took him away from the meeting briefly, letting an awkward silence set in.

'Sorry. I was saying? Yes, guys, I think that this is a really special project. It's really at the bleeding edge of financial services, and I'm sure that once you have gone through our numbers here you will find it truly irresistible.'

It was time to end the meeting. The three bankers left, all smiles and assurances. M thanked his team and then thanked the assorted models who had been looking busy in the background. And that was that. Now all he had to do was wait.

IX

WHAT GOT M HIS LAST PROMOTION, what finally made him the kind of person who was thought to have a future at Hilliard Drake, was a project he spearheaded that involved selling carbon credits to international oil companies.

The UK had proposed a carbon credit solution, allowing companies to buy the right to emit carbon dioxide by buying credits off someone else who would then reduce their emissions accordingly. The energy sector was agreeable to this solution as it allowed them to make ad campaigns where they could announce how green and eco-friendly they now were while not having to actually reduce their emissions in any way. This also allowed countries like the US, China and the UK to claim they had positive per-capita carbon credits and put the focus on the countries with the biggest carbon debt, such as Belize, Papua New Guinea and Zambia.

It was to these last three countries that M would travel, finding local communities, giving them a thousand dollars or so for a signed document that they were not going to develop their forests, which they in most cases were not planning on doing anyway, and exchanged the pledge for carbon credits that he could then sell on to ExxonMobil, Shell and BP for hundreds upon hundreds of thousands of dollars. He sold air, essentially, he explained to Tatiana, back when the bonuses that ended up in his bank account permitted him to date her. 'Well,' he clarified, 'promises, rather. I sell promises related to air.'

This continued for over two years, M having sold off the forestation rights of almost a fifth of Zambia, when two things put a stop to his business. First was an incident involving his interpreter, Abdrazak, who refused to work for him unless he received part of the fees that were being paid to the locals, a refusal that escalated into a full-blown argument which resulted in, i.a., a broken rib, a stolen passport and a trashed hotel room.

M did not return to Chipata after this, but he had plans to venture to different parts of Zambia when the second thing happened: international banks – HSBC, JPMorgan Chase, Barclays – began offering their corporate clients the option to purchase carbon credits. The game had been discovered by the big boys, which meant that the game was up. And soon the world economy would collapse and the environment would be seen as a worry for better times.

When his revenue stream dried up, there was a month or so when M feared for his job. He would stay at the office well after everyone else had left, knowing that the productivity-monitoring software would let everyone know just how hard he worked.

But when it came down to it, M knew that he was unlikely to find another project that would bring in revenue, as the wheels were by this time well and truly coming off the whole capitalist machinery, so instead he took out the money he had kept in his savings and paid a PR firm to pen a profile of him, describing him as an integral part of Hilliard Drake. When the piece appeared in the *Financial Times* later that week, he was called to Allencourt's office and congratulated. 'We were obviously thinking of making you redundant, but this, this shows moxie, my son.'

And so he stayed on at Hilliard Drake, his firing being too much of an embarrassment in light of the hagiography that had appeared in print. Jane, who had been looking for a new job on the offhand chance that M would be fired, since team members were usually dispensed with as collateral damage, claimed M's gambit to have been a miracle, 'Right up there with the bread and the fishes, honestly.'

'That's me,' M had said, sitting back down at his desk with the knowledge that his position at the firm was, for the first time in many months, secure. If only for a short while. 'The Miracle Man.'

X

Men and women stood huddled by the platforms at London Bridge station, looking up to the skies, hope in their eyes. The board above them listing the departing trains did not show platform information until a few minutes before the departure, requiring everyone to wait, focusing intently on the numbers flickering above them. The 18:02 to Brighton, platform 12. A group was prompted into action by this command, filled anew with purpose: to get to their platform in the two minutes that they had before the train would leave. They pushed through the remaining people, hurrying to their platform, orange travel cards ready. Excuse me, excuse me. The panels flapped and shuffled loudly, a shake-up of the entire board. Now it was Sevenoaks, platform 9.

M, waiting to catch Trevor Jones, Structured Trade & Export Finance at UBS, had some time to kill and so, not being in a hurry, was out of step with the others in the station who all had places to go, time to keep. People kept bumping into him as he sauntered about, muttering under their breath, insults caught only when they were too far away for M to respond, and so he went into a small pub inside the station to join all the others who needed to endure some uneventful time.

The floor of the pub was sticky and a cloud of stale beer and a vague hint of piss filled the air. In a corner a man was playing on a loud and bright gambling machine, its epilepsy-inducing lights creating an atmosphere entirely at odds with the rest of the pub. M rummaged in his pockets between receipts, chewing gum and lint to find some pound coins with which to purchase a pint.

'Doom Bar, please.'

The bartender, a gruff bald man who poured an immaculate pint, took the coins from M, handed him back his change, and turned back to the football that was airing on a muted television in the upper corner.

'This is yesterday's game, right?' M asked, knowing enough about football to know the derby had already taken place.

'Yep,' the bartender said, putting a quick end to any chat M could have initiated.

M checked his phone. Four minutes until Jones was supposed to come, having 'maybe time for a quick coffee' before he got on a train out of the city. Deutsche Bank had intimated that it would be best to structure this deal as a consortium of investors. 'We are happy to take the lead, but we'll need one or two other banks to come on board before we take this any further,' had been the last email received, which meant that M had to return to his business cards and make another round of awkward phone calls. He had pestered Jones enough that he relented, making room for this quick meeting. Considering that the last time they'd met was after the Emirates deal closing celebrations at the Spearmint Rhino on Tottenham Court Road where Jones had spent thousands of pounds on bottles of champagne, cocaine and private dances which ended in him vomiting all over a dancer's platform heels and requiring M to help him home, it was the least Jones could do, the little shit. Of course, M did not remind Jones of this night, expecting him to remember and accept his request for a meeting without M having to actually say anything.

'Do you have any crisps?'

'Cheese and onion. Salt and vinegar.'

The bartender, still looking at the game which he had to know the score of, seemed annoyed at the extended conversation. M chose salt and vinegar, a few more coins exchanged hands, and M went to a small sticky table set up between the door and the frenetically blinking gambling machine. He made sure his phone was not on silent, its screen facing up so it could catch his attention, and took out the day's *Financial Times* from his briefcase.

'We decided not to focus on vertical services any more. We only deal in horizontal services,' said a man drinking Guinness at the table opposite M. His hands were stretched out on the table, palms tilted upwards as though asking his interlocutor to hold hands with him. His body language read as desperate, even as his words conveyed the positive outlook all City firms had espoused when faced with their immediate obliteration. If we could all start thinking positively about the economy and really believe that it was going well, then it would go well. The market is nothing but the reflection of our hopes and fears, after all. 'Our products have been re-tailored to better match the needs of the emerging markets. That's where we see growth; we aim to be at the bleeding edge here.' This was the man opposite him, his arms crossed tight to his chest, a glass of white wine in front of him. They were both selling, neither was buying. The Guinness-drinker took a sip of his pint, the beer-advertising coaster sticking to his glass and creating a temporary cardboard stem. 'It's really vital to streamline, we agree. It's really our core competency. Let me send you some of our analysis, you guys can peruse at your convenience. We'll be sure to send you our market data on Luanda. It really is the future.' The coaster flopped back onto the table.

M tried to focus on an article on US sovereign bonds but found himself glancing at the screen of his phone to make sure he had not missed the text from Trevor Jones, and so instead read the first paragraph of the article over and over again.

'You should come to our office, I'd be happy to show you around.' 'Oh yes, you should definitely come by ours as well. We have the best coffee.' 'Oh, our cappuccino is exceptional.' 'We're also just across from the Ivy. We can just expense a lunch there.' 'Let's touch base on this soon.' 'I'll be sure to action it.'

The crisis had made it obvious that what they all spent their time packaging and selling to one another was not actually necessary. Sure, when the market was doing well, these products could be used to generate more money, but when nobody had any money to spare it turned out that nobody needed any of it. The world would be fine without yet another Single-Premium Investment-Linked Insurance Policy or an obscure Collateralised Debt Obligation.

His phone rang.

'Hi, Trevor?'

'Trevor? What is this thing? You don't recognise your own mother's number?'

He had answered reflexively, not checking the caller ID. Whatever this was, he didn't have time for it.

'Hi, Mum, how are you?'

'Oh. You know. Old age and its thousand ailments.'

M took a sip of his ale. Why could she not just say 'fine', why could she never just pretend to be fine?

'Kak Ali died, may God forgive him.'

'Who?'

'Ali! Your father's brother!'

He only remembered meeting his uncle once, when they went back to Kurdistan to bury his father, and wasn't sure what was appropriate for him to say. He knew Kurds in general and his mother in particular were fond of excessive, quasi-operatic declarations of grief, but he could not remember any of the standard phrases. Something about being martyred for his soul?

'I'm sorry to hear that, was it sudden?'

'I put a message of condolence on my Facebook. You should comment; as Rafiq's oldest son it is the right thing to do.'

'Sure,' he said, not having the force to argue with her.

'Have you spoken to your brother?'

M rolled his eyes. Ever since he was a child, his parents had badgered him to take care of Laika, to show him the ropes, to take him out. 'I am afraid he is just not equipped for this hard city,' Rafiq had once told M. 'You must take responsibility for him; he needs to be told what to do.' Why their father could not just do this himself was never explained. As for Xezal, at least she provided a solid argument: 'Your father won't take the time to teach him how to be a man. I'm afraid my darling Laika will grow old in his room, on his computer, with no purpose in his life.'

'Hama, can you hear me?'

'Yes, Mother. I sent him an email for his birthday.'

'All these emails and memails. You kids these days would get married by email if you could.'

M checked his watch. Jones was now fifteen minutes late.

'Mum, I'd love to talk, but I'm in a meeting now actually, so . . .'

'He misses you. Laika misses you so much, he is always telling me.'

'Well, we'll call him together when you come.'

'That is a week from now. You can't talk to him sooner?'

'Well, fine, tell him to call me, Mum. He's the one that changes his number every ten minutes. I've had the same number for how many years.'

'I'll tell Siver to send you his number.'

M sighed. 'Fine. She can send me Laika's number by SMS. I really have to go.'

'Fine, fine. Sorry to have bothered my oldest son.'

'It's not a bother, Mother, I am just sitting in a meeting here.'

'Eh. May God watch over you.'

'Um. Thanks. You too.'

M hung up, and quickly checked his voicemail to see if he'd received any messages while talking to Xezal. Nothing. He made a call to Trevor Jones's mobile, but couldn't get through. Maybe he was on the tube.

'Another pint, please.'

It wasn't so much that his parents delegated responsibility to him that bothered M; after all, God knew that Siver had had to deal with every bill payment and phone call in their home for decades and she never complained (though, yes, she did up and flee to an actual war zone the moment she saw a way out, so, yeah, there was that). It was more the fact that M had always felt that his younger brother resented him for some reason, that whenever he tried to do what their parents had asked of him, Laika would just stare at him with utter disdain, as though it were beneath him to clean the room, to just once pick up after himself. He had barely spoken to his brother since he left for New York, and though he blamed this on time zones, the truth was he was almost relieved that he did not have to pretend to care any more. If his brother didn't show any affection towards anyone in his life, that was his choice.

His phone vibrated. Siver.

> *Mum is being super weird*
>
> *she just called shouting at me to send you Laika's number do you know what's she's on about?*
>
> *xx*

While he was on his phone, he decided to make good on at least one of the coerced promises he had just made his mother. Opening the Facebook app he typed in his mother's name, trying a few different variations since he could never remember how she had transliterated her name. Khajal, there she was. Her profile photo consisting of a bunch of tulips (Kurdish women seemed to always have flowers while Kurdish men had mountains; only those active in politics had their own faces, their own bodies). He clicked on the 'translate' link at the bottom of her squiggly post, knowing that Facebook's translation software was generally awful for Kurdish, but at least he could find out if he was writing his condolences under Ali's obituary and not, say, his mother's rants about one of her telenovelas.

> It is with great sadness I am hearing the death of a dear Mr Ali Hardi Kermanj, who received the death of the cigarette. We share our condolences and sadness. Truly, this news shocked all my heart because Mr Ali had a lot of experience. He build a Marxi Linen community in Sulaymaniyah for our parish meeting. Mr Ali's work, struggle and struggle are wide. May he reach all his dreams in the name of bringing all the rights of our people, may his soul rest in peace and may God fill Mr Ali Wife, and all the relatives of the deceased family with paradise.

Under Xezal's post, people probably somehow related to M posted photographs of Ali, with a black diagonal line across one of the upper corners. Ali sitting in plastic chairs in various gardens, or standing by one of his many cars. His uncle had become quite wealthy in Kurdistan, owning the largest car import company in the city. When they went back for Rafiq's funeral M was surprised at how lucrative this business seemed, with Ali handing out wads of money to M and his siblings. M never understood why Rafiq insisted on sending money back to his family when they evidently did not need it.

Rest in Peace. He was a great man, he typed in the app's little box and hit enter.

Another text from Siver, instants later. *lol I see mum forced you to write on her facebook post as well*

M finished his second pint; Jones was now forty-two minutes late. M kept waiting.

XI

DEUTSCHE BANK WENT SILENT after their last, tentative-sounding, email – *We'll get back to you as soon as we have an update* – and eventually M's staff stopped ignoring M's tendency to stare at the Outlook icon and began actively pointing it out to him, in the hope that they could shame him out of whatever he was doing. 'All right, I'm off, let us know if you manage ascension to Nirvana or whatever it is you're trying to accomplish,' Jane quipped as she left the office while Naveen kept informing M of various Hindi proverbs.

'The reputation lost on a betel nut won't come back though you donate an elephant,' he said, nodding sagely.

'Naveen. What the fuck is a betel nut?'

'It's something you chew in India. You make pan masala out of it. Like tobacco.'

'And this has to do with Deutsche Bank?'

'Exactly.' Naveen smiled, putting a hand on M's shoulder and leaving him to stare at the screen for the rest of the evening.

Across the office Chamberlain instructed Charlie to buy a few bottles of champagne for when the social club deal closed. 'Keep it cold, it's likely to happen any day now.'

M walked home, staring at his phone, bumping into people and poles. Just answer, you bastards. Just answer my fucking emails.

As he changed out of his suit and tie, he kept an eye on the black rectangular glass of his phone, struggling out of his shirt, collar blackened by the City of London. A notification. Subject: Deutsche Bank; sender: Jane Tilly. M waddled over to his bed, his trousers down to his ankles, and swiped on the message. Please, please, please.

> In case you're still waiting for them to get back to you . . . here's a
> pic of two otters holding hands to make you feel better.

He kicked off his suit trousers in frustration, letting them splat against the wall like the slime hands he had been obsessed with as a child. He really would have to have a word with her about professionalism, he thought, as he went over to the living room.

The board meeting was in two weeks' time.

Two weeks, and he had nothing to show for himself. While Chamberlain was chasing signatures at Locanda Locatelli over plates of overpriced pasta and getting Charlie to ensure the Belle Epoque was chilled to his exact specifications, M was sitting at home in his underwear, angry at his staff for sending him pictures of otters.

M had sent not one, not two, but three grovelling emails to Deutsche Bank for feedback. He understood what their silence indicated, of course, but he was desperate. This was no time for self-respect.

He checked his phone once again, knowing full well that if he did in fact receive an email he would receive a notification to that effect. Still, maybe it had gone to spam. (That had been the pretext for his last email: *Sorry, am sending this again, just discovered our servers were down the other day so am not sure whether you received this email.*) It had not gone to spam. He tossed the phone aside, went to boil some water to make himself dinner. It wouldn't be Locanda Locatelli pasta, but Tesco's tagliatelle with a jar of ragu sauce would do just fine. It was no more than he deserved for not being able to close a single fucking deal.

He went on LoveFilm to find something to watch while he ate (invariably, his dinner would be well eaten by the time the opening credits of any show ended), contemplating selecting a cooking show that he somehow had watched three seasons of, one of a seemingly endless array of shows consisting of millionaire chefs shouting at aspiring cooks for not being able to sear a scallop.

All he knew was that for now things were on the back burner. They would get back to him, which, he knew, was a sign that they would do no such thing. And every so often Shahab Al-Shafiqque, the owner of the Islamic Card, would call him for an update. Did he really think that M would just be sitting there, neglecting to return his calls, if the card was on the verge of being financed? Al-Shafiqque's mandate granted Hilliard Drake exclusivity for three months, so even if it didn't close before the board meeting, there was still time to get the money, but most banks had turned M down and the few that remained weren't banks at which he had any contacts. He had told Jane to cold call some of the Islamic banks with London branches, but she had been shot down. He really should have a man make those calls, but Naveen had a thick Indian accent and if there was one thing that Middle Eastern men hated more than women it was non-westerners who weren't them. He could call himself, he supposed. Yes, he would start calling himself.

He finally decided to finish watching a brainless movie he'd started the previous day. He flicked through the menu until he found the film and clicked on the RESUME button, a spinning circle appearing on his screen and then:

THE RENTAL PERIOD FOR THIS ITEM HAS EXPIRED. DO YOU WISH TO RENT AGAIN? £2.99

M switched off the TV.

A message from his mother. *Did you cal Laika?*

Fine, he would give his brother a call. He dialled the number his sister had sent him.

The customer you are trying to reach isn't accepting calls at this time.

Well fuck him, then. M looked at the time. It was too early to go to bed, too late to go out. Japan would open in an hour, he could watch the Nikkei's ups and downs in real time, pretend that it mattered to him.

XII

THE WEEKLY AFTER-WORK DRINK SESSION at the Counting House, a former bank that had been refitted as a posh pub for City boys to
celebrate or drown their sorrows in, was in actuality more of a bi-
monthly event, depending as it did on someone from upper
management wanting to join in, which made everyone else at Hilliard Drake cancel their plans with loved ones and head right on over,
as though this was indeed something that they did on a regular basis.
When the weekly happy-hour session did take place, several people
would mention how nice it was to let off some steam every once in
a while, just to have a beer and gab after a long hard week – chewing
the fat, so to speak. Not everything has to be about work all the time,
the employees of Hilliard Drake would echo to one another, raising
their glasses.

During happy hour, the Counting House offered three beers on
tap, house wines and prosecco at a discounted rate. Mixed drinks
remained full price and bartenders would voice their dissatisfaction
with a customer ordering a cocktail, ensuring they would not do so
again. As the television show *Mad Men* had recently become popular
in the UK, the suited bankers had begun ordering Old Fashioneds
wherever they went, leading to the most disruptive upsurge in cocktail requests since *Sex and the City* had been cancelled, taking with it
its endless demands for Cosmopolitans. *It's happy hour, mate,* the two
bartenders who staffed the Counting House bar would say if someone ordered something deemed too complicated. *Have a pint or come
back after seven.*

Every Thursday that the post-work drinking session took place,
the seating arrangements would be the same: a group of senior people
looking for a promotion would ensure they sat as close as possible to
the attending VIP, laugh at every joke and tell one or two interesting

anecdotes that showed the wide breadth of their knowledge. On adjacent tables the juniors would talk about which TV shows they watched and what embarrassing sex situations they had got themselves into recently, unless they were within ear's reach of someone senior to them, in which case they would discuss IRR rates and what they thought about Lucy Kellaway's latest column in the *FT*.

At some point in the evening someone would, almost always, get drunk enough to show off their watch, casually drop how much they'd paid for it below the listed price, and then, almost as casually, ask Charlie how much her boyfriend was making. The boyfriend, everyone at Hilliard Drake knew, worked as a nurse and probably took home in a year less than the cost of a casually flaunted timepiece on the wrist of a mid-level Hilliard Drake employee. The goal of this ongoing humiliation of Charlie's boyfriend, whom none of the Hilliard Drake employees had ever met, was – ultimately – to seduce Charlie. The fact that nobody, as far as the office knew, had managed to bang her only made the sexual harassment more blatant. 'You don't ever wonder what a dick made of money feels like?' someone would say with an exaggerated eyebrow flash. 'I mean, I'm sure pleb dick is nice and all, but you gotta aim high, you know. Aim high.' Rumours circulated among the Hilliard Drake employees regarding Charlie's breast augmentation surgery (if indeed she'd had one), and after enough pints someone would be brazen enough to ask her flat out, which would result in an eye-roll or a slap, depending on the mood. In the rare occurrence someone got too grabby, she would throw the remnants of her shandy in their face and then come Friday morning everyone would act as though nothing had happened.

Jane only rarely came to the after-work drinks, even when there was a VIP in attendance. She liked where she was and what she did and did not intend to advance to another level in order to do boring-as-fuck nonsense, as she'd once told Naveen. She was a due diligence officer, she *liked* being a due diligence officer. Also, she had a child and a husband who, it was clear from her occasional outbursts at work after receiving a barrage of frantic calls, could not be trusted even with the most minor responsibility, thus requiring Jane's mother take care of the girl whenever Jane had to go out of town. 'An evening out means my kid eats buttered bread, and that's if she's lucky,' she'd shrugged once when M said Allencourt was going to be at the after-work drinks and she should not miss it at any cost. When she did come, however, the atmosphere at the pub changed. Suddenly the men were confused as to whether they should continue their jovial sexual harassment of Charlie as they usually did or try to get in on Jane. 'You can just tell she's filthy, she looks like she knows how to handle a cock, right?' as John eloquently put it to M.

Jane did not converse with anyone during office hours unless she absolutely had to, which gave her already quite striking looks an air of unattainability. 'How can you work with her?' Chamberlain had asked M once. 'I lose my concentration just by looking at her.' M shrugged: he found Jane attractive, yes, but he was also used to her, which erodes people's beauty pretty quickly.

Naveen would not drink, as he had made a promise to his dying father that he never would (this he had not told anyone at Hilliard Drake, who simply presumed that he did not drink due to his religion), but instead acted out in extravagant ways to indicate that he, too, was fun, even if he didn't drink. He was telling Gary from IT about the time his father had been offered Gandhi's sperm. 'It was being offered to all the investors of India. Someone had a vial of what they all said was Gandhi's . . . seed. And that this could be used in a few years to clone a new Gandhi. It was actually being considered at the highest levels, when the government intervened and announced that if the seed was used to impregnate someone, they – the government, that is – would have to approve the woman and nobody could agree on what the criteria for a host of Gandhi's clone should be. It was crazy, the whole country was debating how this would be done, and there were actual arguments in parliament over this, until they reached a stalemate. Nobody knows what happened to the vial. Someone probably still has it, an art collector maybe.'

'Right,' Gary said, taking a gulp of his ale. He'd heard this story before, but didn't want to embarrass Naveen (who was, technically, a superior). Unwilling to ask any follow-up questions, an awkward silence fell upon the table, and Naveen wished that he still drank alcohol.

'So what's new with you?' Naveen eventually asked.

'Oh nothing much, same old same old,' Gary said, darting his eyes across the bar to see if there was another conversation that he could join. Naveen, knowing that Gary leaving would mean that he – Naveen – would sit at a table alone and would be seen as alone and would be judged as someone who nobody wanted to talk to, was desperate to keep the conversation going.

'Come on. I'm sure there's something you can tell me.'

Gary, perhaps opening up after finishing his fourth beer of the evening, shrugged. Could he tell Naveen? He seemed trustworthy enough. Besides, who was Naveen going to tell?

'Well, there is this. When we'd just got together, Jennifer and me, and Lara, her daughter Lara, right? This was years ago, I was only like eighteen or whatever. She was beginning to walk. I was sitting in the living room watching TV, drinking my coffee, and my robe – Jennifer's robe, really – had slipped open, and I was naked underneath. No boxers, nothing. These were the early days of constant sex, so whatever clothes we had worn to bed would be off by the time we got up in the morning, usually requiring a hunt for the odd sock, the vanished boxers. Jennifer had showered first that day and I was watching the news, it was something about the Balkans, I remember it still, it's when Clinton bombed that Chinese embassy because he'd been using old maps. Was that Clinton?

'Anyway, that's when Lara comes in. She's like what, almost two, and she's got that Godzilla-waddle small children have. Now, as it so happens, I have the slight remnants of a morning boner, not that bombed Chinese people get me hard or anything, but it was early and so yeah, I had an erection. And when she walks in, I don't think to cover myself because I don't know, it's a bit like when a pet walks in on you naked: you feel observed, sure, but it's not that big of a deal. I just didn't see this child as inhabiting the same universe as an erect penis, right? But so Lara, what she does is, she waddles towards me and grabs my cock with her hand. She puts her hand on the top of my penis and gives it the slightest squeeze and goes "bop-bop", at which point I jump up and recoil instantly but like what am I going to do? Shout at her? For what? So when she repeats it, bop-bop, I can't think of anything to say but to repeat "yes bop-bop" as I pull Jennifer's robe shut.

'But then for several months afterwards, every time she would see me, Lara would do this little squeezing gesture with her hand and say "bop-bop" and I'm both revolted at myself and utterly terrified. I mean, what if she remembers later on? What if she remembers having touched my penis or, worse, misremembers it and tells Jennifer that I molested her? So right then I begin avoiding her. The girl is almost fifteen now and I'm still unable to be in a room with her. I can't talk to her about anything but the most meaningless shit, because it's there, somewhere in her, this thing that happened. And the worst part of all this is that Jennifer thought that the squeezing gesture was a wave and bop-bop meant papa, that here is this child thinking I'm her dad, right, and she told me later, Jennifer did, that she knew we had something, that it was worth giving us a shot when she saw how attached her daughter was to me. So. What do I. I mean. What do you do with that information?'

Naveen blinked. He had no idea what an appropriate response to such a story was. 'That's . . .' he began, as if merely making a sound was sufficient.

'No, I'm sorry, mate, I've had a lot to drink, I shouldn't be spouting off this stuff to you . . .'

'No, no, that's OK, I'm glad you did,' he said and realised that this was an awkward thing to say considering the topic at hand.

'Naveen!' Chamberlain's voice, from across the pub. Naveen muttered a prayer of gratitude under his breath for being saved from this conversation.

Chamberlain strolled over to Naveen, putting his arm around him, his cheeks flushed with wine and good news.

'Have you seen Mo?'

'Uh, he was here just before.'

'Right, right. So how is that Islamic Finance thing going, matey? Because I just got a call that my guys are ready to sign next week.'

'Oh. Congratulations,' Naveen said, suddenly wondering if Gary's company was preferable to Dan's gloating.

'We just went and ruddy well did it! Here, matey, here, have a drink! Mo, Mo, come over here, drinks on me!'

M gave up trying to get a bartender's attention and pulled out his phone, pretending not to hear Chamberlain, acting as though he was very busy indeed. And then, just as he was about to pretend that he was receiving a call, he saw he had two missed calls from a number he didn't recognise. Before he'd had a chance to return the call, his phone rang again. Same number.

Could this be Deutsche Bank? Could they have finally come to a decision?

'Hello, this is M.'

'Hama, where *are* you?'

'Mum?'

'I've been waiting in Heathrow for an *hour* now.'

Fuck.

XIII

EVEN BY THE END OF XEZAL'S WEEK IN LONDON, in the cab ride on their way back to the airport, her complaints about M had not abated: how he had left her stranded at the airport, how she had had to get into a stranger's car like some common prostitute.

'Mum, I got you a chauffeur. You were in an S-Class. It's not like I asked you to hop into a random minicab.'

'Still, who *forgets* their mother?'

It was a fair question, to which M did not have a satisfactory answer. Rushing out of the pub, he was left scrambling for an excuse as he realised that despite the dozens of reminders, he had forgotten the date his mother was arriving. As the silence on the other end of the line grew oppressive, he flipped through his alternatives. He couldn't be at the hospital, he would need to demonstrate any broken bones, he could definitely not be stuck at work . . . but he could have been in a car crash. Yes, someone had run into his cab and he had to stay to give a report to the police, and he didn't know how to reach his mother and he was so sorry but that's why he wasn't at the airport. He had booked her a car, though, it should be there at any moment.

Satisfied with the lie he'd told, he proceeded to call a concierge service he'd long paid £19.99/month for but only used once before, and quickly managed to get a chauffeur at Heathrow to pretend that he had been waiting at the wrong terminal. Just as he hung up, allowing himself to relax a little, he realised the state his flat was in.

The bed was sprinkled with crumbs from meals eaten in its duvet-protected embrace. Strewn across the bedroom floor were a dozen crumpled cum-filled tissues, post-masturbatory remnants that had yet to be discarded. The bulb in the bathroom needed to be replaced, and had needed to be replaced for days, leading M to urinate with the light of his mobile phone as guidance, the darkness hiding the streaks of excrement that now ran down the bowl.

M pictured his living room with its half-empty bottles of beer and oil-stained pizza cartons. The kitchen was rarely for cooking: it was a storage space for plates and cutlery upon which he could eat the delivery meals that would arrive thirty to forty-five minutes after clicking the order button on Hungryhouse.co.uk or Domino's, the flimsy plastic bags arriving with their too-few napkins and enough plastic cutlery to make him feel, ever so briefly, terribly alone, since it was clear that whoever had filled the plastic bag with his order had assumed this amount of food was for more than one person. The fridge had not been opened in days, but he knew that inside there was a pint of milk that housed a lifeform of its own and a cucumber purchased during an ill-advised foray to Waitrose during which M had convinced himself that he would be the sort of person who would eat more vegetables, a cucumber that would have by now lost its solid biological structure entirely. The stack of plastic takeaway rectangles filled with remnants of Chinese, Indian and Japanese food balancing atop a full bin bag had attracted ants that formed a solemn march across the edges of the kitchen walls. M saw before him the pile of plates perilously stacked in the sink, a thin layer of fuzzy mould covering the tomato sauce on the top plate that had not been scraped off.

Could he get a maid in to clean his entire apartment in the time it would take for Xezal to get there from Heathrow? He called a firm he had previously used, pleaded with them, offered hundreds of pounds, but there was nothing that could be done.

In the end he booked Xezal a deluxe junior suite at the Connaught, charged it to his credit card. It would take months to pay off, but what else could he do?

Not that Xezal appreciated it: as soon as she saw the room her nose wrinkled in disgust. 'I have to be inside this coffin all week?'

His mother's face still looked young, even with the scowl she had presented to M ever since she got out of the car. Once, while shopping for presents for Tatiana at Selfridges, in a fit of somewhat

Oedipal nostalgia, he'd called his mother to ask what face cream she used. 'Only Nivea. All the expensive creams are filled with lies, Nivea is better than all of them put together.' (M bought Tatiana a moisturiser from La Prairie.) But there was something duller about her now, a lustre that he'd never noticed she had until it was gone.

'It's one of the best hotels in London, Mum. I thought this would be nicer than you sleeping on a mattress in my tiny apartment, make it like a little holiday. Treat yourself to something nice.'

He'd spent the past few weeks imagining things they could do together, a London he could treat her to that she never could experience during the years she lived here herself, but seeing her standing in the middle of a posh hotel room, with its baroque chest of drawers and generic abstract art, made him realise he had no idea what to do with her now that she was here. What did she like to do? He almost asked her, but felt it would be inquisitive, like a border guard asking the purpose of her visit.

Xezal, still wearing her coat, was flipping through the channels on the television by the sofa. 'No Kurdish channels?'

'No, Mum, I doubt they have Kurdish channels, sorry. They might have Al Jazeera?'

'Arabist propaganda. Here, this will do,' Xezal said, settling for the World Aquatics Championships on BBC2.

She finally took off her coat and sat down on the powder-grey sofa. M saw that she was wearing one of her old jackets, one she must have had for thirty years at least. Its sleeves were frayed; the buttons sagged loosely off its threads. The sight filled M with pity.

'You like swimming?'

'Huh? Oh, your father always promised me we would learn how to swim one day. We just never had time. It looks so freeing, don't you think?'

'Sure. I mean, I guess. I always found it a bit annoying; the water's either too hot or too cold.'

'You can swim?'

'Yeah, we learned at school.'

'Oh.' Xezal fell quiet then, kept looking at the swimmers tearing through the water.

'Hey, are you hungry? We could order something to the room? They have chicken, or salad, or whatever you're in the mood for.'

'Hama. I will not eat in my bedroom like some teenager.'

They went to the hotel's main restaurant instead, a Michelin-starred venture named after its famous French chef who spent one week at the Paris branch of her restaurant and the following week in London. M had hoped his mother would enjoy a nice meal after years of greasy kebabs and overcooked meat. He was wrong.

'Are those real?' Xezal said, pointing a fork in the direction of the art behind M, who turned around to see what she was referring to.

'Yes, I think they're real butterflies. It's a very famous British artist who has done this.'

'And they call us savages.' Xezal sighed, digging into her squid risotto.

The rest of the week was similarly comprised of failures. He took her to the British Museum, imagining it would please her to see some of the Mesopotamian art, but all it did was enrage her at all that had been stolen. 'If it is the British Museum, they should have their own little pebbles and bits of wood. Why are they pretending our civilisation is theirs?'

He walked around Covent Garden, but the crowd made her think someone was going to steal her purse, the second-hand clothes on display around Portobello Road disgusted her. She refused to get on the London Eye, and found *Les Misérables* grotesque. 'All this singing and dancing, this is not what war is. This is not how we survived.'

Then, when he suggested they have an early dinner at J. Sheekey, she interrupted him.

'No, let's go home.'

'Back to the hotel?'

'No, Sutton.'

So they took the tube to Victoria, where they pushed their way through the underground station into the railway station, through the crowds who flowed through as though they all knew exactly where they were going, and how to get there. At the station, Xezal made M ask someone which platform the Sutton train departed from. She could never just trust that he knew what he was doing, every action had to be confirmed by various passers-by, whose opinion she seemed to value more than that of her eldest son.

'I know which one it is, Mum,' he said. 'It says so right there on the board.'

'Just ask. Why is it you kids never ask?'

On the train, he had to tell her where to sit, as she stood confused in the middle of the carriage, the three available options seemingly too different to choose between. M cleared a seat of a *Metro* newspaper and an empty bottle of Lucozade, and gestured for his mother to have a seat, as though he were the maître d' at a restaurant.

'I guess this will do,' Xezal said, looking at the six seats with an empty, disappointed look, as though there were infinitely better seats somewhere on this train.

He started leafing through the discarded *Metro*, an article about some Roman artefacts being found in Devon.

'What has happened that is so important you have to read about it now?' Xezal asked him, irritated.

'Um, nothing. They just found some old Roman coins and cloths. Did you know the Romans had a specific war flag? That they used when they went to war?'

'All flags are war flags,' Xezal said and turned to look out the window.

'Sometimes I think by God this is an ugly country,' Xezal said as they approached Clapham Junction. 'You know all my life as a child they told me, oh London, London, like it was made of diamonds. Why are they so proud of this? What is there to be proud of?'

'Yeah, I don't know, Mum. People are proud of where they come from.'

Sutton High Street had not changed in the five years since his mother had moved out of the flat. The same Zizzi, Nando's, Waterstone's, chicken bones still on the pavement. They walked the path from the high street to their old apartment in silence, and it wasn't until they reached the squat little apartment complex where they'd spent decades of their lives that Xezal turned to M, acknowledged his presence.

'Were you happy here?'

M was taken aback, not sure of what Xezal wanted to hear. 'Honestly, I don't know. I wasn't *un*happy.'

'I wasn't very happy here.'

M wanted to ask why, then, had they taken an hour-long journey here, but elected to stay quiet.

'We should try to see if whoever lives there now will let us have a peek inside.'

'Oh . . . I don't think we should do that. It's awkward.'

'We could offer them some money.'

'Mother, I don't think that bribing them is appropriate.'

Xezal shrugged and began walking back towards the station.

A few days later, when she disappeared through the security line at Heathrow, M realised he still did not know if his mother had enjoyed her time in London at all.

XIV

A MUFFLED POP, AN AWKWARD CUPPING of a palm to prevent the orgasming foam from spilling over the Hilliard Drake rugs, followed by scattered applause, the faint enthusiasm of distant fireworks. M was late to the office, still exhausted from the chaos around Xezal's visit, and by the time he made his way through the glass doors to Hilliard Drake, unkempt and unshaven, Chamberlain's team was already celebrating, with Daniel doling out foamy pours of champagne, surrounded by employees who were there either to celebrate that their jobs were now saved (and, perhaps, that a promotion would be in order) or simply because it was a Friday and there was champagne being offered.

'I have half a mind to go up there myself, that's a good bottle, you know?' Jane was saying, eyeing the group awkwardly huddled in a semicircle before returning to risk assessment analysis and email writing.

'If we close the Islamic Credit Card deal, I'll buy you a crate of that stuff.'

'Well, Mo, you know what they say: a glass of Perrier-Jouët in the hand is worth two in the bush.'

'What's with the bloody proverbs with you two. This one over here was trying to get me to eat betel nuts.'

'What's a betel nut?'

'Don't you start.'

'Boss. No news from Deutsche, then?'

M shook his head.

Several hours later, the celebrations over on Chamberlain's side of the office had yet to recede. M – not being able to withstand any more joviality – picked up the phone and called Deutsche Bank once again, the receptionist dismissing him with the same evasive excuses that M himself instructed Charlie to give whenever a pestering client called for updates when there were no updates to give.

While trying to click his way through to a human on the byzantine phone tree that the receptionist had beckoned him into, assuring him that on the other end of this maze of automated responses and tacky renditions of Vivaldi lay an answer to his queries, M reached for his well-read copy of a business book that he had turned to many times when his faith wavered. The two authors maintained as their thesis that it was in fact hard work that would get you to the top, not some misplaced belief in yourself as other books of the genre seemed to attest, and it was refreshing to M to find a book that addressed inequalities and presented the possibility to make adversity an asset, and for becoming more successful if there were hardships to overcome. Sure, the two authors were old white Americans who were CEOs of successful companies, so when they spoke of hardship they meant economic downturn and business-unfriendly regulations, rather than structural inequalities or the colour of their skin, but they profiled and interviewed people who had overcome actual inequalities, and though M knew – of course he knew – that each of these success stories hid millions who were not quite so lucky or exceptional and who were relegated to being the demonised poor, it still felt good to read of these people, to know that it was possible, there was a chance.

Jane came by his desk and asked if he knew how much Chamberlain's closed deal was for, to which M snapped that no, his telepathic powers were not quite operating at full capacity that morning, and Jane went away, muttering something about this bloody place and everything in it.

He hung up the phone, after being unable to reach sentient life in seventeen minutes, and told Jane and Naveen that he would go out for lunch. He had initially only intended to walk over to Il Mulino on Birchin Lane for their escalope sandwich, but he found himself walking towards Gracechurch Street instead, towards the Deutsche Bank offices, weaving through the throngs of men and women in business attire who were walking between office buildings and Prets, EATs and Tesco Expresses. Projections of logos for various stores were swirling about on the pavement, and the cookie shop further ahead was attracting customers by pumping out an artificial scent to remind passers-by of freshly baked cookies. M walked past one beggar, turned down two leaflets and ignored three charity workers until he reached Winchester House at the junction of London Wall and Old Broad Street, a sinuous wave of sand-coloured limestone and aggressive anodised windows, confused about exactly what architectural style it wanted to emulate: all 1960s public school exterior mixed with neoclassical pillars and a postmodern ripple superimposed over the facade.

As M made his way to the entrance, he passed a tourist who was being given a stern talking-to by a Police Support Volunteer. Anti-terror laws were referred to more than once as the Police Support Volunteer made sure that whatever photographs of the building the tourist had just taken were deleted from their camera. 'Don't let me catch you doing that again,' M heard as he stepped into the building.

The receptionists were two young women, one seemingly of Afro-Caribbean descent, the other blonde, white. They both smiled at him as he emerged from the revolving glass door and M realised that he had to choose one receptionist over the other and, worse, that both receptionists would know that one had been chosen over the other.

In the end, M stood between the two women, and addressed his query to them both. They looked at each other so as to ascertain which one was to help him but then the phone rang and one receptionist answered it and what had been only a few seconds ago an ordeal was now a straightforward social interaction.

'Do you have an appointment with Mr Erdinger?' the receptionist now tasked with assisting M asked, tapping away at her keyboard.

'Not as such, no. We had discussed my coming by but not specified any time.'

'Right. Well.' Tapping. More tapping. 'Mr Erdinger seems to be in a meeting until four o'clock.'

'Oh? Do you mind if I just sit here? I will try to reach someone else that I have been liaising with.'

The other receptionist, having now hung up the phone, exchanged a briefly worried glance with her co-worker.

'You are more than welcome to leave any message that you may have with me, and I will make sure that Mr Erdinger gets it as soon as possible.'

'No, I mean, it's fine, I can just email him, but I'll see if I can just reach, what's her name . . .'

'Sir, you're not actually allowed to wait here.'

'But you have a couch here.'

'That's there as part of the decoration, sir. We have to ask you to kindly wait outside.'

M looked at the wide sofa, the little table with the latest issues of various financial magazines. A space intended merely to give the impression of a waiting room.

An elevator pinged, and out of the glass gates leading to the elevators came a throng of young men, pinstripes and tan briefcases. The one in the middle was, M reminded himself after taking a quick look at his inbox, Benjamin from that first meeting at the restaurant. M turned away from the reception and ran after them, shouting out to Benjamin before he had the chance to exit the building.

Upon hearing his name, Benjamin turned back towards M, his face twisted into a question.

M's hand shot out for a handshake. 'M. M. Hardi, we had dinner a few weeks ago, at . . .'

'Islamic Finance guy. Yes. Yes. Hi there. Listen, I'd love to chat but we've really got to—'

'This will only take a second, Benjamin. I was trying to see James but it seems that he is double booked.'

'Right . . .' Benjamin looked over at the other two, who were lingering at the door, one of them gesturing with his index finger at the part of the wrist where a watch would be. 'I'll be right with you, guys. Just give me a second, yeah?' He then turned back to M. 'You'll have to be quick, yeah?'

'Literally, only a second, Benjamin,' M said, giving the evil eye to the two other bankers, who barely looked out of their teens.

'Basically I was wondering what kind of update there was on the Islamic Credit Card project.'

'Right . . . right . . . I mean, I'll be honest with you, because I like you, but that project, it's just not going to happen.'

'And . . . sorry, why is that exactly? I thought that the corporate finance team—'

'Oh yeah, I mean, they thought it was OK, but compliance said no. So, that means no.'

'Could I perhaps meet with the compliance team, or . . . ?'

'I'll be honest with you, there's nobody to meet with. Compliance puts the numbers into a computer and it comes out with a yes or no. That's it. This project got a big fat no. Sorry to have to be the one to tell you. But listen . . . it was good running into you again. Now, I am sorry but I do really have to go.'

And Benjamin was out of the door, following the two child bankers. To avoid having to walk a few steps behind them, thus compounding his humiliation, M decided to wait in the lobby for a few minutes and the receptionists, having witnessed the mortifying interaction, were kind enough to not ask him to leave.

As he stood there, waiting to be able to leave the lobby that wasn't a lobby, he scrolled through his phone, allowing himself the pretence of appearing busy. There was, he now knew, no point in pursuing Deutsche Bank. He pressed the compose button on his email program and filled in hr@hilliard-drake.co.uk in the address field.

Hi Patricia,

I'd like to take a week's leave of absence, starting tomorrow. Please confirm that this is OK with you.

He clicked send.

(MONTAGE)

HI BILL, THIS IS M. M. HARDI FROM HILLIARD DRAKE. We spoke last month at the RBS/AXE Anarchy conference? Hi. I don't know if you remember, but I briefly mentioned to you a project that we at Hilliard Drake are working on, an Islamic credit card. We are currently putting together a consortium of investors, and I wanted to meet up with you or someone on your team to discuss this opport— No? Sure, I understand. No, of course, I know what the market is like these days but you know, the right project at the right time can help balance this, and Islamic finance has proven— Sure. I'll send it across to you in an email. Of course. Bye, then.

Tom, hi, this is M. M. Hardi, Hilliard Drake. From the Dunhill horse-riding workshop, exactly. Listen, I am just calling you up because I remember you saying your firm was looking for new products to get involved in, and I have something for you here. Sure, sure, I can call back. When would be a good time? OK, I'll be sure to call then.

Hello? Sam? Can you hear me? Hi! Yes, this is M. M. Hardi, from Hilliard Drake. Hilliard Drake? No I'm not selling anything, we're a corporate finance firm at— Hello? Can you hear me? Hello?

Trevor? Hi, it's Mo, Hilliard Drake. How is UBS treating you these days? Nah, no worries, I understand these things happen. I thought we could reschedule . . . this week maybe? The consortium is shaping up for the Islamic finance project I told you about and I did promise you an in on this, wouldn't want you to think I was leaving you behind. Actually, yeah, we've got two banks on board, 20 per cent capital each, for 3 per cent equity. It's really shaping up to be something pretty amazing, let me tell you. Shall we say lunch on Tuesday?

Tom, hi! I was returning the call from earlier . . . is this a good— Oh, no, no that's fine. I can call again. Tomorrow? Sure. No worries.

So where we off to, then? OK, hop right in. Not a nice day to be walking, is it? Pissing down, it is. I'm just glad I don't have to be out there. Oi! Watch it! Yeah, that's right, keep walking, mate. Keep walking. Did you see that? Nearly got himself killed, he did, jumping in front of the cab like that. You can tell he's up to no good, though, all these kids with these hoodies, don't know why we allow them, to be honest. You just don't know who these people are, do you, what they want, can't see their faces, I don't know what's so controversial about a law that allows you to see people's faces, you know what I mean?

Hello, my friend, where do you want to go? Euston? No problem . . . Where you from, my friend? Ah, but mother father also from London? Iraq! Assalam Aleykom, brother. Baghdad, or? Ah . . . *Kurdi.* Like Salahuddin Ayyubi. Mashallah. You speak Arabic? No? You should learn Arabic, my friend, if you want to be good Muslim.

Where to? Right. Nah, fam I'm wit you, just driving. So then what she say? That's not right. You tell her, fam. Nah, she ain't gonna do right by you, I told ya. Hang on, one minute, one minute, bruv. You prefer to go through Park Lane or Piccadilly? Up to you, but I think this time of day there'll be more traffic on Piccadilly. No worries. Blud? You there? Right, so what she text you?

The train departing from platform 16 is the delayed 10:04 Midland service to Northampton. Calling at
  The train departing from platform 12 is the 09:20 Virgin Rail service to Manchester Piccadilly. Calling at Milton Keynes Central, Stoke-on-Trent
  The train departing from platform 8 is the 09:37 Midland service to Birmingham. Calling at Watford Junction, Hemel Hempstead, Berkhamsted

No, they're not homeless. We don't have any homeless people here in Northampton; we don't tolerate that kind of thing here. No, they work over at the Amazon warehouse. Something to do with zero-hour contracts: by the time they get a text saying that they are needed for work, it's too late for them to get the bus to the warehouse. So they sleep at the station, hoping that they will be needed tomorrow. If not, they just go home. It's a nuisance, frankly; we are trying to get the National Railway or the police or someone to kick them out of there. Anyway, do you want some tea or coffee? Our investment team should be here any moment.

Sorry about the weather. Yeah, I mean as long as it keeps raining over Old Trafford later in the day, haha, yeah no we're City, if it were up to me anyone who does not support Man City in this bank would be looking for a job. So here, we can use this meeting room, after you . . . Oh thank you, yes, we just moved to this office. We may be a local bank but we've found that our clients trust us rather than a big anonymous corporate bank down in London, you know, especially with everything that's happened, you know, with the credit crunch and all, so we've actually been doing really well, hence the new office. Oh, I'm sorry, yeah our Wi-Fi isn't up and running yet. They said they'd install it last week, but you know how it is. If you need to hook the presentation up to the projector, I'll call someone from IT over.

Yeah, the elevators are terrible, aren't they? I honestly don't know how it is that we haven't invented a better way to navigate ourselves in buildings. We keep building higher and higher structures, and yet the only way we have of travelling within these buildings is the same elevator that was invented hundreds of years ago. Did you hear about this skyscraper in Dubai? Its elevators broke down and they had to fly in the parts from the manufacturer in Europe, which took a week, so meanwhile people who lived on the 78th floor were supposed to walk up and down the stairs every day to get to work. I think if we just had more advanced elevators . . . Oh, this is our head of Investment Banking here in Birmingham, Thomas Drew; this is Mr Hardi, from Hilliard Drake in London. He wanted to present a project that, well . . . I guess you explain it better than me.

That's very interesting. Thanks for coming by, I appreciate it's a long journey all the way from London. So, like I said, we will have to run this by our finance people, and have to budget accordingly, but we'll be sure to get back to you within the week.

Well, thank you very much. I'm not sure, I'm not sure this is all part of what we do here, but it was definitely an enlightening presentation. I think we can all agree on that.

Wait, say that thing about the 2.5 per cent again?

We have a special offer today: would you be interested in a Twix or a Bounty for just ninety-nine pence?

Sorry, we don't offer the rustic baguette toasted. You can have our regular ham and Emmental baguette if you want, we can toast that one for you? Yeah? And what drink would you like with that?

The apple pie will take five minutes, is that OK? And what dipping sauce would you like with your nuggets? We have barbecue, sweet and sour, honey mustard . . . sweet and sour. For here or takeaway? OK . . . that'll be 12.99. Thank you.

The next stop is Euston, our final destination.

The next stop is King's Cross St Pancras, our final destination.

The next stop is Euston, our final destination.

XV

'So THIS IS IT, this is the card.'

M pulled it out of his pocket with a flourish and slid it across the cracked wooden table. He was meeting with Ian White, one of the bank managers at the Blackburn Building Society, at a local pub that had once been a post office before it had been rebranded as a Wetherspoons. In the days since he took a leave of absence from work and started criss-crossing through the UK, he'd been able to set up meetings with virtually no effort, just a quick call informing the local banks that Hilliard Drake in London was looking at a project that could benefit local communities and did they have time for a quick meeting and, lo and behold, they'd wheel out an actual bank manager to sit with him.

The bank manager took a sip of his ale and lifted the card carefully, as if he were in the process of defusing a bomb.

'We wanted it to feel exclusive, like the Visa Infinite or the American Express Centurion. Feel how heavy it is. We're calling it the Emerald card.'

'It certainly feels . . . exclusive.'

M smiled and took a sip of his pint. He'd requested to meet at a pub near the train station so as to impart the fact that he was really very busy (this was at least partly true: he was booked on the 13:48 service to Manchester for a meeting with Manchester Credit Union) and also because he wanted Ian White to see him drinking alcohol to allay any fears the man might have about M as a Muslim.

'You know, we have quite a large Muslim population here in Blackburn, and we're always on the lookout for something we can offer our, um, more diverse clients,' Ian said, still holding the card in his hands.

'I think this is a perfect fit, you know, because Islamic banking has a lot of the same values as local banks . . .' This was a risky move, M felt as soon as he said the words, as Ian glanced up from the card and was suddenly focused on what M was saying. In London he knew that everyone at least paid lip service to the fact that Islamic banking was an advanced form of finance, but he didn't know if Ian White in his beige blazer and check shirt would appreciate the comparison. 'Both were industries that came out stronger from the financial crisis, because – and you don't need me to tell you this, Ian – you know the value of the local market, of not taking risks to make yourself rich at the expense of your customers.'

Ian was nodding, but it was unclear whether M had lost his interest. 'So we're setting up a consortium, right now, to deliver this card to the customers who will value it the most . . . not the London bankers, but good people like yourself. We've already got banks in Manchester and Burnley . . .'

At the mention of Burnley, which M had yet to even meet let alone sign, the bank manager's brow furrowed. M had hoped the long-lasting sporting rivalry between the two cities would spur Ian into action.

'Well, I'm not sure what sort of structure you have in mind, but we could certainly be interested in this.'

M smiled and shook the bank manager's hand. 'I'll be sure to send you across our investment memorandum. Now, I'm really sorry, but I do have to go. I'm meeting another two potential investors, the goal is to have this all rolled out before Eid, which is the—'

'Yes, my wife is from Bangladesh, I know what Eid is.'

At the train station, some teenagers made a hand-gesture in the general vicinity of M to indicate he was a wanker, in his three-piece worsted wool suit and his Northampton-made brogues. M did not let this get to him. He was Making Things Happen.

XVI

'WHY IS NATHALIE SITTING in the boardroom on her own?'

'Is she?'

'She's been sitting there for five minutes, just staring into the void.'

'It's not— Shit. Is it the fusion meeting?'

'We're still doing that? Allencourt was always the one to preside over it.'

'I mean, I guess we are. I guess she thinks it's her job now to arrange it.'

'Maybe, I don't know, tell us?'

'This is so embarrassing. Should we just go in?'

Nathalie Hardy, COO and acting CEO at Hilliard Drake, had her office not on the third floor but on the second. Hardy's office being a floor away from the CEO office was, officially, due to the tenets of Punctuated Equilibrium, but many gossiped that she was on the lower floor primarily because Allencourt could not stand her. Originally brought in from the parent company in New York as a mentor to Lloyd W. George, Hilliard Drake CEO between 2001 and 2005, Nathalie Hardy had twelve years of experience at Rothschild & Co in London and had subsequently developed a substantial network to assist the then-CEO, who had quickly proven himself to be out of his depth (but was kept on since the London subsidiary had changed CEOs twice in the past five years already and did not want to give the impression of a company in chaos). When George was eventually ousted and Allencourt was brought onboard as CEO, Allencourt did not appreciate that there was a COO who acted as though she were in charge when he had specifically been brought in to demonstrate that he had the right experience to lead the company. After an attempt to rid the company of Nathalie Hardy failed (the board supported her over the as yet unproven Allencourt), her office was moved to the lower floor, in line with the roll-out of Punctuated Equilibrium. Hardy had, as far as the employees of Hilliard Drake knew, never mentioned this slight and pretended as though it was her suggestion to move floors so that each and every team could be under the supervision of at least one company executive.

Her presence in the third-floor boardroom on Monday late afternoon was confusing, then, until employees began realising that it was time for the monthly run-through of all the active mandates, a meeting previously supervised by Allencourt and which, subsequent to his death, most had assumed was a thing of the past. Why Hardy had not sent out a calendar invite for the meeting was not immediately clear: perhaps she sat in stillness for the better part of fifteen minutes as a demonstration of her influence? That she could will a meeting into existence by her mere presence? In any case, the monthly Hilliard Drake fusion meeting began at 16:30, Nathalie Hardy acting as though it was always meant to take place, as though everyone had had the meeting on their schedules.

'As you all know, the board convenes this week, where a new CEO will be appointed. As it will be my job to present to the board the current position of the projects we have in progress, it is vital that we demonstrate the viability of our mandates, to ensure that whoever the board chooses doesn't have an excuse to bring about redundancies.'

someone thinks theyre up for ceo clearly hahaha, someone wrote on one of the eight BBM group chats currently in use by Hilliard Drake's employees. *Doesn't she look tired?* someone else wrote, to which a reply came, *Tired or old?* followed by an emoticon representing a face sticking out its tongue.

'So, let's get straight into it. John, how is your team doing on the financing for the mine in . . . Kuala Lumpur, is it?'

'We're still waiting on a response from Barclays. They have given us a soft assurance that they are interested, but we have yet to cross the t's and dot the i's, as it were.'

'So, you've done nothing, is what you are saying.'

lol sick burn there jonno
she got you good

Team leader after team leader was called upon to present any developments in their projects. Chamberlain appeared especially pleased to describe in minute detail how much money would be coming to the firm in light of the closed deal.

ugh we GET IT he closed a deal jfc can he stfu already

guys you know i'm on this group chat right?

By the time Chamberlain had finished talking, it was already half past five and there were still five team leaders left to discuss their projects. Those not senior enough to get a seat in the boardroom were shifting the weight on their legs and leaning awkwardly against the glass partitions surrounding it.

guys i think jeremy is looking at like japanese cartoon porn

What made this message do the rounds of a group chat was that Jeremy, an Investor Relations Officer from the second floor, by the full name of Jeremy V. Turnbull, was googling Hello Kitty images rather than staring at the master project list on Excel that he was supposed to be focusing on, his knee restlessly twitching, hitting up against the bottom of the table as though he were composing a telegram indicating that he had to leave. It was his daughter's fifth birthday and he needed to find her a Hello Kitty doll before heading home. Eventually he shut his laptop, wrapped up the charger cords.

'Do you have somewhere to be?' Hardy asked him, an eyebrow slightly cocked.

'I'm sorry, I need to go home. It's my daughter's birthday and I need to find a Hello Kitty doll before the shops close.'

The others were incredulous and voiced said incredulity with a mix of faux outrage and actual outrage. 'Why don't you just get your wife to buy a present?' Chamberlain snorted, while John Morris, all shit-eating grin, pointed out that 'We still have to finish discussing several aspects of the Excel sheet. Is it really that important?' Richard Dawes, the numbers guy on John's team, who had been answering emails furiously on his phone throughout the meeting, glanced up to ask what is a Hello Kitty.

'Listen, if Jeremy thinks his social life is more important than his job, by all means, he should go,' Hardy said, a wry smile on her lips making it impossible for Jeremy to know whether or not she was being serious.

'I'm sorry, I have to go. I have to go,' Jeremy said before rushing out of the boardroom. M, two seats down from Jeremy, felt a strange sort of admiration: as pathetic as Jeremy seemed, there was a quiet dignity in his refusal to stay. The others exchanged shocked glances, unable to fathom what had just happened.

Once Jeremy had gone, the rest voiced some light emasculating barbs. Some wondered what kind of ball-busting wife he must have at home to feel obliged to be present for a little girl's birthday. 'Can you even remember your fifth birthday? Like, does the kid even care?' M was unable to shake the urge to speak up, to say that he hoped to one day be the kind of person to do such a thing even though he would be ridiculed for it, that we should probably all spend a bit more time look-ing at Hello Kitty pictures rather than multi-sheet Excel documents.

'Mohammed? Is there anything that you want to add?'

Nathalie Hardy, having written a well-received report on how to use body language to drive negotiations in business school, kept her eyes on M, who had betrayed some form of ambivalence to the mock-ing of Jeremy V. Turnbull's priorities. M sighed.

'I guess . . .' No, this wasn't a battle he was willing to fight. Not today. 'I guess now is as good a time as any to tell you that my team and I closed the Islamic Credit Card deal this morning.'

The others stopped tapping parallel running commentaries of the meeting in their various group chats. 'I didn't even know we were taking that one seriously,' someone said, to which Chamberlain looked up from his phone, a confused look on his face.

'Does that thing even *work*?'

'Sure. And yes, we had pinned a lot of our hopes on Deutsche Bank financing this thing but once they pulled out, we managed to build a consortium with UBS at the helm and five local banks who want to reach out to their Muslim communities and be able to offer them services, targeting their specific needs. We've been busy, going to Blackburn, Manchester, Birmingham . . . all over the place, really.'

'Weren't you on holiday last week?' Nathalie enquired.

'I didn't want to do all this travelling on company time, so I took a holiday, yes, in order to close this deal as quickly and as efficiently as possible.'

'So they've signed?'

'We're drawing up papers today. I'm not an authorised signatory so you could do me the honour?'

'Well, this is splendid work, Mohammed. Good job.'

tosser. obviously he'd be able to close this deal, he can just reach out to his muslim mates right?

After the meeting, which continued for another excruciating two hours even though the relevant information relayed could have fit on a Post-it, Chamberlain came up to M, flashing his expensive teeth. 'Excellent work, old chap, I honestly didn't think the Islamic card was even worth pursuing. You sure proved me wrong,' he said, thumping M on the back in a gesture that may have been intended as a display of camaraderie, but which felt like an act of violence. 'Listen, if Thursday goes the way we are hoping, I could sure use someone like you on my side.' This was the first time Chamberlain had stated out loud that he was in fact hoping to jump straight to CEO. M didn't know whether he should be happy that Chamberlain saw his value and wanted him close or angry that someone with the same job title as him was talking down to him in this manner.

'What about Nathalie. You don't think she'll get it? The board like her, and she is a C-level executive.'

'Oh, that's a possibility. Of course. But they need someone to steer this ship through choppy waters. Nat's not a war-time consigliere, you know this, the board knows this. They need a fighter who can take some punches until the market sorts itself out. I've got Lord Harbinger on the board to nominate me.'

'Well. Best of luck, I guess.'

Taking the elevator down he took a breath and decided he wasn't going to let Chamberlain ruin his mood with his wild plan to become CEO. M had, after all, managed to put together a consortium to invest in a £12 million project in a single week. With the 8 per cent success fee for Hilliard Drake, that amounted to £960,000 that he had just made his firm. His end-of-year bonus would likely be 10 per cent of that success fee, £96,000. More than enough to pay off his credit card bills, put some money into savings. He'd done it. He'd fucking done it.

That night he called his sister to tell her of the good news. The phone line was terrible, as calls to Baghdad always were, and he kept having to repeat himself, that he'd closed a nigh-impossible project, that things were looking up for him.

'I can't hear you, do you need help?'

M hung up, decided to text her instead.

So happy for you. Karim says he always knew you would be successful, she replied. Then, after over a minute of the thought bubble in his message program indicating that she was typing, she sent *Rly proud of you xx.* M stared at that message for a long time, not knowing how to answer.

When is Zara's birthday by the way? I keep forgetting and I want to buy her a nice present.

Siver did not respond to this message. M did not know if she just hadn't seen it, or whether she was insulted that he didn't know his niece's birthday. After ten minutes he sent another message:

?

XVII

ALTHOUGH THE CONFERENCE ROOM in the Hilliard Drake offices at Lombard Street was both officially and colloquially known as the 'boardroom' it was not a room in which the board actually sat. Rather, they rented out one of the conference rooms at the Lancaster Hotel and only sent out the results of said board meeting to the Hilliard Drake offices in London, New York and Singapore by email later that day. It was customary for M to read about what had been said in the press well before he ever received an email.

The day the board convened, the Hilliard Drake employees spoke in hissed whispers to one another, throwing nervous glances at their phones, asking their co-workers if they'd heard anything. At lunch, M went downstairs to get a box of hard, refrigerated sushi from the Sainsbury's Local, and, as he walked back into the building, he saw Nathalie Hardy, having returned from the board meeting, waiting for the elevator.

'Nathalie! How was the meeting?' he asked as he walked up to her, to which she shot him a look that contained such dejection that he immediately knew she hadn't been promoted. They waited for several minutes for the elevator to reach the ground floor, and she got off at the second floor.

'Bye, then,' she said as the doors closed behind her.

On the third floor everything seemed normal. 'Guys, I just saw Hardy in the lift,' M said to Naveen and Jane in their cubicles. 'She didn't get the gig.'

'Well yes, because God forbid a firm promote a capable woman.'

'She was virtually crying in the elevator, I'm not sure she's all that capable.'

'Honestly, Mo, you did not just say that.'

'I'm guessing nobody knows who got the job?'

'Share price is going up, boss, I think someone knows,' Naveen said, observing the curve on his terminal rise.

M glanced over at Chamberlain. Could that fucker have pulled it off? He walked towards the fruit basket that was located between the two of them and pretended to consider a peach, catching Chamberlain on his way to the restroom.

'Dan, my man. How go things?'

Chamberlain looked around, as if looking for people who would be listening in on the conversation. 'I haven't heard anything. I was assuming Nathalie would message me if my name came up.'

'I don't know. I just saw her in the elevator.'

'And?' Chamberlain grabbed M's arm then, as if the force of his grip served to indicate the importance of this conversation.

'Pretty sure she didn't get it. She was crying.'

'Well then, who did?'

'Not sure, honestly.'

All the phones and computers in the office made sounds indicating that an email had arrived. 'That's gotta be it, right?'

The two men drew their phones as though participating in a duel and proceeded to scroll, scroll, scroll down the press release.

'Shit,' Chamberlain sighed.

'Yeah.'

'Shit.'

'Who is he even? George . . . Gibbons?' M searched the name online. 'Oh. Shit. COO of BNP Paribas Corporate and Institutional Banking Division in London.'

'Yeah. Fucking *Gibbons*. Fuck.'

'Well, you didn't think it was really going to happen, did you?'

Chamberlain looked up from his phone, his face twisted into something that M no longer recognised. 'What did you say?'

'Nothing, I just mean you and me have the same job title, and I sure wasn't expecting to be given CEO out of the blue. I have some sense of reality. Maybe you don't, and more power to you.'

Chamberlain stood silent in front of M, his BlackBerry in his palm tilted as though he were begging for money. His eyes narrowed.

'The *fuck* is wrong with you?'

'What?'

'Why do you always have to be this antagonistic? Why couldn't you just say, "ah, sorry, mate, better luck next time?" Why do you have to be such a *cunt*? No, no, I'm serious. Months I tried with you, *months*, asking you out for a drink, trying to connect with you, trying to help you here, and what do I get in return? Just endless fucking snark, not a single word of congratulation when I closed that deal, by the way, the whole office came by and you didn't say a thing. What, you're too good for me, is that it?'

M stood agape, taken aback by this outburst. 'Dan. Honestly . . . I have no idea what you're—'

'My life! I've given my entire life to this firm, and for what? For what? Not even a quarterly bonus? I haven't seen my kid in a year, I haven't seen *daylight* since the nineties. And this is the thanks I get? After I closed the country club deal in under two weeks, might I add! Oh, I'm out. I'm so out. May this place burn straight to the ground.'

Chamberlain tossed some papers into the air and walked out of the door, making a point of bumping into M as he did so.

'You can have this shithole.'

'What *was* that?' M mouthed to Charlie, who gave an exaggerated shrug and a shake of the head. The employees of Hilliard Drake were staring at each other in disbelief. What had just happened? Outside, the metallic clang of Chamberlain kicking the elevator door subsided and was replaced by Chamberlain shouting, 'Don't touch me. *Don't touch me!*' at someone.

XVIII

M HAD BEEN SO FOCUSED on finding out who the new CEO was that he didn't even notice that the press release informed them that bonuses were frozen for the year. It wasn't until Jane mentioned how she regretted having put a pair of eye-bleedingly expensive shoes on her credit card that M wondered what she was talking about and, as she told him, felt as though a dentist's drill had hit a nerve. He opened the email again and skimmed until he reached the part Jane was referring to. *As his first act, George Gibbons introduced a motion to not pay out any bonuses to Hilliard Drake Capital PLC employees for the 2009 calendar year, and to only resume bonuses once the company balance sheet surpasses that of Q4 2006. The board approved this motion unanimously and firmly intend this gesture to demonstrate that Hilliard Drake Capital PLC's foremost responsibility lies with maximising shareholder value.* The £90,000 he had been counting on had just evaporated.

'Fuck.'

'I'm sorry, boss. You should be proud you closed that deal, though.'

'Sod pride, Naveen. I need to go out. I need a drink.'

'Be careful, Dan could still be out there wanting to punch your face in.'

'Oh, fuck that ponce. I need a drink,' M said and walked towards the elevator, turning back to the other two. 'You coming or not?'

'Honestly, guys, just order whatever you want, I'm fucking expensing this. Naveen, have something. No? Fuck it, more for me. Jane? Attagirl. Gin and tonic for the lady, single malt for me. A double. Naveen? A Coke? A Diet Coke for this one. Cheers. Yeah, just keep the card, we'll open a tab. Thanks. Is here fine, guys? Or do you want to sit over there by the window? Anywhere is fine. Well, cheers, cheers to getting fucked in the arse. You know, there's this clip of

George W. Bush taking a moment out of his busy schedule bombing the Middle East back to the Stone Age, while giving an address at some university in Dallas, where he states that he is proof that even C students can become president. Watch that clip and now watch Condoleezza Rice in the background, look at her face. Honestly, Jane, you can find it on YouTube, check it out. You know that when slavery was abolished in the UK, in France, in the US, when this happened the *slave-owners* were paid for their lost revenues. The fucking slave-owners. And the slaves often had to work the rest of their lives for significantly reduced pay in order to repay their former masters. Can you believe that shit, honestly? Still we keep our heads down, try our utmost not to be confused with "one of those", we dress like them, eat like them, not that weird smelly food, and you try to keep up in a game that is rigged against you. Until of course one day when you realise that there is nothing that can be done. The gig will still be given to George fucking Gibbons, or Daniel fucking Chamberlain. Cunts, the lot of them. Another drink, Jane? Come on, one more. Come on.'

Naveen and Jane, not wanting to offend their superior, indulged him as they both thought of all the work they still had to do before they could go home for the day.

XIX

WITH A NEW CEO came new routines. Security protocols were updated, consultants brought in for tens of thousands of pounds to tell them how to do things ever so slightly differently. It was decided that all employees should acquaint themselves with the company's new HR manual on how to interact in reality-based environments. Charlie was appointed Fire Warden, after it turned out that the previous Fire Warden had been included in an initial round of redundancies in 2007 and the company had neglected to appoint someone else.

When M emerged from the bowels at Bank he rushed to the office, only to have his access card be rejected: new rules, new cards. Charlie had to come down to identify him, even though the building receptionist had seen him every workday for the past seven years. A new card was produced, M instructed to look into a mechanical eye at desk level, a black plastic globe that housed an equally dark lens that briefly shuttered before sending a file to a hard drive. The photo that was printed on the card was washed out, M reduced to a pale, ghost-like figure. He was finally handed his card – his name misspelled because that's how it was spelled on the previous card – and only then was he allowed through the sliding glass gates to the elevators.

'Thanks,' he said to Charlie, who was checking her phone.

'Sure,' she said, not looking up until the elevator slowed down and she moved to get off but realised that it had stopped on the second floor for the FedEx delivery man to get on. She looked embarrassed and tried to intimate that she was just trying to stretch, not get off the elevator. M pretended not to notice. 'Gibbons is looking for you, by the way,' she said as she exited on the correct floor.

Since the management at Hilliard Drake had changed, so had the instructions to decorate one's desk. What was previously encouraged (to a minimum: evidence of a happy family or a prestigious university or some sporting activity was sufficient, certainly no hint of a wild social life outside of the firm) had now been scaled back as a futurologist firm had been hired to revamp the workstations and make sure that the Hilliard Drake office was forward-thinking. As such, focus now lay on the transience of workspaces. A Hilliard Drake employee was supposed to be able to plug in their laptop at the office in New York or Dubai or Singapore and be at home.

Of course, everyone at the firm continued using their own desks as they had done previously, only now they were a little bit harder to identify. M dropped off his bag and trench coat at his now empty desk and made his way to George Gibbons's corner office.

No sooner had Gibbons settled into his office, got the IT department to set up his phone, his email, his email signature and given him a pass to enter the building than he called a meeting announcing new, exciting changes. In order to move up, he said, they had to focus, focus on their core competencies. They needed to get back to what made Hilliard Drake great, and lose the projects that would not lead to growth, and what everyone at the firm needed to do was to ask themselves how were they creating value and what could they improve?

The next week he leased off half of the remaining Hilliard Drake offices and instructed HR to make 20 per cent of the staff redundant. Not pulling your weight, HR would tell the 20 per cent. A new direction. Not wanting it enough.

Considering that every single element of corporate capitalism was suffused with paradoxes, it was never hard for HR to find a reason to get rid of someone. After all, to be a successful employee at Hilliard Drake, you needed to ensure that you had hobbies and well-adjusted families but also that this job came first, ahead of anything else. You needed to overcome sleep, but look healthy. They had actually brought in experts to talk to them about mindfulness, about how ten minutes of meditation every morning and remaining mindful throughout the day could cut down on up to three hours of sleep (most just took Dexedrine). The younger employees, those who still believed you could have a life on the side of this, would nap in the toilets around 3–4 p.m., and join friends at pubs or bars afterwards.

When you got to M's level that was shunned, as much else was. You were meant to shed and shed and shed to reach the top, the very top.

M knew what Gibbons was doing: his responsibilities were to the shareholders, and he could demonstrate short-term profits by leasing off property, by reducing payroll costs. Long term this was a disaster, but Gibbons had no responsibilities beyond providing reassuring quarterly results.

At M's knock, Gibbons waved him into his office and asked him to present to him what it was that he was working on at Hilliard Drake.

'Well, you know I closed the Islamic Finance deal, which brought the firm—'

George Gibbons had the unfortunate facial features that made him look perpetually angry, a mouth turned downward by the weight of his jowls, his eyes – small, round – buried deep into his sockets, obscured by wild brows casting a shadow over them. He was used to being feared, and a raised finger made M stop his retelling of the minor miracle that was the closing of the Islamic Credit Card deal.

'I'm going to stop you right there,' Gibbons said, a voice so quiet listeners would instinctively angle themselves closer to him. A misheard sentence was deemed a lapse of concentration, rather than an inability to hear the man's voice. 'There's no point in focusing on the past. We need to constantly be looking ahead. I don't need to know how you've created value in the past, what I need to know is how you're going to do it in the future. I know that Allencourt, rest his soul, was an easy boss – I'm not going to be that lenient with the staff. I have a responsibility to the shareholders, you must understand.'

M recalled the time that Allencourt had lobbed an employee's laptop across the room because he didn't like the header font on a particular investment memorandum and tried to reconcile the memory with this posthumous revision of him as an easy boss.

'So what are you working on? Right now.'

M had a terrible roster of projects, none of which were likely to ever close. There was a solar plant project which depended on the (corrupt) assistant to the (corrupt) minister of electricity in Bangladesh not losing his job in the coming five to seven years, there was the expansion of a refinery in the United Arab Emirates that required hundreds of millions of dollars in investment when Dubai World had just collapsed, and there was a project in Luxembourg so convoluted, nobody in his team actually understood what it consisted of. M gave a quick shrug and explained that his own projects were currently at a standstill and maybe if he had access to the projects that were previously on Chamberlain's desk . . .

'Can't do that. They're being redistributed internally.'

M nodded, beginning to realise where this meeting was heading. Not even a month ago, he had closed a deal that was meant to get him a hefty bonus and secure his future at the firm; now he had no bonus and was being told that he was on a short leash, that he needed to pull another rabbit out of his hat or that would be him outside, holding a cardboard box, relinquishing his mobile phone and laptop.

'I hope that I've made myself clear,' Gibbons said, gesturing for M to leave his office.

XX

At the centre of the photo commemorating the signing of the Islamic Credit Card project financing is a handshake between Shahab Al-Shafiqque and Michel Latour of UBS, folded outward for the camera, the handshake of politicians and celebrities, an awkward contortion to unfold a gesture intended for two participants outward for a spectator, a lens, now as distorted and deformed as a map projection. Behind them stands George Gibbons, the flash making his eyes seem demonic red in two of the three photographs, his hands on the shoulders of the two men whose deal was valued at £12.6 million, ensuring that George Gibbons would stay on for at least a full financial year as CEO. On the right stand Jane and Naveen, their expressions a mix of boredom and bewilderedness. A group of representatives from the local banks round up the photograph, all smiling. M's arm is visible behind Jane, but his face is mostly obscured in all three pictures, the only photo that shows any part of his face at all has one white eye appearing from behind the head of one of the bankers. It is impossible to tell from his eye what facial expression M had when the photographs were taken.

After Charlie had pressed down on the shutter of the digital camera three times, she showed the photos to George Gibbons on the camera's viewer. 'Lovely, that's just great,' he said, angling the camera so that Michel Latour could also approve it. The memory card on which the three photos were saved filled up a few weeks later, and its contents were uploaded onto Charlie's desktop's hard drive, where the photographs remained, never to be looked at again.

The memory card was then erased, to allow for new photographs.

Change (2011)

CITIES DRIBBLED DOWN THE SCREEN for a moment before the monitor flickered anew and the same cities appeared, this time in Arabic script. Departures. Arrivals. Departures. Arrivals.

Xezal Razaq Rahman stared intently at the flight information display system at Dubai's Terminal 2, which had been designed to look like the rotating split-flap displays of her youth, even though it was fully electronic. Still no flight to Slemani. She looked at the ticket in her hand, the departure date and time hand-scribbled by the people in New York. Could they have written the date wrong? Could they have been so incompetent?

There was a listing beneath those to Lahore and Isfahan, which consisted exclusively of a series of question marks. Could that be it? Xezal looked around for an information desk and pushed her luggage cart over, interrupting a young woman mid-yawn.

'Excuse me,' Xezal said, catching the woman's attention. She had found that her voice had another timbre here, more authoritative than it had been a mere fourteen hours ago when she boarded the flight in New York. 'Could you tell me when the flight to Slemani is departing? I do not see it on the board.'

The woman was dressed in a uniform that reminded Xezal of that American television show she used to watch in Iran, *I See Jeannie in My Sleep*, a westerner's idea of Middle Eastern clothing. Long and sloppily home-painted fingernails clacked on a keyboard for a few seconds.

'What is Slemani? I have never heard it.'

Xezal corrected the woman's Arabic grammar and showed her the flight ticket. 'The flight is supposed to leave today, at eight thirty. Look here.'

Her voice rose so that it seemed as though she were shouting, which she did not intend to, and the woman recoiled a bit. Xezal realised she was still carrying some aggression from her taxi ride over to the terminal.

She had landed at Terminal 1 a few hours earlier, and discovered that the only way to get to Terminal 2 was by taxi. The taxi driver, who had waited over an hour for a passenger only to be told to drive a few minutes for the minimum fare, had proceeded to complain, in English to Xezal then in his own language to himself, for the entire ride. Xezal explained it was not her fault she needed to get to Terminal 2, or that there was no shuttle or bus service that could take her there for free. 'I don't want to take taxi, but I have to,' she explained as the driver continued to insult her in a tongue she did not understand, but the tone of which was unmistakable. She tried to explain that if he would just behave professionally, she would give him a good tip, but this seemed to anger him all the more, and by the time they arrived at the terminal Xezal felt that he did not deserve a penny more than the thirty-two dirhams he was owed.

She had never been to Dubai before, and was surprised to find nobody there spoke Arabic. Even the woman at the counter, who was, Xezal assumed, a local, spoke as though she had just learned the language from a villager last month. She did not know what she expected of this place, which was still a sandpit inhabited by nomads by the time Baghdad was listed prominently beside Paris and London on expensive shopping bags beneath designer logos, but she at the very least thought they would have enough pride to ensure their language was spoken.

'I don't see anything in the computer, I'm sorry,' the woman said and, rather than argue with her further, Xezal sighed and manoeuvred the luggage cart with its infuriating tendency to veer left to the only coffee shop before the check-in counters and the security check. It was a chain she recognised from London, though she had never been in one, and it took her a few minutes to understand what was being offered. She just wanted a coffee, and yet the employee – a small, effeminate thing – kept asking her questions as though he were the Great Sphinx of Giza. Did she have a loyalty card? Did she want one?

She stood for a long time deciphering the numbers on the bills and coins that she had exchanged at one of the airport's many bureaux de change. Pounds weren't like this; you could tell by the size whether one bill was more valuable than another: a twenty-pound note bigger than a ten-pound note but smaller than those giant red fifties. One of Rafiq's guests one day told them that he could sell them fifty-pound notes for half the price. 'By God, it is impossible to tell the difference,' the man had said, holding up one of the counterfeit bills for their inspection. Rafiq had seemed intrigued by the prospect, pretending that it was an efficient way to demonstrate the arbitrary value of money, and though Xezal kept politely telling the guest (Kak Abdulrahman, she suddenly remembered his name being) that they would think about it, Rafiq kept pressing the notion, until Xezal saw no other option but to bluntly tell her husband and his guest that she was the one doing the grocery shopping in the household, not Rafiq, and so she would be the one taking the risk every day of being caught. 'I would rather die; I would rather starve than be shamed so.' The men rolled their eyes at her histrionics and began talking about Tariq Aziz's upcoming state visit to France instead. Xezal resumed her wifely duties and later, when Kak Abdulrahman had left, threw the chocolates that he had brought as a gift in the trash. What a thoroughly disagreeable man he was.

A week or so later, when cleaning the apartment, she saw the back panel of the radio looked like it had been opened. That goddamned radio, and all the suffering it had caused her. When she looked into the compartment she saw a stack of fifty-pound notes, and for months she held on to this knowledge, ready to assail Rafiq with it whenever they were in a fight. Of course someone of his nature would have been scammed by this conman and his forged bills. Of course he'd rather hide the money than tell Xezal what he had done. She would have held on to that grudge for ever, if it hadn't turned out he used that money to take them all to Paris. And to sleep with some floozy, sure, but he did not have to take the entire family to Paris if his only purpose was to cheat on her.

'Just give one of these,' the coffee-shop employee said, pointing to a pink bill in her hand, after noticing Xezal was struggling with the money. He handed some coins back to her, which she proceeded to drop in the tip jar next to the cash register, grateful to him that he had saved her from embarrassment.

The coffee purchase complete (although she was forced to drink her coffee from one of those disgusting paper cups), she sat at an empty table, folded some napkins to put under its legs to stop it from wobbling, and retrieved her phone from her purse, hoping she would be able to call Siver to let her know she was in Dubai. Maybe her daughter could come have a coffee with her before she checked in, bring little Zara with her. She looked at the screen, devoid of bars. Still no signal.

The purpose of her trip had been to visit Laika in New York. A full day it had taken her to fly through that god-awful Istanbul airport named after the vilest man who ever lived, only to be taken into a room at JFK airport and told to wait. There were no toilets, no water, no telephones, she wasn't even allowed to read a magazine, just had to sit there with a handful of Muslims and a very confused westerner. It was an hour before her name was called. She tried explaining that she was not one of these crazy Muslims, that Kurds hated Islamists more than Americans.

'Ma'am, we don't hate anyone,' the immigration officer had said. She had prayed she would not get this one, she had seen how he talked to the people before her. The other one, the woman, she seemed much nicer.

'You filled in this form when you got an ESTA, do you recall filling this in?' he said, shoving a piece of paper towards her.

'Yes, I have ESTA. I am British citizen.'

'That's not what I'm asking, ma'am. It says here, "Do you seek to engage in or have you ever engaged in terrorist activities, espionage, sabotage or genocide?" You answered no.'

'Yes, we not terrorist. We Kurd. We not like Islamists.'

'Was your husband a Rafeek Karmanj? Founder of the Communist Party of Kurdistan?'

'Yes. Yes my husband Rafiq. He died now ten years ago.'

'And were you not a member of the Communist Party of Kurdistan?'

'Member? Maybe, long time ago. This when Baathists come. When we live in Iraq. My husband was politician. Me, just housewife.'

'And do you know, ma'am, that the Communist Party of Kurdistan is listed as a terrorist organisation by the United States?'

'No, no. We not terrorist. Saddam terrorist!'

The man stamped her passport then and before she'd had a chance to say anything further, she was being deported, back to Slemani. They made her buy an extortionately priced ticket via Dubai. Four days of air travel, and she was about to end up right where she started.

Not that her children would care enough to be worried. Even when she moved away from London, when she asked which one of her sons would accompany her to the airport, they had both sheepishly glanced at the pavement.

'Mum, you don't need us there. We'd go with you all the way to the airport and say goodbye at the check-in, and then we'd have to take the train back; it's unreasonable, the whole thing would take hours.'

She didn't know when they had become so selfish. In the end, Laika feebly offered to go with her but she forbade him from coming. 'I don't need you. If you don't want to do goodbyes with your own mother, it is your own choice.' Like the westerner he had become, her son did not argue, let her get into the taxi alone, and turned back towards the block of flats as soon as the car had started rolling out of the driveway.

She had thought that things would be different after their father died, all those promises of honouring his memory, of ensuring things would change, and yet no sooner had they returned from the funeral than they all went their own ways again. As if Rafiq's death was just another inconvenience they had to soldier through before returning to their actual lives.

After Rafiq's death, she gradually came to realise that she had to return to Kurdistan. Her children would not take care of her, this was becoming quite clear, and she could have a better life, a dignified life, if she moved back. There was no shame in going home; her husband had died, after all. Whatever journey they had been on, it was his journey, and he was in heaven now. So she reached out to her sister in Slemani, telling her that she had a plot of land that had been granted to Rafiq years earlier by the Kurdistan Regional Government for his contribution to the Kurdish cause, and she was willing to give half the land to her sister and her brother-in-law, if they paid for the construction of her house.

'Nothing fancy, just a few rooms. And you can sell your part of the land or build your own house there. Wouldn't it be wonderful to be neighbours after all this time?' (Her sister sold the land.)

A year or so later, once construction on the house was nearly complete, Xezal contacted some cousins living all the way out in Saratapa, the village she was born in, and suggested that, if they had an unmarried girl too old to find a husband, she would take care of her – give her housing and some pocket money in exchange for cooking and cleaning. They arranged a call a few days later with Ala, a girl almost thirty years of age. The girl was silent as Xezal explained what was expected of her. When she thought she heard a snivel on the other end of the line, Xezal decided to drop the formalities. 'Come, it's not such a bad fate. Usually the only options for a girl are to be in prison under the eyes of a father or those of a husband. I don't care what you do, where you go, as long as the house is somewhat clean and I don't starve,' Xezal told the girl. She was presenting her case, of course, just as she had to her sister when she had given her half the land, but she was also telling her a hard-learned truth. Xezal's father, God rest his soul, was a hot-tempered man who took out his feelings of powerlessness in the world at large on Xezal and her sister, insisting on total control in at least one area of his life. When she met Rafiq she knew that the only way out from under her father's drunken slaps, the violence of his words, was to get Rafiq to marry her. And no, it wasn't perfect: at the height of his renown, Rafiq frequented the brothels, and she knew of his relationship with another communist's wife. Still, it was better than having stayed at home. Rafiq did not abuse her, he did not swear at her, and when he had money, he spent it on her. He was a doting husband and a kind father, despite his shortcomings.

When she'd tried to tell Siver about Rafiq's infidelities, once, to impart upon her that the world was not fair, certainly not for women, Siver had barely looked up from whatever gossip magazine she was reading and gave a shrug. As if Xezal had deserved it. They never saw things her way, her children, no matter what she did. Like that damned computer: she had worked like a dog for months to build up a buffer, just some money so they would not be on the verge of starvation every month, and what does Rafiq do? He takes all her money and buys a computer with it. And of course the children thought she was a nag, that she was being unreasonable. When she pawned the video camera someone had given Rafiq to buy the children Christmas presents, she was still at fault.

An announcement for a flight to Qom. Final call. Xezal glanced up from her coffee, saw a family staring at the board. Kurds. Xezal was sure of it before she'd even heard them speak. It was the shape of their skulls, the flat back of the head. Rafiq had once told her that because Kurdish babies slept swaddled on stone floors, you could always tell a Kurdish head. She didn't know if this was true: whenever she would ask him a question, he would always give her an answer even if it was wholly made up; they spent thirty-five years together and he never grew comfortable enough with her to just say that he did not know.

The wife of the family wondered (in Kurdish, affirming Xezal's suspicion) why the flight to Slemani was not listed.

'See that row of question marks?' the husband, moustachioed and with his trousers belted well above his waist, said. 'That's our flight. The Arabs were more than happy to start flying to Kurdistan, but they cannot bring themselves to write our cities on their screens, so they just leave it blank, or, like here, write some nonsense. They would rather everyone here missed that flight than write the names of our cities, by Allah.' Xezal recognised that voice, the arrogance of a man-god who pretended that he had all the answers. The arbiter of his family's reality.

Relieved that there was indeed a flight to Slemani, Xezal returned to her coffee, as the parents went to get teas to go for themselves and sodas for their children. 'Wollah, this tea is just water,' the wife complained, and Xezal had to bite her tongue so she wouldn't ask what she expected from a coffee shop. She too had grown up drinking tea, like everyone else in Kurdistan, but the moment she moved to Baghdad with Rafiq she made a point of only drinking coffee, like the consuls and emirs of the city did. The flat bitterness of tea, bridled only by heaps and heaps of sugar, felt unrefined, vulgar almost.

She kept the family in her sight, letting them deal with the difficulties of finding out where to check in, when neither the screens nor the information counter were of any assistance, deciding she would follow them at a safe distance so as to know where to go.

Oh, she was certain that were she to introduce herself, they would be more than happy to take care of her, but she did not like their uncultured demeanour, and wondered what people would say if she was seen consorting with the likes of them, so she contented herself with seeing them slowly push their luggage cart towards the row of check-in counters, a cart atop which they had perilously stacked several boxes, all wrapped in plastic with strings to carry them. Why couldn't they just have suitcases, like everyone else? Why did they have to bring shame to their entire people by travelling like mountain smugglers?

She too had once had her belongings wrapped up like that, but that was a long time ago, when they had to flee for their lives. Of course Xezal hadn't prioritised packing over survival, but what excuse did this family have? Clearly they were not fleeing anywhere, they were going home.

She had hoped life in Slemani would feel like home again, she truly had. But her family there treated her as though her leaving had been a betrayal, as if she had wanted to spend her life in poverty in London. Her sister brought food to her but barely said anything, merely exchanged polite platitudes as though they were complete strangers, except once when Xezal asked if they could go to her father's grave and she became quite agitated.

'That's right, you've never been. You left me with him and never once showed up once he'd passed away. And still, you were the only one he liked.'

Xezal tried to explain that before 1992 there was no way she could have returned without being targeted by Saddam.

'Oh, yes, I forgot, you're so important, Saddam Hussein himself was looking for you.'

Her sister didn't visit much after that. But it wasn't the loneliness that got to Xezal, it was the sense that in her absence, the city had become unrecognisable to her, the people spoke of things she could not fathom, were obsessed with whatever car so-and-so was driving. And they had such ridiculous names for everything. A Land Cruiser was a Monica, after Monica Lewinsky, a Chrysler was an Obama, the yellow taxis were Pikachu. It was like they were speaking an imaginary language, laughing at her outmoded vocabulary. In the time she had been away, there had been a concerted effort to rid the Kurdish language of Arabic loan words and use neologisms instead, though why the English word 'actor' was deemed more Kurdish than the Arabic 'mumasil' she had no idea. If Slemani was home, it was home in name only. Anything that had ever made it a home had been hollowed out and replaced.

Once a month, she would go to the hawala to get whatever money her children had sent her; every month the teller would make a snide comment about how it must be nice to have wealthy children in Europe. She would then spend the money on fuel for the generator, paying the girl and the driver their salaries, and the rest she spent on food and phone cards. But she knew what people thought of her, that she was some well-to-do old lady who kept money for herself, never helping anyone else. She'd lived most of her life abroad, and with that came the assumption of wealth.

Eventually she began entertaining the idea of leaving Kurdistan. She was tired of the oppressive heat, of the petty squabbles and gossiping, of the electricity constantly cutting off. But where could she go? It wasn't even possible to visit Laika, because apparently she was a terrorist in the eyes of the Americans. She'd visited Mohammed, who forgot she was coming, didn't even deign to let her see his apartment, who kept taking her to museums as though she were a tourist. Siver had made it very clear Xezal would be an imposition, and yes, there was no role for her to fill in her daughter's fancy new life in Baghdad (and look where it had gotten her). Xezal checked her phone again: no signal. Her phone was supposed to have international roaming, her driver had talked to the phone company himself. It was ridiculous to be in the same city as your only daughter and not even be able to speak to her.

Xezal drank the last of her coffee. The Kurdish family seemed to have found the correct check-in counter. She threw the cup in a nearby bin and pushed her cart in their direction.

'Slemani?' the man at the check-in counter asked.

'Slemani, yes,' Xezal said, grateful to hear the name of her city spoken aloud.

'You don't have an Iraqi passport? Just British?'

'Just British.'

'OK. It's Gate Three, boarding starts at seven fifty.'

Once she passed the security line she looked around. Four gates, a McDonald's, a small duty-free shop, a cart selling beverages. Compared to the luxurious Terminal 1 with its exclusive stores filled with expensive souvenirs, this was a much more modest affair, befitting the more modest destinations that flew from here. She went to the small duty-free shop, picked up chocolates for her nephews, cigarettes for her brother in-law.

She should get something for her neighbours in Slemani as well, she realised. They kept inviting her over for dinner, and a few months in Xezal had run out of excuses and so said yes, walking up to their door with a tray of baklava her driver had bought from the bazaar. The couple was the most obnoxious kind of nouveau riche, children shipped to Sweden to 'study', marble on every single surface, Swiss watch catalogues conspicuously placed so that guests would see them. They didn't watch Kurdish television, it was too 'embarrassing', no they watched the Turkish shows. They holidayed in Amman, they went to the doctor in Tehran. They were just so awfully predictable. The husband, who owned a housing complex south of the city, would blather on about how most Kurds were just too lazy to become successful in business, they just didn't have the work ethic that they did in China or in America. 'You know this better than anyone, Xezal xan, with all your travels,' he'd say and she'd smile politely. They kept inviting her over, as well, as though she were expected to dine with them once every two weeks. 'Feel free to come over to use our swimming pool any time,' as if she would take off her clothes in the house of some strangers.

But then, when they left to visit their daughter who had just had a baby (she'd married a non-Kurd, of course), the wife left Xezal the keys to their house, asked if she could possibly consider watering the plants, once a week. Xezal said yes, because what else could she say, and expected to tell her girl to do it, but then started thinking of their indoor swimming pool. She'd always wanted to learn how to swim; Rafiq had promised that one day they would take lessons, but of course they never did. She found the bodies she saw on the television so free when they were swimming, so liberated from the world. So one day she brought a nightgown and a towel and, after making sure none of the windows faced the pool, slowly waded into the water, her gown billowing up like a squid. She would look up some videos on her phone, she vowed, she would learn how to do this.

Yes, she should get them something: a bottle of cognac perhaps, they wouldn't know what cognac was probably. She looked at the price tags on the various bottles, tried to calculate what she could buy to spend as much of the local currency she had on her as possible, seeing as she did not intend to return to Dubai any time soon.

Another announcement: the flight to Lahore was boarding. She put down her duty-free bags and sat down near her gate where more flat-headed Kurds had arrived, staring at the screen that was still pretending they were all flying to ?????, and fished out her phone. Still no signal.

In front of her at Gate 3, a young Kurd sat down, plopping down a messenger bag in the seat next to him, and screwed open a bottle of water, taking a loud swig as though he had not had a drink in days. He had sunglasses on, and clothes swarming with various logos that Xezal did not recognise. One of these European Kurds, no doubt, who was involved in petty crime but expected to be given positions and high-paying jobs in Kurdistan, who pretended his mere existence in Europe meant he went to the Sorbonne or Oxford.

Xezal licked her lips, realised she too was thirsty, and went over to the stand selling drinks before she noticed that she had spent all her money at the duty-free. If only she hadn't given the coffee shop all her change. She wondered if the tap water in Dubai was safe to drink. Probably not; this wasn't London. She went back to her seat and checked the time. Ten minutes until boarding. They were bound to give her water on the plane. She could wait.

She'd never enjoyed airports; they were always spaces where bad things could happen to her, where the wrong person looking at the wrong document could make her disappear. Maybe she had been happy when they got on the plane to London that first time. She should have been. But she couldn't remember. She didn't remember much of that first year. She knew that she should remember the flight to London, the rental of their apartment, their first months there, but it was as though that entire year was a void. Everything after what happened at the border had blurred in her mind, as though an aquarelle had been submerged under water. Her first memory after the night they left Iran was of the children fighting over leftovers in Sutton, Mohammed shouting that Siver had eaten far more than her share, that he was hungry. Xezal remembered the realisation that they would not survive if they had to rely on Rafiq, who had grown sullen, resigned, as though he had accepted his lot in life and was just waiting for death. So she sold her jewellery, she sold Faisal II's ring, at a local pawn shop. She thought she would feel anger or despair, but what she felt most of all was relief. Then one day, when she saw an ad for a cleaner pinned to a board at the Woolworths she tore one of the flaps off, kept the number. Back home she looked up the word cleaner in Rafiq's dictionary to ensure she had not misunderstood the job, and when the kids were at school one day she called, reading aloud from a note where she'd translated word-for-word her interest in the position.

For over a decade she cleaned homes in Sutton, Croydon, Wallington, for ten pounds, then fifteen, then twenty, always when the kids were at school, always ensuring she was home by the time Rafiq picked them up. She never told them about this, not wanting to subject her children to the shame of servitude. They needed to remember who they were, Xezal believed, they were a family who had servants, they were not servants themselves. Rafiq obviously knew she did *something* but never enquired, knowing that the question did not have an answer he could live with. He remained happily ignorant, willing to take her money, which, combined with his welfare benefits, allowed them to live. Once her English improved, she began befriending the other maids in the area, nice older women all, who would swap houses to cover for one another when there was a family-related emergency. As Xezal could not clean when the kids were on holiday from school, she needed someone reliable to go to her houses for her. That someone was Olga, a Polish woman who kept talking about her daughter, who was the first person in the family to go to university, how proud she was of her. Sometimes they would clean a house together, splitting the money, knowing they could broaden their client base if they pooled together. 'This is good work,' Olga told Xezal one day when Xezal complained about their lot in life. 'We provide for ones we love; what is more honourable than this?' Xezal did not know what to say. 'What more is there to life?' Xezal thought of her three maids, her cook and her driver who drove her around Baghdad in her very own Mercedes before she'd had to flee; she thought of the clothes she had flown in from Harrods and Le Bon Marché. 'Nothing. Just this,' she shrugged.

A few airline employees appeared, dressed in cheap Iraqi Airways uniforms, pulling their tiny suitcases behind them. Xezal checked the time. Boarding was scheduled to commence any moment now.

The same man who had been at the check-in appeared at the gate, logged into a computer at the desk. It was always surprising to Xezal to see the same people on this side of the airport, it felt as though the gates were a separate space entirely, a pocket out of time. And yet there he stood, a link to the world outside. The microphone crackled as he announced that the flight was ready for boarding. He invited business-class passengers and passengers with small children to board first.

The crowd rose to their feet, ignored the airline's preferred order for boarding, while Xezal remained in her seat, waiting until the rest had boarded, never understanding the need to hurry, as if they did not all have their assigned seats. She kept waiting as the people around her all vanished down the umbilical cord that led them to the plane.

'Final call for flight IA124.'

Xezal opened her purse, located her passport and boarding pass and stood at the end of what was now a very short queue. The man who had checked her in was a Kurd himself, she now realised, welcoming the people ahead of her in Kurdish. 'Baxer ben,' he would say, the use of the formal plural for welcoming in Kurdish, as he handed each passenger their green Iraqi passport and their boarding pass. 'Baxer ben.' Xezal wondered if this was something he was supposed to do, or if he could get into trouble for speaking Kurdish.

It was Xezal's turn. She handed over her documents. The man looked down at her British passport and gave it back to her with a smile and a rip of the boarding pass.

'Welcome.'

THREE

Reckoning (2011)

THE SKY A PAINFULLY BRIGHT BLUE, cloud-threads hanging low, threatening to dissolve across a vast uniform desert. The whine of the wind incongruous to the stillness of the scenery, as though it were a stock effect, added in post-production. A narrow, paved road slashes through the dunes, and on the horizon a row of cars become visible, couched in the blurry shimmer of a mirage.

The first car begins to decelerate, its red lights an indicator for the following cars in the convoy to do the same. They slow down, they stop.

Ahead of the cars, two men are walking a tribe of goats down the road, a stubborn tribe that does not heed klaxons, necessitating that two of the drivers get out to help the goat herders shoo them away. While the drivers wait for the road to be cleared, two children exit one of the cars, keen to play with the animals, the carefree playing of toddlers who would never hear the word no. Their mother, wearing large designer sunglasses and a light headscarf, carrying herself with the casual glamour of the infinitely wealthy, is watching them from afar when an American businessman lowers the window of the car he's sitting in and tells the woman that if she wants, she can swap cars with him, to sit next to her husband. The American's business partner, dressed in a white Arabic thawb, thanks the American as his wife and the two children get into his car, the back seat of the Land Cruiser now alive with the flouncing of children.

From a satellite camera this change of seating arrangements is observed by an intelligence officer seated in a Sensitive Compartmented Information Facility halfway across the world, his hand on a joystick, his thumb hovering above a red button. The intelligence officer looks over at the others in the room, a nervous glance performed in the direction of his superior. The wife and children had not been identified as targets.

While they contemplate this new set of parameters, a black Nissan SUV is noticed on the satellite feed speeding through the pixelated desert, the vehicle bobbing up and down the dunes, trying to reach the convoy. An intelligence officer's finger identifies the vehicle on a screen, asking who the hell that is. The car is now driving parallel to the convoy, the driver waving for the cars to stop. Bodyguards are pointing handguns out of their windows at the white man who is shouting something inaudible to them. A decision is made, somewhere, and the convoy block the man's car between them, a dozen soldiers in camouflage spilling out of the vehicles, pointing rifles. The man carefully exits the vehicle, holding his hands high in the air. He has a ruggedness to him that almost but not entirely masks his magnetism. The soldiers bark orders at him as he tries to explain the convoy is on the verge of being blown up.

In the Sensitive Compartmented Information Facility, a suited man tells the intelligence officer to take the target out.

'Roger,' says the intelligence officer, who proceeds to position a digitised crosshair over the vehicle in which the man and his family sit, and presses the red button on his joystick. 'Four miles.'

The white man carefully approaches the vehicle with the targeted family. He is not saying anything, keeping his arms up in the air. The man in the car recognises him from somewhere, a meeting he's had. Before he understands what is going on, the drone's missile reaches his vehicle and,

no,

wait,

a constellation of pixels deforms the car, the chassis now separated from the wheels. The world dissolves, breaks into coloured polygons as a circle of dots keeps spinning, spinning.

Laika Hama Hardi wiggled two fingers across a trackpad to make a cursor appear above the almost exploding vehicle, a cursor that dove to the bottom of the screen, dragged a rhombus-shaped icon back through the scene's timeline, the dead becoming alive again, as the video buffered, the red of the visible future edging ahead. The laptop was connected to the same network as his server, which was in the midst of processing several financial algorithms, eating up available bandwidth. A yank of the ethernet cable from the side of the laptop followed, cutting off the tongue of the cable's 8P8C modular connector, a tiny piece of plastic that would have to be retrieved and disposed of later. Scrolling down through the randomised poem of wireless network names – BringWeed, Drop it like its Hotspot, Belkin 2.4, John's Network, dlink, Mom Use This One – Laika located his own: 2WIRE982. Click, play, click, the car exploding yet again. It had less of an impact this time, the attack that was intended as the climax of an otherwise pretty dry geopolitical thriller. It felt unavoidable. Soon enough the movie's credits scrolled past. He closed the video player, logged back into his terminal.

For the past few months, Laika had been working on an algorithm, one that mirrored the Goldman Sachs high-frequency trading bots. Whatever Goldman Sachs purchased, or sold, his bot would purchase or sell microseconds later. Initial attempts had resulted in failure, and he had lost tens of thousands of dollars before he realised that since he lived in Brooklyn, the lag-time from his apartment to the New York Stock Exchange was too high. (This was, of course, something that he could have looked into before he wasted nearly a hundred thousand dollars.) The New York Stock Exchange allowed for corporate traders to rent server space within the building itself, thus being able to offer any registered trading firm a platform that averaged 99 percentile latency with a round-trip time of 125 microseconds, allowing for algorithms with ever more complex variables to decide on whether to sell or buy, resulting in thousands and thousands of trades a minute, operating on a timescale that made the speed of human thought seem outright geological in comparison. The world may be connected, we may be able to communicate with each other through 'instant' messages (a misnomer if there ever was one, a trader being able to make over 250 trades in the 'instant' it takes to receive an instant message), but proximity to the centre still matters, even as information is being transferred close to the speed of light, those fractions of milliseconds are what separates us. They are everything.

The internet was meant to democratise trading, to make the economy truly global, and yet it had resulted in a more site-specific economy than ever before. Since what mattered now was how quickly one could send a buy or sell order, and since data was transmitted through fibre-optic cables at a speed that approached that of the speed of light in a vacuum, a trader's physical distance from the stock exchange's servers mattered enormously. If your order took longer to arrive, due to the fact that the information had further to travel down fibre-optic cables, it was like conducting business with someone in the future. You were bound to lose.

This apartment — a former office building remodelled into condominiums by a famous architect and kitted out with a corporate fibre-optic internet line, across from the stock exchange — was advertised on a website catering to Wall Street workers. It belonged to a hedge-fund manager who had used it when it was too late for the hour-long commute back to Cove Neck or for when he wanted to have sex with someone who was not his spouse. The hedge-fund manager, who was now a former hedge-fund manager courtesy of the collapse of Lehman Brothers Inc., had put the apartment up for sale but in the current economic climate he could not find a buyer and so he reached out to people willing to be a show-home manager. The arrangement forced Laika to be pedantically clean, making the bed to hotel standards every morning (he had learned how to do this by watching a YouTube video), wiping the shower after every use. Until someone wanted to buy an $18, 900,000 apartment at 15 Broad Street, this was his home.

New tab. On Twitter, someone had written, 'The awkward moment when your Arab friend says, I'm the bomb!' It had 990 retweets. Someone had replied with a 'lol if only they didn't live in mudhuts . . .' and an ASCII drawing of a plane crashing into a building. Laika wondered if this was something the sender of the tweet had created themselves or if it was copied and pasted from another corner of the web. He clicked on a button to report the tweet but when the options appeared, asking whether the tweet was suspicious or spam, abusive or harmful, Laika wasn't sure what exactly he wanted to report.

Xezal would always tell Laika how afraid he was of the Iraqi jets that flew over Slemani, how the dim roar of a passing airplane would terrify him even when they were in London. Laika, having been born in Iran well after his family had left Slemani behind, never knew what it was that Xezal was referring to. I wasn't even born then, he would tell her, and his mother would just shake her head. 'You were so afraid, my love. So very afraid.' He wondered what children were afraid of now, when the enemy was invisible, when the person who could kill you sat in an office halfway across the world. In the movie he'd just watched, the intelligence officer who triggered the drone attack was depicted as an automaton, a hand on a joystick not unlike the villain in the *Inspector Gadget* cartoons, and of course it's probably accurate in terms of how drone operators are seen by the military, as mere extensions of the machine. But the operators zoom in on the faces of those they kill, they press the button. There are trauma counsellors who specialise in the effects of being a drone operator, just as there are motivational quotes and images of sunny beaches hung above the monitors. Rafiq would always tell his children that capitalism would like nothing more than to turn the oppressed classes into machines, and that we needed to fight to retain our humanity, our dignity. Rafiq said a lot of things.

Laika gave a can of Coke Zero a little shake to see if there was any more left. Just enough for one sip, which he slurped before walking over to the kitchen to get a new beverage, his bare feet slapping against the Brazilian walnut floors, crushing the old can in his fist before throwing it in the white plastic bag by the apartment door. He returned, drink in hand, the *tschitt* of excess gas emerging from the now open can, the *crnk* of the tab being pulled back, followed by the metallic dance of bubbles raging against the rim, trying to get out. He took a gulp, let out a sound of contentment. 'We must rethink the machines,' Rafiq kept insisting to Laika throughout his childhood. 'These were made by the capitalists, so when the revolution comes it will be your job to rethink the machines. You are so good with computers, just keep in mind that the tools of the master cannot dismantle the master's house. Remember that.' Laika clicked on the video of a news clip purporting to show a drone strike in Iraq, uploaded by BBC News onto their YouTube channel, only to be met by a black screen and *the uploader has not made this video available in your country*. He stared at his own face, visible due to the lack of content, his already weak jawline rendered invisible in the dimmed reflection of his laptop screen. A face his ex-girlfriend Lotti had once called 'vacant'. He thought of googling Lotti, finding out what she looked like now, what she was doing. She once told him that she hated the way he breathed, a sound she described as a fart in reverse. He was sure she also said nice things to him, sometimes, but he could not remember any of them. Sod it. Sod her.

Command + N, new window, Applications, a scroll through word processors and browsers before he found the icon he was looking for. He logged onto his VPN, chose London as the server for his IP address and suddenly his computer was, for all intents and purposes, based across the Atlantic Ocean, the YouTube video now available.

The sweating can of Coke, droplets trickling down its side, had left a ring of condensation on the powder-coated steel desk he was using, and Laika hurried back into the kitchen to get a paper towel. A quick swipe across the desk. Good as new.

The ads on his social media switched to UK ads, the Taco Bell offerings replaced by Nando's Peri-Peri chicken, Saks Fifth Avenue morphing into the online retailer Farfetch.

Click.

The video, in the end, was not as spectacular as its all-caps title seemed to suggest. The footage, recently leaked by a Specialist by the name of Manning, who had smuggled a CD-ROM on which 'Lady Gaga' had been scribbled to escape the curiosity of the NSA, was more reminiscent of Paris Hilton's night-vision sex-tape than the crimes against humanity Laika had just seen portrayed in a well-regarded Hollywood film. These acts had become so commonplace that even their documentation seemed dull, uneventful. The movie seemed infinitely more realistic than this anaesthetised drone foot-age, more responsible in the manner it depicted death, in all its gory reality. No wonder people weren't more outraged: this wasn't the Vietnam War's Napalm Girl, this was merely a primitive video game.

When Laika was a child and the chemical bombings of Halabja took place, Rafiq began a campaign to inform western media of what had happened. He had thousands of postcards printed bearing the horrific photograph by the Iranian photographer Kaveh Golestan, showing a little girl frozen mid-cry, her eyes dead, her skin somehow no longer skin at all. For months, Laika would walk around their apartment, turning over the postcards so that the informative text would face upwards, rather than the dead girl's face. When boxes of these postcards were stored under Laika's bed, he told his mother that he was uncomfortable with the image, that it scared him. Xezal looked him in the eye and said, with surprising harshness, that this was the world. This was how it looked. Laika did not have the luxury to look away from it.

Of course, the postcards did nothing. The news kept discussing the Broadway success of the *Les Misérables* musical. The IRA attack in the Netherlands which killed three British soldiers was analysed by a hundred pundits, revisited by politicians who swore Never Again. The CIA kept peddling the – temporarily expedient – conspiracy theory that the bombings were not orchestrated by the US ally Saddam Hussein, but rather by Iran, a conspiracy theory repeated years later by Edward Said in a newspaper wherein he stated that 'the claim that Iraq gassed its own citizens has often been repeated. At best, this is uncertain.' ('When it comes to Kurds, the brightest minds consciously make themselves dim,' Rafiq said, tossing the paper across the living room for effect.) There was no interest in 5,000 lives lost in a Kurdish village.

At one of the many demonstrations Rafiq dragged them to, in front of the Iraqi embassy, a young blonde woman came up to them asking them what the protest was for. Laika remembered thinking she was pretty, like she belonged on a billboard. Rafiq, in his broken, aggressive-sounding English, launched into one of his passionate tirades about the injustice suffered by the Kurds, about the need for solidarity amongst the working classes of the world to stop the ravages of imperialism. 'Your problem is with Iraq. Why are you blocking *our* streets, then? Go back to your own country and protest,' the woman spat and shouldered her way through the crowd. 'We don't have a country! This is what is the problem!' Rafiq shouted to her back.

Laika remembered the thrill he felt when his father clicked through Kurdish phrases on Encarta, an acknowledgement from the world that they existed. This enthusiasm was contagious to Laika, who would cherish any odd references to Kurds in pop culture. The prologue to William Peter Blatty's *Exorcist* taking place in Mosul, the characters asking Father Merrin whether he wanted tea in Kurdish. The movie, of course, had the characters speaking Arabic. 'They're Kurds, though, children. Don't forget that,' Rafiq said, clearly proud enough of the brief allusion to the Kurdish people (an allusion that indicated that Kurds had some primal link to demons, at that) that he made his three children sit through a film wherein a demonically possessed girl fucked herself with a crucifix. The character Sniper Wolf from the video game *Metal Gear Solid* whose backstory was that she was born in Iraqi Kurdistan in 1983. The reference in Zola's *The Ladies' Delight* to the 'beautiful Kurdish carpets'. Laika dog-eared that page, cherished it as though he had discovered something special. 'The French used to have an idiom,' his French teacher said when Laika said, *Je m'appelle Laika, je viens du Kurdistan.* 'As generous as a Kurd. *Généreux comme un kurde.* My parents used to say this.' Generous demonic snipers who wove beautiful carpets. This is who they were.

Every time there was a war in the region, newspapers ran articles explaining what Kurds were and why they were being killed. 'They write of us like we are strange animals,' Rafiq kept saying. 'Something you can only see in a zoo.' Still, as someone who had more than once had to explain the consequences of the British mandate in Mesopotamia to British people who asked where Kurdistan was located, he understood that the military found it easier to just resort to the night-vision abstractions of drone warfare. Fewer explanations required. Years earlier, Baudrillard had reached a similar conclusion in *The Gulf War Did Not Take Place*, namely that 'the absence of images' of actual humans was neither 'accidental nor due to censorship but to the impossibility of illustrating this indeterminacy of the war'.

What Laika remembered most of the first Gulf War was his mother crying every time the news showed footage of Baghdad being bombed. 'I wonder if our home has been hit,' she would say to Rafiq, who would be reading about the F-117 stealth bomber, which had become one of the war's main protagonists. 'Our home is no longer our home, my dear,' he would mumble, turning the page in his issue of *Time Magazine* featuring an American soldier with his eyes closed in pain or ecstasy and the headline 'What War Would Be Like' on the cover, and a long article about the development of the stealth bomber. The 'invisible aircraft' was featured strongly in accompanying US propaganda, leaflets dropped among the Iraqi army containing constant references to the might of the invisible plane destroying high-value targets accompanied by the warning 'Escape now and save yourselves' in State Department-vetted Arabic. A precursor to the contemporary drone, the F-117 stealth bomber was the first appearance of a near-mythical enemy that could strike from above, strikes that evoked a notion of divine retribution which fuelled so much American war rhetoric. 'They think they're gods,' Xezal would tut. 'If they rid the world of Saddam, I will worship them as gods for as long as I live,' Rafiq would reply.

The first target to be destroyed by the F-117 was, fittingly, the building that housed the Baath Party's communication centre. Old media destroyed by an agent of new media. As Virilio claimed in an interview, the Gulf War was 'a local war in comparison with the Second World War, with regard to its battlefield. But it was a worldwide war on the temporal level of representation, on the level of media, thanks to the satellite acquisition of targets, thanks to the tele-command of the war. [. . .] For the first time, as opposed to the Vietnam War, it was a war rendered live, worldwide – with, of course, the special effects, all the information processing organised by the Pentagon and the censorship by the major states.' Laika remembered how he came home from school one day to find a map of the Middle East stretched across their dining table, with Siver's Barbies, and Mohammed and Laika's GI Joes standing in for various factions now that Operation Desert Storm had commenced. 'This is the end of that tyrant, my son,' Rafiq had said, placing Great Shape Barbie on top of Baghdad, positioning her next to Cobra Commander. Laika remembered his parents watching nothing but CNN for months, the looped voice of Darth Vader intoning that this. is. CNN, that the skies over Baghdad had been illuminated. (For years Laika misheard this as *eliminated*.) They had such hope, Xezal and Rafiq, that this life in exile would soon be over. That these were the final days of Saddam Hussein.

The home was always a world unto its own, with distinct moods and priorities. When Laika first kissed a girl (after school, against the wall of the gymnasium, trying in vain to twist his pelvis so that the girl – Stacy her name was – wouldn't notice the bulge of his erect cock in his jeans, perilously close to her thigh) he was skipping home, worried that his parents would notice his dumb grin, his mindless bliss, and ask him what had happened. He needn't have worried: once home he saw the map of the Middle East spread out over the kitchen table, the action figures representing armies. 'Sargallu, Bargallu, Gwezeela and Chalawi, all these villages have been destroyed, the men dead, the houses bulldozed,' Rafiq said when Laika asked if there was anything to eat. 'Thousands of our brothers and sisters. Thousands, dead.' Laika, suddenly ashamed of the joy he had felt only minutes ago, now finding his feelings embarrassing, went to the room he then still shared with Mohammed and cried, though he was not sure why he was crying. That Monday when he went back to school he avoided Stacy. As far as he could recall, he never spoke to her again.

Command + T. New tab.

Someone tweeted a photograph of a blue square they had painted on their property to make it look like they had a swimming pool on Google Earth. 'Fake,' someone else replied. A thread about Roger Fisher, a Harvard Law professor, who had once suggested that the code needed for a nuclear launch should be kept in a capsule that would be implanted next to the heart of a volunteer. 'If ever the President wanted to fire nuclear weapons, the only way he could do so would be for him first, with his own hands, to kill one human being. He has to look at someone and realize what death is – what an innocent death is,' Fisher proposed. 'Blood on the White House carpet.' The Pentagon's reaction was one of horror, and they dismissed the proposal swiftly. 'Having to kill someone would distort the President's judgment. He might never push the button.' Instead, for almost forty years, the nuclear launch codes were 000000. It was deemed safer, in stressful moments, to not run the risk of forgetting the code.

Laika typed in 'collateral murder' in the browser window's search bar, the title of the WikiLeaks drone strike video. But before the search engine would allow him to complete the search, he was made to complete a Completely Automated Public Turing Test to Tell Computers and Humans Apart, to successfully impersonate a human for a machine. He no longer had to transcribe squiggles as he once did, the browser now preferred for him to identify street signs on a grid of 3×3 square photographs in order to prove that he was not a robot. A real-world Voight-Kampff test. This happened whenever he browsed with a VPN turned on, his search engine sensing there was something not quite right about the connection, and he was happy to oblige, clicking three of the nine photographs. Laika knew that it didn't matter which squares he pressed, really, as long as his cursor moved in a way that was deemed to be that of a human. There were rumours in the tech media that the company that developed the search engine was also in the process of developing software for self-driving cars, and that this ritual of clicking on cars and road signs was merely a way for them to perfect their algorithm, honing their machines all while pretending that the users needed to do so to prove that they themselves were not machines.

Click.

In the first few links, he found a response to the leak by a US spokesperson, who had told Fox News that the video only gave 'a limited perspective', as it 'only tells you a portion of the activity that was happening that day. Just from watching that video, people cannot understand the complex battles that occurred. You are seeing only a very narrow picture of the events.' Beneath the video, an ad for a jacket he had looked at once that was now following him across the internet, a digital stalking. Open tab.

In the run-up to the Iraq war, Siver would often come by the house and question the logic for the invasion. Saddam had given up his weapons of mass destruction, she would say in a rehearsed monotone, stealing glances at her engagement ring as if still surprised to see a diamond on her finger. This was a war over oil, which would lead to the death of hundreds of thousands of civilians, most of whom had nothing to do with the Freudian squabbles between the boy Bush and Saddam, who tried to kill his dad. Of course, she only said this to Laika when Xezal was out of the room. She knew better than to speak her mind in front of her mother.

In a sense she was right: civilians had died. Though it was impossible to know how many. This, too, seemed to Laika to be a feature, not a bug. Link after link merely provided estimations. A cluster sample survey by UNDP stated that the number of deaths of civilians and military personnel in Iraq in the aftermath of the 2003 invasion was as low as 18,000 people. A survey published in the *Lancet* estimated excess Iraqi deaths as a consequence of war to be as high as 943,000. Nobody knew, just as nobody knew the number of dead Kurds in mass graves, the number of Kurds gassed to death. Nobody cared to know. An article in the *Washington Post* claimed that the Pentagon had altered the 'Department of Defense Law of War Manual' so that journalists who died accompanying armed militias or terrorists could be counted among the 'enemy combatants', since 'journalists may be members of the armed forces, persons authorized to accompany the armed forces, or unprivileged belligerents'. The number of enemies were amplified, the number of civilians obfuscated. Some lives mattered this little, with not even a dataset to serve as monument. All the while, the earth's technosignatures would remain far longer than any corpses, the method of devastation more lasting than the devastation itself, echoing its warning to other planets. Here be savages. We were, indeed, seeing only a very narrow picture of the events.

'To be a Kurd is to be intimately acquainted with injustice, an injustice so heavy that it cannot be carried alone,' Rafiq had told him, worried that Laika spent too much time in his room, unwilling to converse with his family, seemingly even without any friends to spend the weekends with. And though Laika didn't see the problem in wanting to be alone, he did understand what his father meant. His most painful childhood memories were linked to the feeling of injustice. When he was in Year Three, someone in class threw a rubber at Nishka, a painfully shy girl who had recently arrived from India and who wore horrid glasses that everyone knew were given out to kids for free by the NHS, instantly singling her out for bullying. The rubber hit the side of her head hard, making the NHS specs fly off to the floor. The teacher demanded to know who it was, and somehow, Laika was blamed. 'Just tell us that you did it, Laika,' the teacher said, as Laika cried and swore he had nothing to do with it. 'Well,' the teacher said as the bell rang, 'I'm very disappointed.' Laika waited for the others to leave the classroom before he collected his things and slunk out. Matthew, the son of a vicar who rarely spoke to Laika, had been waiting outside, and put his arm around him. Laika burst into tears at the hug. 'Jesus loves you,' Matthew said. 'And if you admit you did it, you will feel free.' Laika wriggled out of the hug, told Matthew to go fuck himself. Fuck you and fuck Jesus. Later that day (this he usually didn't want to dwell on too much), he spat at Nishka, calling her an ugly cunt.

Ping (from his torrent client, an episode of a TV show had just finished downloading, something to watch with dinner).

Click. Hyperlink. Click. An image of the situation room where Obama had given the order to kill Bin Laden, where everyone in the room was wearing Princess Beatrice's Royal Wedding Hat. An image of Disney's Little Mermaid, wearing hipster glasses with a macro stating Don't Call Me Ariel, My Name is Helvetica. A GIF of Honey Boo Boo retweeted into his feed, wherein she said that sometimes she didn't know whether she was real or not. 'Honestly, same,' someone replied who had received hundreds of stars.

New tab.

He found himself reading an old piece from *The New York Times*. In it the journalist, Ron Suskind, quoted a presidential aide, a paragraph that Laika copied and pasted into a program, Evernote, that functioned like an extension of Laika's memory.

'The aide said that guys like me were "in what we call the reality-based community," which he defined as people who "believe that solutions emerge from your judicious study of discernible reality." . . . "That's not the way the world really works anymore," he continued. 'We're an empire now, and when we act, we create our own reality. And while you're studying that reality – judiciously, as you will – we'll act again, creating other new realities, which you can study too, and that's how things will sort out. We're history's actors . . . and you, all of you, will be left to just study what we do."

It only took one set of parameters (aide + 'reality-based community') to uncover the identity of this aide. A few clicks later, another quote by the same person, again to Ron Suskind but this time for

Esquire: 'We will fuck him. Do you hear me? We will fuck him. We will ruin him. Like no one has ever fucked him!' The quote did not clarify whom the aide was referring to, and the *Esquire* article was behind a paywall. Laika did not care enough to pay.

A cursor over a red circle, a click, a browser window closed.

15:52. Normal trading hours were almost at an end. Almost.

When Mohammed went into finance, Xezal and Rafiq would moan through the night over their eldest son's bad life choices. Yet they always supported Laika for his interest in 'computers', not understanding that he, too, was learning about money, that money was all there was. Why were agrarian societies in Western Europe grain-based during the Middle Ages? Because the king's tax collector could easily see the crops, easily decide how much should be given to the crown. Why did so many regents find the reformation appealing? No more taxes to be paid to the Pope. Everything was money.

When the first user of the online virtual world Second Life began selling penis add-ons for the equivalent of five US dollars, enabling avatars to have penetrative sex in the game for the first time, he quickly became a multi-millionaire. Laika decided he would cash in on this phenomenon: after all, the Maldives and Sweden had already built embassies, Adidas and American Apparel had shops selling virtual clothes for the game's avatars. Laika invested in a porn store, not realising that a society where everyone was free to have sex with whomever they wanted had little need for virtual pornography when real pornography was only a few browser clicks away. He lost a considerable portion of his money during his Second Life venture.

A chime.

The market was closed. The laptop reconnected to the ethernet once again, the cable wobblier now that the connector had snapped off. After 3.8 million transactions made between 09:00 and now, the $518,374.83 he had started the day with had turned into $502,840.12. Goldman Sachs had, during the same trading hours, made money. Something was still off.

In the beginning, he had been obsessively watching the trades as they happened, but not only was this pointless – his bot being able to make over 500 trades in a literal blink of an eye – but it gave him too much anxiety, seeing money appear and disappear before he had even had time to process what had happened, let alone why. What mattered was not whether he made money on an individual trade, it was whether his algorithm worked. And it didn't. There had to be something he was missing. It could be the Exponential Moving Average, or perhaps he needed to improve the candlestick patterns in his pattern-recognition parameters.

A Google search for 'pattern recognition' led to a video on Vimeo, a poor phone recording from a Bristol gallery where Hito Steyerl's piece *In Free Fall* was screening. The badly centred projection showed a junkyard filled with discarded planes being sold for scrap metal, the financial crisis having rendered the planes redundant. 'These are all ghosts,' the junkyard's bearded owner says, before the film focuses on one plane in particular that had been blown up in the 1994 film *Speed* and its remaining parts sold to China which used them in their production of DVD discs.

The video continued, its sound muffled as the person recording had put a finger over the phone's microphone, but the point it made was clear: contemporary reality was a tangle of timelines and increasingly the orchestrated artifice of a Hollywood movie felt more real than reality itself. We have had bot wars and algo wars, programs pitted against each other, able to make over two trades every microsecond. It takes a full second, so over 2 million times as long, for a thought to register in the human mind. An employee at the gallery hissed at the person filming to turn off his phone and the video went dark, before it was replaced with thumbnails of other videos that the site's algorithm suggested to Laika. Before he had a chance to think about which one he wanted to see, a clip auto-played.

An interview, a dimly lit studio, Charlie Rose's grim face, a bearded man waving his hands. 'Men ruled the stock market. I don't mean humans, I mean men. Women weren't allowed into the London Stock Exchange until 1973, we didn't have a female trader at the New York Stock Exchange until 1967 when Muriel Siebert was deemed eligible. They had to build a toilet stall for her, since there were no women's bathrooms. Men ruled the stock market. And maybe Thatcher felt this was unfair, that men were flawed because humans were flawed, so we built machines to be able to have a perfect system without realizing that men would be the ones to build the machines. And not even men, boys.'

Close tab.

He noted the NYSE's value, to compare with what it would start at next morning, after traders had spent the night trying to understand why the algorithms did what they had done, adjusting the prices accordingly. We still applied these artificial opening and closing times to our stock exchanges when in reality the machines could go on for ever, trading at all hours of the day. It was important to retain a semblance of control.

Of course, Goldman Sachs had a distinct advantage in that the New York Stock Exchange leased them access to a server in the building itself, ensuring the fastest lag-time to the exchange's servers. The Goldman Sachs server was connected by a fibre-optic cable that was measured to be exactly as long as all the other trading-firm servers housed in the building, so that no single actor would have the advantage of even a fraction of a microsecond. Laika, being a sole trader with no industry clout whatsoever, couldn't even reach a customer service representative to as much as enquire about renting server space within the New York Stock Exchange. Still, he was geographically close enough. There had to be a way to mirror the trades being made efficiently enough so that he could make money if Goldman Sachs did.

www.forexforums.com, 'mirror trading', search. 472 results. **BigCh33seFastCh33se:** I've found my algo works best when my mirror trader account has over 50000 usd in it, I think the higher balance makes more flexible trading possible. **Myothercarisahelicopter:** I've developed a platform that is 100% foolproof, DM me if you want in! **$exBot:** the music video to Celine Dion's It's all coming back to me now is WILD y'all.

Quit Chrome.

A siren.

Whenever the UK would test its remaining civil defence sirens between August and September each year, Xezal would be on edge, stealing cigarettes from Rafiq and making the children promise to never speak of this. 'Nothing good ever comes of a siren. Somewhere there is a tragedy.' Mohammed tried to explain that they were just tests, that there was nothing to worry about. 'We saw a lot of things, children, we saw too much,' she'd say, inhaling a stolen cigarette and staring out of the window.

Laika wondered if the sound he'd just heard had anything to do with the bodies scattered across the pavement outside. He walked over to the window, his feet leaving brief, ghost-like sweat marks on the wooden floor. No, the bodies were still there. Police, decked out in futuristic assault gear, paced between outstretched limbs, military-grade machine guns in hand, clearly not intending to do anything about them, for now.

It was an eerie sight, hundreds upon hundreds of anonymous people just off the stairs of the stock exchange, victims of a world economy that did not and never would consider their plight. A passer-by briefly stopped, raised a phone, and took a photograph. This picture would be cropped, filtered, aestheticised, before it was shared, sent across the world with a hashtag, a caption, optimised for likes. Laika took a picture of the person taking the picture, not quite knowing what to do with it other than save it in his Evernote folder.

A whistle.

Slowly, the bodies on the street below started to move, stretching into life. The protest, a highly publicised lie-in, was over. The activists hugged each other, as though they were survivors of some awful tragedy, which, in a way, they were.

They began their march back to Zuccotti Park, holding up their signs, starting chants about the unfairness of the system, the stranglehold that the 1 per cent held over the other 99. They disappeared from view, as they returned to the encampments Laika had only seen in photographs, several buildings obstructing his view of the park itself. He understood their anger, but there was no way to stop the machinery, there was a reason Marx called capitalism a vampire. When Naomi Klein's No Logo came out, the world was appalled at the rampant consumerism, at the inhuman conditions in which mass-market clothing was produced by children. He, like many others, boycotted a number of brands, assiduously checking where each item of clothing that he purchased was made, made sure to be a conscious consumer. And then, within a year, the collective outrage was gone. People went back to buying trainers made by Bangladeshi children and fast-fashion T-shirts cheaper than ought to be possible. Even as badly maintained factories burned down, as more and more reports showed the shell-game corporations played to remove themselves from any responsibility vis-à-vis their subcontractors, even though we all knew, we kept consuming. Not even finding SOS notes hidden in our clothes changed anything, notes sewn in secret pockets by the labourers who had made them, we kept going back, attempting to accept as truth the corporate excuse that these notes were simply part of a hoax. We knew what was happening, of course we knew, but we didn't know what to do about it. Just as we knew how animals were being treated so that we could have low-price cheeseburgers, just as we knew that our time on earth was ending, and soon, if we kept flying, driving, consuming the way we did. And yet there were no solutions, except individual ones, moralistic choices to be a vegan, to not own a car, to recycle, while the rest of the world careened further out of control. The machine cannot be stopped; corporate interests always win. A first-world country could outsource its factories to the third world, patting itself on the back for being climate neutral while ensuring pollution would continue somewhere else. To be an amoral consumer was simply too convenient, too easy, too cheap. Laika sympathised with the protesters, of course he did, but he couldn't think of anything save the complete destruction of the world as we knew it that would have an actual effect.

A sharp metallic drilling sound. Doorbell.

He went out of the study, into the impractical but visually impressive circular hallway that led to the apartment's seven doors, catching a glimpse of himself in the full-length mirror that was propped up against the wall. He quickly looked away, not pleased with his slouching posture, his flapping limbs. To think of himself as having a body at all was not something Laika enjoyed, the flesh and skin he was constricted in something to overcome, rather than indulge in. It was so limiting, to have a body, to be restricted to a time and place. Dressing in the same clothes every day (dark grey sweatpants, of which he had four, black oversized T-shirt, of which he had eight, and a dark grey cable-knit cardigan, of which he had two) was a way for him to dismiss the body, instead of obsessing over what clothes to wrap it in.

Laika opened the door to the apartment and picked up the brown paper bag that had been left there, the delivery person nowhere to be seen (as per Laika's instructions to the company). The bag contained his dinners for the upcoming week, calibrated in accordance with his estimated daily calorie needs. He put the bag down in the kitchen and checked his menu. Tofu with broccoli. Organic vegan stir fry with wild ginger rice. Fennel risotto. Thai lemongrass tofu. Tilapia with scallion sriracha pesto. Okra and lentil soup. Chickpea tagine with couscous and peaches. A bag of fruit, which was an add-on that he had selected. He had no idea what tilapia was, and he disliked fennel, which reminded him of an old man's cough. The stir fry would have to do for today. He put the box in the oven, setting a timer on his phone, and put the other meals in the fridge, empty but for nine cans of Coke Zero.

Notification.

An email from a company called DiJiFi, informing him that the VHS tape he had sent them to digitise was in bad shape, that they could not guarantee that all of the material would be transferred accurately. Laika wiped his hands and tapped a reply on the phone's screen. *This is fine, please proceed. Please find attached my card information.* He fished his card holder out of his cardigan and tapped in his debit card details for them to charge.

Payment details sent, he pocketed his phone and card holder, and went back to his laptop.

BREAKING: Charity invested millions in arms manufacturing company. Charity Executive: 'We did not know what the banks were doing with our money.' Read more:

Related Stories: Global Conservation Charity accused of funding guards who torture and kill.

Click. Hyperlink. Click. Hyperlink. An actor talking about tiger blood. A sponsored post, almost indistinguishable from a real news item, inviting him to invest in Cyprus. Click. Recently he'd seen more and more of these ads, offering passports to St Kitts and Nevis (USD 250,000), a golden visa to Portugal (USD 90,000), an investor visa to the United Kingdom (USD 1,500,000). All the rules that restricted much of humanity could be, legally, subverted with enough capital at hand. He skimmed over the details, knowing that the British passport in his duffel bag by the door had only been granted to him through exile and the willingness of a Home Office employee. New tab. 'Visa-free countries to visit with Iraqi passport'. Click. Svalbard, Bermuda, Dominica, Micronesia, Niue, Cook Islands, Pitcairn.

Timer.

He tapped his phone silent and went back to the kitchen, sliding the container out of the oven using only his fingertips, making sure not to burn himself (there was an oven-mitt, but he didn't use it so as to not get it dirty), and unwrapped a pair of chopsticks that had been sent with the food (an extra $2 per order). He placed his dinner on a trivet and carried it, along with a new can of Coke Zero, to the study, eating while watching the latest episode of a TV show about a corporate executive who has a meltdown at work and is sent to a holistic rehab clinic. She returns full of desire to change the world for the better but is constantly hindered by her own imperfections and the built-in dysfunctions of the corporate world. It was surprising to see this topic – how to be a good person in a world where 'good' is often seen as gullible or naïve – play out in a prime-time television show. It was less surprising to him that the ratings for the show were dismal. The episode opened with an establishing shot of Woodland Hills, in California, and the modernist Warner Center Plaza III skyscraper, which served as the location for the show's evil corporation. There was something unsettling about the building, its mirrored exterior making it look as though it were in camouflage, akin to the alien's invisibility system in the 1987 movie *Predator*, the rawest commerce hiding in plain sight, blending in with the topography of the Santa Monica mountains. 'Of course, the world is vast, and complex,' the lead actress breathed in the voiceover, as though she were whispering secrets to the audience, or holding a yoga class. 'To understand it, you can reflect your whole life away. And what have you done? Nothing. At some point, you must do. It's not enough to have good intentions. You must act on them.' What struck him as he watched this odd little show was how its main character communicated almost exclusively in bromides and self-help clichés, and yet, somehow, was able to use these blunt, overused tools to say something meaningful. It was unclear how the show managed this, but perhaps it was true, the more vapid the cliché, the sharper the canines of the real truth it covers. Eating alone, scowling in the low California sun, the main character looks at her oblivious co-workers, laughing together over lunch. It is not clear how much of her actions are from a sense of moral obligation and how much she simply wants to get back at her co-workers, who have shunned her since her meltdown. In a fantasy sequence, four SUVs drive up to the building, and out walk a dozen government agents, all African-American, many with natural hair and headgear redolent of the Nation of Islam. They begin arresting the members of the corporation's board, in slow-mo, as a dramatic operatic score plays. Later in the episode, a Muslim character, fired for an offence he did not commit, screamed *fuck this place* up towards the building. This was an astute choice: more and more compart-mentalising and outsourcing, there was no longer an adequate way to voice your dissatisfaction at a corporation. Anyone you talked to was either a robot or an underpaid worker who was being more abused by the corporation than you, the complainant, could ever be. Scream-ing at buildings may be futile, but at least it was better than screaming at a minimum-wage zero-hour-contract employee with bills to pay who was just trying to get through the day.

In their household it was Siver who was in charge of the bureau-cracy. Calling banks, doctors, the Home Office, trying (failing) to get someone on the line who could provide Rafiq and Xezal with some dignity. It wouldn't surprise Laika if she, too, screamed at buildings.

Not that there weren't legitimate, non-metaphorical reasons to shout at buildings. Composite materials and advances in engineering and computer rendering increasingly meant that for the first time in human history, the engineering bottleneck was the fact that humans had to be able to live in these towers. Our phones and Wi-Fi still need to work, we still need to be able to take elevators up into the sky, and to get out in the case of a fire. In more ways than one, this was the reason behind all of the protests that circled around Wall Street: the slow realisation and pain of oncoming obsolescence. It was poetic really: for over a century our gadgets and devices had been relegated to drawers, to trash heaps, as we made way for newer and better things, but we were fast reaching the point where our manufacturing, our buildings, our economy even, no longer needed us. And unlike the Tamagotchis and Game Boys and Discmans, which were discarded in silence, we could voice our displeasure at becoming obsolete. We could scream. Not that it would make much of a difference.

Episode finished, the dinner receptacle was put into the trash bin and the trivet was replaced on the dining table where it was supposed to be. Back at his computer Laika checked to see whether RedMinx, his favourite camgirl, was online. (She was not.) YouTube, click on video recommended by the site, a satirical news clip where a man behind a desk told the news while pretending to espouse political opinions he did not, in fact, have. The clip had been seen over 1.3 million times. Once the clip ended, another video started auto playing, a weird PowerPoint presentation given by an unkempt man with a broad American accent, a low-budget TED Talk. Laika's finger hovered above the white cross in the red circle that would close the tab, but then, seeing the video's title, 'This Technology Will Change The WORLD', and the view count (9.2 million), decided to keep watching. He clicked the icon comprised of two arrows pointing in opposite directions and watched as the video buffered and glitched for a moment as it strained to fill the entirety of his screen.

'Well, our greatest accomplishment as humans, that which will live on long after we've all died, is not our buildings and bridges: it's our waste. You've seen pictures like this, I'm sure, mountains and mountains of debris and waste, the things that we reject and throw away, the things that make us human. What will remain of us is waste. And for too long we've seen it as an inconvenience, something to be hidden away, to be ashamed of. Scientists all over the world analyse waste, of course, archaeologists learn about prehistoric men by looking at newly discovered waste, biologists learn about diseases by looking at waste. They know that there is something inherently valuable in what we leave behind, but the financial markets have not yet been able to monetise this.

'Until today.

'What we have is a cost-effective, versatile, waste-to-energy solution. We call it Purity. This — let me just see if I can change the
slide — *this*, is the Purity project.'

Laika closed the browser window, wondering what had led the
website's predictive algorithm to decide he would be interested in this
particular video. He had been thinking about waste a lot recently, due
to the fact that his existence in this apartment was meant to be imper-
ceptible, but as far as he knew he had not searched for any of this on
the internet. It was unclear how smart machines had become: yes, the
predictive text that would appear in Laika's search engines had gotten
demonstrably better at reading his mind from only a few keystrokes,
but it wasn't evident how various apps and search terms communi-
cated with each other. He had read that Facebook partnered with a
firm that sold them data from loyalty cards, so that they could know
which user was interested in what brand, but had also read on a forum
someone's claim that shops now used beacons in their stores that
would identify a person's phone, which would allow for more precise
advertising. Laika had identified academics at Yale and MIT who
were working on digital advertising developments, but he knew that
by the time they had finished their books, reality would have moved
on, and the books would be of no other use than a historical one,
merely able to tell us how the world worked a few years ago. There
was no time to accurately define reality as it was happening, as reality
had been moving faster than the human ability to make sense of it for
quite some time already. It reminded him of a letter that was found in
the compound in Abbottabad where Osama Bin Laden was found and
killed. It was a reply to one of his couriers who had asked why they
had to deliver messages in such a time-consuming and archaic way,
and if they couldn't simply use encrypted emails instead. 'Just because
something can be encrypted doesn't make it suitable for use,' someone
in the US State Department had translated the response, 'as you know,
this science is not ours and is not our invention. That means we do not
know much about it. Based on this, I see that sending any dangerous
matter via encrypted email is a risky thing.' This science is not ours
and is not our invention. Cf. also the Kurdish dissidents who had been

265

arrested due to a single pixel: a particular chat application had been widely used by critics of the Turkish regime, and tens of thousands of people were rounded up for having used this app. Except, it turned out, many hadn't. Several other apps had been infected with a line of code creating a 1x1 pixel that redirected to the chat app's server. Thousands of people languishing in prison for a pixel that was too small for the naked eye to see. The technology was not theirs, and they had been punished for it. This could be applied to all technologies with its proprietary underpinnings locked away and used with glee by people who did not mind being sold, as long as the dopamine kick of a star, a like, a heart filled their feeds.

Rafiq always lauded Mikhail Kalashnikov's 1947 invention, the Avtomat Kalashnikova, aka the AK-47, as the only piece of modern equipment made not for profit, but to work as intended. 'Without it, the Kurdish independence movement would have been crushed,' he would say, struggling with the multi-device remote control, trying to find mention of the ongoing wars in the region on a channel, any channel. 'What made this weapon so suitable for guerrilla warfare was that this was a true communist invention: unburdened by the needs of market capitalism wherein new models would need to supplant older models in order to allow for continued profitability, Mikhail Kalashnikov was instead instructed to create the most durable rifle he could.' There was no planned obsoleteness, no new and improved model, just a killing machine made to last. Contemporary landmines and weaponry can be deactivated by the vendor if licence payments are not made: what matters now is the code, not the machine. It wasn't a coincidence that the only person who had been charged with a crime during the 2008 meltdown was a Goldman Sachs trader who, upon leaving the firm, took with him a flash disk containing code that the bank argued belonged to them. A hundred years of wealth was lost in twenty-four months, 500,000 people with their homes foreclosed in the US alone, 5.5 million people who lost their jobs, and the only person who wound up in prison did so because he took a string of numbers with him, in his pocket. 'If man succeeded without much labour, in transforming carbon into diamonds, their value might fall below that of bricks,' Rafiq would say to them, quoting his beloved

Capital. And yet here we were, with invisible bricks worth more than all the diamonds in the world.

Laika took his phone with him to the bathroom and had a shit while scrolling through his Twitter feed, reading jokes and memes about an event that he had not heard about. He searched for some of the key words used in the memes but was unable to find out what it was that was being made fun of. Afterwards, he made sure that the toilet was clean, and washed his hands, wiped the sink, before returning to his desk. Still no RedMinx. He left the camsite open, waiting for her to come online, and opened a new window to kill time, logging onto a website that showed the feeds from unprotected webcams all over the world. As the rectangles on the camgirl site updated to show the models who came online and those who disconnected, he observed a gym in Dublin, an office in Odessa, a boulangerie in Boulogne-Billancourt. It was soothing, in a way, to watch people who had no idea they were being observed, working out, talking to customers, preparing a spreadsheet.

Notification. RedMinx was online. Laika quickly shut the other window and entered her chatroom.

A year ago, RedMinx had gone from being one of 6,000 women on CamTube to the only camgirl that he interacted with. The amount of available women on the site had begun to make him feel anxious, and overwhelmed, and he wanted to somehow devote his time/money to one person, so he selected ten of the women he saw regularly (the ones he had, for whatever reason, set up notifications for, so that he would be alerted when they came online) and sent them each a request for a custom video, the same custom video.

The prompt: *I am thinking a blackmail scenario. I'd like it to start with us hanging out, you wearing a sports bra and me telling you that I know you are doing cam shows behind your bf's back. You get angry with me, but eventually you calm down a little, and tell me I have to promise not to tell anyone about this. I say OK . . . if you do something for me. I tell you you need to suck my dick. Before you've said yes, I take off my pants and you see my dick. Your reaction is one of mild surprise /a hint of excitement and you say something like 'wow, your dick is bigger than my boyfriend's'. This whole build-up should be half the movie. Then you start giving me a blowjob with lots of eye contact,* *starting slow, hesitant, then gradually getting into it. After a few minutes (no fewer than 3) I say I want to fuck you. You start fucking me (cowgirl / reverse cowgirl with the camera pointed up towards you, I'm thinking like 09:47 in this video <u>here</u>). After a while (6–8 minutes), you end up cumming – dirty talk here is key, please be creative. In the end I can't hold myself any more and cum inside of you. You pretend to be mad at me, and say next time I can't cum inside of you. 'Next time?' I say. 'Don't you want there to be a next time?' you ask with a smile. Do you think you can do this? I'm thinking c. 15 minutes. The longer the better (will pay $$$).*

Nine weeks and 3,800 dollars later, the ten videos were in his inbox, all following his prompt to the letter, 173 minutes of his fantasy being repeated over and over again. He watched them for four days before he made his decision. He did not know what it was with RedMinx's rendition that he preferred to Leesa Lee's or Jenni Raw's, but there was a playfulness to her approach that he appreciated, never allowing the scenario to feel *creepy*. He had not spent money on anyone but her since then.

'Hi guys, how is everyone doing tonight?' RedMinx said, looking into her high-definition webcam. She was wearing a flattering black lingerie ensemble, one that Laika had seen on her Amazon Wishlist but had elected not to buy her (he usually got her more useful items: phones, books, winter boots, things that he assumed her other fans were less likely to buy her). RedMinx was a radiant brunette from somewhere in Illinois (for obvious reasons she did not disclose her residential address) who was as good at pithy repartee aimed at the lens of a webcam as she was bringing herself to orgasm using a Hitachi vibrator.

'Hey, Lenin! How are you?' RedMinx said, seeing Laika's username Lenin44 scroll past in the chat window. He typed in hi, you're looking stunning today!

'Aw, thanks. Yeah, I'm wearing a brand-new bra. What do you think?' she replied, writhing up against the camera to a flurry of heart-eye and aubergine emojis.

gorgeous, Laika typed in the window's chat box, amidst requests from other users for her to take her top off/flash her tits/show her feet in free chat. TankDick6969, another regular, enquired what music she had on in the background, a languorous electronic track she was, ever so subtly, writhing to.

Laika left his laptop to get a box of tissues from the kitchen. When he came back the conversation had moved to the patriarchal structure of the Smurfs.

'Smurfette was a robot, created by Gargamel to create friction among the all-male Smurfs, did you guys know that? It's almost biblical, the woman introduced only to create chaos in an otherwise perfect society.'

wait, how do smurfs procreate then??? asked TankDick6969.

'Yeah, it's unclear. I've seen theories ranging from parthenogenesis to asexual reproduction to Smurfs being some sort of hermaphroditic race. I don't buy the asexual explanation, though, because they clearly all want to bang robot Smurfette when Gargamel creates her.'

so she's a robot?

show us your tits!

'I think Papa Smurf gives her some sort of potion to turn her into a real Smurf eventually, so that she is no longer controlled by Gargamel.'

i am googling this as we speak and omg you're not kidding!

'Would I lie to you, Tank? So, guys, who wants to play?'

wanna go pvt? Laika typed.

'Sure, honey, I'm ready for you,' RedMinx said, blowing him a kiss. Laika clicked on the button that said Exclusive at the bottom of the screen, making her only visible to him, at a rate of $8.99/min. An animation glittered across the screen, indicating to them both that they had gone from one form of interaction to another. RedMinx immediately began undoing her bra, and moved her breasts closer to the camera, a nipple brushing up against the lens.

'Do you want to turn on your camera for me today?'

sure, but would prefer the sound to be off

'Whatever you prefer, baby. We're going to do whatever you feel comfortable with.'

Laika clicked on the c2c button on the window, and pressed OK on a pop-up box indicating that the browser was requesting access to his webcam. A green light lit up at the top of his laptop's screen and soon he saw himself, doughy, pale, balding, in a small rectangle in the lower right corner of the screen.

'There you are,' RedMinx said. 'I've missed that gorgeous face of yours.'

i've missed u 2

'I'm working on your video, by the way, you should have it by the end of the week.'

thanks. no hurry obv.

Laika had recently come to an agreement with RedMinx that custom videos should go for 2,000 coins of the website's currency, which came to approximately 750 dollars. This last video had required him to write an eight-page-long prompt and scene description, to instruct her to play the role of a friend's wife who admitted she had had a crush on him for years and begged him to let her give him a blowjob, a blowjob where a custom dildo served as a replica of Laika's penis. He had sent her the schematics of a mould of his own erect penis that she 3D-printed into a dildo. RedMinx was always game to try out new things, it was one of the things he liked about her. Sure, variants of his scenarios could be found for free on a multitude of porn streaming sites, but there were strict turn-offs for him that made normal masturbatory sessions fraught: first he needed to find a pair of actors that he found attractive, then he needed to make sure that the video did not include a to him repulsive shot of the woman's breasts jiggling in such a way as to make her implants visible. He also needed to check that there was no gagging during any blowjob, as the sound reminded him of Donald Duck and was a total turn-off. Also, for some reason that Laika suspected had to do with the popularity of that new TV show about tits and dragons, more and more porn clips had as their premise some incestual attraction. Boy and stepmother, brother and sister, man and stepdaughter, and so on and so forth. These were not a turn-on. It seemed to Laika that porn followed trends and the people in charge or their algorithms believed that people watched these new trends because it was what turned them on, when in reality it was simply that these were the videos promoted on the Pornhub homepage to begin with and therefore the ones that were most watched. It was much easier to simply dictate what he wanted in a clip, featuring a woman he knew he was attracted to.

'Oh, and thanks for the snow boots, by the way! They'll come in handy during the winter. It gets so friggin' cold here, you have no idea.'

welcome bby, wouldn't want u getting cold, now would we?

'Exactly, I much prefer it when I'm hot . . . So . . . what are you in the mood for today?'

joi?

'Sure, we can do that. Why don't you take off your pants then for me, baby, let me see that big cock of yours. I'm going to make you edge today, you're going to cum so hard you're going to lose your fucking mind. Mmm . . . yeah, that's it. You're already hard for me, I appreciate that. Don't touch it yet, not yet. First you're going to just look at me.'

When Laika came, twenty-one minutes and over 200 dollars later, he let out a cry so loud he was relieved that his mic was off, as Red-Minx would probably have laughed at him or otherwise reacted in a way that would fill him with shame.

'Mmm, look at that lovely mess you made, you dirty dirty boy.'

that was fantsstic, i love u, Laika typed with his cum-free hand.

'I'll see you here tomorrow?'

u bet xxxx

'OK,' RedMinx said, giving the webcam a loud kiss.

And she was offline, the video feed of her replaced with the profile picture she had chosen, her arching her back upwards in a suggestive yoga pose.

Laika sent her an offline tip of a hundred gold coins and, after the soft sneeze of tissues being pulled from the box, proceeded to clean himself up.

His mind clearer than it had been all day, he spent the next few hours tinkering with his algorithm. As he couldn't mimic the Goldman Sachs algorithm at an adequate speed, he elected to forgo smaller purchases and sales, to single out the bigger transactions, which he assumed were based on more reliable data.

He hadn't really thought about what he would do if he got it to work. Part of him was intrigued by the idea of creating an open source algorithm that anyone could use, that would grant the user some of the revenues that the world's largest banks were currently raking in, maybe that would be a worthwhile endeavour.

Certainly Lotti would have thought so.

He'd met Lotti when he left London for Berlin, living off money he'd made from a domain sale, renting a dirt-cheap apartment in Neukölln and spending his days in a dérive. Lotti was an environmental activist whom he'd seen once at a party that was held in the building where he lived, where she was arguing with a man in the corridor, poking her hand-rolled cigarette in his direction as she shouted at him in German. He then saw her again collecting funds for Greenpeace by the Turkish market, at which point he gave her a hundred-euro bill and listened to her talk about how western governments promoted artificial pesticides and fertilisers to South East Asian countries. A fertiliser manufacturer had even genetically modified their product so that the crops could no longer use any fertiliser but that of the brand, operating like drug pushers in the way that they donated tonnes of this fertiliser to poor Asian and African nations, locking the farmers into their overpriced product by making the soil otherwise worthless. Laika, genuinely interested in what Lotti was telling him, having never spent much time thinking about fertiliser before, asked her to join him for a kebab nearby to continue the conversation once she was done for the day. She ordered a falafel, he chose a doner, they shared a plate of chips. It was only halfway through the meal that Laika realised that he had chosen the worst date-food there was, it being absolutely impossible to eat a doner kebab in any dignified fashion. But there was something reassuring about it, they had already witnessed each other embarrassed, unattractive, gloops of garlic sauce on their chins and struggling to contain gradually dissolving pita breads. Next time they went to an Indian restaurant, and the time after that they watched a DVD of *The Wages of Fear* on his couch. Since he had a spare room in his apartment that he didn't use, he let Lotti move in with him for free. She fascinated him: refusing to fly, composting, ensuring that every food item she purchased was organic. Obviously, she was a vegan. Laika appreciated the insight into a world he had inhabited but not given much thought to, and quickly read Lotti's tattered paperbacks about climate change, the meat industry and agricultural developments by giant corporations. He had not considered himself political before meeting her, thinking that the world was a mess that would not be solved by politicians, that the democratic process was too slow and too beholden to corporate interests to do what was necessary. But he got infected with her passion, her optimism that the earth could be saved. Having nothing to do during the day, he began volunteering alongside her and after a few months she told him in a conspiratorial whisper that she was part of an activist eco-group. Laika had laughed. So he was dating an eco-terrorist.

Lotti had narrowed her eyes at him. 'We are not terrorists, Laika.'

He began following her across the country, helping in their covert activities where they would sabotage various factories. He was impressed by the care they put into ensuring that no employees were ever inside, that nobody would be hurt by their homemade (and often quite ineffectual) explosives.

It ended in London. It was Lotti's suggestion they take a train to Paris and from there the Eurostar, that way she could join some old friends in an action to destroy an anhydrous ammonia plant, and, she said, Laika could catch up with his family. His mother having moved back to Slemani, his sister in Iraq, this left Mohammed. Laika hinted that he would be happy to join Lotti on the sabotage mission but she made it clear that she wanted some alone time with some old friends. So, Laika texted Mohammed, awkwardly announcing that he was in town, and would he like to hang out? Mohammed answered almost immediately, suggested he bring Lotti and meet him at Cipriani's for dinner the following evening. Laika was stunned, and a bit apprehensive at what Lotti would think of a restaurant which was bound to not be her scene, a suspicion confirmed as he looked up the restaurant on his phone and read about its 'high-gloss wood interior', its 'signature brown leather chairs'. It was the first time Laika would introduce someone to his family, and he grew anxious imagining Mohammed in his three-piece suit blathering on about finance while Lotti tried to find something on the menu she could eat. Laika briefly considered answering the text by mentioning that

Lotti was a vegan and suggesting they go somewhere else, but restrained himself. Mohammed was reaching out. An amendment to the suggested plan would be seen as a rejection. *I'm paying*, Mohammed texted after a few minutes, believing Laika's silence to do with the price of dinner, and cementing the fact that they would indeed be having overpriced pasta in a glitzy London basement. Lotti didn't want to go, having already made plans, but relented after Laika impressed upon her how important this was to him. 'I thought you did not like your brother.' Laika said it wasn't that simple.

He sensed that things were not going to go well as soon as Lotti arrived, twenty minutes late and visibly drunk after meeting friends, eyes wildly darting across the restaurant with its Russian oligarchs sat next to bored, expensive-looking dates. Laika had neglected to tell her anything about the restaurant, fearing she would be self-conscious and bail, but from the look she shot him as she sat down, he realised this had been a mistake. She was surrounded by women in glittering designer wear, while she wore a faded baby-blue T-shirt with an image of a wind turbine and the words 'I am a big fan'. She berated the waiter for not having more vegan options, scoffed at Mohammed's business venture (which sounded, admittedly, ridiculous, consisting as it did of literally buying air), and rejected every one of Laika's attempts to steer the conversation into calmer waters. As for Mohammed, his idea of socialising was to tell an off-colour joke about a bear turning a rabbit gay. 'You're into animals, Lotti, right? You'll like this joke. So a bear is chasing a rabbit through a forest when a genie shows up . . .' She did, in fact, not like the joke. It could have been just a bad date, however, something to be laughed about years down the line, until Mohammed said his mother had mentioned over the phone that Kurds had begun naming their children Bush in honour of the president. That's when they crossed the Rubicon.

'Why would they name a child after a war criminal?'

Mohammed took another bite of his pasta al forno. 'They see him as the man who got rid of Saddam, it's as easy as that.'

'You seem a very short-sighted people, swapping one dictator for another,' Lotti said, downing her third glass of Barbaresco, which made Mohammed put his fork down.

'Well, I guess we're just an inferior race, aren't we?'

And they were off.

By the time Lotti left the restaurant, the argument had evolved into a full-blown shouting match, with Laika, Lotti and Mohammed taking turns to shout at each other. 'Why are you not *defending* me?' Lotti said at one point, turning to Laika in exasperation. He'd half-bellowed that it was because she was wrong. He had tolerated his sister's complaints about the war in Iraq for years, never saying a word, but to hear Lotti speak of things she clearly did not know about he could not abide. After she'd left, Laika started apologising to Mohammed, who thought this was a good time to lecture Laika about his life choices. 'This drama is fun, sure, hell, I've had my fair share of crazy girlfriends. I get it. But, mate, you really need to get your shit together at some point. You need to start thinking about what you want to actually *do* with your life.' Laika decided to leave the restaurant then as well, leaving M with three half-eaten main courses and a fourth bottle of wine.

Later that evening, he tried to go back to the apartment they'd rented for the weekend, knowing he would have to apologise. He'd muttered something about his brother being an asshole, and she said she was sorry, that she was drunk, but by the time they got on the Eurostar to Paris, they both looked out of the train window, knowing that whatever they had was over.

Having withstood the temptation earlier in the day, he now decided to google Lotti, quickly finding her Facebook profile, even though she didn't have a profile photo of herself or even her full name. He scrolled through the posts she had made public: doomsday predictions of an impending mass extinction; protests against oil companies; an animated cat with the body of a pop tart, flying through space. He was about to send her a message, when he saw her relationship status. Engaged. Too much time had passed.

He closed the browser.

He had been sitting in front of his computer for so long he did not notice that the sun had set. He checked the time: 22:38. The algorithm would have to do.

He shut his laptop, pulling out the charger cord in honour of Lotti.

He remembered to PayPal twenty-five dollars to the person delivering his coffee and bagel in the morning, and left the garbage bag outside for them to dispose of (the removal and disposal of his trash was not something that the coffee shop around the corner usually offered as a service, but the delivery people working there were more than happy to do so for a ten-dollar tip). He washed his hands, brushed his teeth, wiped the sink clean of any toothpaste residue and went to bed, taking his phone, his tablet and a pair of headphones with him.

The bedroom was starkly minimalist, an interior design that was probably in vogue when the apartment had been decorated, but that now seemed both dated and alienating. A futon was in the middle of the room, and aside from a single bamboo stalk jutting out of a clay pot, there were no decorations or adornments. The walls were painted in a light grey, which wasn't visible now as the blackout curtains were drawn, and the floor was the same polished wood as the rest of the apartment.

Laika took off his cardigan and crawled into bed, set the Sleep Cycle alarm on his phone – an app that measured his sleep patterns to wake him up at the lightest sleeping point of a given thirty-minute interval – and plugged his headphones into his tablet. He opened the YouTube app and scrolled among his subscriptions to see if anyone had posted a new ASMR video.

He had discovered ASMR by chance, as during a public Gold Show, RedMinx had been softly sighing into the microphone and one of the people in the room wrote 'what is this ASMR shit'. Once the show was over, Laika searched online for the acronym, finding it to mean Autonomous Sensory Meridian Response, and quickly became obsessed with these YouTubers with their high-end, often binaural, microphones, making a variety of tapping, whispering, brushing sounds to elicit a tingling sensation, beginning at the top of the head and travelling down the spine. And no matter what kind of day he had had, watching an ASMR video for twenty minutes or so before going to sleep would provoke in him a sense of calm, as if he were receiving a massage, his muscles relaxing, the 'triggers' giving him a pleasurable sensation that was not entirely unlike having feathers brushed against his skin. He also liked that this was a way to have eye contact with people without feeling awkward about it.

The genre had its limitations, however: there were only so many triggers that a YouTuber could reasonably do videos around, and increasingly the videos weren't about the sounds themselves but about the attractiveness of the YouTuber, about sponsored content, about outlandish roleplaying scenarios that sexualised the young women in a way Laika was not entirely comfortable with. He would prefer endless variations on the comforting friend putting you to sleep, or relaxing triggers being whispered from ear to ear, but he understood there was a need to stand out from the millions of videos being uploaded, and so ASMR as a genre was careening further and further away from that which made it special. Nowhere was the deleuzoguattarian reterritorialisation principle more evident than in terms of pornography. Everything wound up as porn, in the end.

Having no desire to watch any of the latest uploads ('Khaleesi ASMR roleplay', 'Girlfriend opening birthday present binaural ASMR', 'Satisfying Slime ASMR'), he clicked on a video he had already watched, titled 'ASMR During A Hurricane (Comforting You Roleplay)'. In it, the YouTuber was pretending to have rushed home to the friend, the viewer of the video, to comfort them during a hurricane. Before the video commenced, there was a message to all those who had recently been victims of Hurricane Irene. The scene was lit by candlelight, and the YouTuber was stroking the lens of the camera, whispering 'it's OK, it's OK, it's OK', as though it were an incantation. Laika felt his skin tingling, the muscles in his jaw relaxing.

'I'm here for you, I'm here for you, I will never leave your side.'

He woke up the next morning with his headphones wrapped around his arm, the tablet on his stomach, a puddle of fresh drool on his pillow. His phone, chirping with the recording of birds that he had selected as his alarm sound, was scalding hot next to his pillow. He turned off the alarm and saw that his sleep quality had been estimated at 89 per cent, well above his average of 74 per cent, but below his personal best of 94 per cent. After making the bed, making sure to do the hospital corner folds on the sheets and smoothing out any

wrinkles by spritzing water over the bedding, he went into the hallway and tossed his sweatpants, T-shirt and underwear into the
laundry bag by the door and took out another pair of underwear,
another T-shirt, another pair of sweatpants from the sports bag. It
was 07:58, his breakfast would arrive at 08:30, and the New York
Stock Exchange would be open for trading at 09:30.

After he had showered and shaved and wiped the shower clean, he
dressed in his fresh clothes and walked back to the bedroom to put on
his cardigan, giving it a quick sniff to make sure it didn't smell. His
card holder had fallen out overnight, and he bent down to put it back
in his pocket, noting how stiff his lower back was. He would search
for a massage service that did outcalls.

Doorbell.

He opened the door, seeing the delivery person down the corridor, still waiting for the elevator, holding the trash bag.

'Oh hey, sorry, the elevator is taking its time.'

Laika waved it off and picked up the brown paper bag with his
soymilk latte and lox and cream cheese bagel.

'Won't happen again,' the delivery person said, stepping into the
elevator.

Laika walked to the window in the study, sipping his morning coffee, and observed the new protests that were just getting under way, a
scurry of factions chanting slogans, raising their tiny ineffectual fists to
the sky. Even from Laika's vantage point, he could see that the dynamic
today was different, more antagonistic: the throngs of people actively
pushing against riot shields, as if daring them to try something. Yesterday evening a video had gone viral of a police officer using pepper
spray on three kneeling women for no reason that was apparent on the
video, the footage shaking as hands went up to eyes, as the kneeling
women fell to their sides, as the protestors were, briefly, shocked into
paralysis by the act. A hastily put-together press conference in the
hours since to quell media outlets that were slowly becoming sympa-
thetic to the plight of the Occupy movement, brought forth the police
officer to read a statement written on a folded A4 sheet of paper, the
language of which had been agreed upon by four lawyers, language
with which the police officer was unfamiliar and so read with the stilted

lack of affect that brought to mind children reciting poetry. The lawyers claimed, through their police officer vessel, that the use of pepper spray had been 'appropriate' and so now, overnight, the mood in the streets had changed. The euphoric sense of togetherness had tightened into a more combative stance; chants about the state of the world economy were now interspersed with anatomically impossible instructions for pigs to fornicate with themselves and the odd NWA lyric. More than one person held aloft a sign that stated ACAB. The police officers sensed that this crowd, largely comprised of the same people they had met on previous days, now presented a different threat and so were huddled closer together, their polycarbonate shields raised in a tight formation that looked almost Roman from the skies. Laika was intrigued by an ostensibly Christian group marching, dressed in flowing white robes that were reminiscent of both Jesus Christ and members of some nefarious cult. Their preferred sign, it seemed, was a photo of a dollar bill and the words FALSE GOD. Another group held a sign consisting of a print of Damien Hirst's artwork *For the Love of God* with 1% in a sans-serif type beneath it. The notorious artwork, made out of a human skull cast in platinum and encrusted with 8,601 diamonds, cost £14 million to produce and was sold to an anonymous consortium, allegedly comprised of Hirst himself, for £50 million, thus making Damien Hirst the creator of the single most expensive work of art by a living artist, even though he had most likely just bought it from himself. It remained a haunting image, the diamond-covered skull, made at the very height of the financial bubble, back when there seemed to be money to be made from literally everything. It was a potent symbol. The diamond and the brick.

Laika thought of the time Mohammed had used his first salary to buy a blingy watch, how disgusted Rafiq was at the sight of it. 'Son, I never want to see you chasing status so vulgarly. Be proud of your heritage.' Mohammed spent that night complaining about their father, with Laika intoning the odd sound to reassure his brother that he was listening, that he was in agreement.

The marimba ringtone that was the default on his phone began to chime.

Only a few years ago, Laika had different polyphonic ringtones for every occasion: Morricone's theme from *The Good, The Bad and The Ugly* for Mohammed, Garbage's 'The World is Not Enough' for his mother, the motif from Beethoven's Symphony No. 5 for his sister, and so forth. And now the world's phones chirped identically, from the same slab of glass and aluminium, as though what people wanted had not been individuality after all. He had once read a Danish study that showed how various birds had begun incorporating ringtones into their birdsong. He'd tried to find the study again but googling 'birds sound like ringtones' only led to various apps and ringtones that sounded like birds.

Laika looked at the screen, saw a photograph of his mother. Laika sighed. He should probably answer.

'Oh my heart, my liver, are you eating well? Who is cooking for you? Those sons of dogs that didn't let me visit my son, I would have made you rice and chicken.'

Laika told her he was fine. He was eating well.

'What well? I know how they eat in America, I have seen the television. You need to take care of yourself, my heart.'

Changing the topic, he wondered if she'd received the money he had sent her.

'Oh my darling, it's too much money; you really shouldn't send me every last fils you have.'

He opened a browser window, clicked on an article in the *Wall Street Journal*. Clicked on a hyperlink. Then another. Then another, until he found himself reading about the way that the lootings following the New York City blackout of 1977 led to the spread of hip hop. People suddenly had access to sound systems to make their own beats; a previously unaffordable technology found its way into the hands of the people. The text he was looking at stated that 'during the summer of 1977, an extensive power outage blacked out New York, and hundreds of stores were looted and vandalized. The poorest neighbourhoods (the South Bronx, Bedford Stuyvesant, Brownsville, and Crown Heights areas in Brooklyn, the Jamaica area in Queens, and Harlem), where most of the looting took place, were depicted by the City's media organs as lawless zones where crime is sanctioned and chaos bubbles just below the surface.'

A beat, he could almost hear his mother thinking on the other end. 'Your sister, she's not doing well.'

Interesting, that the most efficient backlash against hip hop wasn't right-wing punditry, moral panic or Al Gore's wife's Parental Advisory sticker, but rather the enforcement of copyrights: the owners of the samples and beats would sue the hip hop artists until sampling became too much of a hassle. Hip hop hobbled for a while, depending on Timbaland-style beats, until Jay-Z brought samples back with *The Blueprint*. He was now rich enough to clear any samples he wanted. He had the money to make any problem go away.

Wait. What was wrong with Siver?

'You know how stubborn that girl is.'

Yeah, *Siver* was the stubborn one. *The Blueprint* came out on 9/11. Click. The architect of the twin towers, Minoru Yamasaki, was afraid of heights, and so he advocated narrow windows. The seventeen-inch windows in WTC 1 and 2 were thus meant to instil a sense of security for those on the inside but ended up reinforcing the horrific sense of claustrophobia that the photographs from that day evoke. Click. Yamasaki built the towers as a 'living symbol of man's commitment to world peace'. Click. The towers' structural engineer, Leslie Robertson, said a week before the attacks that he designed the Twin Towers so that 'a 707 could crash into them'. All four hijacked aircraft were Boeing planes.

'I've told her a thousand times, just come home, come take care of your mother, I'm all alone here in Slemani.'

Laika took a sip of his coffee, rolled his eyes at the dramatics. His mother had a maid working for her. She had a driver.

'Because you send me all that money! Otherwise I'd be out on the street, and my only daughter would still prefer to gallivant out in the desert.'

Throughout his teens he had thought that if only his mother had some money, if only she had the one thing that she always complained about not having, then she could finally be happy. Now he knew, it wasn't the money, it was never about that. Xezal objected to her life because it wasn't how she had expected it to be, and money was, if not entirely irrelevant perhaps, not nearly enough to force the world to fulfil her dreams. It seemed to Laika now that what she really wanted was to be who she was before her family had been uprooted not once but twice due to her husband's political activism; she wanted her children to fulfil predefined roles, as though they were all dolls whose wants and wishes could be decided by their mother. For her to be happy, she would need to master time travel and/or somehow become omnipotent. Nothing less than total control would please her. It was, frankly, exhausting.

So. Siver?

'She has no money. She just lost her job and I'm afraid she's so stubborn that she'll return to that betraying husband of hers.'

Wasn't that exactly what Xezal had wanted? Huh: *Zoolander* had come out a week after 9/11.

'I never said that, when have I ever said that? I just said it was hard for a young child like little Zara to grow up without a strong father figure. You don't think I could have left your father a thousand times? A good wife knows when to stay.'

Laika could send her money. He, too, now had money to make problems go away.

'Oh, she wouldn't accept it. You know your sister.'

Bret Easton Ellis claimed that *Zoolander* had cribbed the plot of his novel *Glamorama*. They ended up settling out of court. Undisclosed amount. Roger Ebert gave *Zoolander* one star and wrote 'the makers of *Zoolander* did some last-minute editing. No, they didn't dub over the word "Malaysia" or edit around the assassination of the prime minister. What they did was digitally erase the World Trade Center from the New York skyline, so that audiences would not be reminded of the tragedy, as if we have forgotten. It's a good thing no scenes were shot in Kuala Lumpur, or they probably would have erased the Petronas Towers, to keep us from getting depressed or jealous or anything.'

'But if you *could* . . .'

The conversation became transactional, account details were passed to Laika, assurances were made that he would call his siblings, promises were made to call his mother more often.

He closed his eight browser tabs about Jay-Z, 9/11 and *Zoolander*. Looked at the time: 09:24. Time to get his bot running for the day.

He ensured everything was in order, that the parameters were correct, and clicked start.

Notification.

A WhatsApp message. A photograph of the account details Xezal had already given him. He googled the time in Dubai. 17:32.

When Siver had chosen him as her confidante regarding all things Karim, Laika had found it both a privilege and a source of grim desperation, indicating as it did that the girl did not have any real friends. Laika didn't have any either, but for all of Siver's attempts at building a social life outside of her dysfunctional family, she still had not been able to accomplish more than him, who barely left the house unless it was to get smokes or Coke. A consequence of Siver confiding in him in this way was that Laika felt that he had to be supportive of her relationship with Karim, to provide a counterbalance to the barrage of shit she got from their parents and the indifference that Mohammed showed towards everything. Not to mention the fact that Xezal, once their father passed away, seemed to blame the old man's death on Siver's relationship. If Laika had to be the one she could confide in, he would have to abstain from criticising her boyfriend, which in and of itself needn't have been a problem. Except, and this here was the rub, Laika thought Karim to be a bit of a dick, the sort of man who had never felt out of place in any room but who thrived off making sure others were uncomfortable. Laika could never really understand what Siver saw in the man, and he was not at all surprised when he decided he was just religious enough to want to avail himself of the right to have more than one wife. Neither was he surprised that Siver was unwilling to accept this, preferring to pack up and leave. Not just because Hardi stubbornness was the stuff of legends, but once when Laika had asked to borrow the laptop Siver had gotten for university to check whether the Game in Croydon had any copies of *Turok 2: Seeds of Evil* for sale, the browser history showed a good dozen lesbian pornographic sites, something that he never discussed with his sister but which made him suspect that maybe Karim wasn't who she wanted to be with.

He decided to wait a bit before calling his sister, knowing that Siver had an acrimonious relationship with their mother, one forged in the embers of Xezal's fading beauty, the sort of beauty that can only be granted by wealth. Laika had never noticed that Xezal treated Siver differently as a child, and needed Siver to present him with necessary revisionism as they'd revisit selected moments from their childhood. Of when she wasn't allowed a second slice of cake on her own birthday, when Xezal would refuse to buy Siver clothes in her own size, telling her that those sizes were too big for her age. Did Laika really not remember any of that? With time he had come to accept her truth, so that even his memories had been somehow re-edited to accommodate the subtle psychological abuse that was taking place in their house, unbeknownst to Laika. As they grew closer as siblings, he let their worlds, their memories, merge.

So, if Siver needed money and was in such dire straits that even Xezal was aware of it, why wouldn't she just tell him? What was it about him that always made his family members think of him as a fuck-up, as someone who could barely take care of himself, let alone others? He'd certainly never had to struggle with money: it just had a way of materialising for him.

In his late teens he got a book on Dreamweaver from the Sutton library and taught himself how to make websites on the Pentium II that his dad and Mohammed had bought, a purchase that had started a small-scale civil war in the family. He churned out a variety of websites for local businesses over the next few years, nothing fancy, but it was at a time when every shop wanted a website of their own, and Laika charged far less than the competition, so he had a regular income stream through his website www.laika.com. In 2003 he received an email from an anonymous consortium offering him 25,000 dollars for his domain, wishing to create a 'digital monument' to his namesake, the Laika that was sent into space by the Soviets aboard Sputnik-2 in 1957. At the time, scientists did not know the impact of spaceflight on living beings, and so to clear the path for a man to be launched into space, a stray dog roaming the streets of Moscow was chosen. According to the paper 'Some Unknown Pages of the Living Organism's First Orbital Flight', by Dimitri C. Malashenkov, 'There had been work done to adapt a group of dogs to conditions in the tight cabin. This had led to keeping dogs in gradually smaller cages for periods up to 15–20 days. In general, it seems that long confinement led untrained dogs to neither urinate nor release solid wastes, which made the dogs restless and caused their general condition to decay.' The consortium wanted a website to match the grand statue of her that had been erected at the Russian Cosmonaut training facility in Russia's Star City. The sort of memorials that matter to humans, but did not matter at all to dogs who had yet to weaponise memory. All that mattered for Laika the dog was that she died from overheating, all alone and terrified in space.

Initially Laika thought that this offer of twenty-five grand was a scam, but when it turned out that it wasn't, and that the buyers had already set up an escrow account for the funds, he sold the domain and took the money.

After the death of his father, his family was adrift, slowly splintering after the person who had been holding them together, who had them invested in being a unit of people rather than disparate individuals, was no longer there to give them a reason to stick together. The outpouring of emotions in the weeks and months following the death had led them all to make various promises to one another, to honour his legacy, to do him proud, to be the family he always wanted them to be, but once the funeral had ended and they returned to London with the last of the bureaucracy taken care of, their previous sense of purpose and obligation began to fade. Mohammed was in the City and rarely, if ever, came to visit. Siver got married and moved in with her husband, and even Xezal had begun wistfully talking about returning to Slemani the day that Iraq was rid of Saddam Hussein's regime. Laika was going to end up in this apartment filled with the ghosts of over twenty years of disappointments, while his family left him behind. So when Siver moved to Baghdad with Karim and Xezal raised the possibility of moving back to Kurdistan, Laika began contemplating his move to Berlin.

Bang.

It was the sort of sound that is more felt than heard, followed by panicked screams, the faint echo of which made it through his windows, still vibrating with the fluttered heartbeat of aftershocks. Laika, from where he sat, could see a sliver of smoke undulating upwards as a charmed snake. Quickly making his way to the windows to get a better view of what had happened, he saw people rushing out of the New York Stock Exchange through a cloud of smoke, emerging with jackets raised to cover their faces, as though hundreds of magicians were appearing out of thin air. A body beneath them, being trampled under the stampede. The police, hitherto concerned with the protesters, quickly moved to secure the building, indicating to each other where they should stand, what they should do. From above, the whole thing looked almost comical, sped-up like a silent movie running at fewer frames per second than needed to be translated into regular motion to our eyes. He scrolled through Twitter to find out what was happening in front of his eyes, and within minutes of refreshing his feed he saw a report that someone had detonated stink bombs on the trading floor. A prank, a protest, or both.

He wondered how many of the protesters running below him grew up with protests as part of their lives. Maybe this was all new to them; maybe it had to be for them to believe in it. When they were younger, Rafiq would drag his three children to demonstrations seemingly every weekend. Freezing in front of the American embassy, the Iraqi embassy, the Turkish embassy. Chants of *down down with Saddam*, chants of *American bombs destroying Kurdish homes*, chants of *Kurdistan Kurdistan Solidarité*. The chants didn't rhyme, barely scanned, and were slightly amended for each purpose. Then the kids would go back to school and hear their classmates talk about what movies their parents had taken them to see over the weekend, the new rollercoaster at Chessington World of Adventures. Laika would often lie, say that he too had seen *Return of the Jedi, The Goonies, Highlander*. He claimed that *Professor Burp's Bubbleworks* was amazing.

The crowds began to disperse now, the news that was on his screen appearing to have reached those who were directly affected. Someone was handcuffed, yellow tape was put in front of the entry. Within minutes, the crowds retook their positions, the police in formation once again, as though the second half of a football match were about to begin.

Laika checked to see that the NYSE had not been closed as a consequence of the stink bomb, and was pleased to see that it hadn't, his bot still buying and selling at super-human speed. He went to the kitchen to get a piece of fruit and a can of Coke Zero and saw that, contrary to his explicit instructions, there was an orange among the apples he had requested. The smell of oranges reminded him too much of the bowl of rotting citrus that infested the small Paris apartment he shared with two students. He could not stand the fruit any more, and used a tissue to toss it in the garbage bag by the door.

After it was well and truly over with Lotti (she packed her bag, left his apartment and unfriended him on Facebook), he left Berlin for Paris, mainly because he had a notion that a person needs to have lived in Paris at some point. Still, he needed to get a job quickly as he was running low on funds. He used an app to find a couch he could sleep on near the République in an apartment that smelled of weed and stale beer. One of his hosts, a scraggly white guy by the name of Benoit with hair in a giant lump on his head in an attempt to grow dreadlocks, told him that if he wanted a relaxing job, he could always be the front desk agent at a hotel during the night shift. 'You know, I basically watch videos on the computer for seven hours, and come home. It is – you say this? – piece of cake?' Benoit offered Laika a drag of his spliff and a phone number to call. The job did indeed turn out to be pretty uneventful, but every so often Laika had to deal with drunk guests making ludicrous requests at 4 a.m. An irate Australian asked him to provide 'a hamburger, an eight-ball of coke, and two or three hookers', not understanding that the hotel kitchen was closed and Laika had neither the knowledge nor the desire to get the other things that were requested. 'I'll have you fired, you blarab cunt,' the Australian said before he waddled away to the hotel elevator. Eventually Laika decided he would have to get another job, the social interactions imposed upon him not something that he particularly wanted out of a workplace environment. He was already forced to share an apartment with two students in the Marais, an apartment that always smelled of oranges and cigarettes, as nobody would lease him an apartment without three months' worth of gas and electricity bills.

One of the students he was sharing the apartment with, a fastidious Danish boy with an unpronounceable name who was doing a master's in IT, was working weekends at a video streaming company,

Dailymotion, and told Laika that there were jobs available if he wanted them. He quit the hotel job and went to work for the streaming company, where he reviewed flagged streaming content to see if the uploaded videos were in violation of the site's terms and conditions. It didn't pay much, but his working hours were pretty flexible, and he could just sit at his computer with headphones on and get paid for watching videos, so it was in many ways ideal. Though it's true that, at first, he was disturbed by the multitude of horrors he watched: beheadings by Islamic fundamentalists, a grown man dressed as a baby and bathing in a kiddie pool while a dominatrix stepped on him with her stiletto heels, drive-by shootings taking place as the assailants cackled at the sight of people going down, young kids slapping elderly women for kicks, men talking about how nobody loved them and how they would kill everyone one day, young girls cutting themselves, and a fuckton of amateur pornography. Every once in a while, Laika would report one of the pornographic clips, especially when they showed or alluded to paedophilia, but mostly he would just delete them from the server. After a while, however, he learned that as long as he wasn't listening to the sound, he could efficiently decide the fate of dozens of videos a minute, neither the beheadings nor the lecherous old men filming young girls having any effect on him at all.

Notification.

An email from DiJiFi, he saw as he fished the phone out of his pocket. He swiped and tapped and found that it contained a link to a digital locker where an .avi file resided comprised of the contents of the VHS tape that he had sent the company to digitise. Laika went back to his laptop and began to download the file, a blue line quickly filling the bar representing the file's 1.4 gigabytes.

He didn't know at what point he had stopped worrying about space. The looming threat of a full hard drive was no longer there, as everything was being uploaded to clouds, clouds that we liked to think of as ephemeral but which had massive carbon footprints. A Japanese study found that by 2030 the power requirements of the country's digital tools and services – all those servers, all those 'clouds' – would be greater than the amount of electricity the country could generate. We restrict our mobility, we eat vegan food, and yet it's the internet that we would need to curb. The energy consumption per internet user was rising at 45 per cent annually, when there was only a gain of approximately 6 per cent of additional users per year. We think our digital consumption is preferable to physical consumption, and yet it is all the same waste. Three hundred hours of video is uploaded onto YouTube every single minute.

At least he no longer had to watch it all.

A *ding*, the bounce of the download folder in his dock.

The file had finished downloading. Laika double-clicked on the file and saw grainy footage of a birthday party.

'Laika? Laika, what day is it today?' His father's voice, from behind the camera. Tears filled Laika's eyes as he shivered with recognition. He had forgotten what his father's voice used to sound like and not even realised it.

'It is my birthday!' Laika said, switching from an exuberant glance up at his father to a suspicious look at the camera's lens, too young to have started to avoid having his picture taken.

The camcorder, a Sony Handycam device they had been given as a gift by some wealthy Kurd who had admired Rafiq's political writings, was sold shortly after this birthday party, the money needed to pay rent, buy groceries, whatever it was that had them on the brink of poverty that week. When his mother called him a few months ago saying that she had found in the box of old video tapes something with 'LAIKA BIRTHDAY 7 YEARS' scribbled on, Laika had a vague recollection of this birthday party being filmed, but since Xezal did not own a VCR, there was no way to tell whether the contents matched the label. There being no functioning postal service in Iraq, a family friend who was travelling to Germany took the tape with him and sent it to New York from there. And two weeks ago, it arrived, a decades-old strip of adhesive tape covering the rectangular gap where the VHS cassette copy protection tab had been removed.

'And how old are you today?'

'SEVEN!' Laika said, jumping up and down, smiling a half-toothed smile. In the background, he could see Mohammed poking at the wrapped presents, before Xezal shooed him away.

'Siver, it's your brother's birthday today!' The camera panned to Siver, eating a bit of pita bread and watching cartoons.

'I know!' she said, mouth filled with bread.

'Why don't you come here and give your brother a kiss!'

Siver reluctantly got off the couch and stomped over to her brother. They hugged each other awkwardly, as if struggling to figure out where their arms should go.

'Do you love your brother?'

'Yes,' she said, visibly embarrassed.

'Xezal, come over here, say something to the camera.'

'Can we just eat the cake already? I'm *hun*gry,' Mohammed moaned as Xezal's face filled the screen, prompting Rafiq to zoom out.

'Stop it, I look horrible,' she said, covering her face with her hands.

It was a shock to see his mother. Of course, he had seen pictures, but it was easy to pretend that they were of other people entirely, that his parents could not possibly ever have been so stylish, so young. And yes, Xezal's face was wet with the steam of the rice she had been cooking, and she wore a shoddily improvised turban on her head and a dress that had not aged well, but it still hurt Laika to see what she had once looked like.

'You are beautiful, my heart; come say something to the camera.'

The film began flickering, the original recording growing visible under the layer of the newer footage, a composite image comprised of some cartoon recorded off The Children's Channel and the only filmed testimony of his childhood. Instead of hearing his mother's former voice, when she opened her mouth a bombastic sound emerged.

'Ah! He-Man! What a prize you'll make for Skeletor!'

Soon the image was comprised entirely of 'She-Demon of Phantos', a 1983 episode of *He-Man and the Masters of the Universe*, known – if it is known at all – mainly for being the only episode in which the villain Strongarm appears. Strongarm had, as the name probably indicates, a strong arm, much like the heroic character Fisto had, yes, a strong fist.

The rest of the tape was just old cartoons. Jerry ice-skating to Tchaikovsky's 'Sleeping Beauty Waltz' while being lit through rotating jelly, the theme-song to *ThunderCats*, Skeletor wondering what the point of presents was if they did not explode. Only at the very end of the fifty-nine-minute recording did some of the home video reappear, a few seconds of Laika and Mohammed fighting over a toy, while their parents told them to stop arguing. Rafiq then turned off the camcorder, and Laika stared at the static, the random dot pixel patterns that Mohammed had once convinced him was a war between black ants and white ants, and if he kept watching he would see one of the colours win.

This wasn't the only television-related prank his older brother pulled. When Laika was about three, his brother convinced him that people lived inside their television set. They only had one channel, National Iranian Radio & Television's TV1, and said channel broadcast one thing and one thing only: the day's news with a rotation of four newscasters. Laika had already shown a propensity for developing odd feelings for machines: a shattered LP record on their way home from grocery shopping made him cry inconsolably for days, and when their brand-new stereo broke and Rafiq took it back to the store, they found pieces of stale bread inside (Laika had been feeding it through the amp's air vent because he thought it was hungry). To make him believe that the people they saw on the screen actually lived inside the television wasn't too much of a stretch, then, and it led to amusing moments when three-year-old Laika would start crying every time either of his parents would shout at the television (a fairly common occurrence in the Hardi household). When Laika one day ran in front of the television and told his parents to stop being so mean to his friends, the entire thing could have ended right there, they could have asked Laika who had put such crazy thoughts in his head and he would have pointed to Mohammed and that would have been that. But what happened instead was that neither Rafiq nor Xezal had any questions for Laika, instead laughing and indulging him, pretending along with him that the people inside the television were indeed living there. After the revolution, the one channel they previously had was closed down and replaced with two new channels, Islamic Republic of Iran TV1 and TV2. Xezal explained how the previous tenants of the TV had to move out to make room for more people than before. Laika was upset that his friends had left without saying goodbye, but later, when they had to flee to the UK, he understood how sometimes one has to leave people behind without telling them. Rafiq and Xezal conjured an elaborate story about what had happened to their friends that they had left behind in the television. By the time they had managed to buy a new TV in the UK, they had already forged several postcards from their TV friends who assured them that they were doing just fine, and not to worry about them. There were also two letters, written by Xezal, describing how the TV friends managed to escape from the authorities. Laika could not remember when he actually discovered that he had been fed a lie for years, a lie that three-quarters of his family were in on. There was, as far as he could recall, no major incident, no confrontation of any kind. Whenever Laika learned the truth, he never asked why they had spent several years indulging this fantasy. However he dealt with the betrayal, he dealt with it alone, and never spoke of it to his family.

The gloriously sharp New York sun escaped from behind a cloud and blinded him, covering his face in cold autumn light, before he noticed a flurry of what seemed like dollar bills falling down from the sky, a green murmuration swooping down in a cascading pattern. When one of the bills stuck to his window, it became apparent that they were forgeries: the corners had the number 1, but it was followed by a percentage sign. Laika wondered where the bills were coming from: had someone climbed to the roof of his building with a bag of forged bills? Was there a helicopter far above, dropping them?

Below, a few of the protesters held signs that said PROPERTY IS THEFT, WE ARE THE 99%, and a popular image macro adapted from a Japanese manga called *Gantz* with the caption TOP 1% Y U NO PAY TAXES. Other than these last stragglers, a handful of police officers in ballistic helmets and modular riot gear, and a pair of underwear that rested on the head of the bull, there was no sign of what had taken place there only minutes before. As the bills fluttered down on the pavement, pedestrians and protesters alike sprung into action, a frenzy that reminded Laika of Mohammed's never-ending war between black and white ants on the screen: noise, signifying nothing other than a disturbance in the signal, and if there were books and essays and think-pieces written about this moment in the future, they would amount to nothing more than evidence of the human pareidolic tendency to distinguish patterns in response to stimuli. All sound, all fury. And yet it was hard not to be moved by the way that the people, realising that the money was not real, raised the bills to the skies and began chanting that they were the 99 per cent. The simultaneous nature of the action brought to mind the conventions of the musical, wherein a crowd appears to know the lyrics of a song by osmosis. The sense of injustice was contagious, it seemed, a virus spreading across Lower Manhattan.

Cities were beginning to adapt to this, of course. The public square had too much potential for dissent, for groups of people to meet outside consumerist forums. It was once a necessary place to deliver information, but it functioned as a remnant of societies long past, wherein instead of the proffered vertical occupation of space which contemporary life had imposed upon us, separating us from one another, there remained the possibility for a horizontal occupation of space, allowing for the individual to gain strength and resolve as a crowd, that most terrifying of threats to the powerful, those to whom the future was meant to belong, as per DeLillo.

But contemporary cities were being formed in such a way that the future could never belong to the crowd. It was no coincidence that revolts tended to take place in and around squares, be they Tahrir, Tiananmen, Azadi, Piccadilly Circus. Just as it was no coincidence that post-communist states in Eastern Europe were dismantling the public spaces, building private structures to deny the people of another opportunity to gather. The cities of the future, Dubai first and foremost among them, had no squares at all. Laika had read something Judith Butler had written, that 'for politics to take place, the body must appear [. . .]. Freedom does not come from me or from you; it can and does happen as a relation between us, or indeed among us.' If you removed the possibility for bodies to appear, there would be no more protests. The activities at Zuccotti Park, so close and yet invisible to him, were the last gasp of something as old as human civilisation itself, rather than the beginning of something new.

Endings were often confused with beginnings in this way: had not Pauline Kael, upon seeing *Last Tango in Paris*, rhapsodised about the dying breath of the American New Wave: 'Bernardo Bertolucci's *Last Tango in Paris* was presented for the first time on the closing night of the New York Film Festival, October 14, 1972: that date should become a landmark in movie history comparable to May 29, 1913—the night *Le Sacre du Printemps* was first performed—in music history. There was no riot, and no one threw anything at the screen, but I think it's fair to say that the audience was in a state of shock, because *Last Tango in Paris* has the same kind of hypnotic excitement as the *Sacre*, the same primitive force, and the same thrusting, jabbing eroticism. The movie breakthrough has finally come.' In fact, it was the dawn of the blockbuster, *Jaws* and *Star Wars* only a few years away, laying to waste the era of commercially successful experimental films, and because those movies turned out to be what people chose to see, they became the movies that studios churned out. The flipside of freedom. We were, after all, freely giving Silicon Valley firms all of our private information, nodes of surveillance that we were willingly pumping our secrets into, exercising our freedom to not be free. And how could these structures ever be dismantled? Part of the problem seemed to Laika to be that the physical bodies below were protesting against something that could not be seen. Synthetic Collateral Debt Obligations and shadow banking systems were not tangible, they merely existed as code, the same way that what separated the 1 per cent from the 99 per cent wasn't necessarily the tangible assets, but the numbers ascribed to them in bank terminals across the world. How could an enemy be fought that had no corporeal form? A spectre was haunting the world, all right.

The New York Stock Exchange was closed.

He connected the ethernet cable, turned on, clicked through, logged in, found out. His $502,840.12 had become $482,104.56. And Goldman Sachs was still rising. Goddammit. He had done everything he could think of, and still he was bleeding money. It made no sense to him: surely a bot that performed exactly the same trades as another bot should have roughly the same result? Were those microseconds that the Goldman Sachs bot had at their disposal really the difference between making money and losing it? Laika did not like being presented with a problem that he could not fix.

Time for dinner. He put the tofu with broccoli in the oven, set a timer. As he did so he saw a WhatsApp message from his mother, replete with misused emojis. *Ples call your brother he miss you.*

He didn't understand why it was always on him to make amends. He did not care if his brother was in his life or not, he was perfectly happy with his life the way it was. Mohammed was the one who was rude to him, who kept insulting him. Ever since they were children, Mohammed acted as though he was Laika's boss somehow, telling him to do things and then taking credit with their parents. 'I got Laika to clean the living room,' as if this was worthy of praise. How once Mohammed had seen Laika holding hands with a girl at school and ratted him out to their parents, calling the girl 'some fat, ugly thing'. How he had not once, not once, invited Laika over to his apartment, even though he knew what the situation in the Sutton flat was like once their father died and Siver left to live with Karim. How Laika was on twenty-four-hour Xezal duty, indulging her woe-is-me narratives, and was never told to take a weekend off, that Mohammed would spend time with her. 'I have work, you know,' Mohammed would say any time Laika would bring up the fact that he needed help, especially now that Siver was barely on speaking terms with Xezal. 'You wouldn't understand, since you've never worked a day in your life.'

Notification.

An email, from someone who claimed they worked at Gizmodo, who was doing a piece for the three-year anniversary of the App Store. *Would love to chat about your app.* Money to Burn *is so infamous it would be great to have some background on how it all happened.*

What was there to say? He was drunk, decided to make an app called *Money to Burn*, which consisted of a GIF of burning money. He priced it at $999, the highest price allowed for an app. People bought it. He made millions before the App Store pulled it. What more insight could he possibly grant the journalist? It was a dumb idea, and it made him rich.

He deleted the email.

One other thing: he did it once Yael had broken up with him, and he hoped the app's ridiculous success would bring her back to him, a laughable notion.

Yael worked in the cubicle next to him at Dailymotion, a quiet sort who had the white cord of her flimsy headphones peeking out from the black hoodie she always had on. One day, while they were both taking a break by getting something out of the vending machine, she swore out loud at the naked German couple who had uploaded three videos of them having sex that day. 'You know, I probably will kill myself if I have to look at another eighty-year-old man's testicles.'

He found her compellingly repulsive. The way her hair was either unwashed or unbrushed, the chipped nail polish that she never removed. Her refusal to stop blabbering as if her every thought was the height of fascination. The way she kept the keyboard clicking sounds on her phone. But repulsion is also an effect of a magnetic field, and so he found her so annoying that one day, outside the office toilets, he announced he was going to kiss her and leaned his body so that she edged up against the wall, her turning her face so that he only caught the edge of her mouth with his lips, touching her crusty lip sore, a feeling that wouldn't leave him for the rest of the day.

He had rushed back to his desk, filled with disgust and shame, and then saw later in the day that she had sent him a video on MSN Messenger. It was one of the amateur videos of the German couple having sex. 'ur a pervert, maybe u like this?' she wrote.

From then on, Laika and Yael would share particularly weird videos with one another via Messenger, with elaborately imagined storylines around some of the uploaders, such as the young man who affixed Play-Doh genitalia on children's toys and proceeded to have said toys have intercourse in long montages as he, the uploader, would do the dialogue and moaning of all the characters involved. Yael named the kid Maximilien, and posited that he was the heir of some grand fortune, some French family with a multitude of hyphens in their family name. They would be in steel, or mining, Laika added, and Maximilien was primed to take over the family business, except his true passion in life was having Donatello fuck Rafael with a four-inch putty cock. There was also a particular sub-genre of the Russian car-accident video (as many cars in Russia had dashboard cameras installed for insurance purposes, there was a flurry of accidents and violent acts of road rage caught on tape): an old Ford, kitted out to resemble something out of *Mad Max* that would purposefully ram cars off the road. Laika dubbed the driver of this car the Judge, and imagined that he was a vigilante who got enraged at minor traffic violations, turning Russia into a safer country for drivers, one frenzied car crash at a time. Yael gave the Judge an origin story: he had probably been late to a job interview after missing an exit due to a driver who had neglected to turn on his indicator, swapping a once promising career in biochemistry for the vigilante life.

Gradually, the jokes became more flirtatious, and the videos they sent each other grew ever more sexually explicit. 'Could u fuck like this,' Yael would say, sending him a video of a rabbit jack-hammering a toy gun. 'She looks like she's enjoying herself,' Laika would say after sending Yael a video of a woman cumming to a loud climax while sitting on a washing machine. This went on for a few weeks, until Yael sent Laika a message on MSN instructing him to 'meet me in the WC in 3 minutes'. After fumbling through sex, Laika began apologising. Yael rolled her eyes at him. 'You are really strange, you know that, no?'

The next night, as they left work at 2 a.m., Yael suggested they go to a nearby bar that was open until four. 'They have the best mojito,' she said as she led him through the Bastille, the smell of piss and rotting trash wafting through the narrow streets and wide boulevards. Yael told him that a few years ago Basque separatists had set off bombs in trash cans around Paris, and so the response was to seal all the bins, leading to people just throwing their garbage on the street. 'The garbage is a sign that we are safe,' she said, and Laika was not sure whether she was joking or being serious. 'Come, this is the place.' The bar, a tiny cramped space with pictures of the Virgin Mary plastered over every available inch of the walls, did indeed have excellent mojitos.

One potent glass of mint-muddled social lubricant was all it took for Laika to feel the tightening in his chest loosen up, to see the person sitting in front of him as someone whom he could be truthful to. The truth had always seemed to Laika an excessively complex thing; when people asked questions like 'where are you from?' and 'how are you?' they were being polite, and wanted short, breezy answers, rather than an exegesis on the plight of Kurds in the twentieth century, or the feeling he had of never truly being understood, heard or even listened to. So he found himself lying, throughout his childhood, his teens and well into his adult life. Lies were a convenient shorthand, he found, where you could give any social interaction only that which was needed to keep it light, polite. The few times he had spoken freely, he found people stifling yawns, trying to steal glances of the time or, worse, found himself offending people. But lying was a minefield in and of itself. He'd recently read one of Lotti's worn paperbacks, a book in which the author claimed that 'the paradox of childhood lies is that we so often tell them out of fear of rejection, fear of separation, fear of being alone, and yet the lie is itself an expression of our independence. We lie in order not to be alone, and yet we cannot lie without accepting the fact that fundamentally, alone is where we are. Our minds are entirely private—and especially so when we lie.' He was unable to stop thinking of this paragraph, and realised he needed to stop lying. But he had found the truth too ungainly, too messy, to accurately be described in words. It seemed speech made any truth a lie, as it forced wide, mutable things into narrow, constricting words. And yet, with Yael, that night, he found it to be easy.

Laika told her of the life choices, or lack thereof, that had brought him to Paris. He spoke of having to leave in the night when the Revolutionary Guard was rounding up known Kurdish Marxists in Tehran, touched briefly upon his previous relationship and, wanting to impress her, exaggerated his part in the eco-vandalism that Lotti's group was a part of (a lie, yes, he could not help himself). Yael laughed riotously through it all, the secondary school teacher who kicked him out of class because she refused to believe that his home country was not on a map, the massive payment he received for the Laika.com domain, the time when Lotti's friend Johann had set a timed explosion only to find that the bomb was a dud and Johann, Lotti and Laika stood in a car park playing rock-paper-scissors to decide who was going to go back inside and retrieve the device. The more he spoke the more he felt that he had things to say, and he realised that this was the most he had talked to any one person since that night it ended with Lotti.

'You're really funny,' Yael said, wiping her eyes for effect. 'I have no good stories, you know? My life is just boring.'

Yael's clothes were stolen from previous boyfriends, she announced with strange pride when she caught his eye lingering on her tattered black hoodie, and it wasn't until she took him home one day that he felt like he began understanding her. She lived in a massive space decorated as though it had come from the pages of *Napoleonic Interior*. All gaudy gold-leafed frames of portraits and hand-woven worn-out Persian rugs, an Afghan rug depicting the drones that were part of their landscape. 'This is not mine, of course. It is my parents' apartment. But they're not here so.'

They began seeing each other outside of work regularly and though Laika still paid for the room in the apartment with the rotting oranges, he spent more and more time at Yael's, in her weird bedroom on the fourth floor of the rue Neuve-Popincourt in what had once been an attic, its eaves slicing down in restricting angles as its living space pushed up against the building's shape. He wanted to ask why she didn't sleep in one of the apartment's many outrageous bedrooms, but suspected that would be a conversation that would not end well. So they slept in the former attic, the bed so close to the ceiling that Laika would, more than once, bang his head against it while getting up in the morning, but it was full of light, dramatically shifting across the floors throughout the day.

Eventually, as the initial passion of discovering one another subsided, Yael and Laika found themselves staring at each other, wondering how their mutual presence could ever have felt so intoxicating. Beneath the thrilling shimmer of endless possibility there were two boring individuals, made of ageing flesh, filled with insecurities, unexceptional in every way. Yael, freed from the illusion that Laika was going to bring some excitement into a life that had been spent entirely in and around the 11th arrondissement, quickly grew annoyed with seemingly everything that he did: his lack of desire to socialise with her other friends, his inability to make any plans whatsoever, his obsession with the game *Virtua Tennis 3* on his portable console. But she tolerated him, the idea of being together preferable to solitude, until the night when she told him about her rabbit.

Laika was staying the night mainly because it was raining and he didn't feel like walking back to his flat in the Marais, while Yael lay with her back to him as she had started to do recently. Laika was playing his tennis game, finding himself stuck at the final match of the World Tour for days, and was trying to press the buttons as quietly as possible so that Yael wouldn't berate him for his gaming once again.

'I had a rabbit when I was a kid,' Yael said, out of nowhere, her voice barely a whisper, which made Laika initially think that she was talking to herself or recording a voice message on her phone. 'I really wanted a puppy, but my father he refused for years. Eventually he decided to get me a rabbit, you know, like a rabbit would be easier or something, which of course it wasn't because the cage needed to be cleaned out all the time, it would just piss and shit constantly. Poupouille, I called him. Silly child name. And sometimes, I would let Poupouille out of the cage, feeling that he was happier when he was free. It's a cruel thing we do, have caged animals for the pleasure of our children. Children sense it, you know, that it is cruel. So. When my father was at work, I let Poupouille out. My grandfather came to visit for a few weeks, not my father's father, who disappeared in the war, but my mother's father, you know? My father was not happy, but my mother said that he was old and dying and my dad said OK finally. I remember they were fighting about my grandfather coming to stay so much. I was maybe eight. Or no, we'd moved to the apartment in rue Moufle already so I was nine or ten maybe. And . . . my grandfather, he was a big man. It was crazy, he was so big. He is dead now, but I think honestly he was the biggest man I will see ever. One day he knocked on the door of our neighbour by mistake, thinking it was our apartment, a boy opened up and looked up like wow. He shouted to his parents that God was there. That's how impressive he was. Children would think he was a god. And so. One day Poupouille went missing. I was shouting his name, you know – Poupouille, where are you? – and our apartment was not so big you lose a rabbit: not like this one, it was when my father had lost his money on . . . Anyway, long story. But so finally we see my grandfather had sat on the rabbit without noticing. He killed the rabbit with his giant butt, which maybe it sounds funny now, but I was honestly horrifié, horrified? I start crying but my mother told me to stop: she said my grandfather was sick, and to see me hystérique would make him feel bad and maybe he has another heart attack or something and so I did that thing that children do when they're told to be quiet: I stomped my feet, I slammed doors until my mother she gave me a slap. My father, he hit me often, but I cannot remember my mother ever hitting me more than this one time. When my father came home he just was angry, of course, I had let Poupouille out of the cage. So . . . I don't know. Maybe what I'm trying to say is that I was so sad, a small child sad for her pet rabbit, but everyone kept telling me not to say this, you know? To hide what I was feeling because it wasn't the right way to behave. There's nothing more impressive to a child than injustice, I was so angry, and refused to eat dinner. I had a hunger strike. Then my father gave me a hundred francs and told me to forget it. Like money fixes everything.'

Laika, finally beating the final boss in *Virtua Tennis 3* in a tie-break, let out a yelp of excitement.

Yael turned over, her eyes having teared up while telling her story, and when she saw that Laika was on his console playing a game, she sat up as though she'd been doused with cold water.

'Are you not even listening?'

Laika looked over. He had: it was a story about her childhood pet, how much concentration did that actually demand?

'Are you fucking kidding? What is *wrong* with you?'

Laika was confused, felt he should apologise but did not know what for.

'You are an asshole, you know. I want you to leave. Get the fuck out of my apartment.'

Minutes after he left, she posted a long quote in French from Monique Wittig's *Les Guérillères* that Facebook's translation function garbled into a confusing mess; a few hours after that, 'The male is a biological accident', from the SCUM Manifesto. He got the gist.

Timer.

Dinner was ready, his phone informed him.

Laika performed the tricky balancing move of transporting the food from the oven to the table in the study without burning his hands. He clicked through videos on YouTube, choosing something to watch while he ate. A celebrity falling over drunk, a make-up tutorial, a news clip. A fifteen-minute compilation of 'top 10 teen life sentence reactions'. Nothing seemed worthwhile. A conspiracy theorist analysing Saddam Hussein's body language during his trial, 'did bush kill a BODY DOUBLE?', which reminded him of how he had for years carried a photograph he'd once found in his father's radio, believing it to be a distant family member or one of his father's old communist friends, until he saw the man on trial one day on Yael's tiny television and realised he had been keeping a photograph of Saddam's Minister of Foreign Affairs in his wallet for the better part of a decade. He clicked on a news item about the one conviction in relation to the 2008 financial crisis. The video buffered and Laika saw the attractive anchor look stern as he asked the journalist present at the courthouse what all of this meant. The journalist, standing outside a Manhattan courtroom, pressed on his earpiece as his hair blew in his face, tried explaining that the former Goldman Sachs trader had been convicted for espionage and theft-of-trade-secrets charges, having quit his job and taken with him a flash drive that contained 32 megabytes of proprietary code, amidst the 1,220 megabytes of open-source material. The former Goldman Sachs employee claimed that this had just been an inadvertent mistake, that he had not known that there was proprietary code on the flash drive, but the attorneys claimed it was 'the most substantial theft that the bank can remember ever happening to it', and the presiding judge had sentenced the former employee to eight years in prison because 'the scope of his theft was audacious – motivated solely by greed – and it was characterised by supreme disloyalty to his employer'.

It felt almost natural that bankers, who worked at firms too big to fail, would be too big to jail. After all, giving corporations the same rights as people did not mean they had the same responsibilities. But he knew this was a recent development: the boom–bust cycle of capitalism, so intrinsic to its very nature, had historically led to crackdowns. The 1929 stock market crash led to the head of the New York Stock Exchange being imprisoned. The burst of the so-called internet bubble led to executives from many companies being tried in court. And yet now, nothing. A former Goldman Sachs trader being imprisoned at the behest of Goldman Sachs itself. That was it. That was all there would be. Yes We Can, except when clearly, we can't. Wachovia had laundered billions of dollars for drug cartels and terrorists for decades, and all that happened was that they got a fine that amounted to 2 per cent of that year's profits. And so why not continue? If there are no consequences, why not keep doing it? It was the core purpose of a public limited liability company, after all, to make as much money for the shareholders as possible. If cheating would get you there, why not cheat?

He squinted at his algorithm. It didn't make any sense, his experiment kept failing and he did not understand why. Since he'd started with high-frequency trading five months ago, he'd lost over $350,000. He still had enough to live off for the rest of his life, thanks to the *Money to Burn* app and a series of investments various financial advisors suggested following that windfall, but this trading thing, which was meant to be a hobby, something to do with his time, was starting to become an obsession. It should work, and it didn't.

Maybe he was thinking about it all wrong. Maybe there was no way to mirror trades as a single agent with a store-bought computer server and some cobbled-together algorithm with open-source components when what you were mirroring operated at an IP-protected complexity that was impossible to gain insight into. Maybe all the big firms were in fact operating behind dark pools, private exchanges inaccessible to regular investors, and what Laika's algorithm was coded to mirror could only take into account a facet of what was actually happening, a 2D entity that saw the indentations of a 3D orb and believed that the indentations were the entirety of what was there. Maybe the goal wasn't to mirror trades but to use the algorithms' encoded behaviour against them. He could, after all, mislead algorithms, spoofing orders. Make them think one thing was happening when it actually wasn't. The market allowed for offers to be rescinded, so he could easily pretend to sell thousands of shares, indicating to other trading bots that the price of that share would soon go down, triggering them to sell off shares due to this intention. If Laika were to cancel the sell order a microsecond before it was to be actioned, his bot could then instead buy up the shares sold for a price he had just lowered by indicating an intent to sell. It was risky, since he had to assume that the big trading algorithms functioned much like his own primitive one did, but if his suspicions were founded, he could make a killing. He started working on a new algorithm immediately, creating parameters to generate large sell orders, tinkering with the time available to him to cancel the order, trying to determine how many shares at the lower market prices it should, in the end, buy. He worked obsessively on the algorithm throughout the night, and it was well past 4 a.m. by the time he was done, too tired even to see the code any more. He went to bed relieved, thinking he'd finally been able to crack a problem he'd seen as nigh insurmountable for months.

Alarm.

He woke up a few hours later, swiped the alarm off, his sleep quality a mere 27 per cent, but he felt more energised than he had in days. He made the bed, a little bit more rushed than usual, and took a quick shower, omitting his daily shave. He realised, as he finished wiping the shower clean, that he had forgotten to order his coffee and bagel last night. Never mind, he could just eat an apple. It was 09:08. Soon the fun would begin.

'There was a man in our village,' Rafiq had once said, noticing how the children were enrapt by the soap opera *Dallas*, which followed the lives of the wealthy Ewing family. 'He was the wealthiest man there was. But he hoarded his wealth, not even helping his family members. The villagers were starving after a bad crop, and still this man would not share his wealth. He died alone, with nobody beside him. His fate was a tragic one, children.'

'What happened to his money?' Mohammed asked him, taking advantage of an ad break.

'His family split it. They are still rich to this day.'

'Doesn't seem too bad to me,' Mohammed said, as the show resumed.

Laika went to the window and looked down at the protests. Fewer people than in previous days, it seemed, but those who remained still held up their signs, the police still stood before them, riot shields up. Laika wondered how much longer this would last. Eventually the media's Sauron eye would stop looking at Occupy, turn towards one of the million other things happening, and the police would be given the all-clear to remove the protesters once and for all.

There had been protests before, after all, and all had been quashed. New York must be littered with people who had believed, or at least hoped, that they would be able to effect change, now wandering around the streets without the force that the crowd gives. Had they grown even more disillusioned, Laika wondered, or did they carry a shard of the protests inside them as they worked, as they applied for jobs, as they met friends for overpriced drinks? At least they'd tried to stop the machine; maybe that still provided a sense of accomplishment?

He took a bite of his apple and checked his phone. Time to see if he would fare any better with his new algorithm. He went over to his desk, glanced through the parameters one last time, and clicked for it to begin, before he moved away from his laptop, to return to his window.

It was astounding to him that in the few steps that it took to get to the window, his bot would have made thousands upon thousands of trades already. And the only direction things could go was faster. Was it Virilio who said that acceleration was leading to the liquidation of the world? People were speaking of the Capitalocene, that humanity's capitalist systems would be able to be seen in the strata of the earth, that the damage that was being done by our use of fossil fuels, essentially combusting millions of years of the earth's history for immediate gain, would be as visible to future geologists, if there were any, as the Permian–Triassic extinction event which led to the extinction of 96 per cent of all marine species and 70 per cent of vertebrates. But it was the term Necrocene that appealed to Laika the most, because this system did not have any other goal, after all, than its own destruction. We were digging deeper and deeper, using ever more resources. The goal of capitalism was not monetary gain, it was the death of humanity.

And the writing had been on the wall for a long time, ever since we started messing with the very concept of time with the telegraph. When information could suddenly travel much faster than a human being and information could be relayed across the world in mere seconds. That was when trading began changing from local markets, selling a cow from one area in another area where they were more valuable, to gambling. We invented futures, and could speculate in not what was happening, because that information was now available to all, but what was going to happen. Time had become polychronic, with all possible events happening at once, history collapsing onto itself.

Once it was all over, what would remain? The poet Simonides of Ceos was known to history not because of his skill, but because he was the first to sell his poetry, and inscribed it on wealthy people's graves. While scholars struggle to make sense of Sappho's fragments, Simonides's stone engravings remain. Our history would die with our hard drives, the most well-documented century in the history of the world a dark age for future civilisations as they would find badly degraded drives and DVDs and floppy disks and be unable to read them. We thought the Dutch tulip mania was odd, an entire nation driving itself into bankruptcy over tulip bulbs, while we worked ourselves to literal death for data, believing the cloud and its servers would last for ever.

When Rafiq had wasted yet another benefit cheque on fliers about the Kurdish cause, Xezal tossed them in the bin. She screamed that Rafiq was crazy, that he would willingly starve his own family for some god-forsaken cause. Laika saw Rafiq go through the trash that night, carefully separating the still-clean fliers from those with food stains on them, lovingly ironing them out with his palms. Laika remembered being disgusted at this sight, at how undignified it all seemed to him. He went to his room and shot space demons on his computer for several hours. How could a man be so unequipped to live in the real world?

Online, people were sharing photographs of a flash mob campaign wherein they arranged their clothes and shoes on the ground in public spaces to make it appear as though they had been raptured. An online search led him to the website of the evangelist Harold Camping, who had declared that the day of Rapture was last week, that he'd made a calculation for 'atonement × completeness × heaven squared' and found the exact date of the Second Coming of Christ. As a response, people had started Post-Rapture Pet Care Services to care for the animals left behind, an eBay user had begun auctioning off post-Rapture life insurance, and everywhere these photos, these arranged clothes like thousands of bodies vaporised. Laika thought of the so-called Human Shadow of Death, the outline of a person who was vaporised by the atomic bomb, leaving nothing but bones and carbonised organs, his shadow impressed by thermal rays on the stairs of a bank where the person was sitting. It was just a coincidence that it was at a bank, of course. The Hiroshima Peace Memorial Museum had for many decades now been investigating how to preserve a shadow.

Notification.

He pulled out his phone and saw it was a news push notification, which he started to reflexively swipe away when he read the headline.

Stock Market Collapse.

He dropped his apple, bits of its white flesh scattered across the otherwise clean floor. Laika blinked, read the headline again. It had not changed. Stock Market Collapse: Dow Jones index loses 9 per cent of its value in seconds.

He rushed back to his laptop, hunched over the table as he put in his login wrong once, twice, before he was allowed in and saw that, indeed, the market was collapsing, the graphic interface a ravine plunging deeper and deeper. He clicked to see the evolution of the market the past month, the past year, the past five years, and still, this dip was unlike any that the market had witnessed before. He quickly terminated his bot and brought up his assets. A slow churn, the loading of the online trading window appearing in chunks. Fuck fuck fuck. He'd lost everything he'd put in the trading account. Half a million dollars, gone. What had just happened?

He sat down, his fingers above the keyboard, unsure of what to type in. News. News would be good. New tab. CNN was still talking about the Occupy protests; Fox News was running a story about genetically engineered cats that glowed in the dark and could somehow stop AIDS; CNBC was covering the crash, but was unable to give him any answers, the anchor kept repeating the facts, that the markets were collapsing, but not why. Nothing seemed to have happened in the rest of the world; nothing seemed to have happened in the US. It was a completely uneventful day, and yet the markets kept plunging down. The rise and fall of colourful curves against a black background, an aesthetic that was reminiscent of an ECG chart's visualisation of cardiac activity, the visual representation of the health of capital, now plummeted towards death.

Laika looked at other markets, using his terminal as a deck of tarot cards or tea leaves, trying to see patterns that had meaning, but he noticed nothing beyond the ordinary. Most of the time the market's movements matched events that occurred in real time on websites and news channels, and yes, the Dow Jones Industrial Average had started the day down a few hundred points, mainly due to uncertainties related to demonstrations in Greece against the economic tightening measures the European Union was imposing upon them. It was almost a perfect correlation: a Pavlovian reaction where the market fell a few points each time pictures of dissatisfied Greeks were shown on television, where the echo of the anxiety induced by the specific situation in Greece disrupted the financial world's stability as an earthquake's aftershock. Investors logged in on various websites and said they had finished playing, that they would take their cash from the market's casino. At the start of the day the Dow Jones Industrial Average had been down 300 points. A bad day, in other words, but nothing catastrophic. And then, a few seconds later, total collapse. It made no sense. What was already looking like the largest stock market crash in the history of the United States, with trillions of dollars gone, was happening, kept happening. And yet there was nothing, no news event in the real world that seemed to indicate such a reaction. What was happening was the sort of market response you'd expect from the apocalypse: even the events of September 11 hadn't resulted in anything like this, and yet there was no apocalypse to be seen anywhere.

There appeared to be no logic in the valuations: Apple Inc. shares valued at $36 per share just a few minutes ago were selling for over $100,000 per share. The shares for a consulting company were being purchased for 1 cent, sold for 2 cents, back and forth hundreds of thousands of times in a minute.

Laika paced the apartment, phone in hand, refreshing feeds on Bloomberg, the *Wall Street Journal*, the *Financial Times*. Eventually photographs of traders holding their heads in their hands appeared to illustrate the news, even though these were stock photos, staged so that newspapers would have something to show, when the reality was that there were no traders on the floor, there were only blinking, whirring hard drives. The markets kept falling, down 20 per cent, 25 per cent, 30 per cent.

And then the machine sputtered, and stopped.

Unable to figure out what was happening, the NYSE had pulled the plug, trading was suspended. Outside black vans had gathered at an impressive speed, suited men rushing into the stock exchange building. On Twitter the world was going on as though nothing had happened, the information still not filtered through to the people that decades of wealth had just vanished in seconds. There were still jokes, performances of outrage, cat GIFs. Laika stood absolutely still, observed what was happening outside without understanding any of it. Suddenly the biblical quote that Samuel Morse chose when demonstrating the telegraph to investors seemed prophetically apt. What hath God wrought?

He brought up the stock application on his phone, before he realised it was pointless. What he was looking at weren't the real values, it was more akin to the light of stars in the sky that died out thousands of years ago. This was not his to make sense of. He was, after all, human, and humans were parasites to machines. Whatever had happened had happened.

Laika's foot touched a piece of the apple he had dropped earlier. He knelt down to pick up its pieces, the flesh now gently rotting. He scooped up the largest pieces and put them in the trash bag by his door and activated the robot vacuum cleaner to get the rest.

As the robot began its motion across the wooden floor, zigzagging in accordance with a pattern that made no sense to Laika but was supposed to be optimised to cover the largest floor area in the shortest time, Laika kept staring out of the window. Everything looked the same. If this total financial meltdown was as big as the markets indicated, you'd think there would be visible signs of it, but other than the three black SUVs, this could have been any other day. The tourists were still lining up in front of the designer store selling $10,000 handbags, the delivery vans and taxis still crawled through the space left to them on the street, the sun sliced across the buildings as it always had, the people protesting seemed to have no idea of what had just happened. A man was walking his dog, talking on the phone. Laika recalled something he had read about planes when they crash: they don't plummet, nose-down, to their doom. They glide.

He regretted not having ordered his coffee the night before. The apocalypse deserves a cup of coffee, after all. Laika swiped to unlock his phone and opened the PayPal app.

A notification appeared, a red triangle with an exclamation point followed by 'Your payment is being reviewed because of regulations.'

Laika squinted, trying to gain more information from the corporation's message than the few sentences provided. 'Don't try to make payments until you hear from us.' Fine, he could just use Seamless, it would cost more but fuck it. He needed his coffee. He browsed through the listings until he found a place he wanted, ordered a soymilk latte, tipped 40 per cent, and clicked on Order. 'That card didn't quite work. Please double check your card information and try again.'

Frustrated, he started to compose a text to his siblings. *Have you guys seen the news? It's madness.* His finger hovered over the send button, then quickly tapped on the backspace key instead, deleting the message. Siver. He'd forgotten to transfer her money.

He tried logging into his Chase bank account but was told that 'this part of our site is not available right now'. Annoyed, he fished his platinum card out of his card holder and called the customer service number printed on the back of it. A woman answered immediately, as though she had been expecting his call. Her accent and cadence was that of someone who sat close by, somewhere in New York, unlike the massive call centres across the developing world that those without platinum credit cards at their disposal were relegated to. He did not know who provided a better service, but he knew that this woman instilled in him a feeling that, whatever his problem was, it could be resolved. People with the amount of money he had in his account did not have problems that service workers could leave unresolved. He proceeded to explain where he was, and how he was unable to log into his account. The woman on the other end of the line apologised as though she had spilled something on him, she was *so* sorry, if there is *anything* she can do. She asked him some security questions, the answers to which satisfied her, and tapped some details into her computer before asking him to hold.

Maybe whatever had happened to the stock market earlier had also led to the banks shutting down? It seemed absurd, but how else to explain his inability to log into his account. Maybe all of his money was, for all intents and purposes, gone.

He remembered when he was a child and Xezal and Rafiq were arguing over money, after Xezal and Laika had returned from the cash machine outside Sainsbury's, and Xezal said there was no money. How Laika had walked up to them and said that there was money, the people behind them in the queue had taken some out, a statement so absurd that it defused the tension and his parents both laughed. 'May you always think of money this way,' Rafiq said and kissed his head, his breath lingering with the smell of liquor.

The woman returned, her voice suddenly different.

'Your accounts have been frozen, sir.'

Laika attempted to argue with her, but found himself incapable of coaxing any further answers out of the woman on the other end of the line, of even being able to voice his frustration coherently. His parents could enter an argument as though they had prepared for it their whole lives, always ready, but frustration and anger had been outsourced, all complaints were now dealt with in the form of a post-interaction rating. In the past few years, he'd barely had to confront another human, a one-star rating had become the solution to any interpersonal awkwardness. And here he was, needing to know what was going on with his account, and he had no idea how to argue any more, if he ever had at all. Laika hung up and stared at his phone.

He tried his HSBC account, only to be faced with a similar error message. 'Your accounts cannot be accessed right now.' His Charles Schwab account that held his investments? 'Sorry, there has been an error. Please try again later.' A quick search on Twitter ('cannot log in') indicated that the rest of the world wasn't experiencing any major difficulties. Was it him? Were all his accounts intentionally being frozen?

One last attempt: this time to log in to the French account where his app earnings had once been deposited, Credit Agricole. He had wanted to close the account upon leaving France, but had found the process too bureaucratically complicated and so had left the account dormant for the past three years. It took him several minutes to find his eleven-digit ID number and his password, but this time it worked. *Bienvenu M Hardi.* He was in. A click on his account, a scroll down. His balance was €204, 393.22. Relieved, he dialled his sister's number.

Outside, two SUVs had parked in front of his building, six armed men in riot gear exiting the vehicle, rifles aimed, a man in a suit behind them. Inside the apartment the phone was ringing, without anyone picking up on the other end. How late was it in Dubai? Was she sleeping?

'Hello?'

'Sisi? It's me, Laika.'

Siver inhaled sharply, as if she'd just been informed of an accident. 'Laika? What's wrong?' When was the last time they'd talked? They'd texted a few times but he wasn't sure they had spoken since he'd moved to the US.

'Nothing is wrong. I mean, if you check the news right now you'll see something is terribly wrong, but that's not why I'm calling . . . Listen, you're gonna hate this, but Mum told me . . . that you had money trouble. I can help. At least, I think I still can.'

A long silence on the other end of the line. Laika walked over to the window, looked down over the street below. He saw the two cars parked in front of his building but thought nothing of them, his eyes instead scanning the newspaper vending machines outside his door, these odd metal remainders of a media distribution infrastructure that had already become obsolete. The following day they would all have the same headline, about the single trader who was suspected to have crashed the financial system, trying to explain stock market spoofing and high-frequency trading to their readers, but which still, today, had headlines about Demi dumping Ashton, or the First Lady taking on the role of 'staff energizer'. Rows and rows of already dated news, competing with the live feeds in everyone's pockets.

'I wish she hadn't said anything.'

'I don't see why not. I've got money, I can help you.'

'It's a lot. I'd need about twenty thousand dollars.' Was she crying? Her voice was suddenly strained.

'Sisi, I'm sending you two hundred thousand.'

A banging on his door. 'Laika Hardi. Open up.' Who knew he lived there? His name wasn't on any lease or any official documentation. Other than the guy from the coffee shop who had his PayPal details, there wasn't a single person who knew he lived there, and the aggressive banging did not sound like the actions of the coffee guy.

'Hang on, sis, one second.'

Laika put the call on mute and scrolled through the conversation with his mother to get Siver's bank details as he walked towards the apartment door, saw the distorted shape of a man through the bulging lens of the door's peephole, flanked on both sides of the corridor by armed men.

Laika stepped away from the door and into a blur, as though he had been violently pushed underwater. Panic, this was what panic felt like.

'Laika? You still there?' His sister's voice emerged faintly from the speaker of his cell phone. He snapped to it. Not much time now.

'Laika Hardi!'

He hung up on his sister and returned to his bank account, copy-pasting the IBAN number, the BIC, the SWIFT. He backed away from the door, through the hall and towards the living-room window, gaining him a few seconds if they broke through the door. Outside, the asphalt carried the ghost of a previous night's vomit, the din of New York street life going on as though it was a world entirely apart from this apartment: the honking of cabs, the squeals of badly oiled brakes, the random outbursts of profanity from pedestrians.

Everyone walking past on the pavement below seemed as though they were auditioning for a part in some cosmic drama – Asian Nurse #3, Angry White Businessman #5, Hasidic Jew #2 – and it struck him, this most banal of thoughts, that the world was actually comprised of individuals, rather than a great unknowable mass, that this organism comprised of millions upon millions of sentient minds was like the neural network of a cephalopod, tentacles spreading across the city, all one, all separate.

One last rectangle to fill in. Amount. He mistyped, had to delete a 1 and make it a 2, then the zeros.

Are you sure you want to make this transaction? Send/Cancel.

The door burst open.

Assets (2001)

A LOW-RESOLUTION STRING RENDITION of the 'Flower Duet' from Delibes's *Lakmé* was looping, cutting off inelegantly after a few minutes and starting anew. The music had been playing for over forty minutes. Siver kept her eyes on the notepad on which she'd jotted down her questions, tried not to look at all the spaces her father had once occupied, spaces that would now forever be empty.

As Rafiq Hardi Kermanj's life ended, his family began the process of arranging the documentation – cancelled passport, legalised death certificate, travel documents – that would allow them to send the body back to Kurdistan, where Xezal claimed he would have wanted to be buried. By the time Siver rang British Airways' customer service to enquire what requirements the airline had to transport a coffin, Rafiq's body had already been embalmed, a coffin had been selected and paid for on Mohammed's credit card, and the surviving family members had cried the tears they had, now too exhausted for any emotion.

It had happened over lunch, Xezal bringing Rafiq his toast, almost burnt as he liked it, with a cling-wrapped slice of Sainsbury's Danish Blue cheese, some diced tomatoes and cucumbers, and a bowl of Greek yoghurt. A regular lunch, for a regular day. Laika was in his room, playing with the computer that had once belonged to the entire family, and had in the last year or so become only his, through a process that was never approved or voiced by any one family member, as though the computer had changed rooms overnight, the new rules regarding its use immediately known to all.

Rafiq had put down his newspaper, yesterday's paper that he had already read, and told Xezal she'd forgotten to bring cutlery. 'I can't cut this cheese with my smile, dear,' he'd said, giving her a wink. Xezal had said something about not being his slave, and gone back to the kitchen when she heard a plate fall to the floor.

'Rafiq, you must be the clumsiest being God ever created,' were her last words to him, shouted from the kitchen. As she got a fistful of cutlery from a drawer, she had a thought then that would return to haunt her in the years to come. *What a small man he turned out to be*.

When she saw him clutching at his chest, her first thought was that he was choking on something. She began screaming Laika's name for help, and, in the midst of it all, while clutching her husband, who was – the doctors would later tell her – suffering from a massive coronary event, she realised how absurd it was, calling out the name of a space dog.

Laika came out of his room, the ambulance was called, the paramedics came, jolted him back to life, and drove to the nearest hospital, while Laika called his brother (at work) and his sister (at Karim's). Come now, he told them. Just come as quickly as possible.

The hospital room Siver stepped into smelled simultaneously of lavender and sterilised death and there, in the first of the room's two beds, something that used to be her father, a decrepit avatar. She had a desire to flee the room, flee back to Karim, and never come back. But it was too late: there was no getting rid of this image now, it had colonised her mind.

Rafiq was tucked in with military efficiency, bringing to the surface verses from a Plath poem about tulips that Siver had memorised as a sullen teenager, wires and tubes emerging from him as though he were a mythical sea creature. His head, barely darker than the surrounding sheet and pillow, remained immobile. Siver, still wishing she could bolt, felt as though she had been punched in the stomach by something she could never punch back.

'Rafiq, your daughter is here,' Xezal said, her voice the condescending kindness reserved for old people, animals and infants. Her face, too, had been drained of all colour; she somehow looked like a hastily sketched version of herself, her features all wrong.

'Hi, Dad . . .' Siver began, her throat suddenly constricted, as though there were words too big wanting to come out of her. She found, to her surprise, that she was furiously angry. She sat down on a chair next to him.

Two hours later he would be dead, and the surviving members of the family would be assailed by a seemingly endless amount of forms and paperwork. It was Siver's job to sort out their travel arrangements.

Someone answered. Finally.

'Hi, you've reached British Airways, my name is John, how can I help you today?'

The voice startled Siver, who suddenly forgot why she had been on hold for the better part of an hour. She looked down at her notes, which she'd prepared before making the call. *Find out how to send a body. Ask about costs. Ask what docs they need.*

'Hi! Hi, so . . . we're, um, my father just passed away. Yesterday. And . . . Yeah, I was wondering what I need to do if I wanted him on a plane from London to Kermanshah, in Iran.'

'Oh, so you should call the cargo department, they are the ones who will be able to help you,' the customer service representative told her. Only a few hours ago he would have been a passenger, now suddenly he was cargo. She hung up and dialled the number the customer service representative had given her, trying to figure out how to navigate the phone tree. There was no option that seemed relevant to her. No 'for information about transporting the bodies of your loved ones, press 5'.

Laika was pacing the flat, asking her if maybe he should go to the hospital as well.

'I don't fucking know. Do whatever feels right.'

'It's just . . . I feel so useless.'

'I've been on hold with British Airways for the past hour, you think I don't feel useless?'

Eventually she got through to someone who was more than happy to answer her questions, asking her to provide coffin measurements. He took her name, Rafiq's name.

'Will you be travelling with the body?'

'Yes, me and my two brothers and my mother.'

Just as she was about to end the call, she heard the sound of the door unlocking: Mohammed and Xezal were back from the hospital. They staggered in, Mohammed holding his mother up.

'He's not dead,' Xezal said, eyes like clouds parting. 'This is all a lie; the man in that hospital is not your father.'

Siver exchanged a worried look with Mohammed, who was holding his mother's wrists as a safety precaution so that she would not hit herself.

Xezal looked over at the table, where Rafiq's lunch was still set, where Xezal had placed it before an ordinary day had become anything but ordinary.

'It'll be all right, Mum,' Mohammed said, knowing full well that it wouldn't.

They landed at Kermanshah airport three days later, after a chaotic domestic transfer in Tehran, delaying the flight to Kermanshah as they refused to board until they had confirmation Rafiq's body had made it on to the flight. Then a taxi from Kermanshah to the Iraqi border, Rafiq's casket in a hearse behind them. For most of the drive, Xezal nervously glanced back, afraid that they would lose Rafiq somehow, but the last hour before the border, as they approached the three checkpoints, she kept her eyes closed, told the children that she was feeling carsick.

'It's because you keep looking backwards, Mum, of course you're carsick,' Mohammed said.

She nodded, told him he was right. But she'd spent her life trying to forget the journey when they fled Iran all those years ago, and here she was, driving the same route again.

She would never forget his face, Rafiq's, the day he came home and told them they had to go, they had to go as quickly as possible. The Pasdaran, the Army of the Guardians of the Islamic Revolution, had begun rounding up Kurdish activists, claiming they were in league with the infidels, the imperialists and the Shah. 'They killed Farouq, right there on Shah Reza Street. Shot him in front of his whole family.'

By the time Mohammed and Siver were back from school, Xezal had already stuffed some of their clothes in a box, hidden her jewellery in the radio, while Rafiq was frantically calling his Marxist friends to find a way out, getting the number of someone at the British Embassy in Baghdad. They are helping Kurds, Rafiq's friends told him. They will definitely help you. And so, while Xezal explained to her children that they had to leave, and that they could bring one toy each, Rafiq had arranged for them to fly out of Baghdad airport on a cargo plane, to London. Someone from the British Embassy was going to meet them at the border past Kermanshah, he said, and to this day Xezal did not know if that was truly what he believed or if he had lied to her to calm her fears.

Rafiq avoided the highways on his drive out of the city, the state radio station that he'd tuned into bobbing above the surface of a crackling sea of static for an hour or so until it was submerged entirely, and they drove on under a persistent storm of white noise, too preoccupied with the journey ahead to turn the radio off. The two wobbling headlights of the car were often the only source of light illuminating their path, except for the times they narrowly avoided death when a truck would hurtle towards them at great speed, bright lights ablaze, forcing Rafiq to drive as close to a mountain wall as possible, praying that there was enough room for the two vehicles to pass one another. By the time they reached the first of the three checkpoints before Iran bled into Iraq, the children were sound asleep in the back seat. Xezal had pretended not to notice the little yelps that emanated from the back, she wanted to respect their valiant attempts at not crying; if they were strong enough to pretend nothing was wrong, then so was she.

The guard at the first checkpoint subjected them to a standard harassment, pretending he had given Rafiq back his papers when he had done no such thing, Rafiq both needing the paperwork to continue driving and not wanting to point the guard's attention to the documents more than was absolutely necessary, seeing as they were forged. Still, nothing that Xezal would even have remembered if it weren't for what happened next. The guard at the second checkpoint, Xezal remembered him still, had the full beard that all men in Iran had by this point, and darting, dirty eyes, lingering on her breasts, the odd strand of hair that had escaped her veil. The moment the car's tyres crackled to a halt on the stretch of gravel where he stood with his rifle clutched, that very moment, Xezal knew he was trouble.

'Tell your woman to cover up!' he'd barked at Rafiq, who apologised as Xezal tightened her veil anew.

'It's been a long car ride, we didn't—'

'Papers,' the guard said, tapping the barrel of his rifle against the car door. Another guard, Xezal could never remember his face, shone a flashlight into the car, across the children's eyes until they woke up. Rafiq handed over a set of forged documents, hoping that they appeared as authentic as the man who had sold them to Rafiq had assured him they were.

The guard pored over the documents, mocking their fake names, but handed them back to Rafiq. He then demanded the boxes strapped to the car roof be looked through. Rafiq brought them down with a 'ya Ali', hoping to impress upon the guards that he was a Shia like them, but all his stilted expression led to was cruel smirks. Xezal saw from inside the car how the guards rummaged through their belongings, tossing the children's clothes on the ground, taking Rafiq's bottle of Old Spice and claiming it was a gift from God. Once they were done, they made Rafiq pack up the boxes and load them on top of the car. Then, just as the guard seemed ready to wave them on, the darting light from the other guard's flashlight landed on the radio in the trunk.

'This is a smuggler's radio. What's in it?'

Rafiq was silent, not knowing if he should confess to what was inside.

'Just some personal belongings, Agha,' Xezal said, having deduced they would slide the back of it open no matter what she said.

'Show me,' he said, bringing the radio up to the passenger window, the other guard lazily pointing his rifle towards her. She uncovered the pouch hidden inside the radio, and unrolled it, showing the rings and bracelets she still had left.

'They're just family belongings, it's nothing special,' Xezal said as King Faisal's ring glimmered under the flashlight's roaming spotlight.

'Why were you hiding them, then?'

'I was afraid, you never know . . .'

'Are you calling us thieves?'

Rafiq set a lightly trembling palm atop Xezal's gloved hand.

'Of course not; we mean nothing of the kind.'

'Shut your dog mouth, I am not speaking to you,' the guard said, angling the rifle now towards Rafiq, before turning his attention back to Xezal. 'This is contraband. Give it to me.'

'No! I promise, it's just some trinkets I wanted to keep safe.'

'Didn't you hear me? Give. It. To. Me.'

She remembered Rafiq's eyes then, turning towards her, shining as bright as the moon, trembling with fear. 'Dearest . . .' he whispered. 'Dearest, please . . .'

She handed over her jewellery. 'Take it then,' she said, tossing the pouch through the window at the guard.

'You're lucky I don't break your wife's whore mouth with this rifle,' was the guard's last words to them before the radio was put back in the trunk and they were, finally, allowed to drive on. The twenty or so minutes until the next checkpoint, neither of them spoke. Xezal was seething with rage, her heart pounding, while the bones of Rafiq's jaw were jutting out as he ground his teeth. In time, he would make himself feel better by finding a way to blame her.

By the time they had reached the final checkpoint, the night had begun giving way to the wine-dark spill of dawn, the nearby crow of a rooster audible as Rafiq turned the crank to lower his car window. At this checkpoint stood an older guard, strands of white gleaming in his beard.

Rafiq handed over his papers, and the guard asked them where they were going. 'To see my wife's sister, who is sick,' Rafiq answered.

'Oh, where does she live this sister of yours?' Rafiq gave their old address in Slemani. 'What's wrong with her?' the guard said, nodding towards Xezal. 'She's mute, your wife?'

'No, no, she's just tired; we've had a very long drive.'

'Where do you live?'

Rafiq began reciting their Tehran address but the guard interrupted him. 'I was asking her.'

Xezal turned towards him, narrowed her eyes. 'That is none of your goddamn business.'

Rafiq flinched as though something had exploded nearby. 'She didn't mean—'

'I do mean it! Who gives you the right to be harassing people who are just trying to get to their sick relatives? What authority gives you the right to behave in this manner?'

The guard cracked a smile, despite himself. 'Madame, I was in no way harassing you. I was merely asking where you were coming from.'

'Not you, maybe, but that other little runt, waving his gun at us.'

'Who?'

Rafiq, flustered, kept tapping Xezal's hand to make her stop talking, which enraged her even more. 'Agha, it is nothing, my wife is just tired, she doesn't mean anything—'

'He stole all my jewellery, that son of a dog did; what do you mean I don't mean anything? You think it's all right that he humiliated us in front of our children, and stole from us? You think that's acceptable?'

The guard thumbed at the gun in his holster, a darkness coming over his face. For the first time, Xezal thought she might end up dead.

'Agha, I beg your forgiveness, she's not usually like this . . . We have not eaten for many hours . . . And she is so worried about her sister . . .'

'This happened at the last checkpoint?'

'Yes, but like I said, it's really nothing, may God bless it, what are material belongings anyway.'

The guard shouted a name, and a sleepy teenager in an ill-fitting uniform emerged from a prefabricated building behind them. 'Take over for me for a bit. You,' he turned back to Rafiq and Xezal, 'follow me.'

The older guard went into his jeep and headed east, back down the road they had just driven along. 'What have you done?' Rafiq hissed.

'Why are we going back?' Siver wondered from the back, squinting through the rising sun.

'It's nothing, dear, just go back to sleep, it's nothing.'

The low sun kept slashing its way between the mountains as they drove back along the serpentine road. 'Should we try to get away from him?' Rafiq asked as he looked for dirt roads he could drive the Paykan on.

'From that Jeep? Rafiq. Where would we go?'

'This is a fine mess you've gotten us into, Xezal. A fine mess.'

When they got back to the previous checkpoint the two guards were sitting down at a plastic table, dipping bread into a small bowl of yoghurt. Suddenly, under the morning light, neither of them seemed particularly intimidating. Children, barely in their twenties.

When they saw the older guard emerge from his car, they both quickly rose to attention, gave him a sharp, angular salute. The thief had a dollop of yoghurt on his chin.

'You say one of these men ordained by God Almighty to protect this land stole from you?'

Xezal, ears ringing from her own beating heart, was too scared to say anything.

'Now she's quiet again. Only a few minutes ago you wouldn't shut up! Tell me. Did one of these men steal from you?'

She considered her options. It would have been the wise thing to do to just say that she was lying, that it wasn't either of these two men. Maybe they would be allowed to just drive onwards, if she just said no. Nobody had stolen from her.

'Yes. Yes they did.'

'Woman, what are you doing? Has God made you mad?' Rafiq whispered in Kurdish, no longer keeping up any pretences about who they were.

'She's lying, the little whore,' the guard who had taken her jewellery spat.

'Yallah, you come with me,' the older guard said, waving at Xezal. 'No, your husband can stay here with the children; just you, madame.' Xezal saw how Rafiq's knuckles whitened as he gripped the car's steering wheel tighter. 'Come along then! You've made a very serious accusation; it is time to resolve this matter.'

Xezal straightened her veil, unbuckled her seatbelt, and exited the vehicle.

'Daya, where are you going?'

She wanted to console her children, tell them everything was going to be just fine, but knew that if she saw their faces she would break down in tears. She looked ahead.

She followed the guards into the ramshackle prefabricated building, all cheap plastic and thin panes of glass. The room only contained two bare mattresses and reeked of sweat, its cracked concrete flooring covered by dirty underwear, filthy ashtrays overflowing with cigarette butts. She felt that she couldn't breathe, every inhalation cut short after a second.

'Which one was it?' the older guard asked, the two younger guards with their hands over their crotch like small children who had been caught stealing candy.

'Madame, I'm not going to ask you again. Which one is the thief?'

She pointed.

'OK, give her back her belongings.'

'Hafez, by God I did not take anything from her. She must be mistaken.'

'Don't you ever take God's name in vain in front of me, do you hear? Give her back her belongings.'

The thief stood silently for a moment, as though weighing his options, before he flipped over one of the mattresses where the pouch was hidden.

'Here.'

'Is this it? Is this what he stole from you?'

Xezal nodded, unable to look him in the eye.

'Open it, make sure that everything is there.'

She rolled the pouch open, pretended to look at the jewellery. 'Yes. It's all here.'

'Good,' the older guard said, pulling his gun out of his holster and, before anyone had realised what was happening, shot the thief, blood and brain splattering over the other guard, over the mattresses and cigarettes before the thief's body fell to the ground with a dull thud.

Xezal's ears were ringing from the gunshot, the smell of gunpowder and sweat making her sick. She wanted to scream, but found she had no voice left, not a single sound she could conjure. She simply stared at what had once been a living human being, who now lay dead in a pool of his own blood, yoghurt still on his chin, all because of the trinkets in her hand.

The older guard holstered his gun. 'Madame, you can go now.'

She banished the memory from her mind as the taxi stopped: they'd reached the border. Xezal opened her eyes. Unable to drive any further across the no man's land, the taxi had to drop them off as they waited for three dusty but new vehicles to make their way towards them from the other end of the desert, two Land Cruiser SUVs and one pick-up truck. Four young men in camouflage emerged, Kalashnikovs loosely slung over their shoulders, and greeted Xezal nervously, before they proceeded to load the coffin on the pick-up truck. Out of one of the Land Cruisers a moustachioed man appeared; it was Rafiq, only fatter, younger. He hugged them all as though he had known them his whole life, administered big sloppy kisses on every cheek.

'You are home now. Brother-wife, may God forgive Rafiq, he was a great man, and he could not have hoped for a better wife than you.'

Xezal nodded, unable to say a word, and stepped into his car. The three children, confused as to where they should go, looked around for instructions.

'They all understand Kurdish?' Ali asked her, to which she gave a quick nod.

'Children, the Peshmerga will travel with the casket, don't you worry about that. Come with me in my car. It's a long drive, you'll get bored.'

The desert turned into mountains and soon they were snaking down roads that looked much too narrow to drive across. They drove with their windows open, and a smell of gasoline and cement followed them, the sun hanging so low that it required Ali to flap the car's sun visor up and down with each turn. Villages made of small rectangular cement houses appeared and vanished. Every now and again Ali would tell them about a place where he and Rafiq had once been, or give them some historical background on a mountain. The passengers nodded politely, uninterested in conversing any further.

'Please don't be alarmed when we drive into Slemani. A lot of people loved your father.'

Mohammed and Siver exchanged looks in the back seat, but they did not enquire what their uncle meant by this.

'How does it feel to be home, children?' Ali asked, giving them a glance in the rear-view mirror. They politely murmured in the back seat, because what could they say? Laika had never even been in Kurdistan before, not even as a child, and neither Siver nor Mohammed remembered a thing about the place. This was their first memory of this place which everyone, from Xezal and Rafiq to various drunken skinheads throughout the years, had told them was where they truly belonged.

Laika found the effect unsettling, he realised. His entire life he had been free to imagine a mythical place where he effortlessly fit in, but now that they were driving up and down the mountains with Rafiq in a coffin behind them, he understood the mythical place did not exist. It was only when he finally went home that he realised he did not have one.

'Kak Ali, what's that mountain over there?' he asked, wanting to think about something else.

'That, my boy, that is Pira Magroon. You see how it is shaped like the face of a man, with the eyes, the nose, the mouth? It is where a giant is buried; if we have time I will take you up there to his tomb.'

'A giant?'

'It was probably just a very tall person, but the people believed he was somehow magical. People still put stones on his grave to make a wish, there's a tree women hang their clothes from if they are barren, so that his spirit can help them conceive.'

'Kinky ghost,' Mohammed whispered to his siblings in the back seat.

'And . . . um, that mountain there, what's that?' Laika asked.

'That is a hill.'

'Oh.'

Mohammed now had to bite his knuckle so that he would not be heard giggling.'

'That's enough blabbering, children,' Xezal said, her tone of voice making it very clear she was not in the mood for their foolishness. 'Your father has died. Show some respect.'

They drove past a rusty tank that had wildflowers sprouting through its chassis and its broken caterpillar thread, a young sheep herder chasing after a runaway flock, an entire family of four riding on the same minuscule moped. All of this they passed over in silence, remaining quiet until they approached Slemani.

'Dear God,' Xezal said as the car turned a corner and the city was visible below. This dust-coloured city with its tiny, hobbled houses and crooked streets where she had lived so many years ago. The crowd barely bigger than ants from where they were.

'What is all that?' Mohammed asked.

'Your father meant so much to so many,' Ali said. 'They have come to pay their respects.'

The car drove down the mountain, through streets lined with thousands upon thousands of people, a sea of men and women, young and old, waving flags: the Kurdish flag with the Zoroastrian sun between stripes of red and green, the sickle and hammer on a red background. Through the car's windows they heard Rafiq's name being chanted, like an incantation, a cry of war, as though he had returned victorious from battle and not in the cheaper coffin available at the Croydon undertaker's.

'I have never seen anything like this,' Xezal said, a filament of tears in her eyes as the car slowly made its way through the parting crowd, flags waving all around them. 'Can you believe this, children?'

There were people everywhere. Everywhere.

Sources & References

The citation style used by Carole Maso in her novel *AVA* felt like the correct format for this book: to attribute sources in a way that they may 'at some point [. . .] enhance the reader's pleasure but in no way interrupt the trance of the text'. When a source is self-evident, I have not added further information here.

vii 'When Anacharsis was asked . . .': cited in volume one of Marx's *Capital*, in Ben Fowkes's translation, Penguin, 1990.

5 'There had been a period of relative calm in Tehran . . .': much of the information regarding the Iranian Revolution that was not given to me through conversations with family members who were present was gleaned from James Buchan's stellar *Days of God: The Revolution in Iran and its Consequences*, John Murray UK, 2012.

9 '. . . to connect the strands of the chaotic events that had brought them there, and weave those strands into a cohesive narrative of their lives.': this is inspired by 'In healthy functioning, the self-narrative (the way individuals think of themselves) is continuous; there is a connection between the life events and feelings, and the life story can be narrated', from Tihamér Bakó & Katalin Zana, *Transgenerational Trauma and Therapy: The Transgenerational Atmosphere*, Routledge, 2020.

26 'a very busy place, far too busy to write in.': the article, which has time travelled into Siver's magazine, is 'The Writer's Room', *The New York Times*, 16 March 2016.

27 'please could you stop the noise I'm trying to get some rest': Text & music: Colin Greenwood/Jonathan Greenwood/Edward O-Brien/Philip Selway/Thomas Yorke; Copyright © Warner Chappell Music Ltd; Published by permission of Warner Chappell Music Scandinavia AB/Notfabriken Music Publishing AB.

27 'you can't illuminate what time has anchored down': lyrics by Fiona Apple, 'Carrion', *Tidal*, The Work Group, 1996.

38 'By the time she reached the mall, twenty minutes later . . .': much of this paragraph is a self-plagiarised mash-up from my short story 'Mirage', published in *BOAAT Journal* (now defunct), and my essay 'Dubai, city of generic artifice', published in *The Towner* (now defunct).

50 'Dubai was much like a generic airport, engineered to make the surroundings feel familiar, effortlessly herding people through its geography . . .': the concept of the generic city was coined by Rem Koolhaas, notably in 'The Generic City', *S,M,L,XL*, Monacelli Press, 1995.

50 'The main import to the Gulf from the West was not western culture, but rather western brands . . .': I expanded upon this first in my essay 'Dubai, city of generic artifice', published in *The Towner* (now defunct).

54 'She enrolled in what was colloquially called the Gold Digger Academy . . .': the concept of the Gold Digger Academy is from Peter Pomerantsev, *Nothing is True and Everything is Possible,* PublicAffairs, 2014.

78 'In creating hyper-specific, exact replicas of the world that surrounded it, perhaps what made Dubai seem particularly artificial was the uncanny valley . . .': this is self-plagiarised from my essay 'Dubai, city of generic artifice', published in *The Towner* (now defunct).

92 'Even a Saudi cleric's well-publicised fatwa against the sport did not make the jihadists change their minds . . .': this was an actual fatwa that made the rounds, first published in the Saudi newspaper *Al Watan*. I have used the edited English translation as it was published in the *Guardian*. 'A fatwa on football', *Guardian*, 31 October 2005.

115 'Marx wrote that "a house may be large or small; as long as the neighbouring houses are likewise small . . .': this quote is from *Wage Labour and Capital*, in Frederick Engels's translation.

125 'The Big Bang – a name insisted upon by the press – was the popular term for the deregulation of the London stock market . . .': much of

this paragraph first appeared in my essay 'Staten och högfrekvenskapitalet', *Glänta*, 3–4, 2015.

125 '. . . Gray's Inn Road, that long and intestinal grey stretch near King's
Cross . . .': a riff on 'If the whole city of London was sliced open all
that would come out would be a mess of intestinal gray', Kate Zam-
breno, *Green Girl*, Emergency Press, 2011.

133 'The joy of finding stable employment made him forget that he earned
less than others at the same firm with the same title . . .': this paragraph
is inspired by Bukowski's 'How in the hell could a man enjoy being
awakened at 8:30 a.m. by an alarm clock, leap out of bed, dress, force-
feed, shit, piss, brush teeth and hair, and fight traffic to get to a place
where essentially you made lots of money for somebody else and were
asked to be grateful for the opportunity to do so?', Charles Bukowski,
Factotum, Black Sparrow Press, 1975.

133 'M began going to the gym and hated everyone there . . .': self-
plagiarised from my short story 'They Insisted All Reckoning Be
Done by Hand', *Minor Literature[s]*, 2014.

142 '. . . spreadsheets, sufficiently advanced to a layman to be indistinguishable from magic': a perversion of Arthur C. Clarke's Third Law,
from the revised version of the essay 'Hazards of Prophecy: The Failure of Imagination', *Profiles of the Future*, Harper & Row, 1973.

158 'Sleep is the only remaining barrier, the only enduring "natural condition" that capitalism cannot eliminate entirely . . .': the notion of sleep
being incompatible with capitalism is from Jonathan Crary, *24/7: Late
Capitalism and the Ends of Sleep*, Verso, 2013.

199 '. . . M reached for his well-read copy of a business book that he had
turned to many times when his faith wavered . . .': the book that M is
reading is J. Barry Griswell and Bob Jennings, *The Adversity Paradox*,
St Martin's Press, 2009.

204 'We don't have any homeless people here in Northampton; we don't
tolerate that kind of thing here . . .': this is in reference to an anecdote
about Cardiff residents having to sleep in the train station in order to
be able to make their Amazon shifts in case they receive the text telling them that they are needed, as told by Dawn Foster, 'Where are we
now? Responses to the Referendum', *London Review of Books*, Vol. 38,
No. 14, 14 July 2016, p 12.

205 'Did you hear about this skyscraper in Dubai? Its elevators broke down and they had to fly in the parts from the manufacturer in Europe . . .': this is a reference to the elevators of the 97-floor Princess Tower in Dubai which broke down due to a water leak, cf. 'Elevators break down in world's tallest resi building', *Construction Week,* 16 June 2013.

218 'You know, there's this clip of George W. Bush taking a moment out of his busy schedule bombing the Middle East back to the Stone Age . . .': though this clip does exist, Condoleezza Rice was not there that day.

246 'The internet was meant to democratise trading, to make the economy truly global . . .': much of the high-frequency trading information was gleaned from Scott Patterson, *Dark Pools: The rise of A.I. trading machines and the looming threat to Wall Street*, Random House, 2013; Michael Lewis, *Flash Boys: A Wall Street Revolt*, Simon & Schuster, 2014 and Matthew Philips, 'How the Robots Lost: High-Frequency Trading's Rise and Fall', Bloomberg Business, 6 June 2013.

246 'Until someone wanted to buy an $18,900,000 apartment at 15 Broad Street, this was his home.': I've given Laika a very luxurious home to be 'home manager' of, but the basic premise is accurate, as described in Sara Ashley O'Brien's, 'Live in a multimillion-dollar home for $2,500', CNN Business, 11 August 2014.

247 '. . . the tools of the master cannot dismantle the master's house': from Audre Lorde, 'The Master's Tools Will Never Dismantle the Master's House', *Sister Outsider: Essays and Speeches*, Berkeley, 1984.

249 'a conspiracy theory repeated years later by Edward Said in a newspaper wherein he stated that "the claim that Iraq gassed its own citizens has often been repeated. At best, this is uncertain."': this quote is not from a 'newspaper' as such, but appeared in the *London Review of Books*: 'Edward Said, an American and an Arab, Writes on the Eve of the Iraqi-Soviet Peace Talks.' *London Review of Books*, 7 March 1991.

250 'Baudrillard had reached a similar conclusion in *The Gulf War Did Not Take Place*, namely that "the absence of images" of actual humans was neither "accidental nor due to censorship but to the impossibility of illustrating this indeterminacy of the war"': the quotes are from Paul Patton's translation, Jean Baudrillard, *The Gulf War Did Not Take Place*, Indiana University Press, 1995.

251 'As Virilio claimed in an interview, the Gulf War was "a local war in comparison with the Second World War, with regard to its battle-field" . . .': from James Der Derian's interview with Paul Virilio, translated by James Der Derian with Michael Degener and Lauren Osepchuk, 1997, https://nideffer.net/proj/_SPEED_/1.4/articles/derderian.html.

252 'A thread about Roger Fisher, a Harvard Law professor, who had once suggested that the code needed for a nuclear launch should be kept in a capsule that would be implanted next to the heart of a volunteer . . .': this proposal can be found in Roger Fisher, *Bulletin of the Atomic Scientists*, March 1981.

252 'But before the search engine would allow him to complete the search, he was made to complete a Completely Automated Public Turing Test to Tell Computers and Humans Apart, to successfully impersonate a human for a machine': the quote 'successfully impersonate a human for a machine' is from Hito Steyerl, *Duty Free Art*, Verso Books, 2017, p. 159.

254 'An article in the *Washington Post* claimed that the Pentagon had altered the "Department of Defense Law of War Manual' so that journalists who died accompanying armed militias or terrorists could be counted among the 'enemy combatants'" . . .: the article is Missy Ryan, 'Pentagon alters Law of War manual to remove suggestion that journalists are combatants', the *Washington Post*, 22 July 2016.

254 'Some lives mattered this little, with not even a dataset to serve as monument': the idea of data as monument is from Amanda Wasielewski, 'Data as Monument: The Dystopia of the Column of Figures', *PEER Paper Matters*, no. 1, 1 February 2016, pp. 53–9.

255 'He found himself reading an old piece from *The New York Times*. In it the journalist, Ron Suskind, quoted a presidential aide, a paragraph that Laika copied and pasted into a program, Evernote, that functioned like an extension of Laika's memory . . .': the piece is Ron Suskind, 'Faith, Certainty and the Presidency of George W. Bush', *The New York Times*, 17 October 2004.

255 'A few clicks later, another quote by the same person, again to Ron Suskind but this time for *Esquire*: "We will fuck him. Do you hear me? We will fuck him. We will ruin him. Like no one has ever fucked him!"': the article is Ron Suskind, 'Why are these men laughing?', *Esquire*, 1 January 2003.

256 'Why were agrarian societies in Western Europe grain-based during the Middle Ages? Because the king's tax collector could easily see the crops, easily decide how much should be given to the crown.': this fact came from James C. Scott, *Against the Grain: A Deep History of the Earliest States*, Yale University Press, 2017.

259 'Laika wondered if the sound he'd just heard had anything to do with the bodies scattered across the pavement outside . . .': with regard to Occupy, I found Yates McKee, *Strike Art: Contemporary Art and the Post-Occupy Condition*, Verso, 2016, and Molly Crabapple, *Drawing Blood: A Memoir*, Harper, 2015, very informative.

262 '. . . while watching the latest episode of a TV show about a corporate executive who has a meltdown at work and is sent to a holistic rehab clinic . . .': the TV show in question is *Enlightened*, season 2 episode 2.

263 '. . . perhaps it was true, the more vapid the cliché, the sharper the canines of the real truth it covers': a paraphrase of David Foster Wallace's 'the vapider the AA cliché, the sharper the canines of the real truth it covers'. David Foster Wallace, *Infinite Jest*, Little, Brown and Company, 1996, p. 446.

263 'Not that there weren't legitimate, non-metaphorical reasons to shout at buildings. Composite materials and advances in engineering and computer rendering increasingly meant . . .': the idea that humans are increasingly the bottleneck in skyscraper architecture comes from Tom Vanderbilt's essay in *The Future of the Skyscraper*, Distributed Art Publishers, 2015.

265 'He had read that Facebook partnered with a firm that sold them data from loyalty cards . . .': see, for instance, Devika Girish, 'How Beacons can help Brands take their Loyalty Programs to the next level', *beaconstac*, 2014, https://blog.beaconstac.com/2014/08/how-beacons-can-help-brands-take-their-loyalty-programs-to-the-next-level/.

265 'It reminded him of a letter that was found in the compound in Abbottabad where Osama Bin Laden was found and killed . . .': the excerpts from this letter are from Ryan Devereaux, 'The Al Qaeda Files: Bin Laden Documents Reveal A Struggling Organization', *The Intercept*, 13 March 2015.

266 'Except, it turned out, many hadn't. Several other apps had been infected with a line of code creating a 1×1 pixel that redirected to the chat app's server . . .': pixel tracking as way to (often incorrectly) identify political dissidents is a practice mainly associated with the Turkish crackdowns after 2016; see for instance Glyn Moody, 'Single-Pixel Tracker Leads Paranoid Turkish Authorities To Wrongly Accuse Over 10,000 People Of Treason', *Techdirt*, 7 February 2018.

266 'It wasn't a coincidence that the only person who had been charged with a crime during the 2008 meltdown was a Goldman Sachs trader who, upon leaving the firm, took with him a flash disk containing code that the bank argued belonged to them.': for more on this, see Michael Lewis, *Flash Boys: A Wall Street Revolt*, Simon & Schuster, 2014.

267 'He left the camsite open, waiting for her to come online, and opened a new window to kill time, logging onto a website that showed the feeds from unprotected webcams all over the world.': the website with unprotected webcams is www.insecam.org. Have fun.

277 '. . . he clicked on a video he had already watched, titled "ASMR During A Hurricane (Comforting You Roleplay) . . .'": the somewhat anachronistic video Laika is watching is ASMR Darling, 'ASMR During A Hurricane (Comforting You Roleplay)', *YouTube*, 11 September 2017.

278 'Yesterday evening a video had gone viral of a police officer using pepper spray on three kneeling women . . .': the video is Aggie Studios, 'UC Davis Protestors Pepper Sprayed', *YouTube*, 18 November 2011.

280 '. . . he found himself reading about the way that the lootings following the New York City blackout of 1977 led to the spread of hip hop . . .': not an article, but rather Tricia Rose's essay 'A Style Nobody Can Deal With: Politics, Style and the Postindustrial City in Hip Hop', in *Microphone Fiends: Youth Music and Youth Culture*, edited by Tricia Rose, Andrew Ross, Routledge, 1994.

281 'The architect of the twin towers, Minoru Yamasaki was afraid of heights, and so he advocated narrow windows . . .': the 9/11 details are from the essay 'Under falsk flagg', *1otal*, Nr 32, 2019.

292 '. . . he noticed a flurry of what seemed like dollar bills fall down from the sky . . .': the falling bills was inspired by the activist group GULF's 2014 actions in the Guggenheim, protesting the labour conditions in the Guggenheim Abu Dhabi.

293 '. . . allowing for the individual to gain strength and resolve as a crowd . . .': the notion of the future belonging to the crowd is from Don DeLillo, *Mao II*, Scribner, 1991.

293 'for politics to take place, the body must appear [. . .]. Freedom does not come from me or from you; it can and does happen as a relation between us, or indeed among us': this is a quote from Judith Butler, 'Bodies in Alliance and the Politics of the Street', a lecture held in Venice on 7 September 2011, in the framework of the series *The State of Things* organised by the Office for Contemporary Art Norway.

295 'Would love to chat about your app. *Money to Burn* is so infamous it would be great to have some background on how it all happened.': Laika's *Money to Burn* app was inspired by Armin Heinrich's 2008 app *I Am Rich*, which sold for $999 on the app store and consisted only of an image of a glowing red jewel.

298 'the paradox of childhood lies is that we so often tell them out of fear of rejection, fear of separation, fear of being alone, and yet the lie is itself an expression of our independence. We lie in order not to be alone, and yet we cannot lie without accepting the fact that fundamentally, alone is where we are. Our minds are entirely private—and especially so when we lie': the quote is from Clancy Martin, *Love and Lies: An Essay on Truthfulness, Deceit, and the Growth and Care of Erotic Love*, Farrar, Straus and Giroux, 2015.

302 'the scope of his theft was audacious – motivated solely by greed, and it was characterised by supreme disloyalty to his employer': as reported in Telis Demos' 'Eight-year jail term for theft of bank's code', *Financial Times*, 18 March 2011.

303 'Wachovia had laundered billions of dollars for drug cartels and terrorists for decades': see for instance Ed Vulliamy, 'How a big US bank laundered billions from Mexico's murderous drug gangs', *Guardian*, 3 April 2011.

303 '. . . Laika's algorithm was coded to mirror could only take into account a facet of what was actually happening, a 2D entity that saw the indentations of a 3D orb and believed that the indentations were the entirety of what was there . . .': this image was inspired by the segment about the fourth dimension in episode 10, 'The Edge of Forever', of Carl Sagan's *Cosmos*.

303 'Maybe the goal wasn't to mirror trades but to use the algorithms'
encoded behaviour against them . . .': the idea of a spoofing algorithm
leading to a systemic crash came from Haim Bodek, *The Problem of
HFT: Collected Writings on High Frequency Trading & Stock Market
Structure Reform*, Decimus Capital Markets, 2012, pp. 2–4; James
Surowiecki, 'New Ways to Crash the Market', *The New Yorker*, 18 May
2015; and Commodity Futures Trading Commission and Securities
and Exchange Commission, *Findings Regarding the Market Events of May
6, 2010*, 'Report of the Staffs of the CFTC and SEC to the Joint Advisory Committee on Emerging Regulatory Issues'.

305 'Was it Virilio who said that acceleration was leading to the liquidation
of the world?': a paraphrase, but it was indeed Virilio, in Jean-Marc
Offner and Agnès Sander's interview with him published in *FLUX
Cahiers scientifiques internationaux Réseaux et Territoires,* issue 5, 1991, p. 53.

305 'But it was the term Necrocene that appealed to Laika the most . . .':
the term Necrocene coined by Justin McBrien in 'Accumulating
Extinction: Planetary Catastrophism in the Necrocene', in Jason
W. Moore (ed.), *Anthropocene or Capitalocene?: Nature, History and the
Crisis of Capitalism*. Oakland: PM Press, pp. 116–37.

306 'And the writing had been on the wall for a long time, ever since we
started messing with the very concept of time with the telegraph . . .':
the ideas about the telegraph and time are from James W. Carey, 'Technology and Ideology: The Case of the Telegraph', *Prospects*, vol. 8, 1983.

306 'The poet Simonides of Ceos was known to history not because of his
skill, but because he was the first to sell his poetry . . .': everything I
know about Simonides of Ceos I know from Anne Carson, *Economy of
the Unlost: Reading Simonides of Keos with Paul Celan*, Princeton University Press, 1999.

307 'Stock Market Collapse: Dow Jones index loses 9 per cent of its value
in seconds . . .': this series of events was inspired by the so-called 'Flash
Crash' that occurred on 6 May 2010.

308 'Most of the time the market's movements matched events that
occurred in real time on websites and news channels . . .': the description of my fictional flash crash is adapted from my description of the
real flash crash in my essay 'Staten och högfrekvenskapitalet', *Glänta*,
3–4, 2015.

Acknowledgements and Debts of Gratitude

My deepest most heartfelt thanks to my family: my mother and father for their constant love and support (and for years of letting me use up entire oceans of toner to print out my terrible manuscripts) and my sister Kalé who, ever since she was five years old and shouted at a complete stranger for being rude to me, has always, always had my back.

I cannot begin to express the depth of my gratitude to Kaiya Shang, who is not only an exceptional editor in every way but also the person you would most want in your corner in the event of a cataclysm that brings about societal collapse and/or the end of days. Deep thanks also to Graeme Hall, managing editor at Vintage, my copy-editor Alison Tulett for saving me from a multitude of embarrassing errors and Maya Koffi for handling publicity. A special thanks also to Johanna Haegerström at Albert Bonniers Förlag, who was willing to acquire the Swedish rights before we even had a UK publisher.

My most profound thanks to my agents: Erik Larsson at Albatros Agency, who fought the world on behalf of this manuscript and who spent more time helping me get it into shape than any human could reasonably ask, as well as Karolina Sutton and Amelia Atlas at CAA, who guided me through whatever circle of hell the submission process is in.

Much of the research for this book was only made possible due to a grant generously awarded by Västra Götalandsregionens Essäfond. My deepest thanks to Göran Dahlberg and Linn Hansén at Glänta for helping me with said grant and for publishing the resulting non-fiction essay 'Staten och högfrekvenskapitalet', which allowed me to work out many of the themes that would make it into this novel.

Thanks to Bella Marrin for picking my short story 'What We Did After We Lost 100 Years of Wealth in 24 Months' out of the submission slush pile, and to Ben Eastham and Jacques Testard for choosing it for *The White Review*'s June 2013 online issue. So much suddenly seemed possible on the back of that one lucky break. The writing of this novel could begin in earnest only after I received that email.

Thanks to Fehmi Konyar, Saad and Tawfeeq Hasan, and Vivek Hans, who taught me everything I know about the world of finance. Everything I got right, thank them. Everything I got wrong, blame me.

Thanks to Ida Therén, Lyra Ekström Lindbäck and Samuel Watson: I could not wish for better people to have had as my first readers. There are not enough heart emojis in the world.

I owe a great debt to the teachers and mentors who made me a better writer and called me on my bullshit: Diane Delon, Ingrid Arnesdotter and Anna-Lisa Edberg.

Much love to my fellow baralas, Arazo Arif and Kaly Halkawt, for providing the community I never thought I would be lucky enough to find.

Thanks to Geel and Dia for . . . well, everything. And to Kudu for being a commie once and for giving me books to read.

Thanks to Zagros Rasch for listening to me babble about this book for years, and for lending me a ritual dagger at a moment's notice. To Shelan Sabir for providing answers to questions impossible to look up on the internet.

Thanks to Anthony Dawes, Simon Isakson, Pamela Jouven, Antoine Metivier and Gabriel Munch Andersen for a thousand things but especially for being my friends back when I dressed in black and wrote godawful poetry.

Thanks to Lena von Bahr for years of friendship, for helping me sort out my living situation upon my return to Sweden and for reading all the misguided manuscripts I have shown her over the years.

To Mephistopheles for being a very good boy.

Van: whenever you're able to read this I want you to know that I love you more than I ever thought was possible to love a human being. (Toddler temper-tantrums and wildly inopportune sleep regressions notwithstanding.)

And, of course, my deepest thanks to Amanda Wasielewski, without whom this book – and everything else – wouldn't be worth much of anything at all.